# THE TASTE OF APPLES

*Rose, Rose, I Love You*
Wang Chen-ho

*Three-Legged Horse*
Cheng Ch'ing-wen

*Notes of a Desolate Man*
Chu T'ien-wen

*A Thousand Moons on a Thousand Rivers*
Hsiao Li-hung

*Wild Kids: Two Novels About Growing Up*
Chang Ta-chun

*Frontier Taiwan: An Anthology of Modern Chinese Poetry*
Michelle Yeh and N.G.D. Malmqvist, editors

*Wintry Night*
Li Qiao

# THE TASTE OF APPLES

○

*Huang Chun-ming*

Translated by
Howard Goldblatt

COLUMBIA UNIVERSITY PRESS   NEW YORK

Columbia University Press wishes to express its appreciation for assistance given by the Chiang Ching-kuo Foundation for International Scholarly Exchange in the preparation of the translation and in the publication of this series.

COLUMBIA UNIVERSITY PRESS
PUBLISHERS SINCE 1893
NEW YORK    CHICHESTER, WEST SUSSEX
COPYRIGHT © 2001 COLUMBIA UNIVERSITY PRESS
ALL RIGHTS RESERVED

Most of these stories were first published, in slightly modified form, by Indiana University Press in the collection *The Drowning of an Old Cat and Other Stories* by Hwang Chun-ming, translated by Howard Goldblatt (1980).

LIBRARY OF CONGRESS CATALOGING-IN-PUBLICATION DATA
Huang, Ch'un-ming, 1939–
[Drowning of an old cat, and other stories]
The taste of apples / Huang Chun-ming ; translated by Howard Goldblatt.
p.  cm. — (Modern Chinese literature from Taiwan)
Originally published: The drowning of an old cat, and other stories. Bloomington: Indiana University Press, 1980.
Includes bibliographical reference.
ISBN 0–231–11260–8 — ISBN 0–231–11261–6 (pbk.)
1. Huang, Ch°'n-ming, 1939– —Translations into English. I. Title. II. Goldblatt, Howard, 1939– III. Title. IV. Series.
PL2865.C56 D76 2001
895.1'352—DC21                    00–060260

*Casebound editions of Columbia University Press books are printed on permanent and durable acid-free paper.*
*Printed in the United States of America.*
c 10 9 8 7 6 5 4 3 2 1
p 10 9 8 7 6 5 4 3 2 1

# Contents

○

*Translator's Note*

o

It is ironic that Western readers were first exposed to Huang Chun-ming's fictional creations at a time when many of his Taiwan contemporaries considered the stories that make up the bulk of this anthology passé. For someone then still so young and so talented, whose writings were considered almost revolutionary in subject matter and in use of language, to become so quickly a transitional figure is unfortunate though not uncommon in a world that is changing so precipitously. In Taiwan, where the ethnic dichotomy between the mainland Chinese and the Taiwanese has not completely disappeared, and where the future itself is very much in doubt, the process of change is even more greatly accelerated. It may be that as a writer, Huang, whose stories of the Chinese in Taiwan were a radical (and welcome) departure from the anti-Communist fiction of the 1960s and the subsequent Western-influenced, often avant-garde novels of the early 1960s, may have fallen victim to a social process that he helped put into motion.

Huang Chun-ming writes primarily of rural Taiwan, a generally closed society. He is thus regarded as a regional writer, a term that, while accurate in the main, is limiting in describing both the contents of his stories and their intrinsic universality. Consistent, clearly defined geographical settings and character types, as the novels of Faulkner and others have shown, can aid an author in more fully developing his world view and in expressing his personal observations of the people and places with which he is most familiar. Huang's characters (who are far more important than the incidents in their lives) are generally uneducated, disadvantaged men, women, and children who must cope with assaults on their traditionalism, hostility or condescension on the part of their urban brethren, and of course all the debilitating effects of poverty. For the most part, these characters are society's rejects, people languishing on the lowest rungs of the social ladder; they have suffered at the hands of their peers or of their betters, and they quite often find life and society passing them by. Witnesses to the inexorable disintegration of the community they have known all their lives, they are in the unenviable position of having to choose between obstructionism and passive acceptance of their own anachronistic existence.

Huang could be forgiven if he were to allow his compassion and concern for these people to influence his writing in the directions of idealization or pathos. To his credit, he does not. Rather, he infuses his characters with dignity and wisdom, attributes on which no class has a monopoly. This should not lead us to expect an uninterrupted series of happy endings, human existence being what it is; despair born of a sense of personal inadequacy or loss of livelihood, overreactions to simple misunderstandings that place too great a strain on love, and the overpowering need to be accepted and respected often lead to tragic ends in the stories that follow.

There is a pattern to Huang's stories, a progression from the small-town environment of his hometown and the surrounding villages to the larger urban areas and finally to the metropolis, Taipei. The supporting roles played by the old-timers in "The Drowning of an Old Cat" and the old bachelors in "The Gong" are replaced in the later works by Japanese tourists ("*Sayonara / Zaijian*"), American military advisors, and foreign-affairs policemen ("The Taste of Apples"). Pedicab drivers, gong beaters, and "ad men" with sandwich boards over their shoulders give way to TV reporters and clerks in large companies. Still, the dominant characters in the stories collected here are deeply rooted in rural Taiwan; the major exception, the narrator of "*Sayonara / Zaijian*," is himself new to the big city and is very close in background, interests, and personal situation to

Huang Chun-ming. In a word, rural Taiwan itself is often the central character.

Lacking an education, speaking only their native Taiwanese dialect, and unable to change their conservative, superstitious, unaffected ways, these people are the unwitting and guileless victims of changing societal values; even when they transcend their humble origins, overshadowing all around them, their victory is only temporary. Certainly the greatest threat to these people, as to so many of their kind throughout the world, is the unremitting, merciless, and irreversible encroachment of "modernization," the introduction of highly appealing creature comforts and the more efficient technology of an increasing industrialized society into increasingly remote areas.

Huang Chun-ming is a humanist of the first order. He is a self-designated spokesman for the culturally disadvantaged and a prod to the consciences of those who would lose sight of the human costs of a blind, reckless adherence to "progress." He comes to writing instinctively and with no formal training. But what his works may lack in technical brilliance they easily gain in sheer readability and humor: the complex sentiments of his characters and their reactions to events are faithfully and movingly captured in lively dialogue and uncomplicated narrative. Huang does experiment on occasion, employing such devices as interior monologue in something approaching stream-of-consciousness style or using his cinematic background in shifting scenes and flashbacks, but he is neither particularly innovative nor trendy where ficitonal techniques are concerned. The success of his stories can be attributed to his being content to let the characters tell their own stories.

Huang, who grew up in a rural Taiwan environment, has witnessed at first hand the old and the new (including the transition from one to the other) and the many and varied outside influences on his homeland—from Japan, mainland China, and the West, particularly the United States. All of this experience is reflected in his short stories and novellas, and in such a way as to parallel the changes in Taiwan over the past few decades. But the reader should not assume Huang's work consists of period literature only (a genre of writing that has diminished relevance and appeal), for the prime element in the bulk of the stories presented here is the author's basic sense of humanity. For the Western reader, the unfamiliar aspects of setting are transcended in most of the pieces by a universal and timeless appeal in the depiction of man's role in life, his contradictions, his confrontations with society at large, his struggles with poverty and prejudice, and his ability to adapt to change. Huang's stories are a reaffirmation of the sanctity of human existence.

In the stories that follow, the reader will find many unfamiliar attitudes, modes of behavior, figures of speech, and interpersonal relationships that may on occasion seem puzzling; however, these new elements are overshadowed by the eminently recognizable emotions, situations, and involvements common to us all. Here is a delicate blend of tenderness and insensitivity, idealism and worldliness, love and violence, humor and tragedy; but mostly honesty, compassion, and all the ingredients of stories well told.

The ordinary people of Taiwan have a devoted spokesman in Huang Chun-ming, and the rest of us who read his stories can discover a talented writer as we rediscover certain aspects of the human condition.

∘ ∘ ∘

The stories in this anthology were written in the 1960s and 1970s. All first appeared in Taiwanese magazines and newspaper supplements and were later included in one or more of the author's short-story collections (see Bibliographic Note). Two of the translations, "*Sayonara / Zaijian*" and "The Taste of Apples," were previously published in *The Chinese PEN*, a Taiwanese translation journal; "*Sayonara / Zaijian*" was subsequently reprinted in the Hong Kong magazine *Renditions*. Translations by others of three of the remaining stories have appeared in print, but for reasons of stylistic continuity, personal preference, and the occasional repair of a mistranslation, I have undertaken to do my own rendering, taking the counsel of my predecessors wherever necessary.

It is lamentable, though unavoidable, that one of the hallmarks of Huang Chun-ming's fiction, the conscious, liberal use of dialect, cannot be captured in translation. Since the two dialects spoken in Taiwan—the "official" language of Mandarin and the indigenous Taiwanese—are mutually unintelligible when spoken and sometimes vary in written form, the language gap among people in Taiwan is often pronounced. Thus, in the stories, we encounter frequent references to members of the older generation who cannot comprehend what is being spoken around them. It is language and not intelligence that makes them so apparently obtuse.

One feature of Huang's writing that can be more or less faithfully re-created in translation is his humorous, sometimes racy, and highly colloquial dialogue. I have attempteed to be faithful to the author's tone, especially in the all-important dialogue. Where a direct translation has not seemed appropriate, modest liberties have been taken with the text to realize this goal.

The reader will notice an apparent inconsistency in the rendering of characters' names—some have been transliterated while others have been translated. My rule of thumb has been to translate only nicknames. Some of these names may seem cruel, but in fact the acknowledgment of physical disabilities is common in rural Taiwan—there are no "closet cripples" in Huang's fiction. I have occasionally slightly altered the spelling of a transliterated name so that the same names do not recur to confuse the reader (in Chinese, the different written characters obviate this problem). One family does appear twice—Jiang Ah-fa, his wife, and several children have starring roles in "Ringworms" and in "The Taste of Apples." Finally, I have used pinyin spellings, except for place names, which follow Taiwanese postal spellings.

H.G.

*Preface*

o

In regard to the mastery of modern Chinese—known as *guoyu*, or "national language," in Taiwan and *putonghua*, or "common language," on the Chinese mainland—Taiwan was a relative latecomer. Guoyu's widespread use dates from the end of World War II, following Taiwan's retrocession to China. But the return of the language after half a century of Japanese colonial rule was accomplished by the transplanted Nationalist government only after a concerted effort to promote it and to force the local dialect into disuse. Like all colonial powers, the government carried out its political agenda with utter disregard for ethnic friction and ideological opposition.

The first generation of Taiwanese to write in acceptable guoyu rather than a Chinese remake of Japanese, and who were permitted to publish their works openly, did not appear until the early 1960s. I was one of those writers. But though we had some proficiency, we were denied a rich environment in which to let our language mature, particularly where ideology was concerned. In middle school, we had an insatiable thirst for literature, even if we were too young to understand and appreciate what we were reading; we devoured any book we got our hands on, just so long as it was literature or philosophy, like a goat that will eat anything, so long as it's green, even a plastic bag. I guess you could call this an age of philosophy and us, literary youth.

In those days, the Nationalist government was troubled by domestic unrest and foreign adventurism, beset by ethnic discord and pressure from the Chinese Communists. So it embarked upon an anti-Communist agenda that set out to accomplish two goals: first, to stamp out Communist ideology and eliminate spies (Communists), and second, to strictly control the activities of the people at large and curtail their freedom of speech. During the nearly forty years of martial law, from 1950 to 1987, a white terror enshrouded Taiwan.

At first, our middle school textbook, *Selected Chinese Texts*, was thrown out because it included writers who had been members of China's League of Leftist Writers in the 1930s. Then at least half the books in our school library were taken off the shelves. All works by League members or by Russian and Soviet writers, whether literary or scientific, original or translations, were banned. What remained were either anti-Communist tracts or nostalgic writing by mainlanders, sentimental yearnings for the good old days back in their hometowns. Luckily for us, some Anglo-American literature was spared, unless, of course, the translators happened to live on the mainland.

And so, at the time, foreign works fed my hunger: Hemingway's *The Old Man and the Sea* and "The Killers"; Mark Twain's *Tom Sawyer*, *Huckleberry Finn*, and "The Celebrated Jumping Frog of Calaveras County"; Faulkner's "A Rose for Emily," "The Bear," *The Wild Palms*; and the like. Most, of course, were American, thanks to the U.S. policy of anti-Communism. Then troubling events took place at school. Some of our favorite teachers began quietly disappearing. My homeroom teacher, who taught literature, was one who met that fate. This unfortunate teacher's name was Wang Xianchun; she was a young woman of twenty-five or twenty-six. I mention her in particular because it was she who set me on the path of creative writing. The most obvious difference between the Taiwanese and mainland students at the time was that we Taiwanese lagged behind in our ability to speak guoyu and to write Chinese with a brush. Once, when I turned in a writing exercise I called "The Autumn Farm Family," Miss Wang shrewdly cautioned me not to imitate other people's writing. Knowing that she thought I'd copied the story from someone else, I protested and asked her to let me write another story.

When she read the second piece, she saw that I had some literary talent and, on the eve of the book bannings, gave me two collections of fiction she'd brought to Taiwan from the mainland: an anthology of short stories by Shen Congwen and a Chinese translation of stories by Chekhov. After I'd finished them, she sat me down to talk about what I'd read. Unfortunately, those heady days didn't last long; one day she simply didn't show up.

During the summer that followed, while on a tour of military academies and the National Defense Medical College, some of my schoolmates spotted her body on a table in the dissecting room. She'd been a member of the Chinese Communist Youth League, and our public security agencies determined that she was a secret agent. Of course, we didn't find this out until later.

There's no doubt that my love of literature is in large measure a result of the encouragement I received from Wang Xianchun. My American translator has written elsewhere that many of my stories are decidedly Faulknerian in style and tone. After mulling this over, I've come to the conclusion that this can be linked to the environment in which I grew up. My hometown and childhood experiences are at the core of my writing. In the sixties and seventies, when the modern world began making inroads into the out-of-the-way town of Lanyang, where I was born, the conflicts between the new and the old created a rich source of powerful and dramatic material. Whenever my antennae detected the new dramas being played out in my old hometown, the desire to write about them raged inside me. The stories in this collection were written during those two decades.

Frankly speaking, translating these stories, with all their rural Taiwanese customs, into English isn't something just anyone with a decent command of the two languages can manage, and I'm sure that Howard Goldblatt has found it necessary to be creative in transforming the stories you will read. He has also never stopped urging me to continue writing. Even now, in my sixtieth year, he keeps at it. For that I thank him. Writers are seldom blessed with friends like that.

HC-M

# The Fish

○

"You told me to bring a fish with me the next time I came home, Grandpa. Well, I've brought one—it's a bonito!" Ah-cang shouted happily to himself as he left the little town behind him on his rickety old bicycle.

A twenty-eight-inch bike was not made for a boy as small as Ah-cang, and as he set out he was tempted to stick his right leg through the triangular space below the crossbar. But then he changed his mind, figuring he shouldn't be riding a bike that way anymore. After all, he wasn't a kid any longer.

Perched on the big bike, Ah-cang could not keep his rump from slipping off first one side of the seat and then the other. The cooked bonito, wrapped in a taro leaf and hanging from the handlebars, swayed violently with the motion of the bike. Ah-cang knew that bringing a bonito back to the mountain would make his grandpa and his younger brother and sister very happy. They'd also be surprised to see that he had learned to ride a bicycle. Besides, riding to and from the foot of the mountain at

Pitou would save him twelve Taiwan dollars in bus fare. That was why he'd pleaded with the carpenter to lend him the rickety old bike that lay unused in the shed.

Ah-cang pedaled down the road with the single-minded purpose of getting that fish home to his grandfather as quickly as possible; not even the clanking sounds of the old bike disturbed his thoughts. The moment he saw his grandfather, he'd hold the fish up high and ask, "Well, what do you say? I've got a pretty good memory, haven't I? I brought a fish home."

∘ ∘ ∘

"Ah-cang, the next time you come home, try to bring a fish back with you. It's not easy getting saltwater fish up here on the mountain. Bring a big one if you can."

"But I don't know when I'll be able to come home again."

"I'm saying *when* you come home."

"That'll be up to the master."

"I know that! That's why I said to bring a fish back with you *when* you come home."

"*When* I come home? I may not have any money when I come home."

"I mean when you *do* have the money."

"That'll depend on the master too."

"When will he start paying you wages?"

"You should know—you're the one who took me there. Didn't he say I'd have to be an apprentice for three years and four months before I got any pay?"

"That's right. You're there to learn a trade. How long before you can nail a table together all by yourself?"

"Nailing a table together is easy. I learned how to do that a long time ago."

"Then you shouldn't be an apprentice any longer."

"I haven't been there three years and four months yet."

"Oh? How long have you been there?"

"I still have a year and a half to go." Ah-cang sighed. "Sometimes I feel I might spend my whole life there without ever finishing."

The old man quickly chided him. "Hush! Children aren't supposed to sigh!"

"Why not?"

"Because they're not supposed to." He paused for a moment. "It's bad luck. You remember that."

"Grandpa." Ah-cang looked up at the old man.

"Hm?"

"When you're really low, it makes you feel good to sigh."

The old man laughed loudly.

"What're you laughing at?"

"You don't look any older, but you talk like you've grown up a lot."

"I mean it! After I sigh, I always feel really really good."

"Don't walk on that side where the road curves. The day before yesterday one of the shop owners from the foot of the mountain got a little careless while he was coming up to collect some bills and lost his footing there."

"Was he hurt?" Ah-cang craned his neck to look over the side.

"Of course he was hurt. The bamboo down there had just been cut, and each stalk looked like a crow's beak. When he went over the side, he was stuck by pointed bamboo all over. He also broke his leg. Okay, that's enough looking down there. That bend in the road has always been a nasty spot."

"Who owed him money?"

"Who up here on the mountain doesn't owe money to the flat-landers?"

They silently skirted the bend in the road.

"Where are you going?"

"Nowhere. I'll just walk you down the mountain."

"You don't have to. I'll be careful, and I'll remember to bring a fish back with me the next time I come home."

"That's great. But if you can't, don't worry about it. Sometimes when the weather turns bad, the fishermen don't go out to sea, and then you can't get a fish even if you've got the money."

"Then I hope there's no bad weather."

As they approached a narrow stretch of road, the old man let his grandson walk ahead of him; he gazed at the boy from behind and asked, "Is it a rough life?"

"What can I do about it? They make me do just about everything in the master's house, even wash the baby's diapers. . . ." The boy began to choke up.

"Then what does the master's wife do?"

The boy just shook his head without saying a word.

"So *that's* the kind of woman she is!" Then the old man comforted the boy by saying, "It doesn't make any difference. You've put up with it so far, haven't you?"

"You told me I had to."

"Then you're doing the right thing. You have to set a good example for your brother and sister."

Ah-cang looked off at nothing in particular on the mountain slope. He saw a herd of goats grazing in the acacia grove.

"How're our goats?"

"Oh, they're just fine."

"We ought to raise a few more."

"That's what I've been thinking."

"Let them hurry up and have some kids."

"That's what I was planning to do."

"After all the time we've been raising goats, we still only have those three."

"That's because they're all males."

"Males are worthless!"

"If they were all females, they'd be just as worthless."

"I figure we should raise a few more goats, then we could swap them for a set of carpenter's tools." Ah-cang casually picked a blade of mugwort from the side of the road.

"Be careful, that can cut your finger." The old man quickly returned to the subject at hand. "Are you ready for a set of carpenter's tools?"

"Sure!" the boy said. "I can do more than make tables—I know how to make wardrobes, doors, beds, and chests too."

"That's wonderful!" the old man said delightedly. "I'll go ahead and raise a few more goats so you can exchange them for carpenter's tools."

"When?"

"What's your hurry? Grandpa'll take care of it right away. I'll swap two of our male goats for one female with a flatlander, and we can start."

"You'd better hurry, because I'll be a carpenter pretty soon!"

"That's what I mean!" the old man said, then added lovingly, "But you'll have to put up with whatever comes along for the time being. You know that, don't you?"

"I know. I'll have to be patient."

Once they passed the acacia grove, they could see the bus sign off in the distance at Pitou. They fell silent. When they finally reached flat land the old man asked, "Do you get enough to eat?"

" . . . "

"Do they beat you?"

" . . . "

"What's wrong? Why don't you say something?" The boy lowered his head and fought back the tears. "Don't cry. Why would anyone cry when he's about to become a carpenter?"

The boy shook his head as he wiped away the tears. "I'm not crying." But he refused to raise his head.

"Hey, do as Grandpa says and take this sack of sweet potatoes along for your master. Maybe they'll treat you better if you do."

"No."

"Go ahead, take it." The old man slipped the sack of sweet potatoes off his shoulder and set it in front of the boy. "Don't forget to bring the sack back."

"I said no! They'd laugh at me!"

"These are the best sweet potatoes anywhere around here!"

The boy looked up at the old man with eyes red from crying and shook his head.

"All right then!" the old man said angrily. "I'd rather feed them to pigs than give them to anyone who'd touch a single hair on my grandson's head!"

"Grandpa, go on back now."

"All right, after I've rested here a minute. You hurry on down to wait for the bus."

Before the boy had taken more than a few steps, he was called to a halt by the old man.

"Are you sure you don't want to take the sweet potatoes?"

"I'm sure."

"Who knows, they might even buy a fish for you to bring back the next time you come home."

"I told you I'd bring a fish back for you."

"Come over here." The old man took a couple of steps toward the boy. "Your grandpa once carried a heavy load of sweet potatoes to market because he wanted to buy a fish for you kids. Is the bus coming?"

"Not yet."

"Tell me when it is. You know that fish costs more than most foods. That day I walked around and around the fish stalls until the fishmongers finally got tired of calling out to me. But I kept walking, trying to make up my mind. You know why?"

"You were going to steal one?"

"Nonsense!" The old man straightened up. "That's something you must never do. I could never do anything like that. I'd rather starve!" Then he bent over again and explained to the boy, "I did it because fish was so expensive and the fishmongers are all crooks. If they aren't tampering with the scales, they're padding the weight. I didn't know how to figure, and I knew if I just asked them how much the fish sold for, they'd reach in to get a fish and weigh it using wet rush stems. Keep your eye out for the bus. Tell me when it's coming."

"Not yet."

"So I kept walking around the fish stalls looking the fish over and trying to find an honest face among the peddlers. Finally I stopped at a stall where bonitos were sold and pointed to one of them. I repeatedly told the fishmonger to give me an honest weighing and not take advantage of an old man. She told me not to worry, over and over, so I bought a three-catty bonito. But when I weighed it at home I found it was a catty and a half light!" The old man knitted his brows. "I should have been able to buy a three-catty bonito with the money I got for a full load of sweet potatoes. . . ."

"The bus is coming! I can hear it."

The old man, having stooped over too long, straightened up with considerable difficulty and looked with the boy off in the direction where the bus would be.

"If you can only hear it, then we've still got time."

"Who knows, maybe it's a Forestry Department truck," the boy said excitedly.

"That's even better. You could hitch a ride." The old man paused. "Let's see now, where was I?"

"You were saying you should have been able to buy a three-catty bonito with the money you got for a full load of sweet potatoes."

"So you *have* been listening to me?"

The boy nodded.

"They robbed me of a load of sweet potatoes. Those people are bandits, pure and simple. I was so upset I fretted over it for days. To tell you the truth, even today I won't go near fish stalls in the marketplace!" He heaved a deep sigh. "Ai! It's not easy for us mountain folk to eat saltwater fish. . . ."

"Here comes the bus."

The old man gazed off, bleary-eyed.

"Over there. See that trail of dust?"

"You're probably right. You go on now. Grandpa'll stay here and rest a moment."

"I'm going now."

"Ah-cang, don't forget . . ."

". . . to bring a fish back with me," the boy finished the sentence.

They both laughed.

o o o

"Grandpa, I didn't forget. I brought a fish back with me—a bonito!" Ah-cang said repeatedly to himself, his happiness tinged with feelings of triumph. As he rode along he envisioned wide-eyed looks on the faces of his brother and sister when they saw the bonito, and he could almost see the tips of his grandfather's trembling chopsticks as they reached out to pick up a morsel of fish. "Grandpa, I'll be a carpenter in two months!"

*Clank!* "That damned chain!" Ah-cang jumped down off the bike, put the slipped chain back onto the sprocket, then turned a pedal until it was once again engaged. The chain had kept slipping off the sprocket the whole way, so he knew he shouldn't ride too fast—but he invariably forgot. This time, after brushing some of the rust and oil off his hands, he discovered to his horror that the fish had fallen off! All that was left hanging on the handlebars was the now-empty taro leaf. He quickly headed back, and a mile or so down the road he found what he was looking for, though now it was nothing but a squashed imprint on the muddy road. The fish had been run over by a truck.

More than two hours later, as he headed back up the mountain, the crestfallen Ah-cang could cry no longer over this freak accident. Off in the distance he saw his grandfather sitting in the doorway weaving implements out of green bamboo. Lacking the courage to call out "Grandpa," he just quietly walked up to the old man.

The old man jerked his head up. "Hey! When did you get back?"

"Just now," the boy answered as he walked into the house.

The old man laid the things in his hand down, then stood to follow the boy inside. But between starting to get to his feet and finally straightening up, he had plenty of time to ask the boy several questions.

"Ah-cang, did you see our goats by the roadside on your way home?"

No answer.

"They're over there in the couch grass. Your brother and sister are watching them. I managed it for you—you'll have your set of carpenter's tools any day now."

That made Ah-cang feel even worse.

"Ah-cang, did you hear what I said?" the old man asked as he walked into the house.

Still no response.

"What's wrong with you? You're acting like a bride who hides in the corner the minute she steps into the house." He walked into the bedroom, then into the tool shed, and finally into the kitchen, where he found Ah-cang taking big gulps from the water ladle. "Ah, here you are! Did you bring a fish home?"

Ah-cang kept drinking.

"The weather's been bad the past few days, so there wouldn't be any fish for sale in the marketplace," the old man said, knowing full well that the weather had been fine. "You can't use our weather here as a gauge—out at sea it's always changing."

Ah-cang purposely got his face all wet so his grandfather wouldn't know he'd been crying. He raised his wet face and said, "They're selling fish."

"Well?"

"I bought one—a bonito."

"Where is it?" The old man searched the kitchen with his eyes.

"I dropped it!"

"Dropped it?"

"Dropped it!" Ah-cang didn't dare look the old man in the eye, so he buried his face in the water ladle again, though he didn't want any more water—he couldn't drink another drop.

"How . . . how could that have happened?" The old man was bewildered. The pain he'd felt that time when he'd been cheated on the weight of the bonito returned.

But Ah-cang, not knowing how the old man felt, argued defensively, "I really did! I'm not lying to you. I hung it on the handlebars of the bike, and it just fell off."

"The bike?"

"That's right. I know how to ride a bike now!" He waited to see if this made his grandfather happy.

"Where's the bike now?"

"I left it in the care of a shop at the foot of the mountain."

"It fell off the handlebars?" The old man spoke every word slowly and clearly.

Ah-cang's disappointment was now complete.

"I really did buy a bonito, but a truck ran over it and squashed it."

"Isn't that the same as not bringing one home?"

"No! I did bring one!" he shouted.

"That's right, you did, but you dropped it. Is that right?"

Ah-cang was angry that his grandfather had taken such a matter-of-fact attitude.

"I really did bring one with me," the boy said angrily.

"I'm aware of that."

"I'm not lying to you! I am *not* lying to you! I swear!" Ah-cang began to cry.

"I know you're not lying to your grandpa. You've never lied to me. It's only that the fish fell on the road," he said in a comforting tone.

"No! You don't believe me! You think I'm lying. . . ." Now Ah-cang was sobbing.

"You can bring one home next time. Won't that take care of it?"

"But I already brought one back today!"

"You say you brought a fish with you today, and I believe you, so what are you crying about? You're acting silly."

"But it never got here."

"It fell off and was squashed by a truck, right?"

"No! You don't know! You don't know! You think I'm lying to you. . . ."

"Grandpa believes every word you're saying."

"I don't believe you."

"What do you want me to say?" Beginning to lose his patience, the old man spread his hands in a helpless gesture.

"I don't want you to believe me, I don't want you to believe me," Ah-cang shouted as he threw the ladle to the floor, then began to sob again, sounding like a calf.

The old man, finding himself cornered, began to fume. He reached behind the door to pick up his carrying pole and began hitting out with it. Ah-cang was struck on the shoulder and quickly darted out of the room, the old man right on his heels.

Ah-cang ran through the tea orchard, followed closely by the old man. He then ran over to the bramble patch and quickly threaded his way in to a depth of five or six feet. From there he hopped down onto the road leading home. The old man stopped at the entrance to the bramble patch. Ah-cang turned and saw that the old man had stopped, so he did too. There was by then a considerable distance between them.

The old man stood there gasping, one hand waving the carrying pole, the other resting on a bramble bush.

"Don't you dare enter my door again!" he shouted. "If you do, I'll beat you to within an inch of your life!"

Ah-cang responded in the loudest voice he could manage, "I really did bring a fish back!"

It was then approaching evening, and the mountain was very quiet. The old man and the boy were both startled to hear the crisp echo coming to them from the valley:

". . . really did bring a fish back!"

# The Drowning of an Old Cat

o

## I. THE LAY OF THE LAND

The out-of-the-way county in this story was designated by the Taiwan Provincial Government as a developing area. Its center was Jiezai, a small market town of forty or fifty thousand people. When the town youth were in the presence of people from the outlying countryside, they habitually put on airs of self-importance to show that they were urbanites; the somewhat older people, with their greater understanding of humility, would go no further than to nod their heads with slightly superior smiles. People from the countryside cheerfully and loudly informed anyone within earshot that their daughters had married men who lived in town. And even though the ears of the listeners rang with this barrage of talk, they felt it only proper, for had they had an eligible daughter, she too would have left the farm and married a townsman (or so they thought). Even greater glory came to someone whose son brought a townswoman back to the farm as his wife, for no matter how their lives together turned out in the end, at least in the beginning there was a great deal of loud, enthusiastic talk.

The market town was only about seventy or eighty kilometers from the nearest big city, and transportation to and from the city—by train or by bus—was quite convenient. The roads were well traveled, since a round trip took no more than four hours; a person could ride to the city, take care of business, and return home all in the same day. As a result, big-city fads easily found their way to the market town. Miniskirts that stopped twenty centimeters above the knee were displayed on local girls, and go-go dancing was popular at parties held by the town's youth. As for their elders, a fear of death led to fashionable trends such as early-risers clubs, which were said to have beneficial effects on one's health.

Someone had recently discovered young children swimming in Clear Spring Village, and before long, men with bulging pot bellies and respectable positions in society got up at the crack of dawn and rode over to soak in the spring. Later, when they discovered they were able to take in their belts one hole after another, their numbers increased. Not even inclement weather could stop them. After a while, in addition to soaking in the water, they learned to propel themselves a bit through it, more or less in the fashion of swimming. Among them were physicians, senior bank officials, lawyers, school principals, assemblymen, businessmen, and many more. Nearly every member of the local Rotary Club participated, except for David and Tom, one of whom had an artificial leg, the other a case of congenital rickets.

o o o

Clear Spring Village had gotten its name from a spring the size of two parcels of land in the middle of the village and was under the jurisdiction of the local Water Control Board. Actually, if one were to have dug a hole three to four or maybe five to six feet deep anywhere in Clear Spring Village, a bubbling spring of sweet water would have risen to the surface in a steady flow.

The sixty or more households who lived there were as pure and simple as the spring water that flowed to the surface; there was little difference between them and the unbroken gush of water as they diligently tilled the more than forty parcels of land they owned, plus the side of Guzai Hill. There had never been a drought over the farmland there, yet for years it had been an impoverished area, which was the source of the people's pure and simple nature. Though no more than two and a half kilometers separated them from the market town, the road crossed the hill and was fairly steep, and since there was no bus line between the two places, the townspeople sensed that Clear Spring Village was a great distance away.

## 2. THE SKY IS FALLING

In the year the Temple of the Patriarch was erected, a banyan tree was planted beside it; now that more than sixty years had passed, fully half of the four thousand square feet of temple ground lay in the shade of this tree. On the portion of the red-tiled temple roof that stood under the shade day in and day out, year after year, a carpet of deep green moss and grass flourished, while on the other half the aged red tiles were in full, sunlit view. For this reason the people referred to the Clear Spring Village Temple of the Patriarch as the Yin-Yang Temple, or the Temple of Dark and Light. This long process of change was mirrored in Uncle Ah-sheng and four or five other old-timers who lived in the village, as they had grown old watching the gradual changes take place. In earlier days they had hitched rides on the back of the oxcart that carried the bricks used to build the temple, getting an occasional taste of the carter's whip. Now they were the oldest people in the village, and on every temple festival the duties and activities of the villagers were under the direction of these few men, led by Uncle Ah-sheng.

But temple festivals only came around a few times a year; during the remaining long days these old-timers congregated in one of the temple's side rooms. In the winter they secured the door, each of them carrying a small brazier to warm himself; in the summertime they swung the door open and availed themselves of cool breezes that passed through the side room and carried up to the heavens the fragrant smoke of incense from black joss sticks symbolizing the people's devotion. For the most part, these men talked of the past, and even though their talk was repetitious, they never tired of it. With great fondness they recalled those early days when they'd struggled with poverty. Memories of the past are always fond ones, and this was especially true for these men in their twilight years; only their past instilled a sense of pride. For them the future was a big question mark; who could say that tomorrow would not be the day they stopped coming to the temple? Last year there had been seven or eight of them, and now, a mere year later, their number had been cut nearly in half.

. The stone block just inside the door pillar to the left had originally been Uncle Tiansong's seat, but it had lost its source of warmth and now stood there in icy coldness. After Tiansong departed, Uncle Huoshu chose this seat for his own and sat on it for a single day. That night Tiansong appeared at the head of Huoshu's bed in a dream, angrily demanding the return of his stone-block seat. From that day on, Uncle Huoshu was tormented by hemorrhoids, until everyone in the village knew about the incident. His hemorrhoids soon became unbearable; he took dozens of medications and applied dozens of ointments, but even the generations-old nostrum of the Kuntian family had no effect. Finally he heeded the advice of several old friends and let them carry his half-dead body over to Tiansong's spirit tablet, where he burned incense and offered his apologies. Uncle Ah-sheng, in his role as eldest among them, stood in front of the spirit tablet and upbraided Tiansong: "Tiansong, when you were alive you were open-minded, so why have you become such a short-tempered ghost? You and I and Huoshu and the others are old friends who grew up together in Clear Spring Village, from the time we were wearing pants with split crotches. Now, just because he sat on your stone block, your hostility has brought him to death's door. The fact of the matter is, that stone block doesn't belong to you. Since it's inside the temple, it belongs to the Patriarch. . . ." At first, many of the startled villagers paled when they heard this, for it was as if Uncle Tiansong were there among them, accepting Uncle Huoshu's apologies and being scolded by Uncle Ah-sheng.

Strange as it sounds, within a week Uncle Huoshu's hemorrhoids inexplicably disappeared. But then two months later he simply up and died. Naturally, no one else ever again dared to sit on the stone block, and in the minds of the Clear Spring villagers it had already been given a special name as a warning—hemorrhoid stone.

o o o

Only when an important matter required his attention would one of these old-timers willingly miss passing the time of day with the others in the temple side room. Their number had dwindled to four or five, and when they talked among themselves, no explanation of what was being said was ever needed. Their interests and topics of conversation were entirely compatible. And so, coming to the temple to chat after lunch had become a big part of their lives.

On this particular afternoon, Uncle Cow's Eye, Uncle Earthworm, Uncle Yuzai, and Uncle Ah-zhuan were all there; only Uncle Ah-sheng had not yet arrived. Usually he was the first on the scene, and even if he had to be late, one would think that by three o'clock at least he'd have shown up. The others were soon so worried and fidgety they were unable to talk about anything for more than a few moments.

"I hope nothing's happened to him," someone said uneasily.

"I saw him leading his ox out to Grass Canal to graze this morning."

"How could that be? I took my own ox out to Grass Canal this morning and I didn't see him there. But I saw you walking along the canal all the way to the end."

"Oh, right! That wasn't this morning, it was yesterday," the first old-timer said, quickly acknowledging his forgetfulness.

"Could he be sick?"

"I don't think so. He was fine yesterday. This morning when I was out at Grass Canal with my ox I ran into his eldest daughter-in-law with an armful of clothes she was taking out to wash. She'd have told me if he was sick." He paused, then added, "She didn't say a word, so there can't be anything wrong."

"Well, that is odd! He couldn't have just disappeared, could he?" A momentary smile appeared on Cow's Eye's face but faded away as a silence fell over the group.

"Oh shit, that's right!" Earthworm suddenly blurted out. "Didn't he say the day before yesterday that he was going into town to find a divinator to select the right date to rebuild his stove? He said the firewood burned too hot."

"Aha, now I remember!" Ah-zhuan's lips parted momentarily into a broad grin. "This old noggin of mine's like a stone in the field—it ought to be thrown away. This morning I bumped into him by the well just as he was setting out for town."

"Well, I'll be damned! Is that the truth?"

"You said it—another stone in the field!" Uncle Yuzai cursed, half in jest.

"Still, if he went to town to select a date he should have gotten back by now!"

"Do you think he might have cashed it in on some whorehouse bed?" Earthworm wisecracked.

"Shit! That'd be the way to go—the old fart."

"You're not so young yourself."

"That's right! What I'm saying is, we're all old farts—right?"

Without Uncle Ah-sheng in their midst, they lacked their leavening agent, and their conversation never really got off the ground. Most of what they'd talked about in the past were subjects he'd introduced. As the day wore on, they dozed in the refreshing cool breeze.

On the magnificent tree that stood near the western side room—that large banyan tree—the ripe figs were bright purple, since it was now the fruit-bearing month of June; the slightest bump sent them splattering to the ground. Beneath the tree a blanket of crushed figs gave off a sickly sweet, slightly acrid but generally pleasant aroma. A group of sprightly birds hopped from branch to branch singing songs that sounded like delicate fingers flowing across piano keys in a musical run. The ripe fruit beat out a rhythmical background as it fell to the ground—*splat, splat*. The twin six-year-old grandsons whom Earthworm had brought along sat astride stone lions at the temple entrance, both of them fast asleep, their arms draped tightly around the lions' necks.

o o o

Uncle Ah-sheng was hurrying home from town. His heart felt as if it were burning a hole in his chest, and the faster he tried to make the return trip to Clear Spring, the longer the road seemed, as if something were deliberately delaying his return. He grumbled to himself, "Won't this be the end of Clear Spring? I won't let them get away with it, I absolutely won't allow it! I'll run home and tell the others." He went down the road as fast as he could; after Kunchi's farm came Mute's farm, followed by Red Turtle's farm. After Red Turtle's farm there was Dragon Eye Well and Clear Spring's branch school. When Uncle Ah-sheng drew up alongside Dragon Eye, the village's natural spring well, after having made a point of cutting across to take a look at the well and the area surrounding it, he muttered angrily to himself, "If we let the people in town get away with this, it'll be the end of Clear Spring's geography. What a spiteful thing to do! A matter as great as heaven and earth itself, and they make up their minds on a whim! Shit!" He turned on his heel and ran to the temple.

The moment Uncle Ah-sheng strode into the western side room of the Temple of the Patriarch, he shouted at the top of his lungs:

"Hey! Let's see how long the Demon of Sleep can hold you in his grip!"

The men were startled awake by this unexpected and unusual shout. Then when they saw his appearance, they knew something important and inauspicious was in the air; otherwise, the red birthmark on the side of his face would surely not have lost color like that. A quick glance showed that Ah-sheng was so winded his nostrils couldn't handle his breathing; his parted lips were quaking.

"Why the hell do you have to shout?" Earthworm said, angry after having been so rudely awakened. But when he saw that Ah-sheng's expression was different than usual, he changed his tone to wisecrack again. "We thought you'd wound up in a whorehouse on the other side of town and decided not to come back." He wiped the drool that had run down his chin while he slept.

"What took you so long?" Ah-zhuan asked.

Ah-sheng slumped down in a bamboo chair, but the moment his back touched the back of the chair, he sprang up into a sitting position and said, "We absolutely can't allow them to do this—it'll be the end of Clear Spring." This time he spread his arms and lay back in the chair, as if he'd expended his last bit of energy in uttering these few words.

The others just exchanged glances until Earthworm said anxiously, "What's going on with you, old man? You say you've brought home bad news. Well, you're going to have to spit it out if you want us to share your concern! Isn't that right? You say two words—'the end!'—then just stretch out there. How are we supposed to know what's happened?"

All eyes, which had been riveted on Earthworm, shifted to Uncle Ah-sheng, who heaved a deep sigh.

"The people in town want to come out and dig up Clear Spring's Dragon Eye."

Everyone froze.

"What does that mean?"

"It means that those people who come here to swim in our spring have scraped up three hundred thousand dollars to build a swimming pool next to our village well." Ah-sheng looked at the others, who had been momentarily stunned, only to note that his revelation had produced no effect. Quickly growing irritated, he said, "What's this! Don't you even care?"

"What's wrong with a swimming pool?" Ah-zhuan asked.

"What *isn't* wrong with a swimming pool? First, it'll ruin our geography here. Have you forgotten that the only reason Clear Spring is such a terrific place is because we've got Dragon Eye Well? My grandfather told me so when I was a boy."

"Sure, everybody knows that. But what difference will it make if they build a swimming pool next to the well?"

"You see what I'm saying! Cow's Eye, you've got no cause to complain when people laugh at you for being a fool. Just think! They'll have to draw water for that swimming pool from the well by motor, and if they draw it dry, what are we going to do with a dried-up well? Won't that be the end of Clear Spring?"

They exchanged glances again and nodded their heads.

"That's right," Cow's Eye said. "This is serious."

"Have you forgotten that year when the killer typhoon hit and somebody threw a bale of straw down the well? Remember how the eyes of everyone in the village, young and old, began to hurt? Luckily that time it was only some straw. If it had been thorn balls,* probably everybody in Clear Spring would have kicked the bucket!" Seeing that looks of distress were starting to show on their faces, Ah-sheng began to experience the grim satisfaction he'd expected. "You see what I'm saying." Ah-sheng had a habit of prefacing his remarks with this phrase or uttering it when he was about to make a concluding remark. "How will we ever be able to put up with a motor in Dragon Eye?"

"Is this all true?" Ah-sheng was the focus of attention. As the others became convinced that he was telling the truth, a mood of grim concern began to settle upon them. Still, they were hoping desperately that the answer might be negative, and it was this hope that had prompted Uncle Earthworm's question.

At this stage Ah-sheng grew more relaxed, sensing that the heavy burden this news had placed on him was slowly being shared by the others. "Some time ago—just when, I'm not sure," he said, "they tested some of our water and concluded that it was special. The fools! Of course the water from Clear Spring's Dragon Eye Well is good. We didn't need any stupid tests to tell us that! But just because our water's good doesn't mean they can come and dig a swimming pool!"

"Then we'll have to fight this," Uncle Yuzai said, so greatly aroused that he sprayed saliva into the others' faces.

Cow's Eye, unflappable as ever, gently wiped the spit off his face and said, "Well, of course we will. We won't stand for this!"

Uncle Yuzai reached up and wiped his face too.

"And there's another reason. You can just bet that if the pool opens,

* Steel barbs formed in the shape of a ball and used in Taiwanese temples.

the people who come from town to go swimming—men and women—will be mixing with each other, wearing next to nothing. Who knows what'll be going through their minds? Here in Clear Spring we've always been simple, decent folk, but this could be the undoing of our sons and daughters and could contaminate the entire village!" Ah-sheng noticed the others nodding in silence, so he added, "You see what I'm saying, we've got no choice but to fight this."

Just then Ah-zhuan, in whose heart anger had been building, supplied yet another reason. "Not only that, it wouldn't be right to let Dragon Eye see all those girls and boys in their indecent, skimpy clothing. The dragon would get restless."

"That's right! So now we have three good reasons. Think hard, are there any more?"

Earthworm jumped angrily to his feet. "What other reasons do we need? With these three it's like saying the sky is falling!"

Just then one of his grandsons fell off the stone lion and began to cry. The timing of the tail end of Earthworm's comment—"the sky is falling!"—made it seem like a reaction to seeing his grandson fall to the ground.


3. THE FUNDAMENTAL KNOWLEDGE IN DEMOCRACY*

Never before had these few old-timers attended one of the village meetings, but on this particular evening they arrived early at the makeshift meeting grounds at Village Chief Xie's grain-drying yard and sat on front-row benches. Everyone in the village knew they had been waiting impatiently for this evening's meeting, and in fact was anxiously waiting to see whether the old men's opposition to the construction of a swimming pool next to Dragon Eye Well would have any effect. Consequently, there were far more people at the meeting than usual. Some families were represented by several members.

The people responsible for conducting and witnessing the village meeting had still not arrived by the time the site was crowded with villagers; from Village Chief Xie's house came the sounds of a local opera on his radio, which had been turned up full blast. Normally so little significance was placed on such meetings that if each household hadn't been

* A book dealing with the procedure of parliamentary rule, written by Dr. Sun Yat-sen.

required to send a representative to stamp the attendance sheet with a personal seal at the beginning and end of each as proof of attendance, no one would ever have shown up. It was normally the children who took the heads of households' seals to the meeting, where they simply played the whole time. This satisfied the adults as well as the children, who earned fifty cents for their efforts. But this time it was different. People felt that the meeting was necessary to solve this problem of theirs, one that had been growing more pressing each day. Everyone in attendance was so stirred up that the slightest provocation could have turned them into a mob.

Uncle Ah-sheng and the others turned back repeatedly to study the faces of their fellow villagers, who were crowding in behind them; smiles showed they were pleased by what they saw. Never before had these few men felt so secure, for at this moment at least, their fellow villagers were standing shoulder to shoulder with them. Their feelings of superiority could be likened to those of a soldier fearlessly facing the enemy and shouting, "Come on ahead, damn you! Anyone who turns and runs is a son of a bitch!"

Cow's Eye turned to his cronies. "Hey, let's not let these youngsters think we're over the hill. Tonight we old-timers will give them a show for their money." The others nodded, determined to do just that.

After the village clerk had raised the flag, he disappeared, following which the village chief also vanished. The meeting had originally been scheduled for seven-thirty, and although it was already more than twenty minutes late, you couldn't have told it from the people's faces; they were transfixed by the Taiwanese opera radio program. Suddenly, just before eight o'clock, someone turned off the radio, bringing the crowd up short. The village clerk and village chief came out through the front door of the house, panting as if they'd been running. As someone in the crowd yelled that it was time to start the meeting, the village chief climbed onto a crate and announced with a slight stammer that it would begin in a moment. He asked everyone to quiet down.

The village clerk kept glancing down the road, and when he finally spotted some figures walking toward them, he shouted excitedly, "Here they come! They're here!" The villagers turned to look. Some even stood up, throwing a momentary fright into the approaching people, who stopped in their tracks, surveyed the situation, then slowly continued toward the meeting site. The village chief jumped down from the crate, went over and shook hands all around, then led the newcomers over to the speaker's area.

To the crowd's surprise, even the district chief had shown up. But what made them sense that something highly unusual was afoot was that Constable Lin had brought five unfamiliar policemen with him. As usual, there was a smile on the constable's face, but there were disagreeable looks on the faces of the five policemen. With them were, in addition, three gentlemen in Western suits carrying paper fans, all nearly identical. The village chief introduced them as special invited guests.

It was eight-thirty by the time the official party was seated; everything that evening was extraordinary, for under normal circumstances the officials were the ones who waited for the villagers to arrive. When the village clerk saw the fattest of the three gentlemen nod his head, he screamed at the top of his lungs, "The village meeting will come to order!"

Before the clerk even got around to asking the chairman to take charge of the meeting, Earthworm nudged Uncle Ah-sheng to get up and have his say. So Uncle Ah-sheng stood up and began in a loud voice, "I have something to say . . ."

Wanting to preserve the decorum of the meeting, the village clerk ignored Uncle Ah-sheng's remark and continued with his parliamentary command in an even louder voice, "The chairman will please take charge!"

When Uncle Ah-sheng saw he was being ignored by everyone on the platform, he called the village chief by his nickname. "Hey! Gander Kunzai, I told you before the meeting I had something to say tonight."

People began to laugh in spite of themselves; even the five policemen with their tight faces smirked briefly. Village Chief Xie Ah-kun turned to look down at Ah-sheng, giving him an angry, exasperated stare. But Ah-sheng thought this constituted an unjust rebuke, so he went on, "I mean it, goddamn it! I told you, we both know that!" This elicited another outburst of laughter.

The village clerk quickly walked over and put his mouth up to Ah-sheng's ear; upon being told that the right ear was no good and that he'd have to speak into the left one, he whispered, "Can't you see that fat guy's a big shot? You shouldn't be trying to break up the meeting with a lot of goofy remarks."

Angered by the threat, Ah-sheng shouted, "What's that? You call it breaking up the meeting just because I want to say something?"

In obvious embarrassment, the village clerk whispered again into his ear, this time saying more politely, "You misunderstood me. We want you to talk, but we're not ready for you yet. I'll tell you when your time comes."

Ah-sheng nodded but added loudly, "How was I supposed to know it wasn't time to talk yet?" Then he gave Earthworm a jab.

"Damn you, it's all your fault. You told me to stand up and talk."

"How was I supposed to know?" Earthworm answered in an equally loud voice.

An argument nearly broke out between them, but the village clerk stepped in quickly to make peace. "Okay, okay now. Whatever it is you have to say, your turn will come in a little while."

The episode produced a good deal of laughter among the villagers, and each time his actions drew laughs from the crowd, Uncle Ah-sheng turned around to survey their faces to see if the people were still standing by him. He was encouraged by what he saw, as his increasingly rustic, somewhat foolish manner proved.

The village chief opened the meeting with a speech in Mandarin that left our old-timers feeling disgruntled, since they didn't understand a word he said. Next the three gentlemen came up and gave speeches, though in the ears and eyes of the old-timers it was little more than an unbearable series of grunts and gestures. The same thing happened with the district chief and the village chief, and finally even the constable got up and said a few words. Assuming he'd have to wait until each of the five policemen had his say before his own turn finally rolled around, Ah-sheng turned to Earthworm and said in a grudging voice, "Shit! We might sit here until our backs are hunched before our turn to talk comes."

But before long, prior to inviting Uncle Ah-sheng up to speak, the village chief recapped in Taiwanese what had been said. He explained that the chief representative had described in detail how all sides concerned had enthusiastically promoted the construction of a swimming pool beside the well in the interest of developing Clear Spring, and how he hoped that the local people would unite their efforts to realize this goal. After the swimming pool was completed, there would be vehicular traffic, the branch school would gain independent status, and Clear Spring Village would prosper. When he finished, not a single villager applauded, but when Ah-sheng eventually stood up, he was greeted by a burst of enthusiastic clapping. He turned to look at the villagers, then faced the platform and said his piece in a challenging tone:

"I'd like you to go back and tell the people in town that Uncle Ah-sheng of Clear Spring says, if they want to go swimming they can stay home and take a dip in their bathtubs!"

This provocative statement produced an outburst of laughter and a nearly deafening round of applause; Uncle Ah-sheng himself had no idea where his inspiration had come from. He continued, "Don't be fooled into thinking that Clear Spring is the place for you to build your swimming pool—the water in Clear Spring is for our use in the rice fields, not for you townspeople to bathe in!" The waves of applause increased the pitch of excitement in the old man's words. "The people of Clear Spring have no use for your 'vehicular traffic'—all anyone needs is two good legs. We're concerned only about our fields and our water. As for the lay of the land, Clear Spring is a dragon's head. The village exit leading to town is the mouth of the dragon, and the well beside the school is its eye, which is why we call it Dragon Eye Well. Ever since the time of our ancestors, the people of Clear Spring have been protected by this dragon, which is why we've been able to live our lives in peace. Now someone wants to bring harm to our dragon's eye, and the people of Clear Spring will not stand idly by and let that happen." He turned around. "Isn't that right?" he asked the crowd. They jumped eagerly to their feet. The people sitting on the platform were shocked by Uncle Ah-sheng's ability to incite the crowd.

Cow's Eye leaned over to Uncle Ah-sheng. "Say, old friend, has the revered Patriarch adopted you as his spokesman?"

"I don't know," Uncle Ah-sheng answered him. "Somehow everything seems as clear as a bell to me."

After the meeting ended, Uncle Ah-sheng was invited by the village chief to his house, where he met several of the special guests in the reception room. The village clerk interpreted what they were saying for his benefit. The chief representative said to Uncle Ah-sheng respectfully, "Old uncle, I truly admire your speaking ability."

"You flatter me. I've never been to school and can't write a word."

"To be able to speak like that without having been to school is even more amazing."

"Don't talk like that. You're embarrassing me," Uncle Ah-sheng said. "I've heard people quote some of the things the master Confucius said, and that's more than enough for my use."

The chief representative then said something to the others, which Uncle Ah-sheng asked the village clerk to interpret for him.

"He's commenting on your speaking ability."

"There's no need for that kind of talk. I'm only being reasonable, taking the truth as I see it and speaking as honestly as I know how. The more you use common sense, the clearer everything becomes. The truth can stand any test, or as they say, 'true gold fears no fire.' Isn't that right?"

"Old uncle, I want to ask you something, and I hope you'll answer me honestly. What is it that makes you so brave, and why do you oppose this matter so strongly? Is someone in the background goading you into doing this?"

"No!" Ah-sheng was angry.

"Then why are you so set against it?"

Uncle Ah-sheng responded without a moment's hesitation and with considerable pride, "Because I love this piece of land and everything on it."

## 4. THE FIRST ROUND

On the day the Reliable Construction Company erected its sign over the twenty-five-by-fifty-meter swimming-pool site in Clear Spring Village, its bosses ran into trouble. They were unable to find a single temporary laborer anywhere in the village to dig the hole. On the second day, they hired fifty outside laborers to come and carry off the dirt from the hole.

Uncle Ah-sheng and the others spent the whole of every day at the work site obstructing the construction company workers, until finally the police had to step in and warn them they were breaking the law. This infuriated Uncle Ah-sheng, who couldn't understand why others received the protection of the law for interfering with his and his friends' actions, while the righteousness of his behavior was considered illegal.

The old-timers split up, each recruiting a group of men who returned to the construction site with poles and knives. The laborers threw down their carrying poles and baskets and fled. The group of men Uncle Ah-sheng had brought with him then piled up all the abandoned tools, set a torch to them, and watched them burn. As the flames burned fiercely, the men gathered around the bonfire, the thrill of victory instilling in them feelings of newly gained glory. Before long, a circle of village women and children formed around them, their admiration causing the men to experience a heroic dignity that showed on their faces.

From the midst of the crowd came some loudly voiced comments by Uncle Ah-sheng: "Since they've fled, well and good. That way they can keep their scrawny hides. We've given them a taste of what the people of Clear Spring can do; now let's see if they dare to come back after this and disturb even a blade of our grass!"

Just then they heard shouts off in the distance. "Here they come! Here they come!" And before they knew what was happening, a fire truck carrying a dozen or so armed policemen had arrived in their midst. The policemen jumped down and quickly penetrated the heart of the crowd, after which they turned and began forcing the people back, scattering them before them. The farmers were disarmed and herded one by one into the fire truck. The whole procedure was carried out with the precision of a military exercise.

After Uncle Ah-sheng stepped into the fire truck, the whole lot of them were delivered to the town's station house. Several of the armed policemen stayed behind to calm down the remaining villagers and urge everyone to quietly return home.

The village and district chiefs ran from place to place over this incident; the construction company officials said they wanted assurances that this sort of thing wouldn't happen again. They were willing to work out a settlement if the safety of their laborers was guaranteed.

Late that evening, word came down to release the men, each of whose tightly drawn face showed the effects of the scare he had been given.

Their apprehensive mood remained with them even after they returned to Clear Spring, and their minds were still on the written depositions and fingerprints they'd left behind at the station house. They fretted over what kind of trouble these things might mean for them later on. This somewhat terrifying consideration hit them especially hard when they arrived home and looked into the faces of their family members. Regret set in, and no matter what thoughts of Dragon Eye or, for that matter, the entire village of Clear Spring came to them, they were powerless to muster any feeling of resistance. In fact, some even lacked the will to resist what was normally hidden in their subconscious.

How had they had gotten so worked up? All Uncle Ah-sheng had done was sound the call and everyone had joined the charge like a swarm of bees. They could not know how proud Uncle Ah-sheng was that they had dared to throw out their chests and step forward on behalf of Clear Spring.

Declared the ringleader of the mob, Uncle Ah-sheng was kept overnight at the station house. This actually brought him the peace of mind of a religious martyr. From the moment he sprang into action because of his ardent love for Clear Spring, he sensed he had changed somehow, and he no longer considered himself a man devoid of purpose. In fact, this matter had taken on a greater importance than his own life. If he didn't do it, who would? It was as if a sort of faith had attached itself to his body and had become personified; somehow others too felt that he was swathed in a layer of something that shielded him from outside forces. His rustic airs began to fall away, and the gap between him and other people grew to vast proportions. This feeling was shared both by those who knew him well and by anyone else who had at one time or another had a serious chat with him. Uncle Ah-sheng was aware only that he spoke differently than before, and was amazed by nearly every sentence he uttered. For instance, when someone who tried to change his mind asked what was so good about the water of Clear Spring, a mystical look came into Uncle Ah-sheng's eyes as he said, as if he were in a completely different world, "If you can talk to fish, ask that question of the fish in Clear Spring. Otherwise, just see how happy they are, and you'll get the answer you seek. And it won't be your Uncle Ah-sheng who gave it to you."

The people around Uncle Ah-sheng were just as confused by all this as he was; the sensitivity with which he felt the changes in himself gradually diminished. The mystery of faithful devotion to a belief can cause a man to approach godlike sublimity. That was likely the case with Uncle Ah-sheng—he had already begun the process leading to that plateau where man as apostle and God exist as one.

In the middle of the night, Uncle Ah-sheng was taken to a larger room. The moment he entered, he spotted the honored guest from the village meeting of the previous night—the fat man who had been sitting in the middle. Everyone was extremely polite to Uncle Ah-sheng, inviting him to sit in a rattan chair at a table, pouring him tea, and offering him a cigarette. They wanted to take down his statement, but before they began, the fat man explained that he was not being detained by the police, that they only wanted the "elderly gentleman" to cool down. As far as they were concerned, the whole incident had started out as a simple matter, even though inciting the superstitious masses and nearly turning the whole thing into a violent affair was something the law could not tolerate. But since the "elderly gentleman's" motives were pure, they were willing to turn a major incident into a minor one and a minor incident into none at all, in hopes that the "elderly gentleman" would go home and enjoy life with his grandchildren. Uncle Ah-sheng thanked them unenthusiastically and began to answer their questions for the written statement.

"What's your name?"

"Xu Ah-sheng."

"How old are you?"

"I'm seventy-nine, not counting intercalary years, and I won't live many more."

They laughed.

"Then you ought to take it easy and enjoy your twilight years," one of them said. "Why bother yourself with matters that don't concern you?"

Uncle Ah-sheng answered in a very relaxed manner, "For the simple reason that I won't be around many more years, and if I don't concern myself with such matters now, I won't have the chance to do it later." He continued somberly, "Whether a matter concerns a person or not depends on your point of view. And I . . . I don't agree with you."

The man taking down the deposition responded abruptly. "Why do you oppose the construction of a swimming pool in Clear Spring?"

Uncle Ah-sheng gave his three major reasons, embellishing upon them quite a bit.

"Then why did you organize a large crowd to disturb the peace?"

"I could hear Clear Spring moaning with each bit of earth those people's hoes took out of her to build the swimming pool, and since I didn't have the power to come to her rescue alone, I had to gather the villagers of Clear Spring around me to stop what was happening."

"Do you realize what sort of criminal act this constitutes?"

"What does that have to do with the geography of our village?"

"I wish you'd just answer my questions. I'll ask you one more time. Do you realize what sort of criminal act this constitutes?"

"No, I don't."

" . . . "

" . . . "

Uncle Ah-sheng was still full of vigor as dawn broke in the morning and they quietly sent him back to Clear Spring by jeep.


## 5. OLD MASTER CHEN'S GRANDSON

The construction work proceeded apace, as Uncle Ah-sheng had by now lost the active support of his fellow villagers. Isolation and worry had aged him considerably, and even though his family tricked him into leaving Clear Spring to visit some relatives in Taipei, owing to his unfamiliarity with flush toilets and a mental block against using them, he returned to Clear Spring the same night with a growing pressure in his gut. He entered his home without saying a word and headed straight for the outhouse located in the pigsty.

Several of his old friends had grown passive over this whole matter, and as he witnessed the work on the swimming pool progressing day by day, he knew that somehow he'd have to stop it soon. Even if he managed to stop the work after all the earth had been scooped out, refilling the hole alone would be a taxing job. After thinking the matter through, he decided that rather than try to interfere directly at the work site, he'd use the more indirect method of calling upon connections. If only he could find someone with some real clout, that would solve all his problems.

But considering Uncle Ah-sheng's circumstances, there couldn't possibly be any bigwig with whom he had a personal friendship. Then in the midst of his disappointment, he thought of County Chief Chen. He still recalled how County Chief Chen had come to Clear Spring during the election campaign, sweating profusely, and had pumped his hand enthusiastically, begging over and over again for his support. He'd promised that if he was elected, Ah-sheng could come to him any time with his problems.

One of County Chief Chen's campaign workers had told Uncle Ah-sheng that people who voted for County Chief Chen were folks with insight, for Chen was not a man to make empty promises. Not only did Uncle Ah-sheng vote for Chen, he urged others to do the same. At the time, he'd been genuinely moved that the owner of that plump, delicate hand had been willing to let it be shaken by his coarse, rustic one.

"That's it!" he thought. "Why not go see County Chief Chen? He promised me I could bring him any problems I had. During the Manchu dynasty, County Chief Chen's grandfather was known as Old Master Chen, and my grandfather was one of his tenant farmers. In the old days, whenever the provincial governor came to recruit soldiers and collect taxes, my grandfather and father always volunteered their services as provisional soldiers. All I have to do is go see County Chief Chen and tell him that our family used to be his family's tenant farmers. That ought to do it." This thought brought a new flicker of hope to Uncle Ah-sheng.

Early the next day he changed into clean clothes and went into town to look up County Chief Chen at the county office.

Only after going to several offices did he finally manage to present himself at the outer office of the county chief, and after surveying the stylish surroundings, he inwardly felt very pleased. The county chief had to be a big shot, since his office was so hard to find and was such a solemn place. He must be in charge of a lot of people. With his approval, anything was possible.

The secretary informed him that the county chief was in a meeting inside, and that he should return in the afternoon. He told her he was willing to wait until the meeting was over; in fact, he was happy to wait, for in his estimation, the harder a person was to see, the greater his stature.

When he finally got in to see the county chief, he gave a deep bow, which, however, was not returned. Since the girl in the waiting room had told him he could have no more than ten minutes of the county chief's time, he'd experienced a bit of apprehension. Where should he begin if he hoped to enlist the county chief's support in ten minutes' time?

He thought it best to first make the county chief aware of their relationship, so after the county chief asked him to take a seat, he began by saying, "My family, the Xus, used to be tenant farmers of Great Master Chen's." He cast a hopeful glance at the county chief's face to see if there was an expression of appreciation. But he merely heard him grunt and saw him lower his head to leaf through a stack of red-lined official documents. Uncle Ah-sheng lapsed into silence, and the county chief raised his head and urged him to continue with what he had come to say. But the whole time Uncle Ah-sheng was talking, the county chief's head was buried in the stack of documents as he mechanically affixed his seal to one after another. Apparently, he didn't even have to read them—there were so many it took all his time just to affix his seal to each one.

Even after Uncle Ah-sheng had hit all the important points and was awaiting a reply, the county chief was still hurriedly stamping documents. As for the matter at hand, the county chief, feeling that it was a dispute involving land and developers, pondered which agency he should assign to settle the matter—the Social Services Administration, the Civil Administration, or the Construction Bureau. Even as he considered the matter, he rang for his secretary, who led Uncle Ah-sheng over to the Construction Bureau.

As things turned out, Uncle Ah-sheng was the butt of a number of jokes at the Construction Bureau before finally being turned down. Since there was no place else to go, he returned wearily to Clear Spring, his original impression of County Chief Chen now completely shattered.

On the road home, he reflected upon what had happened, cursing inwardly. "Shit! So that's Old Master Chen's grandson! The old master would certainly weep if he knew this."

## 6. A CAT IS NOT A DOG

After Uncle Ah-sheng lost the support of his fellow villagers, he found he was no longer able to translate his beliefs into action. Gradually he lost the religious aura that had enveloped him at the beginning, so that on the day the swimming pool was finally completed, he had reverted to his old rustic self.

A great many people crowded up to the chain fence around the swimming pool to watch the splashing and hilarity inside. Local children ran home, whining and cajoling until they were given a dollar to go swimming. Youngsters who should have been out tending the fields had put their hoes aside and were staring, as though mesmerized, at the bras and short red pants of the swimsuits, their desires aroused. Greatly troubled, Uncle Ah-sheng paced back and forth outside the pool enclosure agonizingly stewing in his own juices. Finally he rushed crazily into the pool area and shouted at the top of his lungs, "If you're going to take your clothes off, why not go all the way, like this?" With that he stripped naked. Girls were so shocked they scrambled out of the pool shrieking, while the boys laughed hilariously and applauded. Uncle Ah-sheng bent over at the waist and dove headfirst into the deep end of the pool, though he couldn't even dog-paddle. When he didn't surface right away, the onlookers no longer thought it was funny. Two girls dove in with a sense of urgency and pulled him to the surface, but they were a moment too late—all that now remained of Uncle Ah-sheng was his name.

## 7. THE SOUND OF LAUGHTER

On the day of the funeral, Uncle Ah-sheng's family had requested that the pool be closed for the day—after all, it had been the cause of his death. The procession with Uncle Ah-sheng's coffin had to pass right by the entrance to the swimming pool, so the manager of the pool had given his consent and had draped black bunting across the entrance. But even before the coffin had passed by, many of the children of Clear Spring, not to be denied, had sneaked into the pool area, and the peals of laughter that accompanied their frolicking in the water washed over the walls like waves.

# His Son's Big Doll

o

In foreign countries there is an occupation called the "sandwich-man."* This line of work one day suddenly appeared in the little town, but no one could come up with a fitting term, nor knew what it was supposed to be called. Eventually, someone—just who is not known—coined the term "ad man" for a person engaged in this work, and once it became known in town, everyone, young and old, quickly grew accustomed to saying "the ad man." Even babies cradled in their mothers' arms would stop crying and fussing and raise their heads to look around whenever their mothers called out, "Look, here comes the ad man!"

The sun, like a fireball rolling along overhead, followed the people, causing the perspiration to flow freely. For Kunshu this sort of hot day was particularly unbearable, for he was attired from head to toe in a strange costume that made him look like a nineteenth-century European military officer. He was the center of attention not only because of the way he was made up, but even more so because of his heavy costume. But that's what this job of his was all about—attracting attention.

* English in the original.

The sweat coursing down through the makeup gave him the appearance of a melting wax statue; the false mustache stuffed up into his nostrils was soaked with sweat, making it necessary to breathe through his mouth. Only the waving feathers atop his high conical hat gave an appearance of coolness. He longed to escape the heat by walking under the arcade, but the movie ads he was carrying over his shoulders made that impossible. Two more ad boards had recently been added below the original ads: the one in front proclaimed the virtues of Hundred-Herb Tea; the one behind plugged a tapeworm medicine. As a result, when he walked down the street, he looked like a puppet on a string. The added load was more tiring, of course, but he consoled himself with the thought that the additional money was worth the greater fatigue.

He had regretted going into this line of work from the very first day, and was eager to find another. The more he thought about what he was doing, the more ridiculous it seemed. He laughed at himself, even if no one else did, and this self-imposed mental torment was forever on his mind, increasing in intensity as his fatigue grew. He'd better find a new line of work. But then he'd had the same thought for more than a year.

In the heat, the glare of the asphalt road ahead made it impossible to see anything. Off in the distance everything was shrouded in a bile-colored haze, which he dared not try to see through. For if he were actually to collapse there, as he feared he might, that would be the end of it for him. He summoned up all his willpower to struggle against a pall of color before his eyes that seemed bent on hounding him to death. *Damn it! This is no job for a man.* But whom was he to blame?

o o o

"Say, boss, since this movie house of yours just opened, it won't hurt to give it a try. If I don't produce results within a month, you don't have to pay me. I can take your movie ads to the people far better than any billboard. What do you say?"

"What sort of costume do you have in mind?"

*It wasn't so much what I said as it was my pitiful look that aroused his sympathy and convinced him.*

"If you'll give me the go-ahead, you can leave everything to me."

*Getting this damned job was the most exciting thing that had happened in my life.*

"Well, you finally got yourself a job."

*Damn it! Ah-zhu was so happy about this job she was in tears.*

"Ah-zhu, now you don't need to get an abortion."

*It's only right that she was in tears. She's a strong woman, and that was the first time I'd ever seen her cry with such helpless abandon. I knew she was very happy.*

At this point in his thoughts Kunshu couldn't keep from shedding tears himself; they flowed unchecked, partly because he didn't have a free hand to wipe them away and partly because he was thinking, *What the hell, no one can tell if it's sweat or tears anyway!* This thought seemed to encourage his tears, which flowed freely. Under the scorching sun he felt the two lines of hot tears streaming down his cheeks, and for the first time in his life he experienced the satisfying relief of an unrestrained cry.

o o o

"Kunshu, just look at you! What in the world have you turned into? You don't look like a proper man or a proper ghost! How could you let yourself come to this?"

On the evening of his second day on the job, Ah-zhu told him that his uncle had stopped by several times already. He was changing his clothes when his uncle came shouting his way in.

"Uncle . . ."

*I should have stopped calling him "Uncle" long ago. Uncle! Uncle be damned!*

"Don't you call me 'Uncle,' the way you're made up!"

"Uncle, hear me out. . . ."

"What's there to say? Is this the only job around? I believe that anyone willing to be an ox can find a plow. I'll tell you to your face—I want you to get the hell out of here and not bring disgrace upon your community. If you don't heed my warning, don't be surprised if you're disowned by your own uncle!"

"I've been looking everywhere for a job. . . ."

"What's that? After looking everywhere, you came up with this ridiculous, dead-end job!"

"What could I do? I tried to borrow rice from you, but you wouldn't . . ."

"Oh? Is it my fault now? Is it? I don't have rice to spare. I bought what I have little by little. Besides, what does that have to do with that ridiculous job of yours? Stop talking nonsense! You . . ."

*Nonsense? Who's talking nonsense? That really pisses me off! Uncle! Big deal! Screw him!*

"Then just leave me alone! Leave me alone leave me alone leave me alone!"

*He's driving me crazy!*

"You dumb beast! Okay, you dumb beast, if you want to defy me, go ahead. From now on I am no longer Kunshu's uncle! We're through!"

"So what! With an uncle like you, I'd starve to death anyway."

*A good comeback. How did I ever come up with one like that? As he left he was cursing a blue streak. The next day I didn't feel like going to work, not because I was afraid of offending my uncle but because I was depressed. If I hadn't noticed the tears in Ah-zhu's eyes, reminding me of my promise—"Ah-zhu, now you don't need to get an abortion"—and how I'd already thrown away the two packets of medicine, I'm sure I wouldn't have had the courage to walk out the door.*

◦ ◦ ◦

Thoughts. They were all that helped Kunshu get through the day; without them, the passage of time would have been agonizingly slow as he made his dozen or so rounds, from early morning till late at night, up and down every street and lane in town. His mind was active as a natural result of his loneliness and solitude. He seldom thought about the future, and even when he did, it was only about the practical problems of the next few days. Mostly he thought of the past, which he judged by present-day standards.

The blazing fireball followed him as he left the asphalt street. The bile-colored pall was still there a short distance ahead of him, and he was disheartened by the sinking feeling engulfing him. The anxiety forced upon him was a little like the feeling he had every morning at dawn: as he lay in bed, watching the first rays of sunlight seep in through the cracks in the wall amid the surrounding darkness, the stillness, and that dampness peculiar to this house, his mood would change from tranquility to fear. Though this was something he'd grown accustomed to, it was almost like a brand new experience each day. His monthly income didn't amount to much, but it was certainly no worse by comparison than the income from other jobs. It was the tedium and the ridiculous nature of the job that nearly drove him mad. But without the money it brought in, his family's modest livelihood would have presented an immediate problem. What was he to do? Finally, he'd force himself to climb out of bed uneasily and, with a certain sense of shame, sit down at Ah-zhu's little dressing table, take some face powder from the drawer, and rub it into his face. As he looked in the mirror, with only half his face painted, he'd smile sorrowfully as waves of vague emptiness surged through his mind.

o o o

He felt that all the water in his body was gone—he'd never been so thirsty! The prostitutes in the red-light district next to the elementary school were standing around food stands snacking in their pajamas and wooden clogs. Others were sitting on stoops making up their faces or just leaning listlessly in doorways or burying their heads in comic books to pass the time. The few families living in the red-light district either barricaded themselves behind tightly closed doors or had put up fences in front of their homes; as an added measure, each house sported a sign alongside the door with the words "Regular Household" in large red letters.

"Hey, the ad man's coming!" one of the prostitutes called out from a food stand. The others turned to look at the signboard hanging in front of Kunshu.

He mechanically approached the food stand.

"Hey! What's playing at the Palace Theater?" one of the prostitutes asked as he went by.

He mechanically walked past them.

"Have you lost your marbles? That guy never talks," one of the other prostitutes said maliciously.

"Is he a mute?" A debate arose among the prostitutes.

"Who knows what he is?"

"I've never seen him smile. His face is always lifeless."

He was so close, only a few steps away, and their words pierced his heart.

"Hey! Ad man, come here! I'm waiting for you," one of the prostitutes shouted as she ran after him. Amid the ensuing laughter, someone said:

"If he really did come to you, it'd be a wonder if you didn't die of fright."

He kept walking, but he could still hear the prostitute's provocative comments. At the end of the lane he smiled.

*I'm willing. If I had the cash I'd be willing. I'd choose the daydreamer leaning up against Xiaoluo's door.*

Passing through the red-light district momentarily helped him forget his fatigue. He saw by a clock on the street that it was nearly three-fifteen. He had to hurry to the train station to meet passengers coming in from the north. This was part of his arrangement with the boss; he also had to mingle with factory workers as they left work and high school students when school was out.

He managed his time so he didn't have to rush or take shortcuts. As he emerged from the Eastern Lights district and turned toward the train station, the passengers he'd come to meet were just then filing out of the exits, so he approached them from the shady side of the street. This was one of his strategies: the heat was still so intense it could bake a potato, so the departing passengers scooted across the open area and quickly moved under the sheltered arcade where the transport company was located. The only people who showed any interest in him were a few out-of-towners. He wouldn't have known what to do if not for the encouragement he received from those few unfamiliar, curious faces. He was confident that he could look into any face and tell whether the person was local or from out of town; he could even say when and where the person was likely to appear.

But he couldn't hold on to this job by relying solely on those few unfamiliar faces. Sooner or later the boss was bound to find out. The reaction of the people in front of him made his heart sink.

*I've got to think of something else.*

A conflict raged in his heart.

"Look! Look over there!"

During his first days on the job, everyone had gaped at him with the astonishment of seeing a ghost.

"Who's he?"

"Where'd he come from?"

"Is he from our town?"

"Can't be!"

"Yo! It's an ad for the Palace Theater."

"Where in the world is he from?"

*I'll be damned! What's so interesting about me? Why don't they pay attention to the ad? Back then I was an object of real interest to them—I was a riddle. Screw them! Now they all know I'm Kunshu, and the riddle has been solved, so no one pays any more attention. What's it got to do with me anyway? Doesn't the ad change all the time? The gleam in those cold, curious eyes!*

It was all the same to Kunshu—being the center of attention and being ignored were equally painful.

He made a sweep around the train station, then meandered back to the main street. Unable to reconcile the conflict of inner cold and external heat, he reacted merely with a few inward curses. The bile-colored pall reappeared some five or six meters ahead, and his throat was so parched it seemed about to crack. At that moment his home exerted a powerful pull on him.

*She won't fail to make tea for me today because of what happened last night, will she? Ai! I was wrong not to go home for lunch, and I should have returned home for tea in the morning. That'll only add to her misunderstanding. Goddamn it!*

o o o

"What are you so mad about? And why take it out on me? Can't you lower your voice a little? Ah-long's sleeping."

*I shouldn't have taken my anger out on her. It's all the fault of that damned cheapskate—he wouldn't go along with my suggestion to change the costume. "That's your affair!" he'd said. My affair? That damned dogturd. This costume, which I made out of a fireman's uniform, has lost its appeal. Besides, it's not the sort of thing to be wearing in sweltering heat like this!*

"I'll talk as loud as I please!"

*Whew! That was going a bit far. But what was I supposed to do with all that anger inside? I was exhausted, and Ah-zhu wasn't using her head. Why couldn't she put herself in my place instead of arguing with me?*

"Are you trying to pick a fight?"

"What if I am?"

*Damn it, Ah-zhu, I didn't mean it!*

"Really?"

"That's enough!" Then he had added gruffly, "Shut up or I'll . . . I'll punch you!" He slammed his clenched fist down hard on the table.

*That must have worked, because she shut up. I was worried she'd defy me and I wouldn't be able to stop myself from hitting her. But I really didn't mean it. Honestly, I shouldn't have frightened Ah-long awake. The way Ah-zhu held the crying child in her arms almost broke my heart. My throat's so dry I can't stand it, and it doesn't look like I'll get any tea today. Serves me right! No, I'm too thirsty.*

Occupied with thoughts of what had happened the night before, he suddenly found himself standing in front of the door to his house. He was shocked back to the here and now. The door was slightly ajar, and as he nudged it with his foot, it swung open lightly on its hinges. He laid down his ad board, tucked his hat under his arm, and entered. The teapot was on the table beside a bamboo food cover, a green plastic cup covering the spout. She had made tea! A warm feeling flooded Kunshu's heart. Enormously relieved, he poured himself a full cup of tea and gulped it down. It was the ginger tea with brown sugar that Ah-zhu had been preparing for him every day since the beginning of summer and that was waiting for him each time he passed by the house. Someone had once told her that ginger tea is a good tonic for a tired man. He was so thirsty he filled the cup again, but he felt his heart swelling with anxiety. Normally it didn't bother him if Ah-zhu was out when he came home for tea, but the thought of his unreasonable loss of temper with her the night before unsettled and distressed him. He put down the cup and looked under the food cover and into the rice pot, discovering that nothing had been touched. Ah-long was not asleep in his bed, and the laundry Ah-zhu had washed for other people was neatly folded. Where was everybody?

∘ ∘ ∘

When Kunshu left that morning without eating breakfast, Ah-zhu could hardly bear the deep concern she felt. At first she wanted to call him back to eat, but she hesitated a moment and before she knew it, he was already across the street. They hadn't spoken a word. As always, she strapped Ah-long onto her back and went out to wash other people's clothes. She was so distraught she didn't know what to do with herself, so she scrubbed the clothes extra hard—so hard that the movements of her body made it impossible for Ah-long to cram the soap dish he was holding into his mouth to satisfy his sucking instinct. He threw it away and cried angrily. Ah-zhu kept scrubbing the clothes, evidently unaware that her son was crying more and more loudly; in the past she'd never let Ah-long cry so pitifully.

"Ah-zhu," the mistress called through the bathroom window overlooking the washroom.

Her head lowered, Ah-zhu continued scrubbing the clothes.

"Ah-zhu!" The kindly woman was forced to raise her voice.

Startled, Ah-zhu stopped her work and straightened up to hear what the mistress had to say. Then she became aware of Ah-long's cries and reached back to pat his bottom with a wet hand. She cocked her head to listen to the mistress.

"Couldn't you hear your baby scream?" Her voice, while mildly reproachful, was as amiable as ever.

"This child of mine . . ." There was really nothing she could say. "He cries, even with a soap dish to play with!" She lowered her left shoulder and looked back at the child. "Where's your soap dish?" Quickly discovering the cast-off dish on the floor, she bent over, picked it up, rinsed it off, and handed it back to Ah-long. Then she stooped down again and picked up the clothes, but before she could resume scrubbing, the mistress said:

"That's a brand-new dress you have there, so don't scrub so hard."

Ah-zhu had no idea how she'd been washing the dress, but there didn't seem to be any call for this reminder by the mistress.

After finally managing to hang up the laundry, Ah-zhu rushed out onto the street with Ah-long on her back. She threaded her way through the marketplace and the main section of town, looking up and down the streets anxiously, searching in vain for Kunshu. She racked her brain thinking of places where she might find him. Finally she caught a glimpse of him in the distance, carrying his ad board high as he walked down People's Rights Road toward Town Hall. She ran after him in high spirits, and before long, his back was fully visible. She lowered her shoulder and put her face up close to Ah-long's.

"Look, Ah-long, there's Daddy." The way she pointed at Kunshu's back and her tone of voice had the qualities of cringing inferiority. There was too great a distance separating them for Ah-long to know what was going on. Ah-zhu stood at the side of the road and followed Kunshu's back with her eyes until it disappeared at the crossroads. At that moment, the outermost layer of anxiety was stripped from her heart. She wondered what he was thinking, for there had been a message in his not eating. Still, she obtained consolation from the sight of him carrying his signs as usual. But the mixture of this relieving thought with those other, disturbing elements produced a confusion in her mind even more unbearable than her original fears. Seeing Kunshu like this only changed her mood—it did nothing to lessen her anxiety. She decided to go over to the next house and wash their clothes.

The moment she came home after finishing her work, she went over and removed the lid of the teapot. It was still full and the rice porridge had not been touched, proof that Kunshu had not been home today. Something was definitely wrong. Or so she thought. She had intended to put the sleeping Ah-long to bed, but now she could not. She rushed back outside, closing the door behind her.

The fireball's heat was intense, and most of the pedestrians had sought refuge under the arcade, making it easier for Ah-zhu to look for Kunshu. At each intersection she looked in all directions until she was sure he was not there. Finally she spotted him near the lumberyard on North Chiang Kai-shek Avenue, heading toward the Temple of the Sea Goddess. She followed him discreetly at a distance of seven or eight houses, being careful lest he turn around and see her. Noticing nothing out of the ordinary about his behavior from the rear, she hid behind arcade posts several times, closing the distance to two or three houses, and continued observing him. Still nothing out of the ordinary. But she remained uneasy about his refusal to eat or drink, and she was not reassured by what she was seeing. Convinced that something was wrong, she feared that a misunderstanding had come between them.

Suddenly she felt a need to see him from the front, figuring that a glance at his face might tell her what she wanted to know. So she followed him to an intersection, and when she saw that he kept walking straight ahead, she ran ahead several blocks and hid behind a peddler's stand near the Temple of the Sea Goddess. The pounding of her heart increased as she impatiently awaited Kunshu's approach. When he drew near, she squatted down behind the peddler's stand, ignoring the inquisitive gazes of bystanders, and looked around the stand to see Kunshu as he passed by. In that brief instant, all she could see was the profile of his sweltering face, the tracks of perspiration reminding her that she too was sweating profusely. Even Ah-long was bathed in sweat.

This pursuit had stripped away some of the worry, but the innermost layers were so sensitive that the slightest touch was painful. Ah-zhu now placed all her vague hopes on the noon meal. After finishing the laundry at the last house, she went home to prepare lunch. Then she sat down to wait for Kunshu, baby Ah-long at her breast. But she began to grow restless when he still hadn't appeared after a considerable amount of time.

With Ah-long on her back, she went out and found Kunshu on the road leading through the park. More than once she nearly found the courage to go up and beg him to come home to eat, but each time, as she started to draw near him, this courage left her suddenly and without a trace. So she kept her distance and tagged along behind him quietly and forlornly. Street after street, lane upon lane she followed him, blaming herself for having talked back the night before, which had so far cost him two meals and his tea as he walked the streets on this blistering day. Every few steps she had to wipe away her tears with the end of the carrying cloth strapped around her back.

When she finally saw Kunshu turn toward home, she was so happy she was on pins and needles. Taking a different road, she arrived ahead of him and stationed herself at the mouth of the lane opposite their place, where she could observe how he approached the house and see whether or not he ate lunch. Here came Kunshu. He stopped for a moment in front of the door. When Ah-zhu saw him finally enter the house, her tears were flowing so heavily that she had to cover her face with her hands and lean her head against the wall for support, feeling a great surge of relief. She could see his every movement inside the house and could guess what he was feeling at the moment—he was probably looking for her anxiously. This thought gave her a sense of well-being.

Just as Kunshu was about to leave the house, feeling depressed and unable to wait any longer, Ah-zhu, with Ah-long on her back, entered quickly, her head down. (At the very moment she was rushing home from her vantage point across the street, filled with happiness at having seen him drink some tea, his feeling of depression had been nearly overwhelming.) They seemed to shed a heavy emotional burden simultaneously—he having seen his wife walk through the door, she having seen her husband drink some tea. Ah-zhu kept her head lowered as she removed the food cover and filled Kunshu's rice bowl. He slipped the signboards over his head and placed them off to the side, then sat down at the table after unbuttoning his shirt. He ate in silence. Ah-zhu filled her own rice bowl, sat down opposite him, and began to eat. Since they didn't exchange a word, the only sound in the room was a munching like that made by hogs at the trough. When Kunshu got up and refilled his bowl, Ah-zhu looked up to catch a glimpse of his back, then quickly looked down again and resumed eating. When she in turn got to her feet, he caught a hurried glance at her back before looking away as she turned back around.

Finally he could stand the oppressive silence no longer:

"Is Ah-long asleep?" He knew very well that Ah-long was sleeping on his mother's back.

"Yes." Her head remained lowered.

More silence.

He looked at Ah-zhu, but when he thought she was about to raise her head, he abruptly looked away. Again he broke the silence:

"The blacksmith shop at Red-Tile Corners caught fire this morning. Did you know that?"

"Yes."

"Two children were killed on the street this morning, right in front of the noodle shop."

"What!" Her head shot up, but she quickly lowered it again when she saw that he was just about to raise his head from his rice bowl. "How did that happen?" She was eager to know, but her tone of voice lacked the intensity of her initial exclamation.

"Some sacks of rice fell off an oxcart and crushed the kids hitching a ride on the back."

Ever since beginning this line of work, Kunshu had more or less become Ah-zhu's exclusive source of local news. He reported to her daily and in great detail everything that occurred in the town. Sometimes he came with a particular news item like, for instance, the time he saw a long line of people stretching from the side entrance of the Catholic church on Park Avenue all the way to the street. He rushed home to tell her that the church was distributing free flour, then returned that evening to find two large sacks of flour and a can of powdered milk lying on the table.

Though a note of awkwardness was discernible in their conversation, they had now reestablished a line of amicable communication. Kunshu buttoned his shirt, checked his equipment, and, to keep the conversation alive, asked, "Is Ah-long asleep?"

*What a dumb question. I already asked that!*

"Yes," she answered.

Kunshu, embarrassed by his own question, didn't hear her response. Wanting to get out of there in a hurry, he left hastily, without even turning back. As Ah-zhu went and stood in the doorway to watch her husband walk off, she rocked the baby on her back and gently patted his behind. The whole reconciliation process had taken about half an hour, during which time their eyes had never once met.

o o o

The wall of the Farmers Association granary was not only high but also seemed to people to be uncannily long. Because of this massive wall the winds swirled around and around the area. The wall also cast a great shadow over the low houses across the way, and this was where Kunshu was headed. He was feeling better now, and there was no longer a bile-colored pall anywhere in front of him as far as he could see. With the numbness gone from his shoulders, he could once again feel the weight of the ads draped over him. Calculating the hour of the day, he cursed the length of time remaining before nightfall, for he wanted badly to take Ah-zhu to bed. Experience had shown him that was all they needed to dispel any bad blood between them. Actually, the removal of these marital ill feelings was an incidental benefit; he didn't know why, but whenever the animosity between them grew to a certain level, his sexual desires were aroused. The sun-drenched day became the object of his curses.

As sparrows chirped incessantly around the granary, he thought back to his childhood, when the land beneath this row of low houses had been vacant. He recalled how he and his playmates had come here to shoot sparrows—he'd been an excellent hand with a slingshot.

He was being scrutinized by sparrows perched on the telephone wires, and though he turned his head to look at them, he didn't slacken his pace, so that the angle of his head and eyes changed with each step. He was suddenly brought up short by the sound of running footsteps approaching from behind. He turned his head, just as he had done in years past when he was watching out for the old man at the granary. This reflex amused him. The old man had died long ago, when Kunshu was still shooting sparrows; they had found his body near the well beside the granary. With these thoughts in mind, he gradually left the sparrows on the telephone wires behind him.

A group of children playing in the mud by the side of the road left their games and ran toward him, giggling and laughing. They kept a safe distance as he walked along, those in front walking backward and facing him. Prior to the birth of Ah-long, he had been angered by the constant pestering of children on the street. But now things were different: now he would make faces, which not only delighted the children but somehow also gave him great pleasure. It was the sort of feeling he had every time he played with the laughing Ah-long.

∘ ∘ ∘

"Ah-long— Ah-long—"

"Go on, get out of here. You don't have to be cute with him."

"Ah-long, bye-bye, bye-bye . . ."

That was how Kunshu took his leave of them nearly every day. Whenever Ah-long saw his daddy walk out the door, he would cry and make a scene, sometimes trying to keep him from leaving by bending over backward in his mother's arms. Then it would be up to Ah-zhu to say something like, "He's your son, and he'll still be here when you get back," before Kunshu would reluctantly drag himself away.

*The kid really likes me.*

Kunshu was very happy. This job had enabled them to have Ah-long, who in turn enabled him to endure the hardships the job forced upon him.

"Don't be silly! Do you think it's really you that Ah-long likes? What he thinks he has is somebody who looks like you do now!"

*At the time I nearly misunderstood Ah-zhu.*

"When you go out in the morning, he's either asleep or else I've put him on my back to go out and wash clothes. During most of his waking hours you're made up like you are now, and when you come home at night he's asleep."

*It's not as bad as that, is it? But the boy is shying away from strangers these days.*

"He likes the way you dress up and make faces at him. It's no secret, you're his big doll."

*Oh! I'm Ah-long's big doll, his big doll!*

∘ ∘ ∘

The child walking backward in front of him pointed and yelled, "Ha ha, look here, quick. The ad man, he's smiling. The ad man's saying something and his eyes and mouth are all twisted!"

*I'm a big doll, a big doll.*

He was smiling. The long shadow he cast ahead of him did not seem like a man's shadow because of the ad boards over his shoulders. The children were making a game of stepping on the shadow. One of the children's mothers called to him from somewhere far behind Kunshu; the child reluctantly stopped what he was doing and looked up, then enviously gazed at his companions, whose mothers were not calling an end to their play.

Kunshu inwardly admired Ah-zhu's cleverness, musing over her metaphor: a big doll, a big doll.

○ ○ ○

"Born in the year of the dragon, what better name for him than Ah-long—Little Dragon?"

*If Ah-zhu had had any schooling, she'd have been a good student. But then if she'd had any schooling, she wouldn't have married me.*

"Xu Ah-long."

"Is this the way you write '*long*'—dragon?"

*The fellow who handled birth certificates was really something—he knew perfectly well that I only asked him to fill in the form because I don't know how to write, so why did he have to ask that in such a loud voice?*

"It's a dragon, like in the solar cycle."

"He was born in June. Why didn't you report it earlier?"

"We only named him today."

"Since you didn't report the birth within three months, there's a fine of fifteen dollars."

"We didn't even know we were supposed to register."

"You didn't know? I'm surprised you knew how to make a baby." *He shouldn't have made fun of us like that. He said it so loud that everyone in Town Hall was looking at us and laughing.*

○ ○ ○

High school students on their way home from school, more curious than adults, carefully read the movie bills on his board. Some even discussed the movies, though one of them remarked, "What's the use? The military instructors won't let us go see them!" Kunshu didn't comprehend what the boy meant, but he was happy just looking at their bulging book bags and he was filled with heartfelt admiration.

*No one in our family has been to school for three generations. But Ah-long will be different. The only thing that worries me is that he might not do well there. I've heard it costs a fortune to put a child through school! What a lucky bunch of kids they are!*

Two rows of trees lined the sidewalks, one of them throwing dappled shadows onto the street. Workers emerging from the industrial district at the far end of the street lacked the enthusiasm of the high school students; fatigue written plainly on their faces, they walked in silence, the few conversations among them carried on in hushed tones, the rare laughter subdued. Before taking on this job, Kunshu had applied for work in a paper factory, a lumber factory, and a fertilizer factory, and he envied these people their work and the regularity with which they walked down this cool tree-lined road at the same time every day on their way home to rest. Not only that, they had Sundays off. He didn't know why he'd been turned down for a job. He'd thought long and hard about it, but the answer escaped him.

"How many in your family?"

"Only my wife and me. My parents are both dead. My . . ."

"Okay, okay, I know."

*Now how could he know that? I haven't finished. Damn him! I waited in line all that time just so he could ask me a bunch of questions. Some of the men weren't asked anything. He just nodded his head and smiled, and they walked off looking satisfied.*

o o o

Dusk.

Kunshu looked up at the sun, which was sinking into the sea. The sight quickly filled him with happiness. When he returned to the Palace Theater, the manager was outside looking at the movie notices. He turned and said, "Ah, you're back. Good, I've been looking for you."

Shocked, Kunshu was momentarily speechless. Finally, he managed to blurt out, "What's up?"

"I want to talk to you about something."

Kunshu tried to grasp the intent of the manager's words and the significance of his cold manner. He carefully leaned the ad signs against the bare wall beneath the theater notices, then removed the boards that sandwiched him. The hand in which he was holding his tall hat trembled. He wanted desperately to postpone what was coming but had exhausted his supply of delaying tactics, and it was time to say something. He turned around with great apprehension. His hair, which had been wet but was now dry, stuck to his scalp; the white powder that had covered his forehead and cheeks had run with the perspiration and was now caked in his eyebrows and the hollows of his cheeks. The skin that showed through was so mottled it looked diseased. Finally, he unmindfully removed his false beard and stood there staring blankly ahead, like a strange muted mannequin.

"Do you think this sort of advertising is producing any results?" the manager asked.

"I, I . . ." He was so nervous he couldn't talk.

*I should have known. This is it!*

"Maybe we should try something else."

"I think so," Kunshu responded without knowing what he was saying.

*If the damn thing's finished, that's just as well. What future is there in this line of work anyway?*

"Can you handle a pedicab?"

"A pedicab?" He was crushed.

*Shit!*

"I, I don't think so," Kunshu continued.

"There's nothing to it. You'll get the hang of it in no time."

"Uh-huh."

"I'm thinking of switching to a pedicab for advertising. Besides riding around on the pedicab, you'll continue to help out when we close at night. The same wages."

"Right."

*Whew! That was close! I thought I was finished.*

"Tomorrow morning come with me to the shop to fetch the pedicab."

"What about these?" He pointed to the signs leaning against the wall, but what he really wanted to know was, could he stop using makeup.

The manager pretended he didn't hear him and walked inside.

*Stupid! Why did I have to ask that?*

He felt like laughing but didn't know just what was so funny. He hadn't a clue. He opened his mouth wide as though to laugh, but no sound emerged. On the road home he casually carried his equipment over his shoulder, which unexpectedly drew astonished looks from passersby; the townspeople had never seen him like this before, with his tall hat tucked under his arm.

"Take a good look, it'll be your last chance." He was so exhilarated he felt he could actually fly.

*What a ridiculous job!* He remembered a time in his childhood when a traveling moving-picture show had come to town from somewhere—oh, right, it was a show at the steps of the church—and he, Ah-xing, and some other friends had climbed an acacia tree to watch. One of the moving pictures had shown an ad man dressed up like him being pestered by a crowd of children. It had left a deep impression on their young minds, and afterward they'd often dressed up like that to play games. *Who'd have thought that those games would turn into reality for me as an adult? That's really funny.*

"Damn that short movie scene and its goddamned consequences. It's goddamned funny." As he walked, head down with his thoughts, he mumbled incessantly. Scenes of past events flooded his mind.

"Ah-zhu, if I don't find a job soon, you'll have to get rid of the baby you're carrying. This medicine is supposed to work during the first month of pregnancy. Don't be afraid—it'll just come out in the form of blood and water."

*Whew, that was close!*

"Ah-zhu, now you don't need to get an abortion."

*If I hadn't seen that outdoor movie, Ah-long might not be here today! It's a good thing I climbed that acacia tree.*

The strange thing was, a job that he had tried so unsuccessfully to give up and that had been the object of his curses, he now viewed with a certain degree of affection. But affection was all it was. The inner happiness he was feeling now easily won out over all other emotions.

"Kunshu, you're back!" Ah-zhu called out with an uncharacteristic exuberance as she saw her husband making his way home.

This took Kunshu by surprise. How in the world could she have found out? If he hadn't been so preoccupied, he'd have viewed this display of affection by Ah-zhu as too sudden and too bold; usually, this sort of thing caused him prolonged embarrassment.

As he drew nearer but not yet near enough to say anything, Ah-zhu blurted out, "I knew your luck would change." She seemed unwilling to hold anything back. This time Kunshu was really stunned. "Can you handle a pedicab?" she continued. "It doesn't make any difference anyway. You'll get the hang of it in no time. Jinchi wants to sublease his pedicab to you. As for the details . . ."

Now he understood the coincidence, and he decided to tease her a bit. "I know everything," he said.

"I figured as much when I saw the way you were walking home. What do you think? It doesn't sound bad, does it!"

"No, it doesn't sound bad, but . . ." He was barely able to keep himself from crowing over the happy news. He stopped just as the words were about to tumble out.

Ah-zhu pressed him anxiously. "What's the matter?"

"If the manager doesn't want us to do things this way, I don't think we ought to accept Jinchi's offer."

"Why not?"

"Look, if not for this job, I'd hate to think what our lives would be like. Ah-long might not be here today. Now if I give up this job the moment a better one comes along, that's going a bit too far, isn't it?"

He had dreamed this up on the spur of the moment, but once it was out, the gravity and importance of what he was saying came to him in a rush, and he grew dead serious. Ah-zhu, in turn, was gripped by fear, not because she understood what he was saying but because of his change in demeanor. Obviously disappointed, she nonetheless gained support from her sense of right and wrong. She followed her husband into the house in silence, feeling, in the midst of her bewilderment, a newborn respect for him. Perhaps she was able to accept his explanation so readily because of what he'd said about Ah-long.

They ate dinner together as usual, the only difference being the silent, mysterious looks Kunshu gave Ah-zhu from time to time. Though somewhat puzzled by these looks, she was reassured by the twinkle in his eye. She was conscious of the fact that she'd already planned their whole future after he began riding a pedicab, without any thoughts for the well-being of the man who was making it all possible, and she felt guilty. Kunshu decided to wait until he came home at night following the last show to give Ah-zhu the good news. He put down his rice bowl and walked over to look at Ah-long, who was fast asleep.

"That child sleeps all day long."

"It's a good thing he does. Otherwise, I wouldn't be able to get a thing done. The Goddess of Childbirth has been a big help by giving us such a good child."

He left to go to work at the theater.

He regretted not having told her the truth right away, because now he didn't know how he'd be able to stand the long, three-hour wait until closing time. Maybe for other people this was just a commonplace matter, but for Kunshu, who could no longer contain himself, anxiety was bubbling up inside.

*I nearly told her while I was taking my bath. Wouldn't it have been better if I had?*

"Why have you flattened out your hat?" Ah-zhu had asked him. *Ah-zhu has always been clever. She knew there was something in the air.*

"Oh! Have I?"

"Want me to straighten it out for you?"

"No need."

*She was trying to look through the hat to see if she could discover some secret.*

"Oh, all right, straighten it out."

"How could you be so careless as to ruin it like this?"

*Go ahead and tell her and be done with it!*

Musing over past events had become a habit with Kunshu. He couldn't have changed if he'd wanted to. He sat listlessly in the office, thinking about isolated incidents in his life. Even thoughts of events that had caused him pain and discomfort at the time today somehow brought a smile to his face.

"Kunshu."

Lost in his thoughts, he didn't move.

"Kunshu." This time it was louder.

He turned around in surprise and smiled awkwardly at the manager.

"The show's about over. Go open the exits, then lend a hand at the bicycle rack."

The day was finally coming to an end. He no longer felt tired. When he arrived home, Ah-zhu was outside walking around with Ah-long in her arms.

"Why aren't you in bed?"

"It's too hot in there. Ah-long couldn't sleep."

"Here, Ah-long, let Daddy hold you."

Ah-zhu handed him the child and followed him inside. But to their surprise, Ah-long began to cry, and no matter how Kunshu rocked or played with him, he wouldn't stop. Indeed, the crying grew progressively louder.

"Silly child, what's wrong with Daddy holding you? Don't you like Daddy? Be a good boy and don't cry, don't cry."

But not only was Ah-long crying hard, he was bending backward, struggling to get out of his father's arms, just as he tried to twist out of Ah-zhu's arms on mornings when Kunshu left for work in his costume.

"Naughty boy, why are you crying? Daddy's holding you. Don't you like Daddy anymore? Silly child, it's Daddy! It's your daddy!" Kunshu kept reminding Ah-long. "It's your daddy. Daddy's holding Ah-long—

look!" He made faces and funny sounds, but all in vain. Ah-long was crying piteously.

"Here, I'll hold him."

As Kunshu handed the baby back to Ah-zhu, he felt his heart sink. Walking over to her dressing table, he sat down and hesitantly opened the drawer. He took out the powder and looked deeply into the mirror, then slowly began making up his face.

"Are you crazy? What are you making up your face for now?" Ah-zhu was mystified by Kunshu's actions.

A momentary silence.

"I . . ." Kunshu's voice was trembling, as if he were holding something back. "I . . . I . . . I . . ."

# The Gong

o

Han Qinzai had not beaten his gong for quite some time now, probably eight or nine months, maybe as long as a year. He wasn't sure himself. He knew only that it had been a long, long time. Whenever this fact crossed his mind a great anger filled him: here he was, the only remaining practitioner of the unique profession of gong beating, and no one ever came to commission his services. By the time he realized what was happening, it was too late to do anything about it. The brass gong upon which his carefree existence had depended for more than half a life-time now suddenly lay there like something that had been frightened out of its wits, resembling the vacantly opened mouth of a mute. It had lain upside down under his bamboo bed since his last job, serving as a catchall.

That doesn't mean that there were no longer any lost children in the town, or that there were no more calls for the Buddhist faithful to offer prayerful thanks on the various temple days, or that the need no longer existed to announce publicly for the people to pay their taxes, or that smallpox vaccinations for the children were no longer given. But now these announcements were the responsibility of a young man who ped-aled his loudspeaker-equipped pedicab up and down the streets. This sight produced more than just loathing in Han Qinzai; there was also an ineffable, persistent pain that gripped his heart. There was something terribly unfitting, he thought, about having such a bizarre contraption anywhere in his little town. The appearance of this *thing* would destroy the town's social fabric—it represented an extreme absurdity.

Back in the days when Han Qinzai's gong was still in use, every third day witnessed a minor event, every fifth a major one. So among the town's old bachelors, known locally as arhat vagrants, he drank wine more fre-quently than all the others, and sometimes when he had a little more money, he'd even splurge and buy some of the more expensive Shaoxing wine. And in the matter of names, why, even among people of distinction there was no one whose name carried the weight of Han Qinzai's. You had only to say the three words, *han—qin—zai*, and anyone—literate or illit-erate, man, woman, or child—would know at once of whom you spoke. But were you to mention the mayor of the town, Brother Futong, or refer to him even more precisely as the old doctor's grandson, well, old doctor's grandson or not, there were no guarantees that everyone would recognize his name. Yes, in those days Han Qinzai could truly lay claim to both fame and fortune.

But ever since the pedicab with the loudspeaker had come to town, quickly monopolizing the public announcement business, the group of arhat vagrants who congregated beneath the *kadang* tree opposite the coffin shop at Southgate was increased by the addition of one Han Qinzai. In order to secure his position in the group, he had methodically and deliberately planned his every move, as though it were an intricate game of chess. For now that fortune was missing from his life, he was left with only his reputation. It was important not only to win this game but to preserve face as well. In his heart he knew that he was going to hang around there one way or the other, and that sooner or later he would have his place beneath the kadang tree. *But I, Han Qinzai, am not that stupid! I still want to take my place in society with other people!* He knew that it was important for a man to play a role in society. So whenever he had the feeling that he somehow belonged, no matter to what depths his spirits had sunk, they would be given a momentary boost.

## THE GHOST SIGHTING*

By now a considerable amount of time had passed since Han Qinzai had last beaten his gong. He had lost his source of income, and although there was only himself to look after, even a marginal existence was proving difficult. He could do without wine, but not without food!

Of the ten or so roads in town, only two or three did not give Han Qinzai a sinking feeling as he walked down them, for on the other roads were general stores where he had run up bills for wine and tobacco. Times being what they were, he felt as if he were being wedged into a long, deep fissure in which he was powerless to budge an inch. For days he had thought of little else, and he could come up with no more practical plan than to squeeze himself into the group in the shade of the kadang tree opposite the coffin shop.

Bright and early every morning he went over to the yam patch in the Alishi area alongside the stream to steal some yams. By now he was sick of the things; in fact, he had recently been bothered by indigestion, which caused his throat to grow parched and hoarse. As he saw it, the shade of the kadang tree opposite the coffin shop offered his only hope for survival. Once made, the decision to go there gained the force of a mandate.

With a jolt he sat up in bed. The bright light shining in through the opening of the air-raid shelter at that moment brought with it revitalized hope. In the brief moment that his gaze was fixed straight ahead, he felt as light as a feather and imagined himself to be flying away on the rays of light.

Before walking out of the little park, he washed his face at the fountain, then went over in his mind once more the route he had planned: leaving the park, he'd cut across the Lans' vegetable garden via the narrow, dark path. No problems there. When he reached the Utopia Hospital, he'd skirt around the marketplace, taking the alleyway in back of the Revival Movie house. He'd be careful to avoid the metal workshop, for it was likely that Stony and the others, whose shop was nearby, might be around. Han Qinzai made a mental calculation: this route would certainly take him to Northgate, to the train station. He'd walk along the

---

* This is a literal translation of the term *huo jian gui*, which is normally rendered "nonsense" or "absurd(ity)." As will be seen below, the author has introduced a pun with this term, and the literal meaning is more relevant to the story.

canal, and from there it would be best to cut across the Youying Public School playground. Once he'd reached the train station, he'd cross the tracks and take Ashushe Road, which would put him on the outskirts of town. *If I run into any of them out there, I'm dead meat.* From there he'd follow the road back to the Buddhist temple at Point Sixteen, cross back over the tracks to the west side of town, then turn south at the rice shop beneath the melia tree.

When his thoughts reached this point, he sucked in his breath. *Wa! That road would take me out of the area altogether, wouldn't it?* He smiled. Using such a roundabout route just to get to Southgate was like taking off your pants to fart!

He scratched his head hard and twisted his mouth. It suddenly dawned on him that he had become very clever. Clever? Crafty was more like it. *Well, since crafty is the same as clever, isn't clever the same as crafty?* He gleefully embraced this sense of self-respect, then crisply spat on the ground. He squinted into the sky to locate the sun's position: it was slanting above his head. He felt terribly hungry. It must be past noon already, he thought, probably after two o'clock.

There was a breach in the northern wall of the park, which most people called "the dog door" but which people who actually made use of it called "the side entrance." There were but three formal entrances to the park; this breach in the wall, the "dog door" or "side entrance," had been opened up by the bean curd makers at Red Tile Shelter as a shortcut for their trips to the marketplace. With the exception of their early-morning passages, few people took advantage of this shortcut. That was because in order to make your way through Mr. Lan's vegetable patch, you had to walk along a narrow, fenced-in lane in the middle of which were two manure pits hidden in the shade of a large banyan tree. From that very tree, one of the Lan family women had hanged herself one day, and the townspeople were convinced that her ghost often appeared there.

Han Qinzai's heart was heavy as he drew up to the breach in the wall. For some reason an old town saying came to him: "The hungry ghost is king of the ghosts, the full-bellied ghost is startled by the winds." And yet he grew bold, repeating this saying aloud over and over as if it were a chant of exorcism. As he neared the manure pits, several papaya trees nearby suddenly attracted his eyes. Three or four huge papayas hung from one of the trees, their stems a pale yellow. What a waste, he thought as he looked carefully around him, forgetting all about his chant. Standing on the edge of one of the manure pits on his tiptoes, he reached out to gauge the distance to the nearest papaya. If the pit weren't in the way, he'd only have to knock the papaya to the ground with a piece of bamboo fencing. But, stymied by the manure pit, he looked around until his gaze stopped at the bamboo fence: a piece of fencing that had fallen over until its tip was touching the ground gave him an idea. He walked over and unhooked the fence wire, thinking as he did so that once he'd knocked down the papaya, he could use the bamboo for a cook fire. The butterfly bushes alongside the fence were as tall as a man. Closer to the ground there was a thick undergrowth of canna plants, and this wild growth of wattle had already replaced the original bamboo fence—there was no evidence of any repair work by the owner of the rotting fence. Han Qinzai removed the last coil of wire, then happily grabbed the bamboo in both hands; but just as he was about to reach out and knock down the papaya, he sensed that someone was coming. Quickly throwing the bamboo into the bushes, he ran to the edge of the manure pit, pulled down his trousers, and squatted there to wait and see what the person would do. Nothing happened.

*That's strange, I'm sure I heard someone coming. Why can't I see anyone? Could he have spotted me first? Maybe he's lying in wait to nab me. To hell with him. I'll just squat here a while longer and see what happens. After all, it's no crime to come here and relieve myself.* He chuckled to himself. *If I don't get my hands on the papaya, that'll make five meals I've missed, and soon there won't be anything left to relieve myself of. Shit!* He laughed again.

His thoughts returned to a few days earlier, when he'd gone to steal yams at Alishi. The owner had discovered him just as he was about to dig into the patch. The man had started yelling as he ran over from some distance away, so Han Qinzai had quickly dropped his trousers and squatted there casually without moving. When the other man was no more than ten steps away, Han Qinzai really let him have it:

"What's this? You coming over here to eat shit? How dare you accuse me of being a thief! Wait till I'm finished here, then if I don't rub your face in my shit, you'll be getting off easy! Anyone who accuses someone of being a thief doesn't know right from wrong. What kind of person do you think I am? How dare you!"

The young farmer had answered doubtfully, almost apologetically, "What's the big idea of coming here to crap?"

"What's that? Are you complaining because I deliver it right to your door? Don't you go into town every morning before sunrise to pick the stuff up?" The young man had walked off without another word, and Han Qinzai had left laden with booty.

At this point his mind was brought back to the present; he carefully sized up the situation. Still no sounds of anyone drawing near, and it struck him that whoever was trying to nab him might just be very crafty. *All right, I'll squat here a little longer.* He laughed to himself again. This was all very funny to him. *There's nothing easier than getting the best of one of these hicks. The people who plant yams in Alishi just serve them right up to people like me. If you get caught, all you have to say is that you're from the Fulunzai area, and that we're all members of the same group. Then the man who's caught you will say politely, "These out here are no good. I've got better ones in the house." Then he'll take you over and let you help yourself to as much as a hundred catties if you want that much, and might even have you stay for dinner. Naturally, if you tell him you belong to one of the other groups from Ashushe, he'll beat the hell out of you on the spot. Um!* He heaved a long sigh. In a matter of a few years a whole new era had begun.

He knew he couldn't squat there much longer, since his legs were cramping, so he stood up and looked around, concerned that he wouldn't be able to see if there was anyone else in the patch. He parted the clumps of butterfly bushes in several places, taking care not to let down his guard. Then he hit upon a plan. He called out, not too loudly, "Someone's stealing papayas! Someone's stealing papayas!" That way, if anyone came asking questions, he could say that he'd seen a couple of kids but they must have run away. He waited a moment—no response. Now he knew there was no one around. So, picking up the bamboo fencing from the butterfly bushes where he'd thrown it, he tried to knock down the papaya. But he'd grown so weak from hunger that he couldn't handle the eight- or nine-foot-long bamboo, which kept whipping back and forth in the air. The harder he tried to hit the papaya, the worse his aim became, until he began to grow anxious and frustrated.

As he saw it, there were some things that required a certain amount of cursing if they were to be done properly. "You fucking thing, you!" A burst of effort, and he actually hit it. But the big papaya he had in his sights fell with a thud onto a layer of dried excrement atop the manure pit and began to sink slowly to the bottom. Han Qinzai stood there transfixed, like a man who has just parted with his lover, following the sinking papaya with his eyes. He swallowed a couple of times, hoping somehow to lessen the pangs of hunger.

When the papaya that had so tantalized him sank to just beyond the halfway point, the bumps and hollows of the skin and its general shape made it look like a human head, with eyes, a nose, even a mouth. Han

Qinzai's heart raced violently, and he blinked hard to clear his vision. Suddenly the heavy end of the papaya sank below the surface as the lighter end bobbed straight up. Terrified, Han Qinzai fled down the lane, screaming out to Heaven, earth, and mother. Some people on the road adjoining this darkened lane were startled by his shouts and cursed him:

"Damn you, have you seen a ghost or something?"*

"Yes . . . Yes, I . . . I saw a ghost!" Han Qinzai stammered in response. On that June harvest day, Han Qinzai was actually shivering uncontrollably.

Han Qinzai had always been a believer in ghosts and spirits, and this experience caused his superstitions to become more deeply entrenched. Seeing a ghost is a very unlucky omen, he thought to himself, especially in broad daylight. He temporarily postponed his plan to go over to the kadang tree opposite the coffin shop at Southgate. To solve his food problems of the next few days, no matter how uncomfortable his stomach was, he'd have to go beg yams from someone at Alishi to stay his hunger.

Beginning on the day Han Qinzai saw the apparition, the ghost of the girl named Lan, which had been all but forgotten by the townsfolk, began once again nightly to infiltrate the minds of those most fearful of ghosts, the town's children in particular.

Since Han Qinzai had seen the ghost, over the next few days many idlers came to the air-raid shelter when they were in the park to ask him about it. He never wearied of giving an animated account, usually winding up by painting a heroic picture of himself. He naturally avoided any mention of stealing papayas. Some of the children hung around the air-raid shelter all day long listening to him answer people's questions and describe his encounter with the ghost; they never got tired of hearing about it. They'd ask all sorts of questions about ghosts.

"Was her tongue this long?" a child asked, sticking his tongue out as far as it would go.

"That's nothing!" Han Qinzai put his hand down on a level with his navel and said, "It came down to here, all the way to her belly button."

"Wa!" The child's face grew pinched and small, though his staring eyes were larger than ever.

"Her . . . her . . ." Another child wanted to ask something. "Whew! I'm afraid to say it."

---

* This line would normally be rendered "Are you crazy?" or something along that order. See previous note.

"He wants to know what the ghost's eyes looked like," one of the other kids said.

"Her eyes! Wa! They were this big." He made circles with his fingers the size of eyeglass lenses. "But I couldn't see the pupils—the eyes were all white, with blood-red lines running through them."

"When she walked, did she float above the ground?"

"Of course she did!"

"Were her nails long?"

"This long. And there was poison on every one of them. Any place they touched a person it turned to blood."

"Aiyo! Weren't you scared?"

"Me? Not too scared. If I had been, she'd have snatched me away then and there!"

Thus earning looks of respect and admiration from the children around him, Han Qinzai grew more and more expansive, eventually convincing himself that everything he said was true. Once he'd gained the respect of these children, for several days they went out and fetched the firewood and water he needed. As a result, he experienced an incomprehensible sensation of floating in air.

## A BLADE OF GRASS, A DROP OF DEW*

A week or so later his stomach had reached the point where it could not tolerate another sliver of yam. He looked down at the pile of yams on the floor by the head of his bed—there were enough left for three or four more days—then, with his hands on his hips, he stepped toward them, touched them with his toe, and said, "So that's the way it is. I always thought the Alishi folks were generous people who would let me take all I wanted."

He thought back to his sighting of the ghost—it had already been eight or nine days at least. By now the bad luck should have vanished, which ought to forestall any calamities for the time being. He could no longer postpone his plan to go over to the spot opposite the coffin shop at Southgate.

After waking from a somewhat troubled nap, he sat in bed and dully scratched himself all over. He was fully awake by the time he was

---

* A Taiwanese expression meaning that there is subsistence for everyone; even a single blade of grass has its drop of dew.

scratching his head with both hands, thinking of the one important matter he had not yet taken care of.

With extreme caution he took a circuitous route to the Southgate area. When he reached the Buddhist temple on Ashushe Road, where there was a small general store in front of which a pot of tea had been placed for thirsty passersby, Han Qinzai walked quickly over to it. Actually, what had aroused his interest was the tobacco and wine sign hanging under the eaves. He couldn't actually read the words, but he knew that any store that displayed one of those round lacquered metal signs was a tobacco and wine outlet. He walked up to the place, poured a glass of tea, and held it in his hands. As he drank the tea, his eyes scanned the inside of the store. He noticed an old man dozing behind the counter, who raised his head as Han Qinzai walked up closer to get a better look.

"Hey, boss, this is quite some tea you have here." He took another swallow. "It must be from Wulaokeng."

The old man smiled and said, "How could we have tea as fine as that? We grow this in our own tea garden."

"Really?" He drank another mouthful. "Where is this tea garden of yours?"

"Over on Thirteen Hills."

"Aha! Wulaokeng is just on the other side of Thirteen Hills. I'm an expert where tea is concerned." He took another drink. "Not bad, not bad at all. This tea is every bit as good as Wulaokeng." As he was talking, he walked into the store and plopped down on the wooden bench in front of the counter.

Hearing someone praise the tea he had set out for pedestrians, the old man was naturally quite elated.

Han Qinzai had spotted the pastries inside the glass-enclosed counter right off; the sight of them made his stomach growl. But each time he was about to ask the old man to let him buy something on the cuff, he stopped himself. The opportune moment hadn't yet arrived, he calculated, so he racked his brain for something to chat with the old man about.

"Shit!" Han Qinzai cursed out of the blue. Before the old man even had time to puzzle over this, Han Qinzai continued, "I saw a ghost a few days ago. My bad luck!"

"Yeah, I heard people talking about it. They said it was at the Lans' vegetable patch."

"That's the goddamn place!"

"That's always been a bad piece of land."

"I know. But I had something important to do that day, so I cut across there to save some time."

"I heard it happened in broad daylight."

"That's exactly when it happened! Right after lunch."

"Wa! That was some evil ghost to actually appear in the daytime."

"You're right there. Who'd have thought it?" Han Qinzai tilted his head back and drained the cup of tea. "I think I'll have another cup," he said as he rose to walk outside.

"A connoisseur like you should drink some of this—it's hot." The old man reached over beside his chair, took a pot of steaming hot tea from a carrying case, and poured some into Han Qinzai's cup.

"Oh, that's great. Lucky, lucky me. Whoa! That's fine, that's fine. It's full."

"Think nothing of it, and if you want more, just help yourself."

"That's plenty." Seeing the happy expression on the old man's face, he added, "It's always best to have a little pastry to go with fine tea like this."

"That's for sure. These pastries here are real fresh—delivered today."

"I've never done any business in this store of yours—too far from where I live. How about the Prosperity and Longevity stores in town—do you know them?"

"Of course I know them! But how could a little store like mine compare with the likes of them?"

"I get all my tobacco and wine and other things at those places. If it's not Prosperity, then it's Longevity. I buy on credit, then pay them off all at once. The day before yesterday I paid off a pretty big bill at Longevity."

The old man walked over to the counter, opened the glass case, and asked, "How many do you want? Round ones or twists?"

"Forget it. I'll go over to the Buddhist temple in a moment and collect a debt, then I'll come back."

"We're not strangers. Why don't you eat some first?"

Han Qinzai thought about politely refusing again as a disarming gesture, but to his own surprise he blurted out, "Okay, then give me four of the round ones." He was feeling a little guilty, but when he saw how willing the old man was to extend him credit he felt relieved.

All together he ate six of the round pastries and drank three cups of tea. He was feeling considerably more comfortable now. But he still wasn't completely satisfied—he longed for a smoke. Looking up at the cigarettes in the glass case behind the counter, he turned his thoughts to ways to keep the conversation going.

"It's been a long time since I saw you beating your gong," the old man said.

This threw Han Qinzai into such a panic that he could only mutter in response. If he couldn't steer the conversation in the direction he wanted, it would be very hard to have his way with the old man. He put the empty cup up to his lips and pretended to be drinking so he wouldn't have to answer at once. Suddenly he knew what to say.

"Tsk, tsk. So you want to know about me and the gong, eh?"

"You haven't beaten it for some time, have you?"

"No, I still do it, but it's awfully tiring. Sometimes I get a youngster to do the shouting for me, but at other times I do it all myself."

"I haven't seen you out there for a long time."

"I was out just the day before yesterday."

"Not over here."

Han Qinzai smiled, then said, "It wasn't good news, so I knocked off after a while."

"What was the job?"

"Taxes!" He smiled again. "If it had been good news, I'd have made sure everyone heard it." Then he added the punch line. "Say, boss, how about giving me a couple of packs of Long Life cigarettes? I'll pay for it all later."

The old man took a look at his cigarette supply. "How about a pack of Red Paradise instead? I only have two packs of Long Life left."

"I'm used to smoking Long Life. It won't make any difference, since I'll probably be back to pay you for them in a little while."

Han Qinzai's belly was now full and his pockets were stuffed with two packs of Long Life cigarettes. Everything's going right today, he thought. He headed toward the Buddhist temple, figuring that within a quarter of an hour or so he'd reach Southgate. He rubbed his slightly protruding belly, now stuffed with pastries and several cups of tea. Looking off toward the horizon, he mumbled to himself, "Hai! The old saying is right on the mark: 'A blade of grass, a drop of dew.' Damned if it isn't true—'A blade of grass, a drop of dew.'" He very cautiously puffed on the cigarette, which was now as short as it was ever going to get, as though he were engaged in a parting kiss. When he could no longer put off throwing it away, he pinched the tiny remainder between his fingers, then looked down at it; there was no way he could put it back to his lips. He blew out the last puff of smoke. Totally relaxed and at ease, he felt like leaping into the clouds and flying over to Southgate.


### THE NARROW ROAD

Usually there were eight or nine arhat vagrants squatting beneath the kadang tree opposite the coffin shop. Whenever a family of mourners came to buy a coffin, these vagrants would go over to hang around and assist the family in its mourning duties. They'd do things like carry banners and floral wreaths in the funeral procession, or whatever other sundry jobs were required. This would earn them the right to join the funeral banquet for two or three days, and sometimes even a week or so. They'd also divide up a little pocket money. These old vagrants were men with no families or involvements who for a long time had passed their days squatting under the kadang tree. There was even a system of rights and privileges that had been established within their small circle. Naturally they were well versed on the quality of coffins. If, for instance, two grieving families came to buy lacquered coffins at the same time, one made of cedar, the other made of the more expensive cypress, they'd immediately catch the scent of the cypress and fall in behind it. If it was a wealthy family, there was always a great show of pageantry and the possibility of food and drink for more than a week, plus a substantial amount of pocket money. But once in a while there was an exception. Han Qinzai knew just about everything there was to know about these men, so when he lost his job of beating the gong, it was only natural that he should decide to throw in his lot with them.

Only a stretch of road separated the coffin shop from the vacant lot beneath the kadang tree. The rhythmic, even sounds of the axe chopping and the two-man saw being pulled by the two coffin shop apprentices lulled the group of men into a mid-day nap. Some of the old vagrants slept soundly in the shade of the tree, their faces covered with wide rain hats; they looked like the red and gray stones of the chess game they played before their nap, which were scattered freely about. Others sat in their customary places chewing the fat with one another. But their conversations were so lacking in compatibility that it often seemed like each of them was talking to himself. Every once in a while a truck would roar past them down the road, causing them to reflect that there was a big world out there, one they had no desire to belong to.

Han Qinzai walked up to a spot beneath the tree, where he saw this group of carefree vagrants spread out in all positions—seated, standing, supine. He was struck by a sense of disappointment as he realized that if he joined up with them, one of those scattered bodies would be his. He'd been able to conjure up visions of what their lives were like, but seeing them now dealt a blow to his self-respect. He had to strain to think of any redeeming features they might have. Finally, pulling out one of his packs of Long Life cigarettes, he walked over to the man called Scabby Head, who was having a smoke, to bum a light. He made a point of showing off the pack of Long Lifes, which elicited from the sleepy vagrants wide-eyed looks of envy—the cigarettes had captured their attention. He handed the matches back to Scabby Head, then offered cigarettes to the others. His heart was pained to see four or five hands quickly stretch out toward him.

"How come we haven't seen you out with your gong?" Scabby Head asked him.

"That's right, it's been a long time," someone else commented.

"I quit," Han Qinzai answered nonchalantly, blowing out a puff of smoke. "Beating a gong doesn't interest me anymore."

But someone else asked in a doubting tone, "Don't you mean the loudspeaker pedicab took your rice bowl away?"

This comment grated on his ears. He glared at the man who'd said it; seeing that the man was smoking the cigarette he had given him, he felt even worse. Wanting to squelch the effect of the man's statement, he said contemptuously:

"What's so great about a grotesque thing like that? It just so happens that old Han Qinzai here didn't want to beat the gong anymore, and that other guy just picked up the slack. Shit! A lot of people are under the impression that this old hand, Han Qinzai here, had his rice bowl smashed by some young punk!"

"Actually, beating a gong's not a bad job."

"Not bad?" His brow furrowed as he took a deep puff on his cigarette. "How would you know? You've never done it. Sometimes I was out there so long I lost my voice and my legs were sore for days. But all that wouldn't have mattered if they'd always paid me for my efforts! Wouldn't that make your blood boil! Good, you say? It's about as good as a fart, that's how good it is!"

"Are there really deadbeats like that?"

Han Qinzai saw that several of the old vagrants smoking his cigarettes were shaking their heads indignantly, which secretly pleased him.

"Lots of them!" he said. "If I told you their names, I wouldn't be much of a man. Some had me beat my gong to find their lost kids, then when I found the kids, they refused to pay!"

"Would it have been okay not to pay if you hadn't found the kids?" someone asked.

"Hell no! If Han Qinzai beats his gong, he's got money coming." Now, although he was a small man, owing to a lifetime of shouting as he beat the gong, once he got excited his every word became a virtual shout; but the louder he shouted, the hoarser he grew and the less clearly people understood him. As he talked on, the men unconsciously began to move closer until they were all gathered around him.

Scabby Head, in sympathy with Han Qinzai, said, "That's how it should be. Whoever heard of a matchmaker who was expected to guarantee a bunch of kids in the deal?"

"If everyone was as good as you fellows, we'd never have to talk about conscience," Han Qinzai said. "There's nothing false about what the ancients said. 'There are two men of conscience: he who has died, and he who hasn't been born.'"

The smiles Han Qinzai had anticipated appeared on the faces of all the men present; not only were they interested in what he was saying, they were also gaining respect for him.

"Old Han Qinzai here is no fool. If beating a gong was such a good life, do you think I'd just hand my rice bowl over to someone else?"

They smiled and nodded their heads.

Han Qinzai was always saying "Han Qinzai here, this, that, and the other," and he'd thrust out his chest or tug on his sleeve—each sentence was accompanied by some sort of action. Scabby Head and the others, feeling that he was something special, were filled with envy.

Han Qinzai then turned the conversation around: "But when all is said and done, what you fellows have here is the good life."

"Good?" Scabby Head, who was leaning up against the kadang tree, straightened up and shouted, "Good like hell! Good, you say?"

The others all laughed.

Just as Han Qinzai was about to say something, he was cut off by one of the other men: "If it stays like it has the past few days, we'll all die of starvation!" It had been several days since anyone had visited the shop across the way to buy a coffin.

"It's still too early to be talking about any of us dying!" Han Qinzai stressed the word "us." "What are you fretting about? We haven't come to the end of the line. There's no need to worry. Sooner or later someone's bound to die—if not today, then tomorrow. Who knows, maybe the day after tomorrow a bunch of people will come to buy coffins all at once!" He felt that this was just the right thing to say.

"God, no, not all at the same time! One a day is perfect." This was Turtle's opinion.

"Is that what you really think?" Know-It-All asked critically. "One a day? I don't know how you'd handle it all. Each one is good for two or three days, so one every two or three days is just about right. That way, as soon as we finish up with one, we can move right on to another . . ."

Before he had a chance to finish, Fire Baby piped up angrily, "Don't be stupid! Do you think you're King Yama of Hell or something?"

Know-It-All was stunned by the severity of Fire Baby's tone of voice. Taking the roar of laughter from the men as approval, Fire Baby proudly hammered his point home: "Don't you interfere with the business of King Yama. You're talking like a fucking idiot!"

Blockhead, who had been sitting there listening to the conversation, grinning from ear to ear and looking like the potbellied Maitreya Buddha, suddenly stood up excitedly and began to babble like a child: "Go ahead and have everybody drop dead! Go ahead and have everybody drop dead!"

His outburst drew curses from the others:

"Fuck you, Blockhead!" one shouted.

"You drop dead yourself!" said another.

"Children should be seen and not heard, Blockhead!" shouted yet another.

But Blockhead had thoughts only for his own laughter, and for the cigarette butts in the hands of his cronies. He reached down and picked up the butt Han Qinzai had just discarded. These men always pinched the tips of their cigarettes lightly between their fingers. They had smoked this way so long that the nicotine stains on their fingers had turned from yellow to a dark brown. And even though the nearness of the lit ends burned their fingers, they continued to smoke them unhurriedly, as if there were absolutely nothing to be concerned about. It was indeed a rarity for this group of men (Han Qinzai included) to smoke cigarettes of Long Life quality. The mildness and aromatic smell of the smoke coupled with the feelings of grandeur he was experiencing had Han Qinzai in their spell. But then the image of five or six hands stretching out to him ruined the moment, and all he could do was swallow hard a couple of times.

The only effect of everyone's curses on Blockhead was a continuous peal of idiotic giggling emanating from his nostrils, since his mouth remained closed the whole time. It was a weird snorting sound. The others' response was a mixture of hilarity and anger. Fire Baby ran over and pulled Blockhead's whiskers, but the idiotic giggling continued, and even when his whiskers were pulled hard enough to hurt, Blockhead would only say dispiritedly, "Don't do that! Don't!"

Scabby Head took a final puff on his cigarette and flipped the butt away. Blockhead, paying no attention to Fire Baby, casually edged his fat body over to the spot, but Fire Baby jumped in ahead of him and stepped on the butt. Blockhead merely tried to shove Fire Baby out of the way, his action more symbolic than substantial.

"If you promise to wash your ass nice and clean tonight, Fire Baby'll move his foot," Scabby Head said.

Blockhead, still in control of his temper, continued shoving Fire Baby and saying, "Don't say that! Don't! Scabby Head, don't say that!"

"Call me 'Daddy.' If you'll call me 'Daddy,' I'll move my foot."

"Don't do that! Daddy, don't."

Hearing him call Fire Baby "Daddy," the others squealed with laughter. Just then the sounds of chopping and sawing from the coffin shop stopped, and this cessation of activity across the street brought the merriment of the group of men under the kadang tree to a halt; Han Qinzai's laughter, alone, hung in the air for an instant as the other men turned their gazes to the coffin shop. What they saw was three pairs of surprise-filled eyes staring back at them. Blockhead's childlike speech and intolerable giggling broke the silence of this moment. Amid the ensuing laughter the voice of the owner of the coffin shop was still discernible: "Drop dead, you fucking Blockhead!"

The few men who had been sleeping soundly through all this were rudely awakened by the extraordinarily raucous laughter.

Han Qinzai's chatter was well received by one and all. In fact, Scabby Head told him whenever he had nothing to do to come over and pass the time with them. Han Qinzai was already aware that Scabby Head was the leader of the group, so he carried a secret happiness with him on the road home. The knowledge that he too would someday have his spot under the kadang tree wiped his mind clean of worries and anger over his loss of a livelihood, and even his concern over his outstanding debts. He nonchalantly turned his steps toward the road on which the tobacco and wine shop whose owner pressed him the hardest to clear his bill was located. He was making mental calculations: if he returned tomorrow and his luck was good, a customer might show up at the coffin shop and he could take part in the funeral procession; with food to eat and a handout as well, he would be in seventh heaven! The more he thought about tomorrow, the greater the possibility loomed. It had been a long time since anyone had bought a coffin, a situation that could not last much longer. His only fear had been that a coffin might have been sold the day before he showed up, which would have meant a delay of several days for him.

So engrossed in his thoughts was he that the sudden appearance of the Temple of Matsu, the Goddess of the Sea, brought him rudely back to his senses—he had inadvertently walked right up next to Longevity General Store. He was about to turn on his heel and get out of there when someone inside the store spotted him. The jig was up. He had a sinking feeling. Quickening his pace, he turned his face away from the store, steeled himself, and walked on. But it was too late. He distinctly heard someone behind him call out "Han Qinzai," although he ignored the shout and kept walking, hoping that the other man would think it was a case of mistaken identity. But the fellow was not fooled. He not only continued to shout Han Qinzai's name but also ran after him. Grabbing him by the shoulder, he pulled Han Qinzai to a halt and cursed him angrily: "Fuck you and all your ancestors! Come on, run—let's see you run away now. I'll bet you can't sprout wings and fly off."

Han Qinzai had been jerked to a stop so abruptly he nearly tumbled to the ground.

"I wasn't running away," he said innocently. "I wasn't."

"You weren't running away? If you weren't running away, why didn't you stop when I called you?"

"I didn't hear you call me."

"You didn't hear me! Ha! Are your ears plugged up with shit? Huh?" With each sentence, Longevity gave Han Qinzai's shoulders two or three rough shakes, so that his frail body rocked back and forth in the man's hands as though he were suspended in air. "You want me to clean them out with the manure spade? Huh? What do you say?"

"Brother Longevity, let me go! Please, I beg you." Han Qinzai cast embarrassed looks around him at the crowd that was gathering, then said to Longevity in a soft voice, "Let me keep a little face in front of all these people, okay? Please let me go."

"Hai! A man like you worrying about *face*! Did you all hear that?"

Longevity smugly turned toward the crowd and, with a laugh, said in a loud voice, "This is what's called 'putting face before life itself!'"

Han Qinzai, with his frail body, was like a mouse caught in the grasp of a cat, tossed around so violently that onlookers were concerned that his innards might get all jumbled up. Sensing that the people gathering to watch all this commotion had formed a huge crowd that covered the handcar turntable, Han Qinzai was so embarrassed he felt like crawling into a hole and hiding. He'd always felt he had some status in this town, but now that was gone. On top of that, what remained of his will to implore for the return of even a little dignity had crumbled. His spirits were paralyzed, his most instinctive behavior consciously repressed; if it was necessary to lose face, all he had to say was, "So what? If I'm broke, I'm broke! My flesh has a salty taste, so what can you do about it?" But he figured he'd beg one more time, and if that didn't work, he'd go ahead and blurt it out and let that be the end of it.

"Brother Longevity, I'm not your senior, though I am older than you. Let me go, please. If I had the money, I'd pay you," he said softly, a weak smile on his face.

"If you had the money?" Longevity laughed as though he were on the verge of hysteria. "If you had the money, then everyone in the world would be rich!"

Han Qinzai could stand it no longer; he was about to wrench himself free of Longevity's grasp and shout out savagely, "My flesh has a salty taste, so what can you do about it?" when he heard someone in the crowd say, "That's Han Qinzai, the gong beater." Suddenly he grew weak, sensing that if he were to take a truculent attitude, this thing called "Han Qinzai" would surely be beaten to a pulp.

"Uncle Longevity," he said, "have a little compassion. Until I pay back the money I owe you, let all my luck be bad. Okay? Worthy Uncle Longevity . . ." He was about to ask Longevity once more to let him go, but he guessed that the more he pleaded to be released, the more Longevity would be inclined to hold fast, so he made up his mind not to ask again. He merely repeated himself: "Worthy Uncle Longevity . . ."

All this evoked peals of laughter from the crowd of onlookers. And finally, Longevity, seeing no alternative, released his grasp.

"If you don't pay me next time, I'm not going to let you off so easily! Next time I'll rip the clothes right off your back."

Amid the laughter from the crowd, someone said, "Longevity is quite the fellow—look how big a grandson he's got!"

"My luck isn't that bad!" Longevity commented in obvious high spirits.

Standing off to the side, feeling very embarrassed and at a loss as to what to do with himself, Han Qinzai merely examined his wrinkled clothes and tried to smooth them out with his hand. He didn't hear a word of the clamor coming from the crowd. Now that the affair was closed, he didn't even have the good sense to leave the scene.

Longevity returned to his store; the crowd of curious spectators surrounded Han Qinzai as he stood there with a vacant stare on his face. Then the whole scene began to resemble a strange type of fruit: the people were the skin, which at this moment began to peel itself off, layer by layer, until all that remained was the pit—Han Qinzai—cast aside there at the turntable. He was still absent-mindedly smoothing a wrinkled spot on his clothing with his hand. Chagrin filled his heart. *I shouldn't have let him do that to me! I should've told him right off the bat, "My flesh has a salty taste, so what are you going to do about it?" Now that he's let me go, I can't look anyone in the face. I really shouldn't have called him "worthy uncle" or "worthy elder brother"! Worthy, ha!* His feelings of regret increased. He knew that no one was watching him any longer, but he simply could not raise his head, which seemed to weigh a ton.

Off in the distance some people were pushing a handcar toward him. They were on their way here to the turntable to get on the track heading toward the ocean. The driver was shouting. Finally coming to his senses, Han Qinzai left in a hurry. As cautiously and alertly as a mouse, he made his way back to the air-raid shelter in the park.

The moment he entered he threw himself noisily onto the bed, and before he knew it, tears were coursing down his face. He began to sniffle and was soon crying. Never before, in the twenty or thirty years of his adult life, had he shed a single tear. After somewhat regaining his composure, he sat up, cursing over and over in a heavy voice, "Fuck your old lady, fuck your old lady. . . ." After a while he reached over to get the rag that was draped over the head of his bed, with which he wiped his tear-streaked face. Sensing a warmth and soreness on his right cheek, he reached up to touch it and discovered that he had two scratches. He paced back and forth in the air-raid shelter until he happened to notice his gong lying beneath the bed. He took it out and examined it.

"All right!" he said resolutely. "If I ever get another chance to go out on the streets and beat this gong again, I'm definitely going to start saving some money."

## IT'S ALL RIGHT TO WATCH PEOPLE DRINK TONICS, BUT DON'T WATCH DOGS FIGHT OVER A BONE

By the following day, Han Qinzai had put together a story of how he'd received the scratches on his right cheek. As soon as he saw the men under the kadang tree he said, "There's truth to the saying that lightning only strikes good men." He rubbed his cheek. "After I left here yesterday, just as I was passing the Cultivation Pharmacy, I picked up some peanuts from the ground to feed to the two monkeys, and who'd have guessed that when I raised my head one of them would grab hold and scratch my face? I hope the damned beast dies an early death!"

"That's for sure! The two monkeys at the Cultivation Pharmacy are famous for their pranks. Not long ago a woman was walking past there when the same thing happened to her—one of them grabbed hold of her head and wouldn't let go," Fire Baby said.

"What happened to her afterward?" Know-It-All asked, his interest piqued.

"You're the horniest guy around. You wake up as soon as anyone mentions a woman," Fire Baby said, his mouth cracked in a wide grin, as he led the others in a round of laughter.

Know-It-All, apparently intimidated by Fire Baby, replied, "Then . . . then why did you bring it up?"

"You want to know, do you?" Fire Baby said. "Well, since you want to know, I'm going to tell you." He puffed himself up, and even his words had a ring of affection. "Afterward, afterward, uh, the woman got married and had some kids . . . ha ha!"

Han Qinzai squatted on his haunches, and when the laughter had just about died out, he said, rubbing his scratched face, "Damn him, I hope the hand that scratched me rots off!" He was thinking about Longevity, but what he said was, "A pharmacy ought to gain a reputation by selling quality medicines, not by having its monkeys scratch people."

"That's right," said Fire Baby, who was now sitting beside Han Qinzai. "Got any of those Long Life cigarettes left over from yesterday?" There was a marked contrast in the tone of the two separate utterances. He thrust his neck out, sort of like a throat specialist looking down the throat of a patient. His eyes were glued to Han Qinzai's shirt pocket.

Han Qinzai patted the pocket and, with a wry smile, said he didn't.

"Does a chicken with a crooked beak get any of the good feed?" the man named Mongrel, who was sitting beneath another kadang tree, spat out.

"What's that got to do with you?" Fire Baby leaped to his feet. "What are you thinking, you damned ingrate?"

"What's it to you? You looking for trouble?"

Mongrel's response was strong; he got to his feet and said with a cunning sneer, "Aha! So you've finally found a pretext."

"Come over a little closer if you've got the guts."

This was said so loudly that the speaker seemed about to explode.

Laughing lightheartedly but with anger in his eyes, Mongrel took a few steps forward, his glare never leaving the other man's face.

"So, are you going to stand there and let me beat the shit out of you, or are you going to mix it up? You'll treat me for free or you'll have it delivered to my door."

Fire Baby's hands were already clenched into fists; his arms hung stiffly at his sides; he took two or three steps forward to show he wasn't backing down.

Only a single pace now separated the two men. Seeing this state of affairs, Han Qinzai began to tremble. He was hoping someone would step in and break it up, but when he looked back at the others, he discovered that they were all sitting or reclining on the ground, so hot they looked a bit dopey. Their eyes were glued to the two men squaring off, and they were enjoying the prospect of a fight that loomed before them. It looked like it was going to start any second now.

"Isn't anyone going to step in?" Han Qinzai asked anxiously, his eyes sweeping their faces. "Hurry, somebody do something!" As he made his plea he walked up close to the two men.

"Why trouble yourself, Han Qinzai? When the weather's as hot as it is today, it takes too much energy to break up a fight," someone said.

Fire Baby and Mongrel were already shoving each other. Their anger was no longer as strong as when the incident had begun, and when they heard Han Qinzai coming to make peace between them, saying "Come . . . come on, listen to me now," they decided to take advantage of these peacemaking attempts to gain a moral victory before the fight was called off. There wasn't going to be any fight now anyway, they thought, so their pushing and shoving grew more heated, to the point that they were both grunting. Han Qinzai, who had had thoughts of stepping in to break things up, moved off to the side when he saw how hard they were shoving. His mediations were limited to the vocal, not the physical variety: "Ai! Ai! Don't fight, don't fight. Someone hurry up and pull them apart!"

"Don't pay any attention to them, Han Qinzai. Don't spoil their fun," Scabby Head shouted.

Han Qinzai just stood there, not knowing what to do.

Both Mongrel and Fire Baby were scrawny men, so everywhere you looked they were small, except for their joints—knees, elbows, chins, and cheeks—all of which jutted out almost frighteningly. This was particularly true with their shoulders: a loose layer of skin covered sharply jutting shoulder bones, and as they bumped each other, not only did they make sounds like stones banging under water, but they felt sharp pains reaching down to the marrow. It was too late to lessen the force of the bumps—having mounted the tiger, it was hard to climb down. Matters having reached this stage, the two could only bump each other even harder to determine who would be the victor, thereby bringing this standoff to its conclusion. Their thoughts were identical. They bumped each other once more, then stepped back before going at it again; this time they both lowered their center of gravity and were almost crouching as they faced each other—this would really do the trick. The stinging pain from the last encounter was most severe in Mongrel's shoulder, but he couldn't stop now. Just as they lurched at each other this time, Mongrel twisted his body slightly and Fire Baby brushed past him, looking like a catapulted missile as he crashed headlong to the ground, where a kadang tree stopped him.

Everyone burst out laughing as they saw him sprawled there. "That's a mighty force," one of them said. "Look at all the leaves he's knocked down!" Fire Baby was fiery mad. He turned around, fists waving menacingly in the air, and without a thought for how things would turn out, rushed forward like a madman. Han Qinzai was more frightened than ever, but before the charging Fire Baby could get to where they were standing, Han Qinzai placed himself in front of Mongrel, spread out his hands, and shouted, "For God's sake, don't! For God's sake, don't! For God's sake . . ." The wild anger of Fire Baby had produced a similar reaction of anger in Mongrel. Ignoring Han Qinzai's attempt to place himself as an obstacle between the two of them, Mongrel tried to push him out of the way, but it was too late—Fire Baby was upon them. With Han Qinzai standing between the combatants, they swung their fists and the battle was on. Han Qinzai couldn't get out of the way. When one of them kicked, the other kneed; when one of them clawed, the other ripped and tore, until they all tumbled to the ground in a pile.

Neither Mongrel nor Fire Baby could get the upper hand, but as they were rolling on the ground in a stalemate, they both suddenly felt comfortably rested. They were still grappling with each other, but a mutual agreement to stop the fisticuffs had been silently reached, and neither wanted to strike the next blow. They puffed and panted as sweat poured down their faces; then, as they suddenly felt how ridiculously funny it all was, their mouths parted as the laughter welling up inside them burst forth.

The person who got the worst of it all was Han Qinzai. With the two men on top, pinning him to the ground, he lay there covering up his head, not daring to move. His eyes shut tightly, he just kept mumbling over and over, "For God's sake, don't! For God's sake, don't!"

"That's enough, now, that's enough!" Scabby Head said as he lazily got to his feet. "You've nearly squashed poor Han Qinzai to death!"

Mongrel and Fire Baby reacted as if they'd been waiting for someone to call them to a halt, for as soon as they heard Scabby Head's shouts, they let go of each other and stood up. When they saw the shape Han Qinzai was in, they started to laugh.

"Ram it up your . . . ! Go ahead and fight! Show me how you can fight! Old Scabby Head here will treat you both to some fried noodles if you're still able to slug it out!" Scabby Head lectured them with the airs of a leader.

Han Qinzai still lay on his side, mumbling over and over, "For God's sake, don't!" unaware that he should be getting up off the ground.

"You've squashed his soul right out of his body," Scabby Head said, walking over to take a look.

The smiles disappeared from Mongrel's and Fire Baby's faces. They just stood there dumbly looking on while the others crowded around to watch Scabby Head examining Han Qinzai.

"The poor guy," Scabby Head said. "Does anyone know how to locate his revival tendon?"*

No answer. The men just stared dumbly into each other's faces, their eyes opened wider than usual.

Scabby Head lifted up Han Qinzai's black shirt and felt around under his armpits; he stopped suddenly, as though he had found something, then pinched down so hard that even his own mouth twisted sharply. Han Qinzai let out a yelp, which instilled Scabby Head with confidence. "So that's all there is to locating the revival tendon!" He pinched again, hard, which elicited a "What the fuck!" from Han Qinzai. This quickly

---

* Pinching a particular tendon under the armpit or on the face of a person who has suffered heatstroke will release the excess heat from his body.

put everyone at ease, and their eyes returned to normal size. Blockhead was the first to break the stifling atmosphere the incident had produced with his unbearable giggles. Know-It-All, childishly hopping around like a sparrow, dashed over behind Blockhead, reached around him, and squeezed his fat, slightly sagging breasts. Life had returned to this tiny section of the world.

Han Qinzai's every movement, from sitting up to getting to his feet to starting to talk, was carefully scrutinized. All this made him feel as though he were invested with some special privileges. The other men watched him with smiling eyes (no, in One-Eye's case you would have to say smiling eye—his left one—for his right eye never opened and, in fact, was recessed deeply in its socket), waiting to see what he would do.

Han Qinzai felt and rubbed himself all over, squealing with pain and filling the air with four-letter words as he did so. More rubbing and feeling, until there was no place he had missed. During his self-examination, the other men received every shout and every curse with sympathy and good-natured laughs, and their sympathy was no less generous just because there was a little exaggeration on his part. As a result, he did not feel too strongly that he had been abused. He did sense, however, that he must take advantage of the moment, now that they were all on his side. Brushing the dust off his clothing, he was of a mind to blow his stack and show them that he was no one to fool with, but after some reasoned reflection, he said fatalistically:

"'It's all right to watch people drink tonics, but don't watch dogs fight over a bone.'" He smiled. "Hai! The ancients sure knew what was what. We can follow their lead. Me, I'm all muddle-headed. Ai! A real muddle head."

"I think you ought to take some medicine in case you have any internal injuries," Fire Baby said. "I'll recommend some herb medicine for you." He cocked his head. "Horsewhip grass is the best. After it's ground into a pulp, if you're a drinking man, you can add some wine; if not, take it with some brown sugar. It's guaranteed. I've cured a lot of people with it."

"Mixing up some horsewhip grass is easy. You can find all you want at Graveyard Harbor."

Han Qinzai turned to look at the person who was making suggestions for his well-being.

"There's something else that's not bad," Scabby Head said. "Banyan bristles pounded into a pulpy liquid and drunk straight is good for internal injuries. It doesn't taste as bad as horsewhip grass and there's no smell."

"If you're going to take something, do it now."

"Right, right," Han Qinzai said.

"It's only fair to have Mongrel and Fire Baby go pick the grass."

"That's all right, I'll get it myself. All they need to do is buy the wine."

"Sure, sure, that's fair enough."

Several of the men voiced their agreement.

"But I don't have any money now," Mongrel complained, scratching his head. "We haven't had a funeral banquet for a long time."

It *had* been a long time, probably a week since they'd last seen a customer at the coffin shop. But it seemed to take Mongrel's comment to force home the seriousness of their dilemma. The sweltering heat had their nerves on edge. Anxieties flooded their minds, and Han Qinzai's injuries quickly faded into insignificance.

"We're not heartless, but it's really been a long time since anyone died."

"What are you so worried about? There's a meal coming right around the corner," Han Qinzai said.

"Who?" Their eyes lit up.

"Scholar Yang. It's sure to be lavish."

"Balls! They were making noises about him breathing his last years ago, and they're still making those noises today."

"That old fart is holding on for dear life," Fire Baby said.

"Eleven of his twelve souls are already gone, and the last one won't let go of the threshold—you'd hold on for dear life too!"

"Ai! He ought to give it up. The old guy isn't very smart—by hanging on like this he's lost the filial respect of the younger ones. What good does that do anybody?"

Han Qinzai's mention of Scholar Yang led to a lengthy discussion, but nothing came of it, and with the weather as hot as it was, the longer the discussion lasted the less spirited it grew.

The clamor of the moment before and their light mood gradually began to settle earthward like dust. One by one they took up their favorite positions and lapsed into a dull-witted immobility. Han Qinzai was not accustomed to this sort of reticence. After racking his brain for a few moments, he came up with a subject for conversation. Tossing a pebble over Scabby Head's way, he said:

"Hey Scabby Head, people say that if there's no business at the coffin shop, all you have to do is strike a coffin three times with a broom, and the next day someone will come over to buy a coffin. Do you believe that?"

"I've heard that, but I've never tried it myself."

"I wonder if the owner of the coffin shop knows about it."

"Everyone knows. If it worked, he wouldn't just let his business peter out like this."

"Maybe he's never tried it," Han Qinzai said, holding out a ray of hope. "What do you say?"

The others didn't want to be left out of this discussion, and although they didn't actually say anything, they had at least snapped out of their gloomy mood.

"Let's give it a try," Han Qinzai said excitedly.

"Who's going to do it?"

"Any one of us, me included."

"Well, speak up."

The others shrank back, their smiles showing that they wanted to be excluded. They cast glances back and forth.

"Look," Han Qinzai whispered, "the coffin shop owner and his two apprentices have knocked off for lunch. And look over there, to the left: there's a broom standing against the wall. If we're going to do it, now's our chance."

"Who's going?"

"Let's draw straws," Mongrel offered.

"Draw straws! They'll be back outside before you've got the straws cut and drawn." Han Qinzai wanted badly to try it himself. This was just what the doctor ordered to get on their good side.

"So what'll we do?" Mongrel was getting a little anxious. So was Han Qinzai. He was afraid that if he allowed Mongrel to be the first to volunteer, he'd lose a ready-made opportunity to distinguish himself. Observing the expression on Mongrel's face and afraid that he was about to open his mouth to speak up, Han Qinzai blurted out, "I'll go!" He looked at the others. "By the time you guys get around to doing anything, you've missed your chance!"

As the others looked at Han Qinzai, the volunteer, respect was written all over their faces, which redoubled his boldness. Taking a deep breath, he made ready to dash across the street.

"Keep an eye on the road for me. If anyone comes, give a yell." With that, he ran across. Looking back over his shoulder, he saw all the men under the kadang tree holding their breath and watching his every move in motionless silence; they were so still they seemed about to pop.

Han Qinzai walked over beneath the eaves of the building, then looked up and down the street before darting on ahead. He picked up the broom, carried it over to the nearest coffin, rapped on it three times— *bang, bang, bang*—then scurried back across the street, still holding on to the broom.

The men had started to roar the moment they saw him pick up the broom, and the sight of him rushing back, broom in hand, had them holding their sides with laughter.

"You guys are real losers. I just risked my life for you!"

They were by now laughing uncontrollably.

"You bunch of ignorant pigs!" He was waving the broom in the air as a symbol of his contribution.

Scabby Head was holding his sides, laughing at the sight of Han Qinzai with the broom in his hand.

"Aiya! Mother! The . . . the broom . . . oh, it's killing me!"

Everyone was aware of the humor of the situation, and the waves of laughter reached the ears of the two apprentices at the coffin shop, who emerged to see what was going on, their rice bowls still in their hands.

"Hey, Han Qinzai, your broom . . ." someone said softly.

By this time the laughter had stopped completely as the men glanced back and forth across the street, then at Han Qinzai. He had been completely in the dark until the word "broom" was mentioned. When he came to his senses and saw what was happening, he froze on the spot.

"Hide it—hurry, they're looking at you."

As he jerked his head around to look across the street, someone came up and yanked the broom out of his hand, threw it to the ground, and sat on it with one of the other men.

The two apprentices continued to shove rice into their mouths as they watched the activity on the opposite side of the street. But seeing that nothing much was going on, they went back inside. Han Qinzai breathed a sigh of relief, then began to sense the humor in the situation.

"How could I have carried the broom back with me?" he said. "What a lunkhead I am."

"I think you were giddy."

"Where's the broom? I'll take it back over."

"Since nothing's happened, just forget it. We'll toss it away later."

"Ai! How . . . how can we do that?"

"Don't worry about it," Scabby Head said. "Tomorrow we'll see if your plan's worked."

"Well, I . . . I've already done my part."

Although no one said anything in response, Han Qinzai could tell from their smiling faces that they had accepted him and that he was covered with glory.

But then, just as he was receiving their accolades, his heart was troubled by a nagging anxiety. He began to regret what he had just done, for if someone were actually to come to buy a coffin on the following day, wouldn't he, Han Qinzai, be responsible for the person's death? *I've already lived half a lifetime, and although I might not be considered a particularly "good" man, I've never been a particularly "bad" one either — and certainly not one to cause someone's death. I can only hope and pray that the whole experiment falls through.* He sat down on the ground with his eyes closed, his back resting against the kadang tree, as he contemplated his situation.

He was completely oblivious to the words of praise, meaningful or casual, with which the group of men were rewarding him, and to their recounting of the rollicksome effects his daring venture had produced. He didn't even feel like bothering with them; he was too wrapped up in the feeling that he had sunk into a deep, dark abyss. He just sat there and thought. A stream of fond memories of events from his past, even those of little consequence, filled his mind. He no longer had to feel badly about his loss of income, but he did lament with considerable pain the cessation of the jobs he had been given, jobs that had filled him with a sense of esteem rather than subjecting him to ridicule.

o o o

A mother stood at the entrance to the air-raid shelter calling out in mournful tones, "Gong beater! Gong beater!" Then a pause. "Is the gong beater here?"

"Yeah! Here I am!" Han Qinzai awoke from his nap and jumped to his feet.

"Please come outside."

"I'm coming! I'm coming!"

As he stepped through the shelter entrance he was temporarily blinded by the bright sunlight. The woman began talking to him before he could even make out who she was.

"My child, Axiong, is lost." After saying the words "my child," the woman choked up and her speech was barely intelligible.

Han Qinzai knew exactly what this young mother was feeling. He consoled her: "I know, I know. Your child is lost, isn't he?"

The sobbing woman nodded.

"Don't worry, just tell me slowly how big he is, how I can recognize him, what he's wearing, and where you think he might be. When did you notice he was missing? That should do it."

"He . . . he . . ." The woman was trying hard to speak, but all she could do was sob.

"That's all right, don't worry. There isn't a lost child anywhere I can't find. You go ask around and see if I'm not telling the truth. And I can find yours just as easily."

The young mother was greatly reassured. "His name is Axiong," she said. "He has big eyes, and he's very cute. We say he's three, but he's actually only two." She stopped and thought a moment, and as she did, her mournful appearance suddenly gave way to a look of sheer love. "I took him with me to buy a piece of material to cut up and make some diaper pants for him. While I was looking over the material in the shop, he was fussing to get down and play, so I told him not to go into the street—he even made a sound that he understood me." The mournful look reappeared.

Han Qinzai took advantage of the break in her narration to ask some questions, until he finally got all the information he needed.

"Okay, that's all I need to know. You go back and look for him. Your best bet is to go down to the big drainage ditch and look around there. I'll start with the gong right away, and everything will be fine."

He turned on his heel and picked up his gong, then fell in behind the young mother and started beating it.

> *Bong! Bong! Bong!*
> *The gong beater's coming your way—*
> *Listen everyone, here's what I have to say—*
> *A child, his name is Axiong—*
> *Three years old, but really only two—*
> *His eyes big as flower buds, cute as a bug's ear;*
> *Barefoot, black open-crotch pants, a white shirt—*
> *Anyone seeing him take him to the police station right away—*
> *Or to the quilt shop beside the Temple of the Patriarch—*

*Axiong's mother is on pins and needles —*
*Bong! Bong! Bong!*

No one in the entire town escaped the sound of Han Qinzai's gong that afternoon. Around dusk, the mother came running up the street, Axiong cradled in her arms, to catch up with Han Qinzai. She expressed her gratitude over and over, then thrust a red envelope into his hand. There hadn't been much money in it, but as he thought back on it now, it had impressed him as a rich recompense.

o o o

*Ai! I hope and pray I haven't killed anyone, and I wish I hadn't done that stupid thing.* The feeling that his heart was bobbing around in a deep, dark abyss would not go away.

It was obvious to the others that the expression on Han Qinzai's face was vastly different than the heroic look of a moment before.

"Han Qinzai, what's wrong?"

He heard them but did not feel like answering.

"He probably really was injured," Scabby Head said, his eyes scanning the faces of Mongrel and Fire Baby.

"I, I'll go get some horsewhip grass for you, okay?" Fire Baby volunteered apologetically.

A smile appeared on Han Qinzai's face and his eyes flashed open. The pale faces of the concerned men who had gathered around him lit up immediately. He had obviously gained acceptance into the group, just as he had planned, except that it had happened more quickly than he'd anticipated. He was not surprised; he just felt a bit degenerate. It was this indefinable sense of degeneracy that by rights should have alarmed him, for it was the one thing he had not counted on. And this unexpected development was fearful enough to alarm him as it began to crush down on him with deadening force. This was the first time Han Qinzai had come face to face with the specter of degeneracy. "It's nothing, just a nagging old problem. I'll be all right after I've rested a moment."

"But don't take it lightly. You don't want something like this to turn into a chronic injury. That'd be a real problem."

He sensed that he was too easily deceived. The scorn in which he had so recently held these men had been completely and immediately obliterated by a few kind words.

"I won't. I'll go get some horsewhip grass in just a moment." There were no pains anywhere on his body; casually stroking his chest, he said, "I don't think there's anything wrong."

Everyone smiled weakly.

## COCKCROW SIGNALS A HAPPY EVENT

He experienced a feeling of lightheadedness as soon as he got up from under the kadang tree, and he never could have gotten to his feet at all if he hadn't been able to close his eyes and hold on to the tree trunk. He sat down on the cement block at the entrance to the air-raid shelter, his face buried in his hands. He figured it was probably because of his yam diet; otherwise . . . *Oh-oh! Here it comes again.* Brightness suddenly replaced the haziness in his brain; it gradually turned yellow, then green, then red; then the encircling haziness returned. At this instant, his entire being seemed to be a mere shell that had had something drained from it. Fortunately, he was sitting down at the moment, or he would surely have collapsed. He readied himself for the next attack, which he knew would surely come. He continued to hold his head in his hands, and his body was tense and coiled—even his toes were curled inward. These dizzy spells had troubled him a great deal of late; sometimes he was able to bring one under control through sheer willpower alone, while at other times the force of his will had the effect of increasing their severity. He had gradually learned to cope with these two situations by trial and error: when the oncoming spell was controllable, he would increase the force of his willpower very gradually; when control was out of the question, he would gradually slacken it, for if he were to let the dizzy spell take complete hold of him with a rush, he would immediately begin retching or, even worse, crumple to the ground like a man losing a judo match. After a long while, and then an even longer while, before the second attack hit him, his muscles began to relax and loosen like lumps of kneaded dough. Once they were relaxed, the spell had passed, but still he raised his head gingerly, the chill sweeping over his body making him realize that he was sweating. The scene before him was too bright, like an overexposed photograph. He propped himself up on the cement, then steadied himself with the aid of the damp wall and placed his hand on his bed. A current of warmth ran up along his arm all the way to his heart. Once he lay down in bed this current of warmth flowed out of his body.

An oppressive darkness surrounded him, which, by comparison, made him fade into infinite insignificance. He was powerless to move. It was as if he'd been placed there expressly to lie on his side and sleep facing the wall. He was totally alert. Amid the darkness, beads of water on the damp wall slowly came into view, reflecting light seeping in through the entrance as they slithered down the wall. Han Qinzai, who had no concept of time, suddenly felt very keenly time's swift passage. *Tomorrow will be here soon. Have I killed anyone? I'll know tomorrow.* He was deeply superstitious and had gone through life comforted by a conviction that the gods were protecting him. Wasn't it true, he thought, that on the day before the birthday of every temple god, it was he who beat his gong to inform the town faithful? And on each of the festive temple processions or excursions of the gods, it was he who led the way, waving his red-festooned mallet and beating his gong. *Shit, now I don't even have this to fall back on.* He was seeing a tradition crumble right before his eyes, as though it were a gigantic statue crashing to the ground. And since it was crumbling through his fingers, the guilt, he felt, was his. Yet all he could do was curse the cause—which was not at all clear to him. "Shit!"

Much of the light from the entrance had faded, so the drops of water on the damp wall were no longer visible. Mosquitoes buzzed around his ears, sounding like the fading resonance of a struck gong—as though the gong that lay beneath his bed and served as a container for odds and ends were making sounds: *bong, bong, bong.* Beneath the scorching sun the gong was reverberating. He wiped his sweat repeatedly with the hand that had held the mallet. He screamed at the top of his voice; the salt from his sweat was stinging his eyes. Golden flashes of light from the surface of the gong were blinding him. He screamed once more at the top of his voice. He still could not hear the sound of his own screams. Sweat continued to ooze from his pores. He tried again: the faces of passersby crushed in on him, huge and threatening, and he ran like a madman, with many people chasing him wordlessly. He could run no farther; holding the gong tightly to his chest, he squatted down on his haunches, exposing his back until it was chilled, but when he turned around, there was nothing. The drops of water on the wall were still not visible. He could hear his heart thumping so that it seemed about to burst through his chest wall.

He wiped the sweat with his clothing as he lay gazing intently at the ventilation opening. Originally a smokestack that had been carried over and buried deep in a mound of earth, this opening now served as the shelter's source of ventilation. Strangely, no matter how hard it rained, the water had never seeped in through it. Sometimes Han Qinzai would use a brick to plug up the opening, but not today.

Through it he could see a circular patch of blue poking through the pitch-blackness above him and moving with his gaze. If he had seen a bright star up there in that patch of blue, he'd have known that the night was still early. But he saw nothing, only the blue that filled the space above him and kept floating past. It did not capture his attention. He rolled over and lay facing the wall, thinking about the coming day. *They're a bunch of disgusting pigs.* He yawned and his eyes watered. He closed his eyes and wiped the moisture away; he didn't feel like opening his eyes anymore. *The fucking pigs!* He could hear Blockhead's inane giggles. *That guy can go to hell!* Know-It-All's grimy, protruding navel— *Whew!* One-Eye's sunken eyelid; the hernia that bumped on the ground whenever Gold Clock squatted down; Scabby Head's pate, which looked like it had been gnawed on by a dog, plus his runny nose and rotting ear lobes. *A bunch of pigs!* He drew his itchy leg up to scratch it. *I never knew what scabies were, but whenever you fall on hard times you run up against just about everything.* He flicked his fingernails, yawned, wiped his watery eyes, made clicking noises with his mouth, and finally swallowed. *I hope and pray I haven't killed him.*

The shelter was hot and stuffy, and by rights he should have been sleeping in the entranceway. But now several bamboo brooms and scoops were piled in front of it. *Damn them!* He had talked to the men who swept up the park about this, telling them to put their equipment inside, for it was only on hot nights that he slept outside. They'd said that if he wasn't going to sleep inside, he should get out, because they were going to put a door and a lock on the shelter. *Who said I wasn't sleeping there? Damn them!* He yawned again. "Go to sleep now." He said this as if he were coaxing a child to sleep. He rolled over; there were still no stars in the patch of blue above him. He listened intently and with total concentration. *Damn it, it's still early for sure.* The only sounds came from the worms, the frogs, and the water in the fountain. A happy thought suddenly struck him: *If it's not the first watch, it must be the second by now, and I haven't heard the crow of a rooster.* The old saying goes: "The first and second watches signal death, the third and fourth signal happy events," and that's right. That thought led him to another: *I haven't killed anyone, I haven't.* He looked up again and searched the patch of blue. Still no stars. *It must be the first watch. Otherwise it's the second, and not a single crowing sound.*

He rolled back over and faced the wall, yawned, squeezed his watery eyes, then noisily licked his lips a couple of times and swallowed. He did not open his eyes again. *Now go to sleep; it'll be light soon.* But he was too agitated to sleep. His escapades involving the desperate search for yams and the debts he'd accumulated were cast out of his mind as though they'd never existed. *I don't have to wait till tomorrow—I know now that I haven't killed anyone! I'm not a bad person, after all.* With happiness filling his heart, he uttered, "Even if someone actually goes over and buys a coffin tomorrow, that doesn't prove it was my doing. Through the first and second watches there wasn't a single rooster's crow." But a nagging doubt persisted even in the midst of this joy. "I *didn't* hear a rooster's crow! I was awake the whole time!" He listened intently once more. He could no longer detect the sounds of worms or frogs, though the sounds of the water fountain and the wind in the trees sent a chill through him. *I'm going to go to sleep. If a rooster's going to crow, then let him.* He yawned. *It's past the second watch by now.*

Just as he was comforting himself with this thought, from way off in the distance came the faint sounds of a rooster's crow. This threw a scare into him; then he heard an answering crow from nearby. He rolled over to look up through the ventilation opening, where he saw a star woven into the edge of the patch of blue above him. He smiled at the star. The cold rays of light from this predawn star seemed more lustrous than ever. *Here comes another fellow.* He heaved a long sigh. *How can I avoid aging at this rate?* A weak smile, looking like the trail of a meteor, appeared on his face.

In the oppressively dark shelter, the last hint of a thought had disappeared. His even breathing was at one with the darkness and tranquility of the night. This was the most blissful time of day for him: all the fears, self-doubts, remorse, contradictions, and miseries seeped from his heart and melted into the darkness, leaving him to return to his beginnings, to the womb, where he was just like everyone else. He was oblivious of everything.

## GOOD NEWS

As dawn broke, Han Qinzai heard the men who swept the park come and pick up their equipment, and he heard them put it back some time later. He was too lazy to get out of his snug bed. If he could just sleep a while longer, he thought, then he wouldn't have to go out so early to wash up and scrounge something to eat. It would have to be yams, anyway. He wasn't at all anxious. *If I can hold off feeding my belly for a while and make it past noon, I'll have saved myself from a couple of meals.* He smiled wryly.

He never anticipated that he wouldn't wake up till way past noon after going back to sleep. He sat groggily on the edge of the bed for a moment, then reached down and fished the Long Life cigarettes out of the gong. Since he had cut each of them in half in order to make them last as long as possible, he still had about a pack left. While he was at it he took a look at the gong. It lay there, resigned to its fate, a receptacle for old nails of various sizes, a big red button he had found, and a ball of twine. The cigarettes were slightly damp and a little harder on the draw than usual. He decided to go over to the kadang tree and see what was up. Taking out two of the half-cigarettes, he put one behind each ear and walked out of the shelter, making some minor repairs to his conical bamboo hat before putting it on.

When the canopy of the kadang tree came into view in the distance, he heard unusually joyful sounds from beneath it. By the time the men came into view, he was surprised to see that they weren't sitting or lying on the ground. All eight or nine of them were standing up discussing something. Just then one of them spotted him. They spun around. "Here he comes! Here he comes!" Han Qinzai was put on his guard and slowed down, being careful to take quiet steps so as not to interfere with his hearing, but taking care also not to show that he was on his guard. He examined the situation carefully. There didn't seem to be any evidence of indignation among the gathered men; in fact, he noticed that one of them was waving to him. It was immediately obvious from the motion of the man's arm that this was a wave of welcome. This put him at ease, and he quickened his pace.

"Hey! Han Qinzai . . ." Mongrel called out when he was about ten steps away.

"Shh!" Scabby Head warned Mongrel, his back to the coffin shop. He pointed surreptitiously across the street. "Don't let on to them."

Encouraged by the smiles on their faces, Han Qinzai walked in among the men, who immediately crowded around him.

"Han Qinzai," Scabby Head said, "you did it!"

"Fuck him . . ." It was not an angry curse; quite the contrary, it was said in praise. They had taken this insulting epithet and turned it into a catchall phrase. "It's a good thing you thought of it. Scholar Yang died! Fuck him!" He pounded Han Qinzai on the shoulder.

Han Qinzai slumped the shoulder that was being pounded and rubbed it with an exaggerated motion. "Hey! Are you crazy? Tsk, tsk, tsk." He laughed. *That's all right, let them go ahead and give me the credit, as long as I know the truth—that it wasn't me who killed Scholar Yang. I was awake through the first and second watches, and not a rooster anywhere crowed.* Putting the respect he was being shown to advantage, he commented, "You should have done the same thing a long time ago yourselves, instead of letting him starve to death."

"You're absolutely right."

"Actually, everyone knows you can drum up business by beating on a coffin with a broom, but no one ever thought of doing it."

"Who *would* have thought of doing it? We all figured it was the coffin shop owner's affair."

As always, before he spoke, One-Eye rolled his sunken eye inward; then he blurted out, "Oh yeah! Well, Han Qinzai thought of it!"

"You said it!" Gold Clock waved his hand. "We're a bunch of dumb blockheads."

Everyone laughed at this, as if no one took exception to his comment. As soon as Blockhead heard that everyone there was a blockhead, he resumed his interminable giggling.

They all sat down, drawing their respect for Han Qinzai back within them, and listened attentively to Scabby Head as he handed out work assignments. Actually, there wasn't much difference among the various jobs, except that those who helped in the kitchen made out a little better in the food department.

"Last time," Scabby Head was saying, his memory temporarily failing him, "last time where did we go?"

"That was when Dewang's son-in-law was crushed under the pile of firewood."

"No," Fire Baby corrected him. "There's been another since then."

"Right. It was when Xishui the fish peddler's mother died."

"No, that was even earlier," Mongrel said.

"What do you mean, no? That's when there was all that fish. Block-head here almost croaked with an eel bone in his throat. I remember very clearly," Fire Baby said.

"You guys love to argue," Mongrel interrupted, spraying the area with saliva. "If I said it's not right, then it's not. You'll drive everybody nuts!"

"All right, that's enough! If you two want to fight it out, go somewhere else and do it." Scabby Head was getting irritated. "Shit, we haven't had a funeral banquet for a few days, and everyone's gone buggy with hunger."

Blockhead stood to the side muttering to himself, "Tailend was crying like a baby, hee hee. . . ."

"Ah, that's right, it was when Tailend's wife over at Westgate died."

"Right! It was when Tailend's wife died." A smile appeared on Scabby Head's face; now the others had all remembered too. "Well! Blockhead's not such a blockhead today!"

Blockhead just giggled, pleased as he could be.

"Who was in the kitchen when Tailend's wife died?" Scabby Head's glance swept past all of them. "Which ones? Whoever it was, speak up."

Still no answer. They all just looked back and forth.

All of a sudden Know-It-All shouted, "Gold Clock, it was you!"

"Me?" He pointed to himself with the airs of one wrongly accused. "Was it me?"

"It sure was, so no funny business." Know-It-All glared at him.

"Your mouth was crammed so full of fish-paste balls you couldn't talk. Am I right or wrong?"

"Ah—" he said embarrassedly. "You know I've got a bad temper, so I'm not about to argue with you."

Everyone knew that this was Gold Clock's way of admitting the fact.

"Fuck your ancestors! You and your big balls! So you wanted another turn in the kitchen! Aren't you afraid we'll slice your hernia off and fry it up as a dish of tripe?" Scabby Head shouted.

Gold Clock muttered angrily to himself, "Big balls? I'll give them to you if you want them." His words were so indistinct that not even the men sitting beside him could tell for sure what he was saying.

Han Qinzai sat there listening to their conversation, at the same time pondering the death of Scholar Yang and wondering if there was any link between it and his broom work of the previous day. But however he looked at it, the finger of accusation never pointed to him. He felt like joining the conversation.

"Hey, hold on a minute, all of you. I've got something to say. At the moment I don't have a suitable job, so for the time being I'm throwing in my lot with you. But as soon as I find a job I'll be leaving. Do you all understand? This is only temporary. I might even be leaving tomorrow. Since it's only temporary, it's hard to make plans." He kept stressing the word "temporary."

"As long as you're willing to join up, there's no problem," Scabby Head said.

"We don't have it so bad here."

"Mm! No, I told you—it's just temporary." Han Qinzai shook his head forcefully, like a man who was trying to shake loose something that had stuck to his face.

"He's right! Nobody who's got a decent job would hang around here."

"To tell you the truth, the brothers here are happy to have you along." Fire Baby said what all of them felt. Their smiles were warm and friendly.

"No, no, no, it's temporary, I say. When the time comes for me to leave, I don't want you to accuse me of having no feelings. I've told you it's only temporary." He was feeling very complacent now, for he had given himself a great deal of face.

## AT PEACE WITH THE WORLD

As the group of men approached Scholar Yang's tile-roofed mansion, Han Qinzai stayed behind for a moment. *He was going to die anyway. I didn't . . .* he quietly consoled himself, though it was hard to strip away all the fear in his heart. Not really wanting to enter the main hall, he managed to force himself across somehow. At first he had wanted to turn his face away, but he found himself turning to look at Scholar Yang's likeness on the image altar. In the shop of the one and only town artist, a great number of portraits, minus faces, were placed in readiness until needed. This portrait of Scholar Yang had been one of those paintings, to which the artist had now added the man's features. It was hard to say whether or not it looked like him. Perhaps in his younger years, or if he had gotten a bit older, there might have been some resemblance here and there. When Han Qinzai looked into those eyes, which were at peace with the world, he breathed more easily. He was willing to stop and take a closer look. But no matter where he gazed, his eyes always came back to that other pair of eyes, at peace with the world. He brought his hands together and bowed before the portrait. "Scholar Yang, you're the lucky one. Please look after me."

Scabby Head and the others were told that since Scholar Yang's family already had plenty of help, their services wouldn't be needed for very many days. So they sat on their haunches under the eaves waiting for the funeral to begin, at which time they could start out with all their paraphernalia. They were cursing in lowered voices, particularly Mongrel and

One-Eye, who had been assigned kitchen duties. Since Scholar Yang's was the most respected family in the entire town and the rites for him should be splendid, they had decided to add one man as a kitchen helper. At the time, Mongrel was in violent opposition, feeling that two was plenty. Everyone knew what he was so nervous about, but the family blocked his arguments. In a burst of anger, he said, "Just another rich person who lived like a damned beggar!"

Han Qinzai didn't want to squat there alongside the others for fear that someone might see him; even though he wasn't sure what they would think, he knew that he'd feel uncomfortable. So he just walked back and forth beside the bier. The local dramatic troupe, the funeral musicians, and the beggars were all waiting nearby. He could even see the town lunatic, Crazy Cai, standing alone by the rubbish heap laughing to herself for no apparent reason. He walked a few steps, then turned his head back to look at her. "What a fucking shame!" In the days when he was beating the gong, this is what he'd said whenever he gave Crazy Cai a fleeting glance.

He walked a little farther off, then took another glance on the sly. She wasn't a bad-looking woman at all: milky white skin, long legs, firm breasts, and nicely rounded buttocks. *What bewitching eyes!* Han Qinzai pretended to be looking elsewhere, then fixed his attention on Crazy Cai. *This summer she's really blossomed, almost overnight, into a young woman. I always knew that, mad as she was, she'd turn out to be a beautiful woman.* His throat was feeling a little dry and he tried to swallow. But there wasn't a drop of saliva in his mouth, and his desire made him uneasy. "Fuck her!" With this brief curse, he walked off as if he were in pain.

Members of the dramatic troupe were tuning their strings and practicing their wind instruments, the funeral musicians were sounding a few tentative notes, and the whole area began to come to life. Han Qinzai walked under the eaves and said to the others, "Looks like it's about time to start out."

"Scholar Yang's own porters are going to carry the coffin out themselves," Scabby Head said, obviously displeased.

It seemed to Han Qinzai that Scabby Head was blaming *him* for having the corpse turn out to be Scholar Yang, as if it were something he never should have done. "What's up, anyway?" He asked forcefully without actually raising his voice. "It's better than nothing, isn't it?"

No one knew what he was talking about. Propped up behind them were colorful banners made of coarse red, blue, and white material. Since there had been five generations of Scholar Yang's family living under one roof, these long cloth banners, slightly more than a foot in width, were fastened to lengths of bamboo that were a bit longer than the width of the banner. They hung in profusion from bamboo poles on which there were still some leaves. The men's appearance as they sat there was strikingly similar to those limp banners.

Han Qinzai squatted down across the street directly opposite the other men, still unwilling to be publicly associated with them. But since the procession was about to begin, he couldn't move off too far, or he might miss the chance to carry one of the banners and share in the handout. He couldn't imagine what had gotten them so steamed up. All they had to do was join the procession, and at the very least they'd get a couple of free meals and some pocket money for their troubles. If they watched their money closely, it would surely be enough to keep them from going hungry for three days or so, until another stiff came along. So what's wrong with that? *Ptui! Just a bunch of pigs.*

One-Eye—the herniated Gold Clock and Mongrel right behind him—walked purposefully over to Han Qinzai and sat down beside him. Han Qinzai felt as if he were on a seesaw, for the moment they sat down, he felt like standing up. He was getting tense. Afraid of causing them a loss of self-respect, he had no recourse but to keep sitting where he was. Know-It-All and Fire Baby came over and joined them.

"A wealthy household like this shouldn't provide such meager offerings for people like us. We depend on these handouts." The sunken eyelid quivered violently. "The death of the renowned Scholar Yang isn't as big a deal as the death of the mother of Xishui from the marketplace," One-Eye said.

"If they're going to carry him out this way, they're going to be criticized by people on the street," Mongrel said, pressing his face up close to Han Qinzai's nose. Han Qinzai didn't move a muscle. "Everyone knew Scholar Yang."

"As I see it, this is the fault of whoever's in charge. We shouldn't be blaming Scholar Yang," Gold Clock paused. "Han Qinzai, how do you feel about it?" After he'd said his piece, he reached down and rubbed himself.

Han Qinzai just smiled, without saying a word.

"This isn't a loss of face only for Scholar Yang's family—people from miles around will be laughing at us folks from Luodong," One-Eye said with growing agitation.

"They're all nuts! Young folks nowadays never consider the consequences of their actions."

"It's the times. As long as they have money in their pockets, they do what they please, and no one can do a thing about it."

"You there, Know-It-All," One-Eye said, spinning around to face him, "you've got it all wrong. Anyone who wants to live in civilized society has to make sure he does things with other people in mind." He turned back to Han Qinzai, his sunken eyelid fluttering. "Han Qinzai, you've got no axe to grind—am I right or not?"

Han Qinzai smiled and looked at One-Eye's single eye, which seemed nearly capable of talking. One-Eye interpreted this smile as one of support, so he really started to talk. As the men debated back and forth, Han Qinzai alone was occupied with his thoughts. He was thinking about putting some money aside and taking care of Crazy Cai properly. Seeing her standing off in the distance, he experienced such a strong desire he couldn't sit still. He felt like laughing but couldn't say why. He picked up snatches of the conversation around him. "You're way off the mark! You haven't got a prayer of ever getting into the matter of society—the first qualification is to have two good eyes!" Know-It-All got to his feet and, aping One-Eye's manner of tossing his head back and forth, walked back under the eaves where Scabby Head and the rest of them were waiting.

Scabby Head didn't even look up at Know-It-All, but before he'd sat down, Fire Baby began to rail at him: "What the hell did you come back for?" The meaning behind this question escaped Know-It-All, who sat down ostentatiously. Fire Baby glared at him, then jabbed him with his elbow. "We don't need your kind over here!"

"Fuck you! A person with one eye is fiercer than those with two!" He still hadn't grasped the meaning behind Fire Baby's comments. "Society, society, corporation, society.* Now what's bigger, society or a corporation? Do you know or not?" He paused for a moment. Actually, he didn't know himself. "If you want to know, I'll tell you. My hernia here is the biggest!" With that he took the wind out of the other man's sails.

Fire Baby laughed in spite of himself. He jabbed his elbow into Know-It-All, who turned around to look at him. Fire Baby's tone had lost its edge as he said, "What the hell did you come back for?"

---

* The Chinese words for "society" and "corporation" are composed of the same two characters, with the order reversed.

Scabby Head cut in before Know-It-All had time to answer: "After this, if you line up on Han Qinzai's side, you don't have to come back over here." Know-It-All was stunned. "You've got to learn to choose between your friends and your enemies." Scabby Head looked across the street, casting an icy look of warning from his seated position.

"Han Qinzai is an ambitious schemer." Fire Baby explained to Know-It-All the conclusions that he, Scabby Head, and the others had arrived at regarding Han Qinzai. Know-It-All bit his lower lip and nodded repeatedly, his eyes cast downward. "And so, don't let yourself be used. If Gold Clock and One-Eye want to go over there, that's their business. We don't care about them."

"That's right, he's a schemer," Know-It-All agreed.

"If he wasn't, then why didn't he hang around with us once he got here instead of walking all over the place by himself, doing whatever it is he does?" Fire Baby asked.

"That's the truth. I could see that too. Just a while ago when we came over here, he didn't want to stick with us but went over there across the street to be by himself."

"Then why did you go over there with him?"

"I just felt like chewing the fat, that's all."

"Open your eyes a little."

Know-It-All kept nodding his head. Blockhead was standing off to the side, giggling. Scabby Head was staring fixedly at Han Qinzai. Wanting to get into his good graces, Fire Baby commented, "Just look at Han Qinzai! I wonder what sort of scheme he's cooking up for us now?"

"You afraid of him?"

"Afraid of him, with you here? Afraid of a prick like that?"

Out of curiosity, they followed Han Qinzai's gaze.

"Hey!" Fire Baby poked Scabby Head and Know-It-All with his elbows. "Now I know what he's hatching in that head of his."

"I know that. Why do you think I've been watching him all this time?" Scabby Head narrowed his eyes as he glared at Han Qinzai.

"I can tell too."

"Tell what?" Know-It-All asked.

"Just look at Han Qinzai."

"That lousy rat! Has he got his eye on Crazy Cai?"

"Now do you see?" Scabby Head said coldly. A feeling of uneasiness settled over the men. They stopped looking at Han Qinzai and, like him, riveted their attention on the madwoman, as a heated emotion gripped their hearts.

MAKE YOUR BEST MOVE

Scholar Yang's funeral procession, from the vanguard to the mourners, stretched a distance equivalent to thirty or forty shops.

Han Qinzai was one of the banner bearers, carrying a blue banner representing the great-grandchildren's generation. Immediately following him were Scholar Yang's image altar and his coffin. The mourners slowly made their way toward the busy part of town, and the men had heard that they were going to parade up and down several streets. Han Qinzai had a jittery feeling he couldn't shake. The route of the procession would surely take him past the stores owned by Stony, Prosperity, and Longevity. What if they spotted him? *Shit! They're sure to cut old Han Qinzai down! If I cover my face with the banner, the cloth is thin enough so that I can still see where I'm going.* This thought perked him up considerably, but as he walked on, a sudden apprehensiveness flashed into his mind. He quickly turned back to look at Scholar Yang's image altar. The expression in the clouded eyes of the portrait was still one of peace with the world. *I know I had nothing to do with this.* He looked back one more time. *Scholar Yang, go in peace.*

When the funeral procession passed by the open-air turntable, even though his face was completely hidden by the banner, Han Qinzai could still see Longevity's store behind the bobbing heads of the crowd of onlookers. Then he saw Longevity himself, dressed in a vest, his arms folded in front of his chest so that his tough, hardened muscles glistened in the sunlight. "Damn him!" he cursed under his breath. There was a distance of no more than ten steps or so between him and Longevity, and the worst thing was that they were on the same side of the street. Longevity was looking his way, his eyes fixed on Scholar Yang's image. Han Qinzai was afraid that Longevity would spot him. Then an idea popped into his head: he began to hobble along like a cripple. This so surprised Gold Clock, who was walking beside him, that for a moment he was speechless. Han Qinzai was now directly opposite Longevity; he closed his eyes and began to chant:

"Oh, Earth God, oh, Matsu, Goddess of the Sea, please bestow your protection on Han Qinzai." When he opened his eyes again, he was terrified to see that he had strayed from the procession and that the onlookers were laughing at him. He ran back like a shot, completely forgetting that he was supposed to be hobbling like a cripple. "Damn it!" He could all but feel Longevity's eyes on his back, and a shiver ran down his spine. He wished he hadn't feigned being a cripple. He wanted to rectify the situation, but as he walked down the crowded street, each time he decided to make things right, he found that somehow he lacked the determination he'd had when he first saw Longevity.

"Han Qinzai, what's wrong with your leg?" Gold Clock asked impulsively.

"Got a damned cramp in it."

"Oh! The poor damned legs!" Gold Clock's glance moved from Han Qinzai's leg up to his head. "Why are you covering your face like that?"

"Don't you feel the heat today?" He kept his face covered. "This makes me a lot cooler."

"Yeah, it's hotter than hell." Gold Clock covered his face the same way. "Hey, it *is* cooler!"

The dramatic troupe came clamoring down the road, tooting horns and beating drums, making a lot of noise. All together there were some twenty different types of musical instruments—the two-man great brass gong, the bass drum, the hand drums, cymbals, bells, trumpets, three-stringed fiddles, two-stringed violins, flutes—and the cacophony produced by all these instruments, which were being played for all they were worth, assaulted the ears of everyone within range. Without straining at all, Han Qinzai could hear the muffled sound of the gong as it was struck by one of the musicians at the head of the procession. That was the only other gong like the one now lying beneath his bed. He listened and he thought, and as he did so, the gong rang out loudly and blended in with his reveries.

> *Bong! Bong! Bong!*
> *The gong beater's coming your way—*
> *Listen everyone, here's what I have to say—*
> *A call for all pilgrims at the Qiding Temple of the Patriarch—*
> *Tomorrow afternoon at two o'clock—*
> *Fire dancers will be there, tallies will be drawn—*
> *Bong! Bong! Bong!*
> *Calling all the Buddhist faithful—*
> *Get ready your spirit money, your crackers, and your candles—*
> *Everyone off to the Qiding Temple of the Patriarch to burn incense*
>     *and bow to the gods—*
> *Bong! Bong! Bong!*
> *Listen carefully, one and all—*
> *Women in their period, or pregnant, cannot go—*

*People in mourning cannot go—*
*Bong! Bong! Bong!*
*Everyone who goes will be given a tally—*
*To take home and paste over the door for protection—*
*Bong! Bong! Bong!*

"Should we prepare a sacrifice?" a woman asked him.

"It's a lot better if you can. But if you've never made a vow for blessings received from the Patriarch, there's no need. All you need is spirit money, crackers, and candles."

"Is it okay to bring fruit?"

Han Qinzai found himself surrounded by the neighborhood women.

"Sure. Fruit and clear tea are fine, but it's important to go with a pure heart."

"Is it okay to go if you've had a baby within the month?"

"Oh! If the month's confinement isn't up, you're not clean, so you can't go."

"Did you say two o'clock? Two in the afternoon?"

"Two o'clock tomorrow afternoon." Han Qinzai was kept busy turning from one woman to another, answering all their questions.

If he didn't get away from them pretty soon, he thought as the number of women increased, he'd find himself answering the same questions over and over. He started beating his gong, made his way forward through an opening in the crowd, and walked off. Naturally, some of the people stayed behind to pass on the news about the Patriarch to the late arrivals, as though they had been invested with some authority.

o o o

*Bong! Bong! Bong!* Beneath the same bright sun, the heat of summer growing more intense, his reveries dissolved back into reality, and as he looked out through the cloth in front of his eyes to see the faces of all the people gathered to watch the festivities, each and every one of them familiar to him, he was truly frightened that someone might spot him carrying a funeral banner. He heaved a long sigh and the emotional excitement he'd been experiencing turned into a great, heavy stone that weighed down on him.

"Gold Clock," he called out. Gold Clock had long since stopped covering his face with the cloth banner. "Have you ever seen me out beating my gong?"

"I've . . . seen you, of course I have." He was walking with his legs far apart so as not to cause pain to his hernia.

"How'd you think I was at it?"

"I never could figure out why you gave it up." Gold Clock cocked his head to look over at him. Han Qinzai had by then already edged over to him until they were shoulder to shoulder. "Beating a gong has got to be a lot more dignified than carrying a funeral banner."

"Dignified, you say?" With his back to the man, Han Qinzai smiled an ambiguous smile; he didn't dare look at Gold Clock.

"Yeah! I just can't figure out why you'd give it up."

Han Qinzai laughed a dull laugh, which Gold Clock found even more difficult to figure out.

The reverberations from the gong, almost illusory in effect, floated in waves of scorching heat and reached Han Qinzai's ears in pulsations. Thus it went until the entire procession was gathered at the oil shop at the end of the street, leaving room for the pallbearers to carry their burden into the cemetery. The banner carriers were resting on their haunches beneath a red banyan tree. Scabby Head coughed dryly several times, then cursed,"Shit! Well, we're all here. Scabby Head, Rotten Ear, One-Eye, Gold Clock, and the Cripple. Have I missed anyone?" It suddenly dawned on Han Qinzai that what he was holding in his hand was not a gong mallet.

"Don't forget me, Blockhead! Hee hee . . ." Blockhead added his name to the list, which broke the others up and lightened their mood. As for Han Qinzai, this round of laughter seemed to isolate him off to one side, and the barren scene before him produced an anguish that no amount of appeasement could drive away. He was beset by self-pity that had lost all its significance. Feeling terribly depressed, he was thinking that the only way to remove his anguish was to show contempt for these men. With this decision, their every action, the way they had isolated him, nothing could bring him any pain. *A bunch of old bums, lower than pigs!* he cursed inwardly. But he was still put out of sorts by their laughter. He raised his hand to rub his chest, then said, looking for sympathy, "Mongrel, you guys really hurt me—I'm still sore." He followed this with another inward curse: *They're worse than pigs.*

"What's that? Didn't they turn you into a cripple?" Scabby Head queried in mock seriousness.

"I'm sore all over."

"Hey, Mongrel, he says you banged him with your head so hard he hurts all over. Go a little easier next time, Mongrel, Fire Baby!" Scabby

Head nodded with satisfaction as the other men burst out laughing, having understood the intent of his comments.

*No matter what, it's a lot better to argue with them than just sit here all by myself.* So he fired off one comment after another, though nothing came of any of it and their interest flagged. In the midst of his bewilderment, he suddenly thought of some dirty stories that rescued him from his predicament.

Eventually Scabby Head broke in on his story. "Han Qinzai, the musicians are coming back. How much longer is this story of yours? Why not wrap it up for now and finish it some other time."

The words "some other time" were particularly pleasing to Han Qinzai's ear, so he stood up and brought his story to an end. "Of course, you all know that when the woman lay down in the grass, her bound feet, which were sticking up in the air, kept moving up and down, until her husband saw them and shouted happily: 'Amei! I caught the turkey! I caught the turkey! I can see its head.'" He still held his audience, and even though they got to their feet, picked up their banners, and fell in behind the musicians in a big hurry to get back to Scholar Yang's home for a free meal, Know-It-All, Mongrel, and some of the others pushed Gold Clock out of the way to move up alongside Han Qinzai and hear some more of his stories. But all the while they kept an eye on Scabby Head, watching the expression on his face.

"Han Qinzai," Scabby Head said with a smile as he turned to look behind him, "these guys can't hold on to their money as it is, and if you keep it up, tomorrow they'll all be broke."

Know-It-All and the others detected a note of approval from Scabby Head that they were with Han Qinzai. So Gold Clock pushed by the others, yelling, "So you want to listen, do you? Well, so do I!" Han Qinzai's heart was warming up. His mouth was split in a broad grin and he was laughing, though not a sound emerged. His face looked as if it had been stamped by the rays of the sun.

## THE NIGHTMARE

After several uneventful days had passed, everything returned to normal: the second rice harvest had been completed, and no dreams invaded his sleep. His life had taken on a fixed routine: rising with the sun, he prepared a simple breakfast, then went over to the kadang tree, joined the funeral banquets, argued, chatted amiably; meanwhile resentment filled his heart more and more deeply. Even his limited supply of dirty stories had been exhausted, and it was unnecessary for him to observe the cold looks in the others' eyes or listen to their conversation to know that in this circle he had lost that certain something. If the situation didn't improve, before too long it wouldn't make much difference whether he was here or not. But what could he do? he asked himself. He'd been born a person of integrity, and there was no way he, Han Qinzai, could stoop to supporting another man's balls as he crossed a threshold! *Who does Scabby Head think he is? I wouldn't even let him wash my feet.* He was fighting mad, and the more he thought about it, the more his heart froze. Every time Han Qinzai's turn to help in the kitchen rolled around, Scabby Head and the others said that he wasn't a real member of the group, so they skipped him and went on to the next in line. Whenever Know-It-All returned from helping in the kitchen, in obvious high spirits, he'd make a big show of saying to the others in front of him, "Wa! There was a piece of lean meat this big," using his hands to describe it. Or he'd say, "I dipped it in soy sauce and in garlic paste and had it with a bottle of wine—oh, shit! Just imagine eating like that every day!" As he carried on, his eyes never left Han Qinzai.

*Ptui! These guys were all raised by pigs, and this big liar here is saying, "Hai! Just think what it would be like!" Fuck him and all his ancestors! Why don't you guys go to the open-air stalls in front of the Temple of the Patriarch to ask about me, about my good old days? What makes you think a lousy piece of lean meat would be such a temptation to Han Qinzai? That makes me laugh. Back in those days, whenever I went to the Temple of the Patriarch, Pine Root, Woody, and Righteous Virtue would call out to me, asking me this and that, to get on my good side. They'd shout, "Han Qinzai, we've already warmed some wine for you." "Han Qinzai, we've got some goose liver here for you." Hmph! I serve no master, and if I feel like it I can eat sharkskin!*

*Bong! Bong! Bong!* Somewhere along the line, it seemed, a gong had come to exist in his mind. It resounded—*bong! bong!*—on its own. In the middle of the night it was so persistent it caused him great uneasiness and made his ears ring. He sat up straight, his nerves so taut his eyes fluttered. He looked at the darkness around him, as if he wanted to stare a hole in it to get a better look. He felt the walls close in tightly around him and eventually realized that he knew the source of this pressure: the darkness was congealing into a hard lump and was about to freeze him solid there in the shelter. He breathed with difficulty until, from the

depths of his confusion, with an agility born of terror, he leaped frantically off his bamboo bed. As he knocked over two empty bottles, the
noise tore through the oppressively thick atmosphere, which quickly
swallowed the sound up again. He stumbled headlong through the
shelter entrance, his outstretched arms supporting him against the concrete walls. "Come here!" he yelled. "Scabby Head, if you've any guts,
come here! Come here, all of you! Fuck you all!" His neck strained to
support his drooping head when suddenly he felt the cool air of an
autumn night, and just as suddenly the faces of the men under the
kadang tree appeared superimposed on his mind, particularly their cold,
hard eyes; he was powerless to drive away those looks. "I told you to
come! Didn't you hear me? If you had any guts you'd have come!" Lines
of laughter showed in the corners of their eyes.

"If you don't believe me, there's nothing I can do. But don't look at
me that way. Let's hear you say something. Let it out, curse me if you
want to."

But they just sat there lazily, though they continued to look at him
coldly, occasionally exchanging glances among themselves.

Han Qinzai looked at each of them in turn but could not detect the
trace of a kind look.

"You all know well enough how Crazy Cai was deflowered beneath
the pork butcher's counter in the marketplace. I felt sorry for her, that's
all." A look of exasperation that confused the men appeared on his face.
"What do you want me to say? I feel sorry for her."

The others glanced at Scabby Head, who smiled. They turned their
cold eyes back on Han Qinzai as they heard him mutter, "I know why
you guys are suspicious of me: you're thinking about how I give her food
whenever we have a funeral banquet, and how I do it on the sly. I know
you won't believe what I say, but I just feel sorry for her." He saw that
they were looking at one another, conversing with their eyes. "But," he
continued, "I did it on the sly because I was afraid you guys would get
the wrong idea. In all good conscience, may heaven strike me down with
lightning if there's been anything between me and that woman."

But no matter how sincerely he said it, opening up his very heart to
show them, knowing glances passed among the men, giving him an even
more unpleasant taste in his mouth.

"I really didn't do a lowdown thing like that!" He felt as if he were
being tortured into self-revelations, one after another, under the
unchanging looks of doubt in their eyes. He continued, "You all want me

to own up to it, but . . ." He stopped, finding it difficult to say what was on his mind. This created a moment of tense anticipation. Finally, in nervous embarrassment, he admitted, "If it's my thoughts you want to know, well, it did occur to me several times, but when the time came and I saw her, I ran away, afraid to go through with it. I might have had the same thing on my mind when I took the food over to her, but the moment I laid eyes on her, I just put the bowl down on the ground, turned, and ran off. I was thinking of her. I *was* thinking of her!" This came out almost unintelligibly and had something of a sob about it. Scabby Head and the others laughed. Sensing that he was still not believed, he cited another instance. "The night before last, she came to the park alone late at night—it must've been at least eleven o'clock, when the place was deserted." Clarity suddenly came to his voice and his mood grew somber. The faces of the men around him were frozen with the attentiveness of people listening fearfully to a ghost story, unwilling to miss a single word. "When I saw her, I was scared and pleased at the same time. I looked all around to make sure we were alone. 'Crazy Cai,' I said to her, 'you come with me to the air-raid shelter and I'll give you something to eat.' And she did, she followed me quietly back to the shelter. I was really getting the itch then. I looked around again, and there was no one, not even a stray dog." When he reached this point in his narration, the other men began to squirm uneasily, as if they would burst waiting for the climax.

"Now you all know that even though Crazy Cai's got a big belly, she still isn't bad. I was constantly on the alert to see if there was anyone nearby. Although she seemed to know what I had in mind, she didn't resist. I figured she needed it too, since she already had some experience. As the saying goes: 'A man enjoys it three parts, a woman seven.' When I was sure we were alone, I . . . I reached out and touched her arm, but then I drew back like my hand had been struck by lightning. I give you my word—all this time that she's been on my mind, the night before last was the first time I touched her." His listeners' faces showed how displeased they were that his narration wasn't going into enough detail. "I started to get scared," he went on, "and I told her to leave—started pushing her away, in fact—but not only did she stay where she was, she even headed into the air-raid shelter by herself, which scared me so much I just climbed up onto the grass covering and waited there anxiously till dawn."

When Scabby Head and the others heard this, they showed their utter disgust, born of disappointment and a sense of having been cheated, with looks that seemed to mean that they wouldn't give him the satisfaction of getting angry. And their disappointment proved a disappointment to him.

"I *did* think of her," he yelled. "Who hasn't? I'll bet all of you have. But that's all it was—thoughts. If you say I was wrong, then the only thing I did wrong was touch her once two nights ago. But I let go of her right away. I really did. Because I was too scared!"

At this point, not only was he subjected to icy stares, he was also the target of silent looks of bitter loathing. He voiced his feelings of injustice by yelling, "If you don't believe me, you can call her over and ask her yourself! If anything happened between her and me, you can do anything you want to! You can take me around to all the town gates, where I'll beat my gong and admit my guilt in front of everyone. How's that?"

Scabby Head expressed all their sentiments with a hateful snort. As far as Han Qinzai was concerned, that was an ambiguous response. He was feeling terribly dejected, unable to understand why he had to give these men so many explanations. He regretted having told them about the incident of the night before last, and of having let out his secret thoughts for Crazy Cai. In sum, he regretted having said any of this to these men.

○ ○ ○

Han Qinzai bought two bottles of 25-proof cheap wine and headed home to his air-raid shelter, making up his mind once again not to go back, ever. *Who cares that there'll be food to eat tomorrow at the funeral at Kelin! I'll just drink these two bottles of wine and get a good night's sleep.* He was mentally exhausted to the point that all desires had left him. He just hid in his shelter and drowned his sorrows in the wine. Before he passed out, the mosquitoes that were feeding on him had all fallen drunkenly to the ground without even getting their fill of his blood. A kerosene lamp constructed of a tie band from a pair of shorts, lying in a small plate and supported by a single split chopstick, burned unwaveringly all the way down to the plate, until the supply of kerosene was exhausted.

The sound of a gong being struck resounded in his ears, but no matter how hard he tried, he could not lift his head. It drooped forward until it could go no farther, and then it rolled back again. In like fashion, no matter how hard he tried, he could not wipe away the persistent images of those cold looks. It eventually got so bad they gave him shivers. Things had deteriorated with Han Qinzai until all he could do was shout in confusion, "Come on! Go ahead and look, what good does that do? Anyone, anyone with any guts, come over here. . . ." He waved his arm in the air, causing him to lose his equilibrium as he stumbled several steps out the door. He lay prostrate on the grass, continuing to mumble in an unbroken stream. He was soothed by gust after gust of cool night air in the open park. Like an infant sleeping soundly at its mother's breast, he noiselessly sucked in the breath of life.

o o o

A road, the most familiar one of all, stretched out before him. Faces so familiar that there was no longer any need to consciously record their names lined the brightly lit roadsides, eagerly awaiting the public announcement of some vile deed committed in town. With this sight in front of him, Han Qinzai balked. The gong felt so heavy he could barely hold it; even the mallet seemed heavy as a boulder. His mind was busily engaged in reflecting on ways of dying. He gave it some serious thought for a while but found that he lacked both the knowledge and the courage. He realized that there were things more fearful than death. But all these impressions, ill defined though they were, took the shape of a torturous anxiety. He turned back to beg for mercy but, seeing pair after pair of staring, frightening eyes, he was rendered mute. Turning back around, he felt those cold glares bore into him until his backbone seemed to recoil. Apparently the only option open to him was to follow through on his vow. At this critical moment, he still had thoughts of changing the wording of his defense, but no matter how simple he made it or how reserved, he would still have to say something along these lines: "The gong beater's coming your way. Listen everyone, here's what I have to say: I, Han Qinzai, have committed the unpardonable sin of seducing Crazy Cai. . . ." He wanted badly to beg for mercy, or for death. Met by the same cold, unrelenting stares, he had no choice but to screw up his courage and walk forward, beating his gong and shouting, "The gong beater's coming your way. Listen everyone, here's what I have to say: I, I . . ." He could not go on, as the full awareness of his discomfort hit him.

His mind was still clouded and confused when he opened his eyes, and he was in a state of total shock. He had no idea why he had walked into the woods—then it gradually dawned on him that the rice stalks that rose unevenly around him as he lay on the ground had made him believe he was in the woods. As he reached a state of awareness, the first emotion he experienced was the self-congratulatory happiness of someone who realizes that a calamity has turned out to be only a nightmare. But this short-lived happiness only increased the mournfulness of his self-pity.

Today was the grand funeral of the rich man, Chen from Kelin, and there would be food to eat. He'd heard that the Chen family owned nearly ten acres of land. Han Qinzai was through making vows. He wanted to go over to the kadang tree. *If they don't believe me*, he thought as he walked, *then they don't believe me—if the roots of the tree are solid, there's no need for the branches to fear a typhoon. How could people like that ever understand me, Han Qinzai? They think I'm the same as them. That makes me laugh! Like that episode yesterday, when Scabby Head and the others gave me those cold glares.* He was not going to give that a second thought. His thoughts moved to the rich Mr. Chen's ten acres of land, the golden grain, the piles of money, the funeral arrangements, the meat on the tables, the generous packets of spending money. And even if the image of Scabby Head and the others should occasionally flash into his mind, he had only to silently curse, *Fuck them*, and that took care of that. As he passed over Southgate Bridge, the canopy of the kadang tree came into view once again. His thoughts having turned to the tree, he spat on the ground. "Ptui! Fuck them!"

## THE RAINBOW WITH NO END

"Ah!" Mongrel seemed to be trying to wrap up all of their comments into a general conclusion. "'In shallow water the dragon is laughed at by the shrimps; in the open plain the tiger is at the mercy of dogs.'"

"What's that?" Know-It-All jumped up shouting. "Is that an admission that he's a dragon or a tiger? And we're a bunch of little shrimps and mutts? If you don't know how to make comparisons, then keep your mouth shut. You're the mutt, and who wants to be associated with you?"

The others all looked at Know-It-All and nodded, some voicing their agreement with "That's right!" or "Good point!"

"Ai! Why make such a big deal out of it? Why do that? I'm only here on a temporary basis, you know." Gold Clock the herniated was making fun of Han Qinzai by mimicking his manner of speaking. He glanced at Scabby Head, then at the others. He was seldom in such high spirits, for it seemed that he never did anything right in the presence of these men. But this time, not only did he escape being yelled at and called "Hernia," he was actually rewarded by their lighthearted approval. "Temporary, I say, just temporary. You know what I mean?"

"Oh, no, don't be temporary! Stay here with us," Mongrel cut in, like an actor on the stage.

But Gold Clock was so beside himself with the joy of not having angered the others that he completely missed the opportunity to engage Mongrel in a mock debate. He just sat there, his arms clasped around his knees, as he rocked back and forth. Mongrel was growing a little impatient, but before the moment had passed, Fire Baby said, in imitation of Han Qinzai:

"No, no, when I say temporary I mean temporary. I'm not like you guys." He had all of Han Qinzai's little movements down pat, and the others laughed at him. They constantly looked over to see if there was any reaction from Han Qinzai. As if he had some magnetic effect that kept drawing their eyes back to him, they seemed powerless to keep from looking his way.

Han Qinzai sat alone in the spot where normally they all sat in a group; while the others had picked up and moved to a spot under another kadang tree, some three or four trees removed from him. Their conversation was intended to drive him away. Their every sentence reached his ears and penetrated deeply into his heart. It was all over for him, he thought. His only recourse was to stay put, whether they wanted him there or not, and see what they would do. He shrugged off the knowledge that it was a very undignified way to go about it. Each time a peal of laughter floated across, he was driven by his curiosity to turn around and see what was happening. But with all the strength he could muster, he forced his will upon his seemingly rebellious neck. When all he could hear was a series of unintelligible mutterings, broken suddenly by an explosion of laughter, the strain was so intense that a soreness developed in his neck. He rested the point of his chin between his knees as he squatted there, not allowing his curiosity to get the better of him. He simply didn't know how else to handle the situation. More than once he was so agitated by what they were saying that he was on the verge of jumping to his feet and cursing them soundly before walking off and washing his hands of them. But for reasons even he did not know, he was unable to jump up, powerless to curse out loud. He just stayed as he was, squatting motionlessly on his haunches, until his buttocks, his legs, and his back were numb with soreness and eventually all that was left to him was the remorseful anger that filled his still-alert mind.

He made up his mind that if he heard any more talk or laughter that distressed him he'd leave at once. But immediately after making this decision, he heard Mongrel say something about "hatching an egg." This produced a round of side-splitting laughter. His resolve of a moment before slipped away and lay there steaming. He began talking to himself. *I'm not stupid! Leave? That's exactly what they want. So I'll stay put and see what they do about it.* He hugged his knees more tightly. Fearing that he wouldn't be able to follow through with his latest resolution, he forced his chin down hard, closed his eyes, and, with all the willpower he could muster, resisted whatever it was that enervated him; thrills of victory came in waves to salve his wounded heart, which in turn inspired him with greater courage to continue the struggle. This in turn increased his fatigue while simultaneously causing him to experience the intoxication of a tragic hero as he held on to this particular spot.

Another burst of laughter hit him like a bayonet thrust. *Could they be laughing at me because I've got no guts? Fuck them! To hell with them! What can they do if I don't leave? So what if I don't have any guts? No! I don't have any guts if I do leave. Right! I don't have any guts if I do leave.* He hugged his knees tightly, pressed his chin down hard, and closed his eyes as the *bong, bong* sound of a gong rang in his ears. Nowhere, not on any street or lane of the town, was there a cruel face or a pair of cold, expressionless eyes. His throat was as parched as if he'd been shouting at the top of his lungs. He noticed that his hands were hanging loosely, as if the left one were holding a gong, the right one grasping a mallet, and both quivering slightly. After hurriedly and forcefully stopping these involuntary movements, he glanced at the thumb of his left hand, which was roughly stroking the callus on the inside of his index finger. This callus had been caused by the constant rubbing of the rope handle of the gong he had once carried. He smiled grimly.

As for Scabby Head and the others, although they'd gained the upper hand by expelling Han Qinzai from the group, now as they watched him sit there so composed, apparently unaffected by what they were saying, conflicting emotions of triumph and defeat assailed them as well. The only difference was the source of these emotions: for them it came from a sense of superiority; for him, from one of inferiority. It was a stalemate. As it turned out, Han Qinzai was able to minimize the effects of this particular stalemate, for he had analyzed his own present situation and the deterioration of what had originally been good relations with the others. Scabby Head and the rest, on the other hand, after spending a good part of the day poking fun and directing heated criticisms at Han Qinzai, found that he was unaffected by it all. Eventually, without being aware of it, they began to lose interest, even though no one was willing to bring the episode to a close. So they let things run their course, waiting for their interest to peter out naturally. Even the comments of Mongrel, Fire Baby, and Know-It-All, who continued to take their pleasure in heatedly baiting and poking fun at him, could no longer get a rise out of the other men. Gradually they too quieted down. But they didn't let Han Qinzai off the hook completely, for in addition to openly isolating him, they were already contemplating what they would subject him to next. In the meantime, Han Qinzai was no longer exposed to the laughter that had so unsettled him.

Suddenly a new thought disturbed him as he sat there in solitude. *What would happen if someone came now to make funeral arrangements? Should I go along with the others? Or shouldn't I? If not, why sit here and suffer? Wouldn't I feel a lot better if I stood up and gave them hell, then just walked away? If I were to go along with these heartless bums, who knows what trouble they might dream up for me?* He thought and he thought, but to no avail. Concerned that some bereaved family member might turn up across the street to buy a coffin, he hoped desperately that at least it wouldn't happen today.

A leaf from the kadang tree fell to the ground in front of him. He felt like someone who had run into a friend so intimate that all formalities could be dispensed with, someone he could welcome or ignore, as he pleased. He looked at it lazily, then picked it up and put it up to his mouth to lick it. He focused his gaze on the leaf until his eyes grew crossed; his face was gaunt and slack. His thoughts turned to his present predicament, the source of which could be traced initially to the death of Scholar Yang. But it was his relationship with Crazy Cai that had had the most direct effect. At first it had been a simple misunderstanding. But after her belly had begun to swell, things started to turn bad. *What a joke! Blockhead can do it, so why can't I? Besides, I only* thought *about it.* More giggling from Blockhead's pursed lips, but he couldn't tell if it came from across the way or was a figment of his imagination.

Blockhead was giggling. "Don't, Mongrel. My ears are splitting."

"Tell us, what did you do with Crazy Cai?"

"Don't. What did I do?" Blockhead stammered. "I . . . I only . . . I only took a piss in her, that's all." Mongrel let go of Blockhead's hand, joining the others in side-splitting laughter. After that, whenever they wanted to have a laugh at Blockhead's expense, they had only to grab hold of one of his ears and ask him what he'd done with Crazy Cai. He would say that he'd taken a piss in her, that's all. Later on, merely grabbing his ear would make him blurt out the same thing without even being asked the question.

One day, Scabby Head suddenly asked, "Han Qinzai, haven't you really ever had anything to do with Crazy Cai?"

"Me?" Han Qinzai was momentarily speechless. Then he giggled and said, "I only took a piss in her, that's all."

At first a few of them chuckled at this, but when they saw the hardened looks on the faces of Scabby Head and one or two of the others, the laughter died as quickly as it had begun. What had been intended as a joke had backfired, resulting in Han Qinzai's complete isolation from that day on.

Crazy Cai's belly had now become *the* topic of conversation among most of the people in town, particularly the women. Han Qinzai was terribly worried that his name would be drawn into the talk. Therefore, bearing his vague anguish as best he could, he stopped bringing her food. And yet, she continued to greet him with that idiotic smile of hers whenever she saw him.

He had unconsciously chewed the kadang leaf into a pulpy mass, and the slightly bitter juice from the leaf entered his stomach, swallow by swallow. He thought, without being totally aware of it, that if that piece of growing flesh inside Crazy Cai's belly was his, then . . . *Wa! Wouldn't that be something! I, Han Qinzai, would gladly jump into a vat of boiling oil if I had a child. I could endure any amount of suffering. That heartless woman of mine; if she'd had any feelings at all, Ahui would be over twenty by now. Shit! But then, what good would have come of it? It served her right, being killed by that guy. It just proves the saying that evil is repaid with evil, good rewarded with good; nothing is left unrecompensed, and your day will surely come.* This thought served to smooth away the feelings of injustice that filled his heart. Except for the sense of isolation they produced, the clamorous sounds that floated over to him were no longer a cause of concern. The rules of Heaven were the guiding principle in the ways of life. He who obstructs another person will be visited by heavenly reprisals. He believed strongly in this principle of retribution and was convinced that in the future, Scabby Head and the others would get their just deserts. This brought a momentary feeling of comfort to him, and the melancholia caused by fleeting memories of past incidents was swept cleanly away, while the inner strength he had mastered in his struggles dissipated. At this moment, he felt himself truly at rest—body and soul.

"Han Qinzai—" A strange sound from Scabby Head's direction came to him. As though shaken out of a sleep, he looked over his shoulder, where he saw Mongrel jerking his chin upward and pointing his nose at him, saying to a neatly dressed man, "Isn't that him over there?" All the men, including the stranger, turned their eyes in the direction Mongrel was indicating to look at Han Qinzai. This threw a slight scare into him. The man stepped onto the pedal of his bicycle and pushed himself over toward Han Qinzai.

"Han Qinzai, are you still beating your gong?"

He couldn't believe his ears. He got to his feet, feeling both flabbergasted and elated. Stooping slightly, he didn't know what to do with his hands, putting them first behind his back, then clasping them in front of him. "Do you mean . . ." he asked cautiously. But before he'd gotten the words out, the other man butted in impatiently, "Well, yes or no?"

"Yes, yes, yes," Han Qinzai replied with a sense of urgency. "Mm-hm, mm-hm!" Although he didn't know what the man had in mind, he didn't dare ask any more questions.

"Meet me at the district headquarters at two tomorrow afternoon. I've got a job for you." Then he added impatiently, "I'll need your services for three days."

"Yes, yes, yes . . ." Han Qinzai stammered, nodding with each word. He kept it up until the man was out of sight. Then it came to him—the district headquarters. No wonder the man looked so familiar; in the past, he was the one who had always hired him when the district headquarters had an announcement. "This head of mine is really something—I even forgot him." As he watched the man's retreating figure, the gratitude and happiness brought by this unexpected opportunity had the effect of slowly straightening his slightly crooked back, like a vine growing at night. Enough time passed while he was in this state of mind to vex the men looking on; then, sensing something in the air, he became aware of several pairs of eyes staring at his back. But there were no more cold shivers up his spine. He coughed dryly, sending the stares back where they came from, then turned around and gave the others a sweeping glance. Much to his surprise, these men whom he had endured for so long, whom he had feared to anger, and whose arrogance he had catered to now resembled little more than a mass of dead cinders. Some of them were blinking involuntarily. Sickened by what he saw, Han Qinzai opened his mouth and released his long-pent-up anger.

"What's wrong with you? Look! Don't you know who I am? Since you want to look, get yourselves an eyeful. I'm different from bums like you, who spend your whole lives gnawing on coffin boards!" So saying, he rolled his sleeves up, and with his arms—both as thin as rails—at his waist, he struck the pose of a scarecrow. Suddenly realizing that this outburst had included him in its invective, he added, "Don't you get the idea that I'm a bum like the rest of you. Maybe I'll just go marry Crazy Cai, and what of it! If I want to take a piss, I'll take a piss, and what of it! I'll take it wherever I want to, and what can you do about it? All you can do is swallow your own spit." And yet for some reason, they still intimidated him. Almost instinctively, he maintained a guarded distance of as much as three or four kadang trees from them.

Scabby Head and the others were speechless, looking as if someone had smashed something valuable of theirs when they weren't looking, and they didn't know what to do about it. At the same time, they were struck by the feeling that a livelihood of gnawing on coffin boards really wasn't a very respectable occupation (prior to this, the thought had evidently never crossed their minds). This impression, however, was only a shallow, fleeting one, and did not enter their relative consciousness. Self-demeaning looks appeared on their faces, but these were nothing more than instinctive shows of self-protection meant to illicit sympathy and help them over this critical moment.

*Marry Crazy Cai?* This shocked even Han Qinzai. How could he have said that? He felt a need to explain, both to himself and to the others. "I . . ." He sputtered for a while, but could never get past the word "I." Finally, growing impatient with himself, he blurted out, "I, Han Qinzai, mean what I say. If I say temporary, I mean temporary. My teeth aren't made to gnaw on coffin boards like yours are." But no matter how satisfying all this was, he couldn't shake the emotional discomfort caused by his comment about marrying Crazy Cai. He was afraid they'd take it in all of its despicability and turn it on him. "Of course, I wouldn't actually marry her; what I meant was *if* I did, what could you guys do about it?" But that didn't make him feel any better. *If I feel like marrying her, that's what I'll do! Having a baby is easy, but rearing a child is a deed of kindness; anyone can father a child, but a parent is one who rears a child, whoever's seed it may be!*

Among the group of men, only Blockhead was a loner, totally unconcerned about what earthshaking incident might be occurring in this circle; he simply continued doing what he did best, which was to giggle foolishly. But on this occasion, he was unable to draw any laughter from the others.

*I've got to hurry back and get everything ready. I'll have to polish the gong with ashes, and the mallet—I may not be able to find it at all, and even if I do, the cloth head has probably rotted away.* But the thought that he was going to let these men off so easily was an irritation, and he was tempted to level one more hateful blast at them. He thought for a moment, then said:

"You guys come over to my place when you're not busy. I won't be able to provide too much, but at least you can have some rice wine and smoke a cigarette or two—no problem there. Now I mean it—you come on over. Han Qinzai will be waiting for you." His intent was to mock them, and as he saw the embarrassed looks on their faces, he knew he'd accomplished his goal. He spat once loudly, then turned briskly on his heel and walked off.

*Later on, if I can really manage it, I'll treat them to a sumptuous meal in one of the open-air stalls in front of the Temple of the Patriarch. Then I'll give them each a pack of Long Life cigarettes and see if that doesn't make them feel just terrible.*

### THE GONG GOES *BONG! BONG! BONG!*

"Hey, it's time to get up." He stretched and reached beneath the bed to take out the gong that he'd been using as a catchall. He examined it carefully. "Wow, you sure have slept for a long time; you've even got a dead lizard in here!" He stared intently at the sunken eyes with the tiny specks of white showing through the lizard's skin. Then he picked out a nail from the junk inside and used it to flip the lizard's carcass onto the floor, after which he turned the gong upside down and dumped everything into a heap under his bed. At that moment he realized that he was holding in his hand a real but badly tarnished gong, and his heart was pounding uncontrollably. He turned the gong over and over in his hands, brushing the dust off as he did. He spat on it, then rubbed it with his fingers as he walked out of the shelter. He examined it carefully once more in the natural light, as the sun glinted weakly off the spots he'd rubbed with saliva. He could envision the gong in all its shiny luster; its sound, which was in his mind always, seemed now to be pounding in his ears.

*Bong! Bong! Bong!* "The gong beater's coming your way . . ." He muttered under his breath, "Once I fall on better days I'll show them. Where do they get off looking down on me?" He'd pulled up a handful of wild grass from atop the air-raid shelter; with it he scooped up some ashes from the incinerator, then gently rubbed the face of the gong. Although it had the scars of two cracks as wide as grains of rice where the hanging straps went, they'd been carefully polished so that when the gong was struck the sound wouldn't reveal any trace of the flaw, nor would its resonance be affected.

"Shit! Damned good-for-nothing!" He remembered the day those cracks appeared as if it were yesterday. It was on the day of the Matsu festival: following the procession, he'd been asked to stay over for a meal by the family selected to keep the goddess at the house for the year. He must have drunk a great deal that night, or else how could his gong have fallen on a cobblestone? Never before, in all the time he'd been beating the gong, had Han Qinzai dropped it. He'd replaced the rope straps about once a month. *What a damned good-for-nothing!* As he polished the gong, he cursed to himself, although only he knew what was being cursed.

As the gong began to shine once again, the lost days of Han Qinzai's past returned in all their vividness, giving a scintillating boost to his spirits. He reflected on how, because of the cracks in the gong, he had manipulated his wrist action as he wielded the mallet and struck the gong at just the right spot so that the sound had the same beauty and resonance as when it had been whole and perfect, and so that the cracks did not grow any longer. He knew the course of these two cracks by heart: they'd meet near the middle; then a tiny triangular section of brass, about one fifth of the gong, would fall off. In the past he'd taken pains to guard against this eventuality, and he would have to continue doing so from now on. As he relished these thoughts of the past, his wrist twitched involuntarily. He could see his reflection in the gong. He laughed inwardly.

"Oh-oh!" He raised his head to discover that someone was standing there watching him. This stunned him momentarily. "What time is it?"

"I don't know exactly; I just came from the marketplace. I noticed by the clock at the district headquarters that it was about eleven-thirty."

"How long ago was that?"

"I just came from there. Why? You back to beating the gong?"

"If I didn't, who would?"

"What's the occasion?"

"You can be sure there's an occasion. You go and tell everyone to keep their ears open." He saw another fellow—a young man—walking down the road. He stood up and called out, "Hey, elder brother!" The young man turned around. "Elder brother, do you have the time?"

"No, I don't," he said, shaking his head. "I'm on my way home to eat lunch."

"Eat lunch? Then it must be somewhere around noon," he said to himself, greatly relieved.

Returning to the shelter, he got some rags and his old mallet handle, then went outside into the sunlight, where he began making a mallet head. Every once in a while he asked the time of day from a passerby, and by the time he'd formed the mallet head out of the rags, he'd already asked three people. Time seemed to be standing still. He looked for but could not find a piece of hemp to twist into a strap for the gong; then he was reminded of the tie band that served as a belt. He hadn't used it long, so it was still serviceable. He went back into the shelter to get the tie band from his black trousers, which were draped over the head of his bed.

He knew he ought to eat something, but he wasn't the least bit hungry. He had brief thoughts of life under the kadang tree, of Crazy Cai, and of the days that were to come, but all these were cut short and superseded by the presence of "two o'clock" in his consciousness. Before actually meeting that man at the district headquarters at two o'clock, there was nothing else he could concentrate on. Should he go at one-thirty to wait for the man? No, one o'clock would be even safer.

Having reached the district headquarters gate well ahead of the appointed hour, Han Qinzai paced back and forth in front. He watched the people returning to work inside, one after another, until he grew a bit anxious. Just about everyone who worked there had returned, so where was the man who had agreed to meet him? Toying with the idea of going inside to ask around, he found he was much too frightened to do so.

"Han Qinzai!" someone called out from behind. He turned around, and there was the man. He told him he'd been there for an hour already, but the man, devoid of expression, simply told Han Qinzai to follow him.

"Are you all set?"

"I was all set a long time ago."

"Didn't you bring your gong?"

"I'll get it right away."

"No need." Every word the man spoke to Han Qinzai was uttered with a total absence of emotion, as if he were impatient with him. Han Qinzai was so guarded he didn't even dare breathe hard. "You see this thing?" the man said as he pointed to a placard leaning against a wall, on which some words were written. (The thing was made of tin.) "Well, I want you to carry it around and beat your gong. Do you know what it says?" For the first time he was looking directly at Han Qinzai, who forced a smile and shook his head, embarrassed. "Okay, then you just announce that this year's property tax and income tax are due by the end of the month."

"Yes, yes, I understand: the propriety tax and . . ."

"What do you mean, 'propriety tax'? Hmph! I'm not talking about taking a woman to a hotel for some hanky-panky, you know," the man said, unable to keep from smiling. But he quickly regained his composure and said with a scowl, "It's 'property,' not 'propriety.'"

"Oh! Property, property," Han Qinzai repeated with great effort.

"Right! Property, hm?"

"Excuse me," Han Qinzai said, cautiously trying to get into the man's good graces, "do I have to pay property taxes?"

"How should I know? Do you own a home?" he asked impatiently.

"I live in an air-raid shelter, the one in the park."

"Then you ought to pay an air-raid tax," the man answered, holding back his laughter by closing his mouth tightly.

"When is that due?"

"Ai, what a chatterbox! Just go out and beat your gong and we'll let you off the hook."

Han Qinzai's response was an embarrassed smile.

"How much do you want for three days' work, beginning this afternoon?"

"Don't worry about that." He didn't mind making sacrifices this time, for what mattered was that the man hire him again. "Forget it; I'll take whatever you want to give!"

"I can't do that."

"Then make it the same as I got in the past, and we won't count this afternoon."

"In the past?" The man reflected for a moment as Han Qinzai lifted up the placard, rested it on his shoulder, and started to walk off.

"Hey, hold on, wait a moment. Do you remember what you're supposed to say?"

"I know. This year's property tax and income tax are due by the end of the month."

"Now, that's 'property,' not 'propriety'! Remember that. Okay, go ahead and start."

Han Qinzai walked off carrying the tin banner, which made a twanging noise in the air. The feeling this gave him was nothing like the one he'd experienced from carrying funeral banners. He was struck by the changing fortunes of life: when luck was not with you, it was like being tied in a knot that could not be undone; the more you tried to free yourself, the more tightly you were bound. But when fortune smiled on you, like a magician's sleight of hand, one-two-three-presto! and all the loosened ends of the rope were laid out in straight lines.

Fortune did not smile upon a man many times in his lifetime, so it was essential that Han Qinzai take full advantage of his prospects this time. He had to make sure that his services would be needed in the future by producing greater results with his gong than the loudspeaker pedicab ever could. Over the next two and a half days, he thought, his beating the gong to urge the populace to pay their taxes ought to result in everyone in town's doing so by the end of the month. *I know what makes these people tick: if they think they can put it off, they will, and if they can get by with forgetting it altogether, they'll do that too. For people like this, who never cry until they actually see the coffin, the only way is to scare the hell out of them.*

Indian summer had arrived during the days following the second rice harvest of the year, before the north winds began to blow. Han Qinzai, hoisting up the placard and holding his gong, hesitated for some strange reason; like a child standing naked on the edge of the shore, about to go swimming in strange waters, he lacked the final spark of courage. In the end, even this child doesn't know at what moment and in what manner he has entered the water.

As he passed through the gate of the park and went out onto the street, he reminded himself that he must do a good job. His thoughts returned to his brief rehearsal of a few moments earlier and the deftness with which he had struck the gong. When he reached Northgate Street, he could not gauge his feeling of the moment—was it excitement or apprehension? Many of the people on the street stopped in their tracks before they even heard the sound of his gong. Han Qinzai quickly went over in his mind several times the text of his announcement: *Property tax, not propriety tax, property, property . . .*

The first sound of the gong accompanied his first step onto the asphalt road. But he was given a shock; with an inward shout of alarm, he quickly hugged the gong closely to his body—he didn't want any new cracks to appear because of the powerful blow he had struck the trembling gong. No one who observed the look of panic on his face could figure out what he was doing. He made a mental calculation to determine the proper force of wrist action to strike the gong again and raised the mallet high, but then his arm froze in the air—he couldn't follow through. He let his arm fall slowly and made more mental calculations. Then—*bong, bong, bong*—three beats of the gong that, though weak, nonetheless were loud enough to bring several people out of their houses.

> *The gong beater's coming your way—*
> *Listen everyone, here's what I have to say—*

He took a deep breath as he puzzled over why he seemed so breathless.

> *This year's property tax—*

He stopped for a moment; assuming he'd said it right, he continued:

> *And the income tax—*
> *Are due by the end of this month—*

He was extremely disappointed in the effect. This was the sort of announcing that had done him in in the first place. If you didn't put a scare into these people, who understood nothing of the importance of paying their income tax, they'd simply ignore you.

The people in this small town, seeing that the gong beater had reappeared in their midst, were brought out by their curiosity. The sight of all the people he was attracting pleased Han Qinzai as he frantically tried to think of a way to add some zip to his announcement. Then his furrowed, troubled brow went slack. Following three beats of the gong that sounded quite satisfactory to him, he shouted out in a loud, confident voice:

> *The gong beater's coming your way—*
> *Listen everyone, here's what I have to say—*
> *This year's propriety tax and income tax—*

*Are due by the end of the month —*
*If it has not been paid —*
*You know how this government office is: they'll come*
     *down on you like a chicken butcher —*

The bystanders began to laugh. Han Qinzai beat his gong three times to drown out the sounds of laughter, then went on:

*Laugh? You can laugh after you pay your taxes —*
*Don't you dare take any chances —*
*If you don't believe me, see what happens when the time comes —*
*If I, Han Qinzai, am deceiving you with my words —*
*I, Han Qinzai, will gladly let everyone here slap my face —*

He paused. *That should do it.* In half a lifetime of beating the gong, this was the first time he had experienced a situation like the one today. No matter where he walked he had a teeming audience, and the more they laughed and carried on, the higher his spirits soared. He was secretly pleased. *Let's see the loudspeaker pedicab match this! Without me, Han Qinzai, to beat my gong, the thing wouldn't get done. I've had all I can stand of days like this. Now I'll show Scabby Head and the others how I've got it made, and I'll be surprised if they don't die of envy. I'll be able to avenge myself in my own lifetime. I'll treat them to a real feast. I'll even give them each two packs of Long Life cigarettes.*

By the time he'd passed the shops along half a block of Northgate Street, he'd made his announcement five times, and there was already a long line of curiosity seekers in his wake, all wanting to hear this comical speech a few more times. He turned his head to look at this crowd of public-spirited citizens and was given a shot in the arm by what he saw. *Just wait until I pass by the kadang tree and they witness the prestige I've gained — what'll they think then?* He had a pretty good idea what the motives of the people in his wake were, and his mind was working at full capacity: as far as he was concerned, the announcement he'd been told to make was of less importance than the embellishments he himself had added. *Oh! I know what to say now!*

A feeling of wonder and joy gushed from his heart, as three gong beats rang out in what was now practiced fashion. He said what he was supposed to say without missing a single word, although he had the feeling that he might have said "propriety" rather than "property." *But, what the hell—property, propriety, what's the difference—it's all about the same thing anyway.* Then came the important part. First three beats of the gong, then:

> *If it has not been paid—*
> *You know how this government office is: it'll come*
> *down on you like a chicken butcher—*

Hearing the roar of laughter these comments evoked, he responded with a serious warning:

> *You people may have never slaughtered a chicken, but you've*
> *seen others do it—it's no laughing matter—*
> *When the time comes, if I, Han Qinzai, have lied to you—*

*Bong! Bong! Bong!* Three more beats of the gong.

> *I, Han Qinzai, will let you cut off my head and use*
> *it as a chair—*

Complacently, he wiped the spittle from the corners of his mouth, feeling that this oath carried great force—how could a slap in the face compare with cutting off one's own head? Yes, that's what he'd say. How stupid he'd been in the past, believing he'd carried out his duties by merely repeating what he'd been told to say by his employer. If all along he'd done his job like he was doing it today, using his imagination to improve upon what he'd been hired to say, he'd never have fallen so low as to take himself to the kadang tree and live off coffin boards, not to mention endure all that abuse from that bunch of pigs.

The tin placard he was carrying on his shoulder, dignified though it may have been, was a lot heavier than a funeral banner. The wooden pole resting against his shoulder hurt like hell. He shifted it to his right shoulder, thereby blocking his vision to the right. When he looked off into the distance he noticed a round lacquered sign above a shop to the left with the word "wine" on it. He realized at once that this was Stony's store. His first impulse was to shift the sign back to his left shoulder, but then the self-confidence he'd so recently regained won out, for what did he have to fear now that he had his gong to beat? He didn't owe Stony too much money, and besides, Stony wasn't as heartless as Longevity. *As for Longevity, let's see what he can do now! I'll be able to pay him what I owe — I'll be a customer now!* But even with his courage pumped up, he was not totally unconcerned: his eyes never left Stony's store.

Before he'd taken but a few more steps, he was directly in front of Stony's store. Seeing Stony himself, he called out, "Stony, I'll pay you off tonight." Then, with a show of how busy he was, he turned away, even though he was frightened stiff, and beat his gong right where he was standing. He said what he'd been hired to say, then followed it with his oath. The laughter from the bystanders grew in intensity. Forcing himself to look over toward Stony, he was relieved by what he saw. Stony was certainly no Longevity: one look at his face showed you that he was a man with whom you could deal. He was thinking (actually, he was making plans, not just thinking): Crazy Cai, Taiwanese opera, good rice wine, outdoor stalls, Scabby Head and the others. . . . His mind was flooded with these disconnected thoughts, coming one upon the other. Sweat poured down his face until his sleeves were soaked from wiping it away. He had exerted himself to the utmost but didn't feel at all tired. He continued walking until he passed by another twenty shops or so. As he prepared to strike his gong again, a piercing screech that hung heavily in the air brought him to a stop. A dark image had darted in front of him, and he found his way blocked by a bicycle. The person on the bicycle was none other than the man from the district headquarters.

"Han Qinzai, stop at once! Go back to the district headquarters immediately!" The man had anger written all over his face, and when he finished he stepped down hard on the bicycle pedal and rode off in the direction from which he'd come.

Han Qinzai looked like a man who has sustained an electric shock; he stood there dumbly for a brief moment. Then as he watched the retreating back of the man, he yelled as loudly as he could, so that the man on the bicycle would hear him, "What's wrong? I beat the gong! Not only that, I made a special job of it!" His voice was so shrill it nearly cracked. But the man's figure was lost among the crowds on the road.

Han Qinzai felt weak all over; he turned and mumbled to the laughing people around him, "I beat it, I really did a good job. You, any one of you can bear me out on that. I beat it . . ." What he mumbled after this no one could say for sure. He just stood there, his head hanging down, his eyes cast to the ground. Both his left hand, which was holding the placard and his gong, and his right hand, in which he held the mallet, drooped like falling drops of water. He was soon surrounded by row upon row of curious onlookers as an atmosphere of seriousness moved outward from the center, infecting them all.

Han Qinzai listlessly took a few plodding steps forward, the crowd giving way for him. He stopped in his tracks after a few paces, raised his gong, much to the surprise of everyone, then lifted up his mallet and beat the gong loudly three times, momentarily forgetting all considerations of what he was doing. The third and final beat of the gong was muffled; a small triangular piece of brass fell to the ground. He seemed oblivious to everything as he called out in a voice tinged with madness:

> *The gong beater's coming your way—*
> *Listen everyone, here's what I have to say—*
> *This year's propriety tax and income tax—*
> *Are due by the end of the month—*

By now the sound had become a wail. He fought hard to enunciate each and every word, but it was impossible.

> *If by that time you don't . . . you don't . . .*

His voice was now quivering so badly that the words were unintelligible, although his mouth continued to move as if he were still speaking. He opened and closed it with great effort. Before long there were no more sounds, but by reading his lips, the onlookers could pretty much tell that he was saying, over and over: "I, Han Qinzai . . . I, Han Qinzai . . ."

# Ringworms

o

The moment Ah-fa walked in the door after getting off work, his wife handed him the baby. Seemingly uncomfortable cradled in his father's arms, the baby began to cry. Ah-fa quickly and clumsily rocked him for a moment, which produced the desired effect of stopping his crying. But the baby was not so much lulled into stopping as he was frightened by the violent rocking. Edging a short stool—actually, it was nothing more than a block of wood—over with his foot, Ah-fa sat down, laid the baby across his legs, and began fumbling through his pockets for a cigarette. Then he recalled that he had smoked the last one after getting off work and had crumpled up the empty package and thrown it on top of the lime pit. It had sure looked good lying there. He had some happy news for his wife, but before saying anything he decided to tease her a little first. This somewhat sinister idea had popped into his mind when he'd discovered that he was out of cigarettes.

Ah-fa's wife was busy cooking dinner, darting from one end of the kitchen to the other. Just then her still-rounded buttocks appeared directly in his line of vision, and as he watched her wriggling rear end, his customary enthusiasm at being home was considerably increased. All this weighed heavily on him, making him a little uncomfortable.

"Ah-gui, I'm out of cigarettes." He knew he was asking for trouble.

"You can worry about that tomorrow." She kept busy with dinner, not so much as turning around to look at him.

"Not on your life. I want a smoke now."

"If not smoking will kill you, then go ahead, drop dead!" Her spatula clanged loudly against the wok.

"Take it easy, will you! What if you break that? I could buy a lot of cigarettes with the money it would take to replace it."

"We could buy all the woks we needed if you stopped smoking for a year."

As she leaned over to scoop some water out of the vat, her rear end stuck up under her trousers, a sight that greatly amused Ah-fa. Since there was no water in the vat, the ladle merely clanged against the sides.

"Are Ah-zhu and the kids out getting yams?" Ah-fa asked.

"She's got it all over you. Yesterday she brought back a whole sackful plus half a basketful."

"Did Ah-xiong go with her?"

"That's the only way I can get him out from underfoot."

"He's still small. Have you forgotten he's only three?"

This brought an angry scowl to her face. She picked up the wooden bucket and marched outside to fetch some water.

Ah-fa sensed that he should get on with telling her the good news, because if she got much angrier things could get out of hand.

His wife returned, carrying a bucketful of water.

"This time luck's with us," Ah-fa said. "When this job's finished in a couple of days, Ah-zhu wants me to go with his group to a job that'll last a full three months." He riveted his eyes on his wife's face so he could see her frown turn into a smile. But she pretended she hadn't heard him and busied herself with pouring the water into the vat. He continued anyway. "The pay is thirty-five dollars a day, five more than I'm getting now. This time I won't have to sit around all day with nothing to do." As his wife walked outside with the empty bucket, he saw that her face was still tightly set, and angry frustration began to well up inside him. This is going too far, he thought to himself, and decided to give her a taste of her own medicine when she returned.

It seemed to him that the stool on which he was sitting had grown thorns, causing him to fidget. He stood up and began pacing back and forth, growing angrier by the minute. *Everything was just fine at first, but she had to go and sour my mood! What's so bad about smoking a pack of cigarettes every once in a while? Since I'm the one who's earning the money, I should be able to spend it any way I please.*

*How long can it take to fetch a bucketful of water? She should have been back by now.*

He walked to the door and looked outside, but there wasn't a trace of her anywhere. Turning back, he resumed his pacing, but just as he was heading away from the door, his wife entered with the bucket of water. Then as he turned to face her, a pack of cigarettes landed on top of the baby in his arms. What really caught his attention was the expression on her face: the warm, apologetic smile she wore quickly melted his heart.

*Boy, that was close. I damn near ruined everything.*

Laughing and giggling as they came, the four children brought back a big load of yams in baskets and in bags thrown over their shoulders. When they were all dumped in a pile on the floor, they presented a real sight. Ah-fa looked at them with mixed emotions.

"Where did you find all those yams?" he asked. "You didn't go and . . ."

Ah-zhu, the eldest daughter, cut him short. "It rained today, so the yams in the freshly plowed field were sticking out of the ground, right in front of our eyes."

"Oh! That's fine, then." Still he was apprehensive, thinking that the children might have stolen them. How could such big yams have gone unnoticed?

Number Two was about to say something, but one look from his elder sister quickly changed his mind.

"Okay, let's get ready for dinner," Ah-fa announced to the children, who were proudly gathered around the pile of yams. "Ah-cang, go buy half a bottle of wine for Daddy, and get a dollar's worth of peanuts."

"With what?"

"Get the money from your mother."

"What kind of wine should I get?"

"Hai! What a dumb question! Rice wine, of course!"

Ah-cang quickly went out and bought the wine, then got eighty cents worth of peanuts, kept twenty cents for himself, stuffed some of the peanuts into his pocket, and hurried home.

Dinner had already started. Number Three stared blankly at the bowls filled with yams and screwed up his mouth. His mother scolded him loudly:

"You don't want any? So don't eat! Anyone who's born into this family can just count on eating yams. What makes a crooked-beaked chicken like you think you can eat rice?"

The child stealthily raised his head to look at his mother. It was futile to argue with her, and if he didn't think he could get away with something, he didn't try. He knew that if he didn't stop he was in for a beating. But in order to salvage a little face, he put on the airs of a spoiled child and said he wanted some peanuts.

"All right, you can all have a few peanuts. Now hurry up and eat," their father said, dividing the peanuts among them. "In two more days it'll be the second of the month, and after we've paid our respects to the local god, we'll all sit down to a good meal."

The children finished their meal on their best behavior. Noticing the gleam in her husband's eye, Ah-gui knew there'd be activity in bed tonight. Lately, after several visits by Miss Li from the Happy Family Planning Association, Ah-gui had begun to develop some misgivings about all this bedroom activity; with the knowledge she had gained, she now possessed a greater understanding and a new outlook regarding sex. But she was troubled by many concerns, and her feelings regarding the matter were mixed; there were even times *during* sex when her mind was on several related and quite scary things. Naturally, they were all things that Miss Li had told her, and she didn't know whether she should be grateful to Miss Li or bear a grudge against her.

As always when they were eating yams, the children—all but the baby—did so spiritedly, pointing at each other and giggling, none willing to acknowledge a fart. They played the children's game "Striking the Gong" to determine who the farter was, pointing to a different child with each word they sang:

> *Bong, bong, strike the gong loud.*
> *Who farted by the doorkeeper, be not proud.*
> *The doorkeeper's mother picks up a steel pole,*
> *And drives the little fart right out the bunghole.*

The song ended on Number Two, who loudly proclaimed his innocence. But the other three were adamant in their accusations, so a loud argument erupted. Finally their father stepped in to settle matters.

"It was me," he said. "So what!"

They all broke into gleeful laughter as their mother cleared the table, giving instructions to Number One: "Ah-zhu, go help your brothers wash up and get them off to bed a little early."

Ah-zhu was only nine, but she was everything an elder sister ought to be. She knew instinctively that her parents were going to do you-know-what tonight, and, for that matter, so did Number Two.

The family shared one large bed, all seven of them sleeping together. But ever since that humorous incident with Number Three, the adults felt that with the children growing up, they'd have to put up a divider. What they did was place a screen made of sugar-cane pulp down the middle. It was low enough that if they sat up they could still see whether the children were covered or not. But even the simple matter of placing a divider in the bed was possible only after Ah-fa had gotten hold of another tattered old comforter, for their single large comforter was just big enough to cover them all if they slept bunched up together. As for the humorous incident with the child, Ah-fa made a big joke out of it without the slightest embarrassment, telling everyone during breaks at work. This is what had happened:

One night he and his wife had startled Ah-xiong awake as he was sleeping beside them. When the little boy saw what was happening, his face contorted with terror. Ah-fa quickly said, "Mama hit you today, didn't she?"

The boy nodded his head.

"Okay, I'm trying to crush her to death." Naturally, this was an exciting prospect to the child, who then got up, saying he wanted to crush her too, and sat astride his father. Ah-fa could tell this story so immodestly because it was clear from their normal conversation that all his co-workers had experienced more or less the same thing themselves.

Ah-zhu put the children to bed, then started to recite "The Old Tiger Woman" to them again. Number Two complained that it was just like their daily fare of yams—she'd told them the same story hundreds of times before. But Number Three said he wanted to hear it and Number Four had no objections, so Ah-cang simply buried his head under the comforter and ate the peanuts he'd stashed in his pocket earlier. Ah-zhu began the story. "Once upon a time . . ."

"There was an old tiger woman . . ." one of her brothers cut in. Their parents were still in the kitchen washing up for bed, and when they heard Ah-zhu telling the story, they whispered proudly:

"Listen to Ah-zhu telling a bedtime story to her brothers."

"She's just like a little mother to them."

"If she'd been born into a wealthy family, at this age she'd still be doted on by her parents."

"That's a bunch of rubbish!" Ah-fa said. "Except for the fact that children from poor families aren't blessed with much of a fate, they're no worse off than anyone else in lots of ways. Poor children know how to do more things! Look at me—I was taking care of my mother when I was thirteen. Those other kids rely on their grandparents to get by, but we rely on the sweat of our own brows!"

"That's because of all the rewards the other people have earned in former lives, so what's there to be surprised about?"

"Well, if that's the way you want to look at things, what can I say!" Ah-fa had the feeling that his tone of voice didn't quite fit what was about to happen, so he changed the subject. "Next month we can buy a piece of sheet metal to put over the leak in the roof. Then when it rains you won't have to wear a bamboo hat when you cook."

"Like hell! Your palms start to itch the minute there's any money around!"

"Now don't make fun of me, okay? This time I really mean it."

"I'll believe it when I see it."

"Besides, I usually win at dice!"

"Win! Then where's the money? Besides, it's all the same whether you win or lose!" Ah-gui's tone of voice grew harsher. "If you lose, there's no money. If you win, you go on a binge."

"Aw, why keep bringing up the past?" He dumped out the water, then wiped his feet dry as he said in a softer voice, "Let's not talk about that. And if you want to know the truth, I just wanted to win so we could have a little extra money around the house." He knew at once that this wasn't the right thing to say either, but . . .

"Just forget it!" Ah-gui said sternly. "All I know is, you're a hopeless case." This was followed by a steady stream of low grumbling.

Ah-fa sat there without making a sound, waiting for his wife to finish. "Come on," he said finally, "you don't have to stop everything just to talk."

The strangest thing of all was that the desire he felt for his wife suddenly increased considerably. To him, a woman who was not genuinely angry was very sexy; or maybe his curiosity was aroused by this unusual fancy of hers. Whatever the case, he was growing impatient over his wife's stalling.

"Hey! Come on, hurry it up."

Sensing a somewhat pitiful ring to his voice, Ah-gui figured that the time had come to put forward a condition:

"The burden of raising five children is already heavy enough," she said. "If another one comes along, it's going to be more than you can handle."

Ah-fa knew she was right, though it was a topic he did not like to discuss. He was worried she might not accept him tonight, and a pained look appeared on his face. Ah-gui knew well enough that this would make him unhappy, but she hadn't finished, so she continued in a gentle voice, "Why don't I have a 'loop' inserted? Miss Li said that once I had a 'loop,' we'd be free from worry." She gazed hopefully at him, but he simply sat there staring at the wall without making a sound, his brow furrowed as he puffed fiercely on a cigarette.

"Well, what do you say?" she asked after giving him ample time to think it over.

Just as he'd done the last time she brought this up, Ah-fa turned and stared at her. But this time his reaction was markedly different. Previously he'd felt that she was going too far, that the whole idea of inserting a "loop" was more than he could bear. Did she think he was unaware that the health center doctor who inserted the "loops" was none other than Ah-sheng's son? *No matter what, Ah-gui is my—Ah-fa's—wife!* But this time was different. *Damn it, go ahead and have it inserted and don't tell me about it! How would I know the difference? Oh-oh, hold everything! If she didn't tell me, wouldn't that be the same as taking a lover? . . .* He simply couldn't decide something as serious as this in the brief time he had to think it over, and there was even less chance that he'd actually change his position. So he continued to stare at Ah-gui, all the while trying to come to some decision. For it was not just contradictory feelings that bothered him—his self-respect was at stake here.

Ah-gui lowered her head and said softly, as though talking to herself, "It's for your own good. What difference does it make to me if I have a few more kids? There were eleven of us girls in my family before Mom finally stopped having babies. I'm sure I could do the same. But once you fall into the children trap you'll never be able to climb out. It's up to you. We'll do whatever you say. It's really no concern of mine, and I'm not going to bring the subject up again. It's not easy for me to talk about this either, so just forget it!" She raised her head briefly to sneak a look at him, then lowered it again. There was no sense in redoing something that had already been taken care of.

All this got through to Ah-fa, but she misread his opinion on the matter. Actually, how could she not, when he hadn't even made his feelings known? Since he had no opinion, what was there to talk about? He stared at the wall with an angry, troubled look. The mere mention of the subject had put him out of sorts to begin with, and his wife didn't know when to stop. He'd been in a happy mood until she'd ruined everything with her nonstop chattering.

"Now get out of here," she said. "I'm going to wash my feet."

Ah-fa turned and walked into the adjoining room, after which Ah-gui put the piece of wood up to block the doorway. When he heard the muted sound of the makeshift doorway being put carefully into place, he surmised that she wasn't really angry, and it pleased him to know that the situation hadn't soured after all. Not that there was any reason for it to, since the thought of having any more children was just as disagreeable to him. *"Should I have it inserted or not?" Stupid woman!* Just then he heard the sounds of splashing water as his wife washed her feet on the other side of the partition, and he felt himself giving in. Wanting her to know that he was no longer angry, he called out in his normal tone of voice, "Ah-gui!" He listened carefully to her reaction.

"What?" She could guess the expression on his face from his tone of voice.

"Are you smelting gold or something in there?"

Although she didn't answer, they both had a good laugh over this remark.

The children appeared to be fast asleep, but Ah-gui sat there for a moment looking at them uneasily.

"They fell asleep long ago, so what are you looking at?" Ah-fa asked with some impatience.

"I'm worried that the baby has a cold. I think he's coming down with something."

"You can hold him when you go to sleep in a little while."

Their daughter, Ah-zhu, grew tense every time this situation presented itself. She lay there now, eyes wide open, ears pricked straight up. But her parents were speaking in hushed tones that made it hard for her to hear much of anything. She carefully rolled over and stuck her head out from under the bedding, then, holding her breath, peeped through a hole in the partition. She was suddenly aware of a slight movement behind her. Turning back to look, she discovered that Number Two was also awake. Ah-cang put his finger to his lips as a sign for his sister not to say anything. Ah-zhu squeezed her eyes tightly shut and twisted her mouth frantically as a sign to her brother to go to sleep. Eventually the two of them struck a compromise; by then they could make out what their parents were saying.

"What in the world is this?" It was their father's voice.

"It's a ringworm!"

"How did you get one here?"

"It had to have come from you," she said in an accusing tone.

"Ugh! What a disgusting thing!"

The minute the kids heard the word "ringworm," the ones on their bodies began to itch. Ah-zhu clawed at her neck; Ah-cang began scratching his head for all he was worth.

"Where else do you have those things?" Ah-fa asked.

"Here."

"Here?"

"A little higher."

"Oh! You've got them all over!"

"Not as many as you. Ouch, that itches!"

"Don't scratch them. They're filthy!"

"What do you think you're doing?"

"I . . . I . . ." He couldn't say it.

"'I . . . I . . .'" Ah-gui repeated, mimicking his embarrassed reply. "You act like a tyrant who plays with fire but won't let anyone else even light a lamp."

"These awful things!" he complained as he scratched with all his might.

"I feel sorry for the kids. The baby's only a few months old and he's already got some."

"When did we start having ringworms around here?"

"Who knows? It's been years."

"Really? Yeah, I guess you're right."

"Of course I am. The next time we have some money around the house, don't bother about sheet metal—what we need is ringworm medicine."

"It's not like I never bought any before."

"Buy some good stuff next time!"

"Good stuff! Do you know how much it costs? We can't afford it."

"You know, it's odd. I've never seen any rich people who had ringworms, so why is the medicine so expensive?"

"If we buy a lotion, it only stops the itching for a little while. Besides, if you took all the ringworms in this family and laid them out on the floor, they'd cover the tatami mat. Buying a couple of bottles of lotion is about as much use as rolling around on the tatami."

"So what'll we do?"

"It's just our rotten luck!" Ah-fa kept scratching out of a sense of exasperation. "Ouch! Ouch! I'm sure I broke the skin. It's all wet and sticky!"

"Mine too."

"That's no good! Is there any water left in the pot?"

"Not much. I'll go boil some more."

"Boil some more, you say? If it's too hot, it'll burn me to a crisp! Ouch! Ouch!"

"It's all your fault," Ah-gui said.

"What'd I do?"

"If you hadn't mentioned them a minute ago, everything would have been fine. As long as you don't talk about ringworms or think about them or touch them, there's no problem."

Ah-fa had to agree with her. "Well, it's not that big a deal. For poor people, ringworms are just part of the family. Go ahead, boil some water!"

Ah-gui was suddenly struck by a fact of life. "Aha! Now I understand. That's exactly how all our kids were born."

"What do you mean, that's how they were born?"

"If the kids are going to come, let them come. As long as you don't think about it, mention it, or touch it, there's no problem."

"That's what you say!" Ah-fa was getting a little irritated. "Tell me, what does all this have to do with boiling some water?"

"Then will you let me have a 'loop' inserted?"

Ah-fa's building anger made him seem like a walking time bomb. The room was so still it was as if everything had frozen to a halt.

The two children slipped back into their places feeling terribly disappointed. They were both scratching without letup.

# The Taste of Apples

○

## THE ACCIDENT

During the early morning hours, as thick layers of clouds were beginning
to send their moisture downward, an automobile accident occurred at the
intersection where the road from the eastern suburbs enters the city. A
dark green sedan with a foreigner's license plate crashed into a rickety old
bicycle like a wild animal pouncing on its prey, crushing it on the other
side of the yellow dividing line of the two-lane highway. A pickaxe was
still securely fastened to the bicycle rack, which protruded from under
the car, but the contents of a lunch box—mainly rice—that had been
tied to the handlebars were scattered all over the street, the solitary salted
egg that had accompanied the rice lying smashed at the edge of the safety
island.

The rain was coming down harder now, and the puddle of congealed
blood in front of the sedan was being washed away. Several foreign and
local MPs were busily trying to determine the circumstances of the
accident.

## THE TELEPHONE CALL

". . . He won't be in this morning. . . . Mm-hm . . . don't worry about it; a junior secretary like me can easily handle a matter like this. Um . . . Huh! Now hold on a moment, listen to me. Don't forget, we're in Asia now! The other fellow is just a laborer. . . . Huh? Well, isn't he . . . That's right, he is! So there . . . he can't afford any trouble. Hmm? Let me finish. This is the Asian country with which we have the closest ties of friendship. Besides, it's the most secure. Huh? . . . Would you let me finish, please? America has no intention of jumping into the middle of a quagmire. Our president and our people all feel that way. Now look, let's not say anything more on the subject . . . just send him there. . . . Um! All right, I'll take the responsibility . . . okay, I'll call right away . . . right . . . right, that's how we'll do it. Good-bye!"

## THE LABYRINTH

A young foreign affairs policeman led a tall, heavyset foreigner up to a district where tiny illegal shacks made of wooden crates and sheet metal were located. There were no clearly delineated streets or byways here—everything was laid out in capricious disorder. They made their way through the area for a while as if meandering through a labyrinth. "Boy, what a great place for a game of hide-and-seek!" said the foreigner with a laugh as he walked behind the policeman.

"That's what I was thinking." The policeman detected a dubious tone in the comment, even though it had been said as a joke. He wondered if the foreigner was mocking him for not being able to find the house they were looking for, questioning his qualifications. He was stung by the injustice of it all. The man was probably unaware that foreign affairs police only assist the local precinct police in incidents in which for-eigners are involved. He regretted bringing him here straight away instead of first checking in with the local police. Now even the foreign affairs policeman was in the position of having to find his way through all this confusion.

He lowered his head slightly to look for numbers on the closely set doorways. The foreigner was a head taller than any of the shacks in the area, so all he could see was a mass of rooftops thrown together with sheet metal and plastic covers, plus some old tires and bricks to hold them down. Some of the roofs also sported an array of wooden crates, birdcages, and the like.

The policeman turned to look at the foreigner surveying the landscape and said in a not-very-convincing tone, "Their new homes are nearly completed—those apartments by the river. Once they've moved these people out, they're going to put up a high-rise here." He felt pleased with himself about his alert reaction but at the same time was uneasy about lying. If the man hadn't insisted on coming to pay his respects to Jiang Ah-fa's family, the policeman would never have brought a foreigner to this kind of place. He was attentive to his companion's responses, but all he heard was the occasional "mm-hm" so common in American-style conversations, pregnant with ambiguities and dubious connotations. In order to show that he was, in fact, listening, he responded with an "mm-hm" of his own from time to time. Meanwhile, his efforts to determine what was on the foreigner's mind distracted him from his painstaking search for house numbers. They had continued for several paces without exchanging a word when they met a little girl standing in the lane with a baby strapped to her back. The policeman asked her a question, but the moment she opened her mouth, he was dumbfounded. The foreigner, standing off to one side, uttered a muffled "Oh, my God!" The little girl, it turned out, was a mute.

They walked off, the mute peppering their retreating backs with a stream of incoherent grunts accompanied by a flurry of hand motions.

## THE RAINSTORM

The rain, which had stopped briefly, began to fall again, beating a resounding tattoo on the myriad materials that served as rooftops and increasing the anxieties the young foreign affairs policeman was experiencing. Just as he was about to recommend that they enlist the aid of the local police—in the midst of embarrassed indecision—he discovered that the house number directly ahead was 21–7.

"Here it is!"

"You don't say!" the foreigner blurted out spiritedly.

Just then the rainfall turned into a downpour, so, without a thought for the niceties that ought to accompany a visit by civilized people, they burst in on Ah-gui and her daughter, who abruptly raised their heads from their work by the pickle barrel to find themselves face to face with this uninvited foreigner. Despite the kindly, embarrassed look on the man's face, as the mother and daughter witnessed the policeman and foreigner rush in on them, they imagined for a fleeting moment that something momentous was about to happen; a shadow of terror settled upon them.

The rain beat down hard on the sheet-metal roof, producing such a clamor that the policeman was forced to shout as he translated what the foreigner was saying. Ah-gui didn't understand Mandarin, so all she saw was the policeman energetically opening and closing his mouth. The motion of his hands caused her to look even more apprehensively toward her daughter, Ah-zhu, hoping she'd clue her in on what was happening. But when she saw her daughter's lips tighten with a look of alarm and sadness, she asked in a terrified voice, "Ah-zhu, what's wrong?"

"Ma . . ." Opening her tightly pursed lips to speak, the daughter burst into tears.

"What's wrong? Tell me quickly!"

"Pa . . . Papa's been run down by a car. . . ."

"Oh! Papa . . . ? Where? Where is he?" Ah-gui's mouth contorted. "Where is he?" This was followed by a stream of incoherent babbling.

The policeman tried to comfort her by saying in halting Taiwanese, "Don't worry, it's not life-threatening." Then he reverted to Mandarin, saying to the girl, "Tell your mother not to be upset, and don't you cry either. They've already rushed your father to the ER." The foreigner stood off to one side with a remorseful look on his face and said something, which he asked the policeman to convey to the others.

"This American says he'll take full responsibility, and he urges your mother to stop crying." The foreigner walked over and put his hand on Ah-zhu's head, nodding repeatedly to make his point, hoping she'd understand.

At that moment the little mute girl with the baby strapped to her back burst through the doorway, dripping wet. Unaware of what was happening inside, the moment she entered to discover the policeman and the foreigner she'd run into a short while before, her eyes widened and she began making loud grunting noises, accompanied by hand gestures. All the while Ah-gui continued to moan almost witlessly, "What'll we do? Oh, what'll we do?" When the little mute realized that a pall of grief had settled over the room, her grunting quickly subsided and she walked softly over to Ah-zhu.

"Is she your sister?" the policeman asked in disbelief.

Ah-zhu nodded.

Feeling ill at ease, the policeman said anxiously, "Hurry up and untie the scarf—the baby's soaking wet." Then he turned to the perplexed foreigner. "It's her younger sister," he said.

"Oh, my God!" the foreigner softly muttered for the second time.

## IN THE RAIN

Ah-zhu covered her head with a piece of transparent plastic and walked out of the squatters' district in a great hurry, heading toward her younger brothers' school.

The heavy rainfall continued, so the clothes stuck to her body on the side of her back that was soaked through. Had she arranged the plastic more carefully on her way out of the house, she wouldn't have gotten so wet. She was accompanied on the way by her thoughts: *If Papa can't work, there'll be no money for the family and Mama will have to adopt me out.* It would be different than before, when her mother had tried to scare her with: "Ah-zhu, if you don't behave yourself, I'll sell you off!"

But this time she wasn't frightened. She never wavered from a conviction that she would be a well-behaved, obedient daughter in her new family, accepting any and all hardships that came her way. They would have no cause to mistreat her and would let her return home to see her younger brothers and sisters once in a while. By then she might even have a little money saved up to buy a toy gun for her brothers and a ball and a doll for her sisters.

But even though she wasn't frightened by this prospect, the more she thought, the faster her tears fell. Before she knew it, she was standing in front of her younger brothers' school.

## CIVICS CLASS

During the morning civics class, not a single student's voice emerged from the classrooms, only the sounds of loud, shrill-voiced teachers, which could be heard even from a distance. The old principal, hands clasped behind his back, moved stealthily down the hallway outside the classrooms like a shadow.

The homeroom teacher of the third-grade White Horse class was standing at the podium leveling a pointer at Jiang Ah-ji, who was being made to stand in the corner as punishment.

"The semester is almost over," she was saying, "and Jiang Ah-ji still hasn't paid his tuition." She turned to look at Ah-ji. "Jiang Ah-ji!" He quickly raised his head to look at her. "You have to stand there every day during civics class," she continued. "Aren't you ashamed of yourself?" He quickly lowered his head. "Lin Xiunan paid his today, so that leaves only you standing there. How do you feel about that?" The children all turned to look at Lin Xiunan, who first lifted his head and smiled proudly, then dropped it bashfully. "Hm, Jiang Ah-ji, when can you pay it?" The teacher walked to the edge of the podium, drawing closer to Ah-ji, then tapped him lightly on the shoulder with her pointer. "Well?" He raised his head to give her some kind of answer, but the instant he looked into her eyes, he lowered his head again. The teacher tapped him once more. "Ah-ji, when are you going to pay?" she asked.

"To—tomorrow," he answered softly.

"What?" the teacher exclaimed loudly. "Just when will this 'tomorrow' of yours ever come?" Everyone in the class giggled. "I don't put any stock in what you say anymore. I'm not asking you to pay tomorrow; next Monday will be fine. Don't get the idea that all you have to do is stand there all semester to get by without paying. Don't forget, if you don't come up with the money, I have other means. Remember now, you must have it by next Monday! Do you understand?" Ah-ji nodded. "Fine, just so you understand."

Bowing his head very low, Ah-ji ran toward his seat without looking up.

"Hey there!" the teacher shouted. He stopped in his tracks in the midst of his classmates and turned back to look at her. His classmates were giggling. "What are you doing? Just *what* do you think you're doing? Come back here! Since you haven't paid yet, you have to keep standing! If you can bring the money tomorrow, you won't have to stand anymore. Otherwise it would be unfair to Lin Xiunan, wouldn't it?" The children turned around in their seats again to look at Lin Xiunan, who felt both proud and sheepish; he lowered his head, not knowing what else to do.

The matter concerning Jiang Ah-ji had just about run its course, so the teacher returned to the podium and asked the students seated below, "Little friends, what moral lesson have we learned from this week's civics class?" She scanned the seats in front of her briefly as every child raised his hand. "That's fine. You can put your hands down. Let's say it together."

"Co—op—er—a—tion!" they said in unison.

"Right, cooperation. Take Jiang Ah-ji, for example: everyone has come up with the tuition except him. Can we call that cooperation?"

"NO!" Once again the class responded loudly in unison.

Ah-ji, who had just breathed a sigh of relief, grew tense again as he heard the teacher mention his name. He thought of himself as an unco-operative child. The very mention of tuition brought with it the memory of his father staring down at him. Then he thought longingly of the rural elementary school down south. He couldn't figure out why, when they were in the south, his father had kept telling his mother how good things were up north. Down south, if they were late in paying their tuition, his teacher, Mr. Yang, wouldn't punish him by making him stand in the corner.

When Ah-zhu reached the White Horse class, the first thing she saw was Ah-ji standing in the corner. Quickly moving up to the window, she called out with undisguised trepidation, "Ah-ji!" His heart skipped a beat and he immediately hung his head low. The momentarily startled teacher rushed out of the room as all the children turned to look outside, those at the rear standing up to do so.

"Is Jiang Ah-ji your younger brother?"

Ah-zhu nodded, then said, "Our papa was run down by an American's car."

"How bad is it?"

The classroom was all astir.

"I don't know," she said, beginning to cry.

"All right, now, don't get worked up." The teacher turned and walked back into the classroom as the students clambered back to their seats. "Jiang Ah-ji, hurry up and go with your sister to see your daddy."

Ah-ji didn't seem to be any more upset over the news than he was over having to stand in the corner. He bowed deeply to the teacher, then walked slowly back to his seat to pick up his books.

From that moment until he walked out of the classroom with Ah-zhu, the eyes of all the children in the room followed his every move.

"Where's Ah-song's classroom?" Ah-zhu asked him.

"Over there," he said, pointing to the door at the end of the hallway.


ON THE OVERPASS

The rain still hadn't let up; Ah-zhu squatted down and arranged a plastic cover over Ah-song. "You ought to be able to do this yourself!" As she thought again about being sold into adoption, she drew back one of her hands and wiped the tears that were streaming down her face. "Don't feel sad. I'll come home to see you sometimes." Actually, neither Ah-ji nor Ah-song displayed the slightest trace of unhappiness; they were in a daze, and Ah-zhu's words served only to confuse them more. "Let's go! Hurry now, Mama's waiting for us." Ah-zhu took Ah-song by the hand, Ah-ji walked beside her, and the three of them passed through the front gate of the school together.

When they reached the intersection near the school they watched the cars passing by in both directions, waiting for a chance to dart across. The shrill sound of a whistle came to them from the car stand across the street.

"Ah-ji, we can't cross, there's a policeman over there. Let's use the overpass."

Ah-ji walked on ahead and lightheartedly jumped up onto the steps. Ah-song cried out anxiously, "Hey, wait up."

"You're the one who's walking so slow. Why should I wait for you?"

Ah-zhu looked up at Ah-ji, who had turned back to face them, the sky above him serving as a backdrop. "Ah-ji, wait for your brother," she said. Then she lowered her head again. "Hurry up," she urged Ah-song. "Ah-ji's waiting for you."

While Ah-ji waited for them to catch up, he looked down at the cars passing below. Then he turned back to look at his sister and Ah-song, who were five or six steps behind him.

"Sister," Ah-ji said with a tone of sadness creeping into his voice, "I don't want to go to school anymore." Ah-zhu stopped where she was and gazed up at him while Ah-song continued climbing the steps.

"Ah-ji!" she said, her head lowered in deep thought as she started up again behind Ah-song. "What would Daddy and Mommy think if they heard you say that?" She grabbed hold of the now silent boy and together they walked across the overpass.

"We can't afford the tuition."

"Wait till Daddy has some money, then we can pay it."

"But the semester is almost over."

"That's all right," Ah-zhu comforted him. "Wait till I've been adopted and I'll give you the money."

"Is somebody going to adopt you?" he asked in astonishment.

"Uh-huh!" Even though she answered him firmly, tears began to course down her cheeks faster than she could wipe them dry.

"Does Mommy want to adopt you out?"

"I'm afraid this time it's for real. Daddy was run down by an American's car."

Ah-ji didn't understand what his daddy's being run down by an American's car had to do with their future. As a matter of fact, his attention was momentarily caught by the fact that Ah-song wasn't there beside them. "Hey! Where's Ah-song?" They jerked their heads around and spotted Ah-song squatting down next to one of the railings in the middle of the overpass, watching the cars pass beneath him.

"Ah-song!" Ah-zhu called out.

"Ah-song really makes me mad! He does this every day when I take him to school. He even throws pebbles down on the cars!"

"Ah-song!" Seeing that he was paying no attention to her, Ah-zhu ran over angrily.

The sight of Ah-zhu dragging Ah-song over toward him made Ah-ji laugh.

"I'm going to tell Mommy when we get home that Ah-ji says you do this every day!"

"He does too—he started it!" Ah-song said as he glared at his brother.

"Who said so?" Ah-ji was still laughing.

"Come on! Let's go! Mommy's probably worried to death. It's taking us all day just to cross an overpass!"

"Sister, carry me down on your back," Ah-song said when he reached the head of the steps leading down.

Without saying a word, Ah-zhu squatted down to let Ah-song climb onto her back.

## IN THE SEDAN

Heedful that her husband had lost quite a bit of blood and was undergoing emergency treatment, Ah-gui cried helplessly and muttered reproachfully, "I told him that jobs are the same everywhere, but he wouldn't listen. He kept saying we should go up north and try our luck there. Now look at the luck we've found! My God! Just what kind of luck have we managed to find?"

She was still crying as they approached the highway, though she wasn't even aware that they'd reached it—she simply followed Ah-zhu wherever she led.

The policeman and the foreigner signaled to them from a big black sedan. "Mama, there's the American. Ah-ji, take the others over there," said Ah-zhu. When the foreigner saw them walking toward him, he jumped into the car and started the engine. The policeman jumped in beside him. As she walked up alongside the car, Ah-gui began crying even more loudly, more than likely intending to make this American aware that he had brought her family to ruin.

The policeman stuck his head out the window. "Get in!" he said. Ah-gui simply stood there and wailed while Ah-zhu stared at the closed door, not knowing what to do. While everyone stood around indecisively, Ah-ji reached out and grabbed the door handle. Nothing happened, so, putting his left foot against the car, he used both hands and pulled on it with all his might. Still nothing. Just then the foreigner, suddenly realizing that they hadn't yet opened the door, turned halfway around in his seat with a little hiccup of surprise, reached over, and opened the door from the inside, nearly sending Ah-ji sprawling backward.

Ah-gui and the children couldn't possibly have managed to seat themselves if the policeman hadn't told them all just where to sit. Fortunately, even with her lack of experience and her apprehensions, Ah-gui bumped her head only slightly as she climbed into the car and was merely startled. That and the unexpected opulence of the interior combined to bring her crying to an abrupt halt.

Before they had driven very far, Ah-gui realized that she'd stopped crying the minute she was seated in the car, making her mournful cries of a moment earlier seem a bit contrived. She soon recommenced babbling and sobbing and before long was giving rein to her grief with loud wails.

The policeman, unable to endure her mournful crying, turned around and said, "There, there, Mrs. Jiang, there, there! Don't cry so hard. Who knows, maybe Mr. Jiang was only slightly injured. But if you cry too hard, you might make him worse—he could even die! Now stop crying." At first he was feeling pretty badly himself, but this little speech nearly made him laugh. He quickly turned around and faced forward, biting down hard on his lower lip.

Ah-gui was crying out of a genuine sense of grief, to be sure; not understanding clearly what the policeman had said, she figured that they must all be in sympathy with her, so she cried even more bitterly, mumbling as she did, "How are the five children and I going to live? How are we going to live?"

The policeman wanted to give her more counsel, but as he turned around he saw her crying so hard she was shaking, and the words stuck in his throat. He could think of nothing to say that might stop her crying. Looking at the situation from a different angle, he realized that for an impoverished woman to give rein to her grief this way wasn't necessarily bad for her emotional health. As this thought formed in his mind, he was struck by his own callousness.

Ah-zhu, holding the baby in her arms, was pressed up close to her mother, though her thoughts were only of what might happen after her adoption. Ah-ji, Ah-song, and the mute girl were all kneeling on the back seat, looking at the scenery out the back window and giggling. For them, their father's accident had quickly been left far behind around one of the curves in the road.

As the car followed a gradually winding mountain road, the three children on the back seat pressed up against the side window that separated them from the scenery outside. They watched the houses at the foot of the mountain grow smaller. Ah-ji and Ah-song kept pointing to things for each other's benefit, excitedly telling each other in soft voices to look here and there. Even the little mute girl was exuberant, but when she tried to speak she only made loud grunts. "Ai ya! Ba, ha, ha, ya. . . ."

## THE WHITE HOUSE

A clean, white, medium-sized hospital stood on the scenic mountaintop. Although the parking lot was filled with cars, no people were out walking. Some white sedans and ambulances were parked among the cars, and there was a short white fence surrounding a patch of Korean grass made dazzling by the recent rainfall.

Ah-gui was still crying bitterly as the car drove into the parking lot.

"All right," the policeman said to her, "all right. We're here now, so you'd better stop crying."

But with the cold, white hospital there in front of her and not another soul in sight, Ah-gui was confronted by a series of images. She knew her husband was inside. Was he dead? Crippled? Or what? Suddenly she could no longer restrain the emotions that she'd been able to keep more or less under control thus far. Covering her face with her hands, she let herself be led along by Ah-zhu, the wails of grief sticking in her throat and making her sound like a dying animal.

When Ah-gui and the others followed the foreigner into the hospital, the grief that had been surging unchecked was contained by the stern atmosphere inside. Having regained control of herself, Ah-gui looked around at her children, who seemed frightened by the strange, new environment. Gathering them all together, she squatted in front of the mute girl. Using sign language, she pointed to her own mouth, then to the mute's mouth, indicating that she wanted her to quiet down. The mute nodded, then grunted loudly, quickly realizing she'd goofed from the angry glare in Ah-gui's eyes. She tried to scoot backward, but Ah-gui pulled her up close and made hand motions of sewing the girl's mouth closed. The frightened mute shook her head spiritedly.

The policeman walked over from the reception desk and told Ah-gui, "Mr. Jiang is in no danger—his legs were broken, that's all. He'll be out of surgery soon."

From his expression and tone of voice, plus the few words she understood, Ah-gui had a rough idea what he was getting at. She glanced at the reception desk as the foreigner, a comforting smile on his face and a foreign nurse beside him, walked up to her. He began talking feverishly, bending at the waist to make hand motions first against his left leg, then his right; then he nodded. Just then, to everyone's surprise, the mute girl, seeming to comprehend what he was saying, walked up to him, patted his leg, and began grunting and gesturing. The foreigner smiled and nodded.

The foreign nurse took them into an empty ward to wait for Jiang Ah-fa. With the knowledge that her husband was in no immediate danger, Ah-gui felt considerably relieved and, like her children, began to scrutinize the hospital and the people walking around in it. Being sick in a place like this might not be so bad, she was thinking. After the foreigner and policeman had left the ward, Ah-zhu asked Ah-gui, "Mama, Papa's going to stay here, isn't he?"

"I don't know."

"How long will he stay?" Ah-zhu asked with growing interest.

"You little imp! What makes you so happy?" She was nearly laughing herself.

Ah-zhu could tell that her mother wasn't really angry, so she said bravely, "I have to go to the bathroom."

To her surprise, her mother said with a laugh, "Me too. I've held back since this morning. This is awful! Where do we pee in here?"

"I don't know."

"This is just awful!" As she was bemoaning the situation, Ah-ji and Ah-song ran into the room. "Where the hell have you two been?"

"We went to the bathroom," Ah-song answered.

"Where is it?" she asked impatiently.

"Over there!" Ah-ji pointed casually. "Go out here, then turn, then turn again, and there it is."

"You little brat, aren't you afraid of anything? Where do you think you are? What's the idea of running all over the place? Now, where is it? Take me there."

"This way!" Ah-ji gleefully threw open the door and started out.

"Wait a minute! Slow down . . . and stop shouting."

Ah-ji and Ah-song took Ah-gui and the others to the toilet; then the two of them ran back to the empty hospital room.

"Hey, everything in the place is white," Ah-song noted with amazement.

"It's an American hospital."

"Their clothes are white, so are their hats and shoes."

"So is the room." Ah-ji looked around. "The sheets are white, the blankets, even the bed. So are the windows and the walls. . . ."

Ah-song was getting a little anxious, since everything in sight, everything worth mentioning, had been covered by his brother. He rolled his eyes as he thought hard, then blurted out, "The place where we peed was white too!"

"Besides, there's the . . ." His thought was interrupted by the return of Ah-gui, Ah-zhu, and the mute. Ah-gui began scolding the moment she walked through the door. "You little imp! Someone would think you were having a baby instead of just taking a pee, you were in there so damned long! There was some American man in there who kept saying 'Noh! Noh!' or something like that. What the hell does 'Noh! Noh!' mean? He had me so nervous I damn near died." Then she changed her tone of voice and asked, "How did you pee?"

"Aren't you supposed to sit on it?"

"You sat on it?" Only after she saw Ah-zhu nod her head did she say with a sense of relief, "Me too." Then she happened to notice a bulge around Ah-zhu's chest. She reached out and grabbed it. "What's this?"

Unable to back away quickly enough, Ah-zhu let her mother reach inside her blouse. "It's terrific toilet paper!" she said awkwardly.

"Ai! What an imp you are!" She pulled a big wad of clean white toilet paper out from under Ah-zhu's blouse and straightened it a bit. "Really!"

she said. "What if someone found out about this?" She turned her back to the children and put the neatly folded toilet paper together with that which she had taken from the toilet. Seeing that it made her belly protrude too much, she reached out to take the baby from Ah-zhu and held it low to cover the bulge. Then she said, "What's wrong with this kid today? She's sleeping like a corpse." She looked herself over and straightened up her clothes.

Just then the policeman rushed in. Ah-zhu and Ah-gui were so rattled that even the policeman noticed it. He quickly tried to comfort them by saying, "Don't be frightened, please don't be frightened, he's not in any danger. You can see him in a few minutes. Take it easy." He'd barely finished when the foreigner and a nurse rushed in, looked things over, and said something to the policeman, who translated for them: "Everyone out of the room for a moment."

Ah-gui led the children out into the hallway, after which two male nurses entered the room and wheeled out the empty bed. Before long a bed carrying the unconscious Jiang Ah-fa was rolled past them and into the room. The sight was enough to cause Ah-gui and Ah-zhu to weep softly. Ah-ji, Ah-song, and the mute stood in the doorway staring dumbly into the room, watching the nurses' bustling activity. The children simply could not believe that this was their daddy. Except for his closed eyes and his nose and mouth, he was completely swathed in bandages.

Unable to shake his suspicions, Ah-song gently tugged on Ah-ji's sleeve and asked in a soft voice, "Brother, is that white thing our daddy?" Then he just stood there, his eyes and mouth opened wide.

THE WINGED ANGEL

By now there was no one in the room but members of Jiang Ah-fa's family, including Ah-fa, who was still under the anesthesia. Ah-gui was again seized by a sense of sadness, but this time it was not caused by imaginary fears. She felt genuinely sad for the head of the family, upon whose existence they all depended. Both his legs were broken, his head and arms had been injured, and it was quite possible that he would become a cripple. What were they to do? Just what were they to do? She mumbled as she sobbed, looking into Ah-fa's face and hoping he'd soon come to. Ah-zhu was holding the baby and crying, thinking of all the hardships she could expect as an adopted daughter. She no longer reacted as bravely as she had that morning, when these thoughts had first occurred to her as she walked with Ah-ji. She was so frightened she nearly began to wail out loud. As for the other three children, with their mother and eldest sister feeling so unhappy, they didn't dare run about or cause a commotion. They stood there quietly, looking here and there, and even when they wanted to ask something, after thoughtfully looking the situation over, they held back.

After a while, a nurse in a Catholic nun's habit walked in, looked at the patient and then at Ah-gui and the children, and asked, "Has he come to yet?"

With the exception of the mute girl, they were astounded by this; they simply couldn't believe their ears. Sensing from their facial expressions why they were so shocked, the nun said with a smile, "I can speak Taiwanese. I'm a Catholic sister. I was working at Saint Mary's Hospital, but in accordance with the wishes of the Lord, I've been temporarily assigned to the American Hospital to take care of Mr. Jiang." She glanced around the room at Ah-gui and the children. "Is your whole family present?"

Ah-gui didn't know what to do except nod her head. If she hadn't been so upset, the sight of a foreign woman who bore no resemblance at all to herself yet spoke the local dialect with such fluency would surely have seemed comical. The children were staring in amazement at the woman, smiles adorning their faces. They were reminded of the winged angels they had seen on greeting cards. Somehow or other, the appearance of this nun suddenly had everyone in the family sensing that their world had grown larger—which was why Ah-gui felt compelled to try to make the woman appreciate her dilemma. But how? After giving it some thought, the old tried-and-tested method seemed the best: having been grief-stricken from the very beginning, she abruptly reverted to how she had been before the arrival of the nun, looking dispiritedly at Jiang Ah-fa's face, touching his hands, sobbing, and mumbling, "What'll we do? Oh, what'll we do? Here we are, seven of us, no food to eat, no clothes to wear. . . . Ai! What's going to happen to us? Why didn't the car hit me instead? Why did it have to hit you?" She grew visibly sadder as she went along, and all the nun's attempts to calm her were in vain; in fact, the nun's admonitions proved an added stimulus to cry. The nun was well aware of the effect this kind of situation had on a woman like Ah-gui: when she was faced with the cruel realities, her ability to go on would quickly be fortified. And so, taking advantage of Ah-gui's sobbing, she quietly slipped away for the time being.

Ah-gui was by then weeping over her own predicament. "Woe is me! What'll we do? What'll we do now?"

"Mama, Mama, the nun's gone," Ah-zhu said tearfully.

Ah-gui raised her head and looked around, then stared at Ah-zhu with eyes red from crying and said in a pained and angry voice, "So what does that have to do with us! Why tell me?" Seeing Ah-zhu lower her head, she continued, "Now you've all seen how your daddy was crippled in an accident, and from now on I expect every one of you to shape up. Keep your eyes open a little wider for my sake."

Ah-zhu's thoughts turned once again to her adoption. She hadn't imagined that her mother would get so angry just because she'd told her that the nun was gone. She'd had the best of intentions, thinking that her mother had been wailing for the nun's benefit. It wasn't fair! These thoughts produced a steady flow of tears from Ah-zhu's seemingly inexhaustible supply.

"Ah-ji! Ah-song!" Seeing the state Ah-zhu was in, Ah-gui felt she'd been too harsh with her, so she turned her attention to the others. "The same goes for you two! Your daddy can't work anymore, so you'll have to work in his place."

For reasons unknown, Ah-ji was so tickled by all this that he had to lower his head and bite down hard on his lower lip to keep his mother from noticing. Ah-song, who was standing off to one side, heard his mother's threat that he'd have to work in his father's place and unexpectedly turned very serious, answering obediently, "Yes, ma'am."

Ah-ji could hold back no longer, and as his mouth opened he began to giggle. Even Ah-gui's angry curses of "What's this? That's just great! You can drop dead, you crazy child! Hurry up and drop dead!" had no effect on his laughing, which would stop only when it had run its natural course.

## BLESSED ARE THE BELIEVERS

The combination of the anesthesia wearing off and Ah-ji's laughter brought Jiang Ah-fa around. He moaned softly, bringing an abrupt change to the room's atmosphere. Ah-gui placed her hand on his chest. "Don't move," she said. "Especially your legs."

Ah-fa lay there, straining to raise his head so he could see his legs. "What's wrong with my legs?"

"They're broken."

When he heard this, Ah-fa let his head drop weakly back onto the pillow, and he let out a sigh. "I thought I was dead for sure." He grew silent as he looked up at the ceiling, his eyes still clouded, then asked, "How about the kids?"

"They're all here, right beside you."

"Papa," Ah-zhu called out softly. Ah-ji and Ah-song also called out, and even though the mute made no sound, she quietly lined up with the others beside the bed, across from their mother. As Ah-gui watched Ah-fa cast a silent glance at each of his children, she was moved to tears. The entire family seemed to have turned into a bunch of idiots, standing dumbly by, unable to say a thing. And the longer the situation persisted the worse everyone felt, as each of them desperately hoped that someone would break the ice and say something. Just then the baby in Ah-zhu's arms began to bawl.

"Give her to me," Ah-gui said, so Ah-zhu walked around the bed and handed her over. "This little imp seems to know that something's happened to you. She hasn't cried a bit all day, ever since morning. She's got to be hungry now." So saying, she exposed one of her breasts and began to feed the baby. The sounds of the sucking baby were the only ones to be heard in the stilled room.

Thoughts of his own injuries and of these people around him made Ah-fa feel miserable. He wasn't absolutely convinced he was still alive. *Why haven't I died? Why not just get it over with? How will they manage if I live on like this?* . . . "Where am I?" he asked with a start, as if the question had just then popped into his head.

"An American hospital."

"Huh? An American hospital? Where . . . where's the money coming from?"

"I don't know. We were brought here by an American and a policeman," Ah-gui answered.

"Where are they now?"

"They said they'd be back in a minute."

Ah-fa didn't say another word but just lay there looking as if he had a great many things on his mind. His expression alternated between concern and relief, which led Ah-gui to assume that, to some degree at least, he was reproaching himself. So she said, "How are we going to manage through the long days ahead?" As she uttered these words, her nose began to ache and tears started to fall. "I told you," she continued with a note of resentment creeping into her voice, "but you wouldn't listen. I said that if it was work you wanted, you could find it anywhere. But you didn't believe me. You said women don't understand, and that we should try our luck in a big city. Finding work isn't the same as opening a business—what kind of luck is there to try? No, there's luck, all right! And we've just found our share, haven't we? . . ."

"Mama, that's enough," Ah-zhu cried out anxiously. She saw her father's face turning livid with anger, though he didn't say a word, and she knew that if her mother kept it up much longer he'd explode with rage, after which nothing could calm him down. Ah-zhu had witnessed such scenes many times—this was how their arguments always started. Ah-gui herself was well aware of the fact, but whenever matters reached this stage, she was powerless to avoid the inevitable results. This time, at least, she stopped her monologue in the nick of time, and in the silence that followed, the only sound was Ah-fa's labored breathing. Remembering the nurse's instructions to press the buzzer by the head of the bed if she needed anything, Ah-gui pressed it, and almost immediately the courteous, friendly nun came rushing in.

"Ah, he's awake," she said when she saw Ah-fa. Then she walked over to his bedside, put her hand on his forehead, and asked, "How do you feel?"

Like the others before him, Ah-fa was shocked to hear a foreigner speaking the local dialect.

"That's fine, his fever must have broken." She took a thermometer out of her pocket, shook it a few times, and looked at it. "Put this under your tongue." She stuck the thermometer into Ah-fa's mouth, then glanced around the room, taking in all the others. "Are you still scared, hmm?" she asked with a smile.

"What difference does it make whether we're scared or not?" Ah-gui answered her. "We're still worried."

"Do you believe in God?" Seeing that Ah-gui had nothing to say, she continued, "There are blessings for those who believe!"

Just then the American and the policeman entered with several bagsful of things in their arms. They exchanged greetings with the nun, and the affairs of God were put aside for the moment.

They put the things on the table one at a time. "Here are some sandwiches, and some milk, and here are some soft drinks, and here . . . here's some canned fruit. Then we have some apples here," the policeman said, identifying each object. "This is your lunch."

The children looked at the bags, absorbed in their contents. The nun took the thermometer out of Ah-fa's mouth. "That's fine," she said after looking at it. "He doesn't have a fever." Then she went to the foot of the bed to make an entry on the chart. The foreigner and the policeman walked up to Ah-fa and smiled. Bewildered, he returned their smiles.

"This is Colonel Grant. It was his car that hit you," the policeman said.

Colonel Grant reached out and grabbed Ah-fa's hand, a stream of unintelligible mutterings pouring from his mouth. From his facial expression Ah-fa could tell that the man was apologetic.

The policeman acted as interpreter. "He said he's terribly, terribly sorry and begs your forgiveness. He said he's prepared to assume all responsibility, and he'd like to become a friend of your whole family."

Like Ah-gui, Ah-fa did not understand Mandarin, but he'd figured out that it was Grant's car that had hit him, so he said accusingly, accompanied by moans, "Aha! So it was you! You ought to be more careful. I saw your car coming a long way away, so I pulled over to let you pass—I never thought you'd come right at me. Aiya! When you smashed into me, you also smashed my family to pieces. . . ." Wanting very much to know what Ah-fa was saying, Colonel Grant looked over at the policeman, who returned his look and shook his head. Eventually it was the nun standing behind them who conveyed Ah-fa's words to Mr. Grant.

From that point on the nun acted as Colonel Grant's interpreter.

"In addition to the insurance compensation, Colonel Grant considers it a matter of personal honor, and for that reason as well as for official reasons, his organization is willing to assume full responsibility in guaranteeing that you will not suffer financially because of Mr. Jiang's incapacitation. Additionally, he hopes that you will permit him to send your mute daughter to a special school in the United States." Everyone quickly turned to face the mute, throwing a scare into her. If Mr. Grant hadn't just then placed his hand on her head and rubbed it, she'd probably have been shaking in her boots. Ah-gui and Ah-fa looked at each other. The nun quickly added, "No hurry—we can talk more about this later. But for now here's twenty thousand." Grant handed her an envelope, which she placed on Ah-fa's chest. "You can use this to live on for the time being. There'll be more later."

Twenty thousand! This nearly made their heads swim, but since the money was right there in front of them, something had to be said. But what, what should they say? All this indecision gave them the uneasy feeling that they'd done something wrong and offended someone.

The policeman, who had been standing off to one side, suddenly broke the silence.

"This has been a stroke of good luck for you," he said, "being run down by an American's car. If it had been anyone else, you'd probably still be lying in the road, covered with a grass mat!"

Ah-zhu bent down near Ah-fa's ear and told him what the policeman had said. Through tears of emotion, Ah-fa said, "Thank you! Thank you! I'm sorry, I'm so sorry. . . ."

## THE TASTE OF APPLES

They ate sandwiches and drank cola as they chatted happily. The Jiang Ah-fa household had never been as harmonious as it was at this moment.

"Ah-gui, when you go home, make sure you don't tell anyone how much money we got."

"What makes you think I'd do that?" Then she turned to the children and said, "Now all you kids got the message, didn't you? Whoever goes and shoots his mouth off will find it sewn shut by me!"

"I wouldn't dare."

"Neither would I."

"Papa, I want to keep these soda cans," Ah-ji said.

"So do I," said Ah-song.

"I don't want any of you kids losing these pretty soda cans," Ah-gui warned sternly. "I'll flay the skin off the bones of anyone who loses them!"

"We know," the children shouted gleefully.

Ah-fa was experiencing an unusual feeling, one devoid of cares or worries. It was written all over his face, and Ah-gui noticed it; she hadn't dreamed that this man for whom she'd borne five children was capable of such an attractive expression. Seeing that he wasn't watching her, she moved her head back a little and stared at him. *Just look at him! When has he ever looked as dashing as he does today? Today he really looks like a human being.*

Ah-fa stole a glance at Ah-gui while he was drinking milk. He was wondering why she hadn't started in again with her grumbling. He was even hoping she'd repeat that sentence, "You said let's go up north and try our luck; now just see what you've run into!" *Wait till she says that, and I'll come back with "Well, if this isn't luck, I'd like to know what it is!" Haha, I'd sure take the wind out of her sails with that!* Ah-fa took another look at her at the very moment her eyes were on him. Knowing smiles spread across both faces.

The happy atmosphere the family was enjoying was interrupted, but not unpleasantly, when Grant brought the foreman and the workers' representative, Chen Huotu, to call on the injured man.

The foreman and Huotu entered the room without a single consoling word; as always, they giggled and laughed and said things like, "Wow! What a life, nothing but lying in bed, eating and crapping. As for the rest of us, nothing's changed. We're still working like animals. Who could have it better than you? Ha ha ha!"

"Heh, heh, we'll depend on you from now on!" the foreman exclaimed.

Ah-fa and Ah-gui were puzzled.

"Hey, Huotu, what are you two talking about? You're getting me all confused."

"Don't put on an act with us. You think we don't know? That American fellow told us all about it. They're even going to send your mute daughter to a special school in the United States. Not only that . . ."

"Who said?" Ah-gui asked.

"There must be a hundred of us at the job, and we know all about it."

"It's only right! Otherwise how could we know if one of our brothers was being taken advantage of? Isn't that right?"

"Sure, that's right. This Mr. Grant, he's a nice guy," Ah-fa said.

"Hey!" Huotu shouted, then asked conspiratorially, "Hey, Ah-fa, did you do it on purpose? Ha ha ha . . ."

"Damn you, Huotu, you had to say it, didn't you? No goddamn kidding . . ." There was nothing Ah-fa could do; not knowing whether to laugh or cry, he simply cursed at Huotu with the trace of a smile on his face. By then everyone was laughing.

"Huotu, if you think it's so great, why don't you try it?" Ah-gui teased him.

"Me? I could never be as lucky as you. Look here. With a pointy chin like this, where would I find that kind of luck?" Everyone laughed again.

Because their jobs were waiting for them, the foreman and Huotu let this count as paying their respects and departed.

"Damn it, what's a guy supposed to do with a bunch of goof-offs like that?" All of a sudden Ah-fa's legs began to ache. "Ow! My legs hurt."

"Call the nurse."

"Not so fast. She was just in here. We don't want to put them to too much trouble." He saw the children looking longingly at the apples, so he said, "If you want an apple, go ahead—one apiece." The children quickly reached out and took them. "And give your mother one!"

"No, I don't, I don't . . ." But Ah-ji had already put one into his mother's hand. "Why don't you have one too?"

"My legs hurt too much, I don't feel like eating."

"Shall I call the nurse?"

"I already said you don't have to—weren't you listening?" Ah-fa said irritably.

Everyone was holding an apple, turning it over, not quite knowing how to eat it. "Go ahead, eat them!" Ah-fa said.

"How?" Ah-zhu asked bashfully.

"Like they do on TV," Ah-ji said, then took a bite to show them.

While everyone was watching Ah-ji take a bite, Ah-fa said, "For what one apple costs you can buy four catties of rice—and not a single one of you even knows how to eat them!"

Following this remark, the children and Ah-gui all began to eat their apples. The silence of the room was broken by the crisp sound of apples being bitten into, gingerly, one after another. As they took their first bites they said nothing, although they felt that the apples weren't quite as sweet as they had imagined; rather, they were a little sour and pulpy, and when chewed they were frothy and not quite real. But then they were reminded of their father's comment that one apple cost as much as four catties of rice, and with that the flavor was enhanced. When they took their second bites, they spiritedly bit off big chunks, with the result that the sickroom was filled with a chorus of loud munching.

Ah-fa, who hadn't wanted one at first, finally succumbed to the temptation. "Ah-zhu," he said, "hand me one of those."

# Xiaoqi's Cap

○

Following three days of vocational training, only twenty-one of the sixty-five applicants who had passed the test were hired on as salesmen for Takeda Gas Pressure Cookers. In order to show how seriously the company viewed this training, on the last day, the chairman of the board and the general manager stood in the doorway as we passed through, solemnly shaking hands with each of us and saying solemnly, "Our company's success rests with you now."

From where I stood at the rear of the line, inching forward, it all seemed pretty comical, and when it was my turn to have my hand shaken I nearly burst out laughing.

*Please*, I was thinking, *shake my hand and let me get out of here.*

"I have a suggestion for you, Wang Wuxiong," the general manager said as he squeezed my hand and waved it back and forth. I felt like jerking it out of his grip. But obviously, that was impossible, even though he was hurting my hand. He was smiling broadly, and I smiled back in spite of myself. He looked like he had something to say but was biting back the words. He'd said he had a suggestion, and I was wondering what he could possibly say that was any creepier than "our company's success rests with you now." So I waited. Finally, still smiling, he said, "Put a little more into it when you shake hands from now on. People will lose confidence in you if you shake hands this way, and they'll doubt your sincerity. Most of the time, of course, you can do it any way you want. But now that you work for Takeda, you represent the company, and when you shake hands, be sure you . . ."

Even I was puzzled by what happened next: before he finished what he had to say, I squeezed his hand as hard as I could. It was immediately obvious to me that the powerful hand of just moments before crumpled in my viselike grip. The shock from that unexpected development drove the rest of his comment right out of him. So I loosened my grip a bit to let him finish what he was trying to say, but he just hemmed and hawed for a moment, then changed his mind.

"All right," he said with a wry smile, "all right. Keep it firm."

Satisfied with how things had worked out, I let go of his hand and was about to walk off when he added:

"Firmness is important, but not too firm. And of course, not too limp either. Heh, heh, just right is best."

I nodded and smiled, noting as I did so the expression of discomfort he was trying hard to conceal. I also saw that he was trying to pry his fingers apart without letting on. This little incident threw such a fright into him that when the next in line had finished shaking hands with the chairman of the board and was standing in front of him holding out his hand, the general manager never took it. The pained look on the face of my new colleague, who'd gone without a handshake and didn't know what to do now, struck me as both funny and pathetic.

What was really strange was that my mental confusion, caused by weariness from the vocational training I'd just finished, and my disdain and helplessness in regard to the job itself, which had been so strong prior to the handshake, suddenly disappeared. Not only that, I was very conscious of the fact that my abrupt lightness of mood had begun when the general manager's hand crumpled in my grip. And the reason he kept his temper in check might possibly have been that after three days of training, forty-four of the original sixty-five applicants had decamped, and he felt that since finding good people was difficult enough as it was, he'd better let it pass. Still, during the final session the general manager had stressed the point that the company had set their quota at twenty new salesmen, and they knew that three days of training would weed out a portion of the applicants, which is why sixty-five individuals had been notified. They'd achieved their goal; one extra didn't make any difference, since it proved that there was at least one more talented individual than expected. Anyone with a lick of intelligence can see that was a silly exercise in self-justification.

By the second day, I'd pretty much made up my mind to pack it in after the construction and functions of the pressure cooker were described. A middle-aged engineer by the name of Chen stepped onto the stage and quickly dismantled a pressure cooker whose exterior design was simplicity itself. Armed with the patience of Job, he picked up one part after another and described its function. This, he said, is the outer pot, and this the inner pot; this is a protective rubber seal, this a pressure regulator; this is the safety switch and this is a pressure release valve. And this, this is the outer lid with its safety lock. This here is the alarm mechanism. He then went on to describe in detail the workings of the cooker, how all the parts fit together. He told us that if the alarm went off, you had to turn down the heat at once. Next he planned to make calculations on the blackboard to show us the relationship between temperature and pressure. Panic quickly set in and I jumped to my feet to say something.

"Excuse me, Engineer Chen, but I've just finished my military service. I was assigned to ordnance, and as I see it, getting some housewife to effectively use this sort of pressure cooker makes our dealing with land mines seem like child's play."

My comment was met with raucous laughter from my new colleagues, some of whom actually showed their appreciation by applauding. Engineer Chen was clearly not amused. I could see he was struggling to keep his composure. His face darkened one minute and turned ghostly white the next. He swallowed hard before he could force himself to respond.

"Since you have no faith in our product, how do you expect to go out and sell it?"

All I could think was, *Why should I go out there and equip the country's kitchens with bombs disguised as pressure cookers?* And that thought gave me the courage to see this little rebellion through to the end. So I continued, "Engineer Chen, it's easy to have faith in one's own invention . . ."

"No," he interrupted, "you've got it wrong. I'm not clever enough to invent something like this. It's a Japanese invention. The Japanese have been using these for nearly twenty years already. It's only new to us!

These are Japanese imports. Get it?" The implication in his rebuttal was
that he was somewhat shamed by our backwardness, a good twenty years
behind the Japanese. He glanced over at the general manager as he spoke,
as if silently pleading with him to drag me out and lop off my head
without delay. The look in his eyes, filled with hidden meaning, shifted
the attention of all the trainees to the general manager, who met their
gaze with a smile, and that was all.

"Tell me this," I went on. "What if your average consumer, the housewife, gives the same opinion I just did?" He froze. I continued, "When
we're out there peddling your pressure cookers, door to door, if a housewife says this, can we give the same answer Engineer Chen gave me—
'Since you have no faith in our Takeda Pressure Cooker, how do you
expect to cook with it?'"

Another burst of raucous laughter stopped me before I could go on.
That and a round of enthusiastic applause.

"All right now, everybody, quiet down," the general manager said
with a rap on the table. I didn't detect any anger in his voice. He walked
up onto the stage. "Wang Wuxiong is quite a gifted speaker, and I like
that. That's exactly what a successful salesman needs to be. . . ." More
laughter, more applause. "Hear me out, everybody, please. Let's give
Engineer Chen a chance to finish what he was saying about the product,
and we can discuss Wang Wuxiong's question during the class on sales
techniques." He turned to Engineer Chen and jabbered something to
him in Japanese. Then, switching back to Chinese, he said, "All right,
let's go on with the lesson."

Now it was Engineer Chen's turn to lack faith, I could see. As he went
on with his description of the pressure cooker, he either kept his head
down or spoke to the diagram hanging behind him. I no longer detected
any implication of mockery of our backwardness in his voice, which now
had a cringing quality. I turned to look at my fellow trainees, who greeted
me with smiles. A few of them even gave me a thumbs-up on the sly.
Sure, I was pleased to be hailed as a hero of sorts, but that didn't dispel my
distaste for the job itself. I was sorely tempted to split with the other
dropouts, but on second thought, there weren't all that many ideal jobs
out there, especially for someone like me who wasn't a college graduate.
After being released from the military, I'd ordered three dozen two-
square-inch head-and-shoulders photos, bought a stack of brief résumé
forms, composed as elegant and flowery a personal history as I could
manage, and begun poring over the help-wanted classifieds, day in and

day out. I responded to ads for every position I seemed even remotely qualified for, so long as it didn't require a college degree. Whatever they were looking for—salesman, cub reporter, temp—it didn't matter to me. Most of the time my inquiries fell into a black hole, and at first I suspected that the postman had misplaced or misdelivered the responses, even though I sent many of them out by registered mail. This sort of blanket mailing led to an occasional interview, but in the end they all pretty much came to nothing. For a few of the jobs that seemed a bit more promising, I sent a follow-up letter on the pretext of retrieving my photograph, but even that was a waste of time. In my quest for work, my hopes and anxieties were as high as they'd go, which made me extremely irritable. My parents scrupulously avoided saying anything like, "Why don't you get a job?" Eventually, it wasn't just a job that brought things to where they wound up. By then, all I needed was an excuse—any excuse—to leave home so I wouldn't have to look at their long faces anymore.

I had the most success with the Takeda Company. Three days after sending them a letter, I was invited for an interview. Then the day after three or four hundred applicants took both a written and an oral test, those who passed were notified to show up for a training session. I was one of the lucky ones. In addition to a monthly subsistence allowance of 1,200 New Taiwan Dollars, there was a base salary of $1,200. All other earnings came from bonuses, $50 dollars for each pressure cooker sold, but only if you met your monthly quota: 50 per month in class A districts, 40 in class B districts, and 30 in class C districts. Anyone who exceeded the quota by 50 percent received an additional $500 bonus. That's what they'd meant by "Take home thousands every month!" in the classified ad. In any case, even if I didn't sell 40 of the things, I'd still take in $2,400 a month, so my attitude was: wait and see. Meanwhile, I could keep my eyes open for a better job. That way, I could put up with all the anger, anguish, agony, and angst that came along.

And that is how I came to be assigned to this little coastal town, which, on the company map, was designated class B. The company rented a tiny building for us to use an office; we were told it was an unused garage belonging to an old doctor. By "us" I mean Lin Zaifa and me. Since he was ten years my senior, he was put in charge: Resident Director of the Takeda Gas Pressure Cooker Company. Concerned that I might not take orders well, the general manager made a show of appointing me Assistant Director. Over the first three weeks, I didn't hand out a single business card from the box I was given. Lin Zaifa, on the other hand, said he'd handed out quite a few. A hundred pressure cookers in cardboard boxes took most of the space in our garage, and that's where they stayed, all neatly stacked. We hadn't sold a single one. In what space was left, we set up a pair of bunk beds, a small desk, and two folding chairs. If we'd tried to squeeze another item in, we'd have had trouble breathing.

Lin Zaifa was as faithful as any salesman could be. Faithful to the company, I mean. He'd drag himself home exhausted yet wouldn't go to bed until he'd filled out the day's report—completely. He took particular care to record the customers' reactions and suggestions, as well as a self-evaluation. I never saw a single report with a space uncluttered by his tiny, cramped handwriting. Sometimes he'd even append a handwritten letter when there wasn't enough space on the form itself.

Every time he filled out one of those forms, he'd ask my opinion. At first I complied, but that got real old real fast. And still he'd ask, until all I could do was fire back, "Let it go, would you, my dear director? You wear yourself out with those things, and how do you know the company even reads them?"

"Why wouldn't they?"

"Why would they? Besides, if anyone reads those things, how come you've never received a single reply?" This hit him like a bucket of cold water, and he had a pained look on his face. "I know you look forward to receiving a letter from your wife every day, and one from the company as well," I said before his pained expression had a chance to disappear. "Your wife's always come, but what about the company's?"

Once I'd finished, he pumped himself up, after a brief internal struggle, and said, "I'm not doing all this just for the company; it's for us as well. But you're barely twenty-three, so you can think that way if you want. I'm over thirty, and I can't think about things the way you do." He appeared to be saying this for my benefit, but I knew it was mainly for his own benefit. And apparently it worked, since he put his head down and went back to work filling in his form.

I lay on my belly in the upper bunk watching him hunched over the desk and couldn't help feeling sorry for him. I was thinking about how conscientious Lin Zaifa was and how superficial the company was. The company's attitude seemed not to register with Lin, but it wouldn't have made any difference even if it had. My head was a welter of confusing thoughts, and I was trying to straighten them out. Then, out of the blue, it came to me, to my great and probably unjustified delight.

"Lin Zaifa," I blurted out, "sometimes the line between faith and deception is as thin as toilet paper."

He looked up and gave me a forced smile. I realized how rash that sounded and at the same time knew that he wasn't sure what I was talking about. Maybe he was too focused on what he was doing to come around in time to get my meaning. But, concerned that he'd embarrass me by not paying attention to what I was saying, he forced a smile in response. It couldn't have been more obvious, damn it! That's the sort of forthright person Lin Zaifa was, which was why I respected *and* felt sorry for him.

Feeling I ought to leave him be, I rolled over to let him get back to work. But my head had no sooner hit the pillow than he blurted out happily, "Wang Wuxiong."

I rolled back and looked over at him. He looked up at me. "You asleep?"

"Not yet."

"Do you believe that a child still in the womb can pound its mother?"

It was a strange question, and it took me completely by surprise. One minute he's hard at work filling out a form, the next minute he hits me with an off-the-wall question.

I laughed politely. "How do you expect me to know the answer to that if you don't?" I laughed again. "I thought you were working on your form."

"All of a sudden I thought about my wife's letter." He laid down his pen. "She said over the past few days the baby's been pounding the inside of her belly with its fists." With the word "pounding" he loosely balled up his fist and punched the air in slow motion. "She also said that if I was home, I could feel the fist by resting my hand on her belly." He laughed gleefully. Here we were in this coastal town, and we hadn't sold a single pressure cooker, which is why he always had a long face. This was the first time I'd actually seen a smile crease his face.

I laughed right along with him, moved by the beauty of their happiness. That and the lovable foolishness of his comments. But even then I was puzzled over how a totally irrelevant comment like that could become a topic of adult conversation. I wasn't bothered by it or anything. In fact, I found it pretty interesting—not something I knew anything about. So I asked the logical question: "Does it hurt your wife?"

"Ah, I'm going to have to write and ask her. But the tone of her letter was light and airy."

"Who knows, this little imp of yours might turn out to be one of our national representatives."

"You mean Little League?" he asked excitedly.

"Why not?"

"Hm, that wouldn't be bad at all." But the joyful look on his face was short-lived. "What if it's a girl?" he said as a shadow fell over his face.

"They've got girls' Little League these days."

I don't think he even heard me that time. The excitement he'd shown when he asked me about the stirrings of his unborn child was completely gone. I knew this would be their first. He picked up his pen and returned to the form on the desk, putting everything else—me included—out of his mind. But he didn't put pen to paper, not that I saw. He was wrapped up in his thoughts. I started thinking my own thoughts. Ever since leaving home, where all my young friends had nothing to do but count utility poles, and teaming up with Lin Zaifa, I'd found myself spending more and more time in self-reflection. He'd be thinking and so would I. But my thoughts were of the curious variety. Why, I wondered, had Lin Zaifa, who'd been conscientiously filling out his form, suddenly started thinking about his wife's letter, then started talking about his child? You know, I've always been one who wants to get to the bottom of things. Like, for instance, when I'm home talking with friends, we might start out talking about basic training and wind up talking about having a party. Then when I'm alone, I'll re-create the conversation from beginning to end, or from end to beginning. In tracing how we got from basic training to parties, I discover how much unrelated chatter occurred along the way. And in just this way I arrived at an understanding of what Lin Zaifa had on his mind.

Or, he thought that maybe the general manager had got it right when he'd said there was a huge market for pressure cookers in Taiwan. With over two and a half million households, even if only one out of ten bought a pressure cooker, that would make two hundred and fifty thousand units sold. So he should go out there and get to work. This was a job with a future. So not only did he fill out those forms with conscientious dedication, if anything, he worked even harder as he went door to door trying to sell the product and responded to the indifference he encountered with a genuinely apologetic smile. The first few days I thought he was just putting on an act, but I came to realize that that was just his way. He bore my mockery and sarcasm with the same smile. Maybe he thought that if he started to produce results in the job, his wife wouldn't have to keep working at the beauty salon at this late stage of her pregnancy. His wife, Meili, wrote to him nearly every other day. He said his father-in-law had taken a risk in naming his daughter Meili—"Beauty"—before even knowing if it was going to be a boy or a girl. Naturally, he could smile when he said the word "risk," since he had dodged a bullet. I had never met his wife, but I assumed that she was a beauty. He told me that her parents had been staunchly opposed to the marriage, which made for an incredibly heavy emotional burden. He couldn't let Meili be a laughingstock, either to her family or her friends, because of him. As far as he was concerned, selling pressure cookers was something he could do, and if he did it well it would be to his credit. It had already been several days and we hadn't sold a single one, but instead of faulting the product, he either blamed our sales technique or our inadequate powers of description and persuasion. He was devoted to self-examination. On the first night of our second week in town, he made two suggestions:

"Wuxiong, we've been at it for a week now, and we've nothing to show for it."

"So what do we do?" I said. "I think it's hopeless."

"It's awfully early to be losing hope. It's too soon to be talking—"

I found his optimism intolerable and didn't even give him a chance to finish. "The people aren't even listening to us, and we don't have near enough time to speak our piece. The only way we can give the whole spiel is to find housewives with time on their hands. Then we can only visit a few homes, one at a time and one right after another, saying the same thing over and over. You know what we're like? At best, a tape recorder!"

"How about this?" he said patiently. "Up till now we've gone out together, a single line. I think we might have better results if we split up into two lines, each of us sell individually. But," he quickly changed his tone of voice, "please don't get the wrong idea . . ."

Knowing him as well as I did, I jumped in to reassure him before he'd even finished: "I won't get the wrong idea, don't worry about that. We can give it a try, but I'm still not hopeful, not at all."

"Then let's try it. And another thing. If we need a day off to rest, let's not take it on Sunday. That's the one day we'll find everyone at home, which makes it a natural for door-to-door selling."

"I don't care one way or another. I don't need a day off."

That night, when he was filling out the day's report, in addition to the usual detailed information, he added a second sheet of paper to spell out these newest strategies.

The next few days proved how unworkable this plan was and exhausted us in the process. He then said that things would improve if the company allowed potential customers to use the product in their homes on a trial basis, and he recommended that customers be allowed to pay on the installment plan. That night's report was crammed full of writing. He fervently hoped for a reply from the company. He didn't get one, not a single word.

"Our company has vanished from the face of the earth," I joked with him. "Which is fine with me. If we don't get our $2,400 at the end of the month, we wind up with the entire stock of 100 pressure cookers, 50 apiece. All we have to do is sell them at a discount, and we still make a bundle."

He was in such a foul mood after that, I don't know how he'd have gotten through the night if not for the letter from his wife. That night he rattled on and on about Meili and himself. That included their plans. He said they lived frugally in a low-rent apartment, and that they had already saved up more than ten thousand Taiwan dollars.

"That means we won't be short on money when the baby comes." He smiled and continued, "I'm not going to go out on a limb like my father-in-law did. I'm going to pick a name our baby can live with."

There was something about the way he was talking that was at odds with the cold, hard facts, and I was starting to lose patience. But he seemed so full of hope that it would have been cruel not to hear him out.

The more I thought, the more tired I got. So I rolled over onto my back. He'd gotten a letter from his wife that day, and when he was filling out the day's report, he drew a blank where he was supposed to fill in the accomplishments; there were no accomplishments, which he found unsettling. So he thought about his wife's letter, particularly the parts concerning the baby, wrenching his focus away from his work and bringing the two subjects together. The merging of his baby and job gave added weight to his sense of gains and losses. It was perfectly understandable that he'd think about his baby as he was filling out the daily report, which he now did with a heavy heart.

The concept of gains and losses had no effect on me, since I was free of any burden. As a matter of fact, this in itself I viewed as a gain. I didn't have to give a moment's thought to the job and could focus on my impressions of the place I'd been sent to. I found I'd developed quite a fondness for the little coastal town in the three weeks or so I'd been there. Naturally, that included the residents, the local color, and the natural setting. I particularly liked the fishing harbor. Not a day passed when I didn't sit on the prow of a fishing boat and smoke cigarettes as the sun set. You see, there was no time to smoke during the day, when I was busy trying to sell my pressure cookers. And besides, during our training, the general manager told us that most housewives wish their husbands didn't smoke and are put off by smoker's breath. Smoking is usually a sure-fire way to kill a sale. Now I didn't put any stock in this. But when you work with a go-getter like Lin Zaifa, there's never a spare minute for a leisurely smoke. A sense of wonder suddenly gripped me. Here I was, lying in bed, thinking about smoking cigarettes as the sun set, and all of a sudden it seemed to me that I was far away from the place in space and in time and was caught up in images of a distant past filtering through my memory. The first cigarette was always the hardest, since the ocean winds kept blowing out the matches. But after that I'd chain-smoke, like keeping sticks of incense burning, flipping the butt of one cigarette away after using it to light a fresh one. When darkness set in, the burning ends looked like bright red shooting stars as they were carried off in the wind. Lin Zaifa called me a poet, the way I carried on about the beauty of a sunset. Sometimes, he said, the sight of the sun going down only served to remind him that he hadn't sold a single pressure cooker all day. After a while, he stopped tagging along. I was pretty sure that, if not for this salesman's job, I'd never have come to a place like this, so far from home, which means I'd never have met Xiaoqi. And any time her name came up, Lin Zaifa would laugh at me for what he called my ten-year plan. It was only a joke, of course. But I did tell him once that I wished he wouldn't say that anymore.

"It's just a joke," he said. "But just so you'll know, I'm twelve years older than my wife. When I was your age, she was about as old as Xiaoqi."

"Stop talking like an idiot, okay? Don't you have forms to fill out?" I didn't know whether to laugh or to cry.

"I mean it," he said without a trace of emotion. "As soon as I saw Xiaoqi, I could tell she was different from other little girls. She's going to be a real looker when she grows up."

Anyone who laid eyes on Xiaoqi would agree with Lin Zaifa. No doubt about it, she was a beautiful little girl. I gave the matter a lot of thought and came to the conclusion that there was more to distinguish her from other girls than just a pretty face. She was only a third-grader, but rather than the cuteness you normally find in girls her age, hers was the beauty of a mature young woman. At the same time, there was something about her appearance that gave you the feeling that fate would not be kind to her. We had moved in on a Sunday, more than two weeks earlier, and in all that time I don't think I'd seen Xiaoqi speak more than a word or two. We saw her just about every day, but she'd never spoken to us without being spoken to first. And even then we might not get a reply. The fact that she didn't talk much probably explains why she was always alone when we saw her, except for one time when I saw her walking by the harbor with a coastal defense officer. I later learned that he was her father. I asked her about her mother, but I never got an answer. One time, as a matter of fact, she actually ran away from me.

Xiaoqi made an appearance on our very first day in town, I recall. The company truck was four hours late. Now moving a hundred pressure cookers was no big deal. The problem was, the intersection to our street was closed for construction, so they had to unload the truck some fifty or sixty meters away; since it was getting dark, we were afraid that with just the two of us doing the moving, there would be no one to keep an eye on things. I was pretty annoyed by the whole situation; I'm sure Lin Zaifa was too. When I was carrying the first box over, I spotted a little girl in the doorway of our branch office, craning her neck to look inside and blocking my way. I was about to yell at her when she spun around, giving me the shock of my life. I swallowed the words, thanking my lucky stars I hadn't blurted out something I'd surely live to regret. Looking at the back of the little girl, I couldn't have imagined that when she turned around I'd be face to face with such mature beauty. Needless to say, my tone of voice couldn't have been more genial.

"Say, little friend . . ." I hesitated. Somehow that didn't sound quite right. "Miss, would you mind letting me by?"

She quickly moved aside and watched me carry the box through the door. I put it down and walked back out; she was still there by the door, watching me nervously. I gave her a friendly smile, but to no effect. I took a step toward her and followed her gaze inside the room. I asked her what she wanted.

With an anxious look at me, she squatted down and looked back inside.

"Are you looking for something?" I squatted down beside her. Before she answered me, I spotted a ball resting under the bed inside. "Ah, you've lost your ball."

She nodded but didn't move otherwise.

"Go on in and get it," I said. But still she didn't move. Instead she gazed at me with pleading eyes. She had beautiful eyes, so beautiful, in fact, that I nearly lacked the courage to look directly into them. "Come on," I said as naturally as possible, "I'll help you get it."

I crawled under the bed and retrieved the ball. That was when I noticed that she was wearing regular clothes but still had on her school uniform cap. She wore it pulled tightly down as low as it would go, until the brim nearly covered her eyebrows. The amazement returned. She was truly a beautiful little girl. When I walked up to her with the ball, instead of reaching out eagerly to take it, like most kids would, she actually shrank back a bit, her eyes glued to the ball in my hands, as if fearful I might not give it back.

"Could you stick around here for a while and watch the place for me?" I still hadn't given back the ball, which she gazed at uneasily. "Just a little while," I said as I handed her the ball.

She took it from me timidly, without a word, before lowering her head, turning slowly, and running away. I watched her run a few steps, then was reminded of Lin Zaifa, who must be wondering what was keeping me. I hurried off.

As soon as Lin Zaifa saw me round the corner, he picked up a packing box and walked toward me. That was how we'd agreed to do it, the only way to ensure we didn't lose any boxes. As we passed each other, I could tell that he was unhappy about how slowly I was moving the boxes. But when we passed each other the next time—me carrying a box, him returning empty-handed—he said excitedly, "There's a gorgeous little girl standing in our doorway!"

"She's still there?"

"You've already seen her?"

"Uh-huh." I laughed and walked on with my box.

Our annoyance was replaced by happiness, thanks to Xiaoqi. Lin Zaifa and I arrived virtually simultaneously at the same conclusion: Xiaoqi was a little bird easily frightened, so in order not to be deprived of her presence, we kept our questions to her to an absolute minimum. She didn't respond anyway.

After we'd finished moving all the boxes, I asked her her name, and not just once. She was too bashful to tell me.

"We're finished. Thank you," I said.

She turned and walked off.

Lin Zaifa said, "We ought to give her a little something."

My thoughts exactly. I called out to her, then ran inside to search through my carryall for a semicircular seashell. It was something I'd found on the beach while I was in the army on the Pescadores Islands. Over a long period of time, I had painstakingly but not very artistically carved a pot-bellied Buddha in the shell. I liked it in spite of its crude workmanship and took it with me wherever I went. I held out to her my little treasure, which she accepted after taking a long look at it. I was disappointed that she didn't accept it with a squeal of delight, and I said to her with warmhearted seriousness, almost as if I were having second thoughts:

"If you look closely, you'll see a fat Buddha with smiling eyes." She studied it with no discernible expression. So I pointed with my finger. "This is his belly button, but I pressed down too hard and punched a hole right through it." I took the shell from her and held it up to my eye. "I can see you through his belly button."

Finally she laughed.

"I want you to have it."

She took it from me, obviously happy.

We saw her again the next day.

I got out of bed and opened the door in time to see a crowd of children hurrying off to school. So I bent down to put on my shoes and go looking for Lin Zaifa, just as Xiaoqi came running in, laid the seashell down on the table, turned, and ran out. It all happened so fast that if not for the seashell I might not have known who it was. With one sandal on and the other only half on, I ran to the doorway, where I saw the rapidly retreating back of a little girl in a student's uniform. It had to be Xiaoqi. Once the back disappeared from view, disappointment set in, and I sat down on the edge of the bed to nurse an inexplicable sadness and gaze at the seashell on the table. Only by strength of willpower was I able to control my impulse to pick it up and smash it. And that display of willpower allowed me to calmly examine the source of my annoyance. Obviously, this wasn't unrequited love. Though I was able to reject any linkage between my brief dealings with this little girl and the word "love," I had to laugh nonetheless. But what part of me was laughing? Was it the calm side? Or was it a bitter laugh from my impulsive side? After a moment of depression, I managed to figure things out. Xiaoqi's family, or maybe Xiaoqi herself, had gotten the wrong idea. And that misreading of my intentions was what had made me so unhappy. But after a bit more reflection, I wondered if that was all there was to it.

Some subtle aspect of my psyche warned me to be on guard against certain emotions. I thought it over from every angle but was unable to put these feelings into words. I was, it seemed, someone who derived pleasure from self-imposed mental torture. Just then Lin Zaifa walked in and immediately concluded that I was mad at him.

"I went out to take a look around," he said cautiously. "I haven't eaten yet. Let's go together. There's a shop down the street that sells soy milk." Spotting the seashell on the table, he picked it up and looked it over. "That little girl give this back to you?" He paused. "Maybe it was her family's idea." A look of surprise filled his eyes.

I stood up and laughed. "Let's go. Where's that shop?"

The next morning I saw her again. It was about the same time as the day before. Lin Zaifa and I ran into her just outside the door as we were on our way to breakfast. But before I had time to think what I wanted to say to her, she ran off in a panic. She was really beginning to annoy me.

"No sesame-seed cake or oil fritter for you?" Lin Zaifa asked me.

"No, just a bowl of soy milk."

"You can't go without breakfast."

I just shook my head.

"One sesame-seed cake and an oil fritter and two bowls of soy milk," Lin Zaifa said to the shop assistant. "Put a raw egg in one." Then he turned and said to me, "The one with the egg's for you. Will that be enough?"

"That's fine."

The momentary silence that followed was broken by Lin Zaifa, who smiled and said, careful not to lead to any misunderstanding, "Wang Wuxiong, now don't get mad when I say that you're like a little boy, I mean simple and uncomplicated. You're a good person, did anyone ever tell you that?"

I smiled back.

"A good person? Not in the eyes of that little girl. That's why she runs away every time she sees me." I paused before going on. "Let's not talk about this anymore. Let's talk about our Takada pressure cookers instead."

"What's that?" He laughed. "My dear young fellow, after all this time you still don't know that the name of the pressure cookers you're trying to sell is Takeda, not Takada? It's Takeda. . . ."

I laughed at my foolish mistake. So did he. Several of the other diners turned to us with peculiar looks.

"Now how about a sesame-seed cake and an oil fritter?"

"Only if you'll add an egg to your soy milk."

The little girl didn't show up on the fourth day, and I put her out of my mind.

Then, on the fifth day, we knocked off early, so tired we lay down to rest almost immediately, just as the children were on their way home from school. Lin Zaifa and I were chatting casually when I saw the outline of a figure at the door. At first I ignored it. But after it had passed by the door several times, I sat up to get a better look. It was a couple of elementary school students; they turned and ran as soon as I sat up.

"It's a couple of kids," I said to Lin Zaifa. I got up and walked to the door.

"I know, I saw them."

I spotted her and one of her schoolmates trying to hide just beyond the doorway. She was hunkering down behind the other girl; they were both giggling.

"What do you want?" I asked with a smile.

She kept giggling as her schoolmate turned around and nudged her. "Go ahead, say it, go on!"

She straightened up and said bashfully, "My daddy told me not to accept gifts from strangers."

"Oh!" I didn't know what to say at first, so I sort of froze. Finally I said, "You're a good little girl who does what she's told."

"She said," the little girl who came with her said, "she wants to see the shell."

"It was you," she argued. "You're the one who said she wants to see it."

I quickly went in to get the shell, which I handed to them. The girl with her took it from me. She roared with laughter when she saw the carving.

"See, I wasn't lying."

"What are you two laughing at?" I knew they were laughing at the Laughing Buddha's belly button, but I wanted to hear them say it.

"Don't say it!" she blurted out. Which only made her schoolmate laugh harder.

"What's your name?" I slyly asked her schoolmate, since Xiaoqi hadn't told me her name when I'd asked her earlier.

"Zhang Caiyun."

"What about you?" I asked Xiaoqi in turn. She didn't answer, so I asked Zhang Caiyun.

"Don't tell him!" she said. But too late.

"Li Xiaoqi."

"Big mouth!"

And so, finally, I knew her name.

After that, we saw her nearly every day, and her fear of me had vanished. But our work kept us so busy, there were few opportunities to talk with her. Most of the time we simply ran into her on her way to school.

Then one evening, knowing I wasn't taking any risk, since Lin Zaifa understood me as well as anyone, I said, "You know, it's strange, but it makes me feel good to see Li Xiaoqi. But when I see her in one of her happy moods, there's this aching feeling that life hasn't been good to her."

"How's that?"

"I don't know, something tragic." I looked him in the eye and continued, "I don't know if you can understand my feeling."

"I think," he said, as if giving this serious thought, "I think I understand it. In fact, I kind of feel the same way."

"You see!" Then I said in a soft voice, "I didn't see her today, and I can't help worrying that something's happened to her."

"Now don't get carried away," Lin Zaifa said with a little laugh.

The next morning we stood in the doorway looking up and down the street. She came walking along in her school uniform and cap, her schoolbag over her back. I called out to her, "Li Xiaoqi, where'd you go yesterday?"

"To lay a wreath," she answered over her shoulder.

Strange as it sounds, I realized how happy that made me. But what really surprised me was the realization that my moods over the past several days had been, to some extent at least, tied to whether or not Xiaoqi showed up. No wonder Lin Zaifa was always teasing me about my ten-year plan.

The more I thought about things, the more energized I felt; I was too wide awake to sleep. I looked at Lin Zaifa, who was bent over the desk, ballpoint pen in hand, single-mindedly writing away. I saw it was already past eleven o'clock, and, sleepy or not, I needed to get some rest. Over the past couple of days, we'd gone out separately, which was much more exhausting than going out together. Besides, we had a new strategy for the next day that was going to be even harder on us.

"Hey there, Director, let's get some sleep!"

"In a minute." He looked up. "Good, you're not asleep. We can go over our plans for tomorrow. Here, let me read my report to the company for you. Tell me if there are any problems."

"Go ahead," I said as I lay there.

"We want to substitute action for talk, since actions speak louder than words. So we plan to change our sales methods by bringing several housewives together for live demonstrations of our pressure cooker. By letting them see with their own eyes how we can cook up a bowl of tasty rice in ten minutes, stew a meal of pig's feet in twenty minutes . . ."

Lin Zaifa read with such feeling I couldn't help but laugh.

"Is there a problem?" He stopped.

"Keep reading, it's very good. No problem."

He looked for his place in the report, then continued reading.

"If someone will let us use their living room, we can probably fit in twenty people or so. We can give the hostess a little something for the use of her living room, say fifty Taiwan dollars. Then, after the pressure cooker's done its job, we can treat them to a meal on the spot . . ."

"Hold on a minute," I interrupted. "The company has to reimburse us for everything we spend."

"I say that toward the end." He continued reading, all the way down to the spot where he mentioned the budget. He stopped and stressed, "Pay attention, now, here is where I talk about the budget. Twenty dollars for rice, forty for pig's feet, fifty for use of the living room, and ten for seasoning. Altogether one-twenty. Double that for the two of us, and you come up with two-forty. This plan of mine is limited to Sundays. Well, that's about it; what do you think?"

"I think there's not enough for rice or pig's feet. What you have will take you through the morning. But what about the afternoon?"

"You're right! We'll double the amount for rice and pig's feet. And we'll need a second location, so we'll double the amount for use of the room."

"Wow! Now you're talking about four hundred and eighty dollars! You think the company will go for it?"

"Who cares? We'll try it out tomorrow. If they don't approve it, we'll scrap the whole idea. It's for the good of the company, after all!"

"Okay, now let's get some sleep. We've got some shopping to do tomorrow morning."

"You go to sleep. I haven't quite finished yet."

We were up bright and early the next morning. After buying the pig's feet, we each started debristling the ones we were going to take with us. He finished both of his before I'd finished one. But I refused his offer of help and told him not to wait for me while I kept plucking.

"I'm leaving, Wang Wuxiong," he said from the doorway.

I looked up to see him with his bicycle, the pair of pig's feet hanging from his handlebars, a funny sight. He flashed me a smile, then said, "Today's the day!"

That comment introduced a note of high seriousness. I waved to him as he rode off. I was fed up with this rinky-dink job but still found it sort of laughable. This was my first time. But sometimes there are jobs you're just fed up with but still find laughable. Even though I am always interested in new work experiences, it was becoming increasingly difficult to resist an upsurge of dejection. As I continued plucking bristles, I was afraid I'd have to do more of the same in the future. From now on, if we were going to stew something, I wouldn't use pig's feet, even if Lin Zaifa opposed the use of beef. He said beef was a lot more expensive and that eating it was taboo in some places in Taiwan. When I'd suggested using beef, it wasn't because I'd discovered the difficulties in using pig's feet. I was halfway through the second pig's foot, but that last half seemed to be taking an eternity. One bristle, then another; I was starting to see spots. On the other hand, perhaps because I was mad at having to do such a boring job, I plucked each hair with so much force that my pincer-holding fingers were sore. I put the pig's foot aside to light a cigarette. When I straightened up, I caught sight of Xiaoqi standing across the alley. I thought she was waiting for someone; she looked like she was, looking at both ends of the alley.

"Xiaoqi," I called out happily. She smiled at me. "Come over here."

She came over, still her usual self, not daring to look at people, so she immediately fixed her eyes on the pig's foot on the ground.

"Who are you waiting for?" I asked.

She shook her head, casting a quick glance at me before staring again at the pig's foot.

"Do you know how to pluck hairs on a pig's foot?"

She smiled at me and looked away hurriedly.

"My fingers are sore from plucking the hair. Could you help me out a bit?"

As she squatted down, she carefully straightened her skirt, under which she concealed her knees, showing only her feet clad in plastic slippers and considerable poise. She quietly picked up the pig's foot and plucked the hairs one by one with the pair of pincers. She actually wasn't working faster than I, but she did it in an even-tempered and calm way. I chatted with her as I smoked, but it was mostly me talking with an occasional response from her.

"When I finish this cigarette, I'll do the rest." I said. I noticed her cap
again. It was a Sunday and she wasn't wearing her uniform, but she was
still wearing the cap that went with it, just like the first day I came to
the small town. She wore it very low and tight, with the brim pressing
against her eyebrows. I thought she would look even more beautiful
without it. As I thought about it, my hand started to move, an action
that not just she but even I myself was unconscious of. I took off her cap
with a swift move of my hand. Just within that brief moment, dramatic
changes occurred that made me nearly pass out. I saw almost nothing
except for bare scalp, but I was never sure, for I only remember Xiaoqi
let out a terrifying shriek while she pounced forward to snatch back her
cap. She didn't have time to put it back on; pressing it onto her head, she
ran back home, crying all the way. Her crying sounded so sad it was
scary. I followed her to the alley outside and called her several times. But
she ran faster and faster, and then she disappeared at a street corner. A
few people ran out of the alley to take a look, but I didn't care what they
might think about me.

I kept calling Xiaoqi and running, when I was brought to a sudden
stop by a thought. Xiaoqi must be terrified of me by now, and she would
run faster and panic even more when she heard me calling her. She would
be scared to death if I caught up with her. But my crude and rash
behavior had made her so sad that I couldn't just let it go like that.
Standing there for a while, not knowing what to do, I finally mustered
enough courage to apologize to Xiaoqi, prepared to accept any consequence. As I took two leaden steps forward, a chill rose from my heart
and plunged me into an extremely unsettled state. I thought I wouldn't
have the courage to face her even if she weren't afraid of seeing me, even
if she could accept my apology. In fact, I wasn't concerned that Xiaoqi or
her father wouldn't calmly and openly accept my apology; on the contrary, I wished they would curse me in anger or her father would hit me
so I could feel at ease with myself. But obviously the fundamental question was how to make up for my mistake. That was how I felt, and I
believed that was how Xiaoqi felt, even if she couldn't explain it. The
problem was, I had accidentally destroyed something perfect, and there
was nothing I could do to reverse that.

I returned to the room. As soon as I stepped in I saw the pair of pig's
feet, one on the newspaper, the other lying on the ground. The sight
immediately drew my attention back to the real world. I knew I could no
longer face Xiaoqi, so I had to leave the small town. That was okay with

me, since I could give up the job of selling pressure cookers. I hadn't realized until that moment that I had always hated the job. My dislike for it was stronger now than at any other time. But the scariest thing was, though I never liked the job, I had stayed with it for two weeks. If not for what had happened that day, I might actually have continued with the job. On the other hand, today's cooking demonstration might turn out to be a big success and in turn make the job something important in my life.

I laid my limp body down on Lin Zaifa's bottom bunk bed and continued my jumbled thoughts. I was well aware of the influence Lin Zaifa had over me, for my disgust at the job would have manifested itself early on and I'd have already quit if I'd worked with someone else. But today even Lin Zaifa couldn't affect me; no one in this world could change my attitude toward this job. I didn't want to do it anymore; I wanted to get away from there. Lin Zaifa would be very unhappy, but there was nothing I could do.

I didn't have the energy or the will to get up. Thoughts were churning swiftly in my jumbled mind; I thought about lots of things but could never forget Xiaoqi, her face, her eyes, her cap, and her scalp with its multihued scars. Every time I thought about her, I turned around in agony. I was prepared for Lin Zaifa's return, prepared to quit, prepared to leave this town. But my most urgent task was to face Xiaoqi's seething father, the coastal defense officer I'd seen walking with her the other day. I was counting time until the appearance of a father who would come to find justice for his daughter. I longed for all this to pass, no matter how embarrassing or how painful it might be. I had no intention of trying to escape. But in that mood, time moved more slowly than usual, and it was a long time before half an hour had passed. I didn't know where Xiaoqi lived, but it couldn't take that long to go from one end of the town to the other. It was about time they showed up. I felt an unknown anxiety. I wondered what to say or do as I faced her father. The most I could say would be, "I didn't mean it, I'm sorry, really sorry." Perhaps I wouldn't be able to utter a word. Hearing someone walking by outside stretched my nerves really thin. If they didn't show up soon, I would collapse from the anxiety caused by people passing through the alley.

*Ah, here they are!* I cried out inside. I quickly sat up and got ready to stand, when I saw it was a mailman, the light behind him. Sitting on his bicycle, he threw in a letter before he pushed his feet against the ground and set off for next door. I picked up the letter, another one for Lin Zaifa. I wasn't expecting mail, since I had just written a letter home two days ago, saying that everything was fine with me and that my job was okay. Now that letter had become a huge lie to my family. I hadn't written to any of my utility pole–counting friends, so they didn't have my address, and I knew they might not write even if they did. I didn't think there were many people like Lin Zaifa's wife, who wrote letters so frequently. He got about one letter every two days. But today's was an express letter. I discovered it was only half sealed as I took a closer look. Laying it down on the table, I was thinking about going to the door to look around but was afraid I might just run into Xiaoqi and her father, so I returned to lie in bed. Lin Zaifa would be very sad when I told him I'd be leaving. This would be a big blow to him. Before he'd left that morning, he'd said, "Today's the day!" He was, of course, talking about our work, but he hadn't thought that what he said had a coincidental double meaning.

I was getting more and more nervous; I could no longer stay lying down, so I got up and started to pace around the room. Since I couldn't walk from right to left, I paced in and out. I felt all right when I paced in but got really nervous every time I paced out.

Another half hour passed, and still no trace of them. My gaze constantly fell on the letter on the table as I paced in and out. The red strip of paper indicating express mail, pasted alongside the stamp, was particularly conspicuous. What urgent matter would require express delivery? As I thought this I picked up the letter to take a look, then threw it back down. It was getting harder and harder to wait. I wanted to take the initiative and turn what must happen quickly into a thing of the past. I wanted to go look for Lin Zaifa and give him the letter. As I put on my shoes and placed the letter in my pocket, it suddenly occurred to me that they wouldn't find me if they came while I was out. Then it would be an even greater misunderstanding. In their eyes, I would become a coward. I didn't dare go out now. Feeling very tired, I collapsed in bed as before, suffocating little by little.

Perhaps it was because I was psychologically trying to divert my attention to reduce my anxiety, but strangely, I found myself drawn to the half-sealed letter. I took it out of my pocket and stared blankly at it. Lin Zaifa never hid anything about his wife from me, and he never tired of relating the little details in her letters. He had always been so sincere that I believed he wouldn't object to my reading a letter from his wife.

Encouraged by Lin Zaifa's attitude, I carefully and slowly peeled open the half-sealed letter, which I would reseal after reading it. I unfolded it.

Zaifa:

I'm so scared. I didn't want to tell you before, but I've thought long and hard about this, and have decided I should let you know. Yesterday, as I was leaving the beauty shop, I tripped and fell. I was bleeding down there when I got home. I hurried to get a shot at the hospital. The doctor said he couldn't find anything wrong and that I should come see him if I bled again the next day. When I got up this morning I didn't feel anything unusual in my belly. It didn't hurt last night either, but there were traces of blood. I'm scared; I'm going to see the doctor. I know we're both looking for- ward to having the baby next month. Zaifa, you just got this job and it can't be easy to ask for leave. But I've been so afraid that I really need you here. Please forgive my unreasonable request. Didn't you say that Mr. Wang, your co-worker, has been very nice to you? Please ask him to take over for you for a couple of days. We'll repay him in the future. Thank him for me.

*Wish you*
*Peace*

*Your Meili.*

My God! I muttered as I finished the letter. I became even more agi- tated after reading it. I wanted to go look for Lin Zaifa but was afraid Xiaoqi and her father would be wasting their time when they came to reason with me. On the other hand, I'd be letting Lin Zaifa down if I didn't go find him. So I took out Meili's letter, trying to make a decision by mulling over what she said. There was one phrase that put my mind at ease somewhat, and I believed I could use it to comfort Lin Zaifa: "When I got up this morning I didn't feel anything unusual in my belly. It didn't hurt last night either." I believed that Mrs. Lin felt worse than her actual condition warranted. So I decided to stick around and wait for Xiaoqi's angry father. But it had been two hours; why weren't they here yet? Maybe he was on duty and couldn't get away at the moment. On the other hand, would it hold up something major if my judgment of the letter were overoptimistic? Now I really regretted reading it. If I didn't know anything, I could have just let things run their course. But now that I'd read it, I couldn't act as if I hadn't. I wanted to go look for him but was afraid that I was making a big deal out of a trivial matter, that my one-time, impulsive behavior might make my good friend doubt my integrity. All this was agonizing, and I didn't know what to do. It was a terrifying feeling to delay action because I was unable to make up my mind.

Deciding to smoke, I lay in bed, puffing on one cigarette after another. Suddenly a man in military uniform and hat walked in; I could see him clearly even though I was facing the door, the light in my eyes. I jumped to my feet nervously. When he came closer I discovered he was a policeman. I was upset to see that the police were involved in this matter.

"Are you Wang Wuxiong?" The policeman looked at a card.

"I, I'm Wang Wuxiong." I was terrified.

"Is Lin Zaifa your director?"

"Yes. What's wrong?"

"Ai!" he sighed. "Something is very wrong."

I held my heart in my hand, waiting for him to finish while I prayed for protection from Heaven above.

"This morning when Lin Zaifa was demonstrating pressure cookers to some women at a house in Minlo Lin, a pressure cooker exploded, killing three and injuring several. . . ."

"What about Lin Zaifa?" I asked anxiously.

"I'm afraid he's in great danger. A broken piece pierced his neck, and he was blinded. Ai!" He sighed again.

"Where is he now?" I forced myself to ask.

"They're all in the county hospital. You'll have to go to the hospital and the station house in a while."

"Can we go now?"

"Where are your pressure cookers?"

I pointed at the cardboard boxes piled up like a wall behind me and said, "Over there."

"Good. We've got to seal them up temporarily." He opened his briefcase and flipped through the paper seals as he took another look at the boxes. "So many boxes! I don't have enough seals."

"Tell you what: there are ninety-nine boxes, including this one on the floor. Why don't you write a note and I'll sign. I'm anxious to see Lin Zaifa."

"Okay." He took out a piece of paper and started to write.

Holding the letter from Meili, I worried about her. Then I thought about myself. It was hard to believe but impossible to deny that within the space of a single morning so much had happened. *My God! My God!* I kept crying in my mind.

After signing the paper, I climbed on the back of the policeman's motorbike. Tears started to run down my face on the way to the county hospital in the next town. Then I thought about that morning, when Lin Zaifa had turned around before leaving to say, "Today's the day!" Yes, today was indeed the day. But what kind of godforsaken day was it?

When we got to the hospital gate, the policeman took his motorbike over to storage as I stood there taking time to prepare myself. At that moment, I lacked the courage to move. I saw the policeman walking toward me from a distance and was afraid to go in with him. Then I thought about Meili's letter, so I took it out of my pocket and held it in my palm. At that instant a brief but determined thought came into my head: if Lin Zaifa died, I'd marry Meili. I knew many people would consider my idea absurd; some might even say I was despicable. But I didn't care. If Lin Zaifa died, what would Meili and the baby do? I'd try my best to convince her to marry me. My tears were coming down faster now. Then the policeman came up to me and said, "Let's go in!"

I followed him silently, no longer afraid.

# The Two Sign Painters

o

I

Following revisions in the building code, the eleven-story Insurance Building was no longer the tallest structure in Qishan, a city lying along an earthquake fault surrounded by volcanoes.

The twenty-four-story Silver Star Hotel rose steeply on the southwest corner of Shengsen Avenue where it crossed the Aibei River, completely occupying the former grounds of the Jipeng Middle School. A huge wall facing east paralleled the west side of the road that ran alongside the Aibei River. Though it had been built slowly, brick by brick, by the time the wall reached its final, massive proportions, it gave the impression of having suddenly appeared out of nowhere.

It also created an illusion for people in cars crossing the Shengsen Bridge from the train station, for the moment they began their descent of the span, this massive gray wall ahead seemed about to topple over on them, and that made their hearts tremble. After having experienced this once, they would mentally prepare themselves for the sight, yet the next time they actually came down off the bridge, a momentary panic would seize them. People to whom this happened often would unmindfully look up at the massive gray wall with vague, helpless grins on their faces.

Before long, there was more activity at the wall: the Jishi Cola Company decided to make use of it by painting a seminude mural of VV, the most popular starlet of the day, to advertise their product. The job was commissioned to the Giant Sign Painting Company, which in the past had only done five- or six-story-tall ads and had painted the names of factories on chimneys. The company was banking all its capital and technical expertise on this one big job.

It took two full weeks for Giant to complete the white base coat, only to discover that legal action was being taken against it. Newspaper reports said that the three-hundred-plus families who lived opposite the wall had signed a petition, complaining that once the wall turned white, it was as if their homes, which faced west, were now facing east, for they were blinded by the early morning glare of the sun's rays off the wall. One of the families was suing the company, alleging that one morning as the grandfather was pointing his cane at the wall and swearing, covering his eyes with his other hand, he suddenly collapsed in a faint and never regained consciousness. The newspaper report concluded with the observation that the wall seemed to be a living object.

2

Ah-li and Monkey were suspended at the seventeenth story. They'd been working on VV's huge breasts for three or four days without making much headway. Monkey brushed on the paint mechanically and evenly, an old folk song from eastern Taiwan on his lips. How many times had he sung that same song since starting work? Over and over he sang it, with such enthusiasm that one would think he could keep it up until nightfall. Ah-li was sick of hearing that song and thought of telling him to stop, but that's as far as he went—thinking about it, never bothering to actually say anything.

Although the white base coat had drawn complaints from the residents opposite the wall, the two men, who were wearing sunglasses as they worked, noticed nothing out of the ordinary.

But once they began to apply color they could no longer wear their sunglasses. The heat of the sun beat down on their backs, its glare reflecting off the painted wall into their eyes; not a drop remained in their water bottles, and the water in their bodies oozed out through their pores, dripping to the ground below or evaporating in the air. Getting another drink of water was not going to be easy. In the three days since they'd been applying color, they'd lost their appetites for everything but guzzling down tea and water. Their bodies had turned dark in the sun, the pounds melting away.

What distressed Ah-li the most was the job before him. They were supposed to be painting VV's breasts, but who could tell? The breasts alone were several stories tall; the two men were plastered up against the wall endlessly slapping on paint, until finally they began to wonder just what they were doing up there. Bucketful after bucketful of paint went onto the wall, but when they looked back, they could see several white spots showing through the places they had just covered so evenly. In the past, whenever they'd put on a base coat, they'd always used a brush to smooth out the rough surface of the wall first. But this time they'd sprayed the base coat on to save time, with the result that the roughness of the wall showed through all too clearly. By the time the boss realized the seriousness of the problem, it was too late. It had taken them several days just to paint the rounded outlines, and now that it was time to start adding the color, they'd just have to use a little more paint and a little more time.

Ah-li's vision was getting blurred. Each brush stroke took great effort, but he was still unable to tell at a glance how the wall looked. Working like this made him feel that he was being cheated and that he was cheating himself. Sometimes it seemed to him that a spell had been cast on him, that he was engaged in a meaningless struggle in a vast, illusory fantasy world. Not far from him, Monkey kept on with the same folk song, though now he was only humming the tune. It still got on Ah-li's nerves. He felt like telling Monkey to shut up, but then he decided to let him continue a while longer.

If he didn't stop soon, though, maybe he'd tell him. He finally just stopped what he was doing and watched Monkey. The man acted as if he was having an easy time of it, his brush never stopping. Ah-li would have loved to know what was going on in Monkey's mind. He looked up above him, then down below; there were more than twenty men on the wall, each of them steadily manning his brush. *Aren't they also wondering what they're doing up here? And the boss told me that since I do such good work, I'm responsible for painting the breasts.* The boss had said that they were the hardest to do and were the essence of this particular ad. He had put his hands up to his chest and made the motions of giving a woman's breasts a hard squeeze. The men standing around waiting for their work assignments had had a big laugh over this, producing an embarrassed look on the face of Ah-li, the man assigned to paint the breasts. He couldn't tell for a moment whether they were laughing with him or at him. Monkey was laughing the hardest of anyone. So when the boss had said that he could choose his own assistant, he had unhesitatingly picked Monkey, though Monkey had loudly protested—"No, no . . ."

The sight of Monkey wielding his brush alongside him now struck Ah-li as funny. Somewhere along the line he had picked up his brush and started painting again, and the bucket was soon empty. He hooked it onto the rope, then gave a few tugs as a sign to the men below. The empty bucket was slowly lowered to the ground. The few puffs on a cigarette he could manage while the refilled paint bucket was being hauled back up would constitute his rest break. He lit a cigarette and reflected on what the boss had said. *Good work? How was my work good? On such a ridiculously large thing as this, what difference could "good work" make?*

Monkey had stopped singing his folk song for a moment, but now he started up again. Ah-li couldn't imagine what was so great about a folk song that the man could sing it for hours on end without ever growing tired of it. Both he and Monkey were from eastern Taiwan, and this was an old song from their district. Although it gave him a warm feeling, he had grown sick of hearing Monkey sing it today. But as Monkey picked it up again, the irritable feeling Ah-li had had when he was about to tell him to stop a moment before surprisingly disappeared. He was amused by the sight Monkey presented. Before he knew it, he had begun singing along with Monkey, who turned with a smile on his face, nodding at him as he sang loudly to let him hear the correct melody and help him over the unfamiliar lyrics. Ah-li paused momentarily to listen to Monkey and quickly got the hang of it. For reasons he couldn't comprehend, this filled him with a refreshing happiness. Monkey in turn was delighted by the happy look on Ah-li's face.

"So you sing too?" Monkey edged his way over next to Ah-li.

"I caught it from you," Ah-li said with a smile.

"I thought maybe you were a mute or something."

"Don't make fun of me, all right?"

"You know yourself that these last few days you've been like a zombie, not saying anything and not eating. Every time I saw that scowl on your face I wanted to come over and slug you."

"Slug away."

"Don't think I won't," Monkey responded. "You wait and see."

Ah-li merely sighed.

"What good does it do to sigh? You ought to tell your mother the truth."

"Did you read my letter?" Ah-li was a little shocked.

"Didn't have to. The same old problem, isn't it?"

"You really didn't read it?"

"Who the hell wants to read your letter?"

"I'm not calling you a liar." He suddenly felt that there was no need to give an explanation. "You know, there's really no way I can send it this month. I borrow two hundred dollars from you every month and I've never paid any of it back. It's been over a year now. How much do I owe you?"

"Whose idea was it to tell her you made two thousand a month?"

"If I didn't tell her that, she'd want me to go back and work on the farm!"

"Yeah, but just think: there's a big difference between twelve hundred and two thousand!"

They were silent for a moment, then Monkey continued. "You still ought to tell her the truth."

"No!" Ah-li shouted, terror-stricken.

"Then what are you going to do? You only make twelve hundred a month, and if you send five hundred of it home, how are you going to live? What choice do you have?" Monkey looked at the downcast Ah-li, then offered, "I'll tell her if you don't want to."

"Don't worry about your money. I'll pay you back sooner or later." For some mysterious reason Ah-li was angry.

Monkey was hurt by this. He turned to move away, then stopped and said in measured tones, "Ah-li, if we weren't old friends, I wouldn't take that kind of talk from you." Then he moved off, humming the folk song as though nothing had happened.

Ah-li had regretted the words as soon as they were out of his mouth, and hearing Monkey say they were old friends made him feel even worse. He couldn't quite muster the courage to apologize, although several times he came close. He attacked VV's breasts with his brush. He couldn't recall when he'd first begun to be so afraid of his mother. At the mere mention of her name, he could picture her tear-streaked face as the words poured out. "You shouldn't treat me this way! When your father died, you were only three and your sister was two. . . ." He wouldn't let his thoughts go any further. He felt very, very guilt-ridden. *But what can I do?* Her letter had stated point-blank that they really needed a cart for transporting things and she wanted him to send a thousand dollars home, since she'd already put down a two-hundred-dollar deposit. This was what was on his mind, and he felt like going over and telling Monkey that this time his mother wanted a thousand, not five hundred. He figured that his friend might forgive him when he heard that. As he looked over at Monkey, he desperately hoped he'd turn around. There was no discernible expression on his profile, and it was impossible to judge his mood merely from the way he was singing.

Before Ah-li had used up a third of his last bucket of paint, it was time to knock off for the day. The other men began edging their way carefully along the wall. He continued to apply the paint, one brushful after the other, again feeling that a spell had been cast on him and that he was in a vast fantasy world, engaged in an endless struggle.

Monkey moved over and asked, "Want to call it a day?"

"I still have more than half a bucket left."

Monkey picked up a brush and began to work alongside him. Ah-li was fervently hoping that Monkey would keep talking so he could explain things to him. But Monkey remained silent, and Ah-li grew impatient. "What are you thinking?" he suddenly blurted out.

"What's there to think about?"

"Are you still mad?"

Monkey looked over at Ah-li, then said rather helplessly, a pained smile on his face, "I've got problems too, you know. You don't feel any worse than I do. You believe me?"

"Haven't you been singing all day?"

"This kind of work makes you feel miserable. It's terrible. After a few days of painting like this, you start to go a little crazy. I'm not even sure now just what it is I'm painting."

"You're painting VV's breasts!" Ah-li was secretly pleased—Monkey was just like him after all.

"Aw, come on! 'VV's breasts' is what everyone says, but I'm not sure we can really paint anything like that." Monkey took a vicious swipe with his brush.

"I thought all along you were having a great time, the way you were singing."

"What else can I do? Cry?"

"Then why have you been singing our hometown folk song about the centipede, the toad, and the snake?"

"I don't know. That's just the one that came to mind."

"Homesick?"

"Are you kidding? You can be sure I'd never miss that place in eight lifetimes. I made a promise I'd never again set foot on the land my uncle shit on."

"But you've been singing the same song all afternoon."

"Yeah! Funny, isn't it? Once I started singing, it was like I was hooked on it and couldn't quit. I stopped and gave myself hell a couple of times, but before I knew it I was humming the same song again. I don't know what damned power it had over me. The more I tried not to sing it, the more it kept popping into my head, until I couldn't stop singing. Hai! Funny, ain't it?"

"I thought you were happy."

"Happy?" Monkey nearly shouted.

"I tell you, if we keep painting like this, I don't know who's gonna flip his lid first."

"You can't take it anymore either?" Monkey seemed surprised.

"You have to ask? Who could take something like this?" He slopped on some paint with disgust. "What . . . what . . . what are we doing here?"

"What do you suggest we do?" Monkey started slopping the paint on like Ah-li was doing.

"What *can* we do? Paint! Who the hell cares how it turns out, as long as they remember to pay us when it's finished!"

"Don't mention money. As soon as I hear the word I get a funny feeling all over. We've worked for Giant Sign Painting Company for two or three years now, and it's been a year and a half since they raised our pay to twelve hundred. Do you know how much the eleven temporary workers hired for this job are making?"

"Do you?"

"A hundred a day."

"That much?" This came as a shock to Ah-li. "How do you know?"

"One of them told me."

"That's ridiculous. What does that make us?"

"Now you know!"

A little paint remained in the bucket, which the two of them carelessly slopped onto the wall.

"Let's go," Monkey said.

"Go where?"

"Down!"

Ah-li thought for a moment. "Let's go up."

"What for?"

"We're on our own time. Let's go sit up on top."

"What about the brushes and buckets?"

"Take them with us."

They cautiously climbed onto the top of the scaffold.

"Let's just sit here," Ah-li said.

"Since we're on our way up, why stop here? We might as well go all the way to the roof."

"There's nothing up there."

"So what? Let's go! Follow me. There are some girders sticking out over there. We can climb on them."

"Take it easy. Don't fall, that'd be a waste."

"If you fall, your mother won't get a penny," Monkey teased.

"Stop talking and watch where you're going!"

"No problem," Monkey responded confidently.

"Here, hand me your bucket." Ah-li took the bucket and watched Monkey climb. "Secure that rope. No, on your right."

Monkey made it to the top. "Here, give me the buckets."

Ah-li turned and looked down to the street. "Wow! We're out over the Aibei River!"

"Come on up before you look."

"How are we going to get back down?"

"The same way we got up."

"I don't think it's going to be all that easy." Ah-li climbed onto the roof, then looked down at the street. "Wow! If you fell from here, it'd be worse than being in a plane crash."

"Don't keep looking down. Let's just find a place here to sit and talk."

"There's nothing here."

They looked around the unfinished roof of the building. "The wind sure is strong!" Ah-li commented.

Monkey walked over to the front of the building. "Ah-li, let's go up there." He pointed to a thick steel pipe that stuck out some two or three meters and was supported in the middle by another steel pipe that jutted out from the wall at a forty-five-degree angle. A heavy steel mesh construction basket hung from the end of the pipe. Beneath it was nothing but street.

"What?" Ah-li's eyes were wide with wonder. "You mean you want us to climb onto that floodlight?"

"If we climb into that steel basket, that'll make it worth coming up here."

"Forget it. It's too dangerous."

"Dangerous? How do you think they're going to hook up the light there? Come on." Monkey got down and started to crawl over.

"Monkey!" He stopped and looked back at Ah-li. "Let's forget it. What's wrong with just sitting here?"

"It's boring." Monkey started to crawl, then stopped abruptly and said to Ah-li, "Most people consider what we do dangerous, but we don't think so. It's the same thing here. Come on. I'll go first and you follow." With that he slid down, wrapped his arms and legs around the support pipe, and crawled carefully upside down.

"Ah-li, hurry up and come over!" Monkey stood up in the steel basket. "Now this is really something! You won't believe what a thrill it is! Leave the buckets and rope there. When you look out from here, it really seems like you're right over the Aibei River. Come on."

Ah-li hesitated for a moment, not really wanting to do it.

"Don't be such a coward! What do you say?" Monkey shouted.

"Don't call me that. If you say that again, I won't go for sure."

"Okay, okay, I won't say it."

Like Monkey before him, Ah-li wrapped his arms and legs around the steel pipe, thinking that if he were to fall from here, it'd be all over. It was so high! He suddenly felt a chill run down his spine. Then he could hear Monkey—he was singing again, damn him. *He's turned into a singing machine.* He swore at Monkey under his breath as he stole a look down below.

"Yo! Monkey, we really *are* right above the Aibei River!"

"What's wrong with you? Why do you keep looking down from there? Get on over here quick, then you can look all you want!"

"I'm here, aren't I?" Ah-li said with a weak laugh. "You're the one who's scared."

"Stop talking and get over here." Monkey couldn't take his eyes off Ah-li as he crawled.

Ah-li looked down again. *Damn! What the hell am I doing looking down all the time? I wouldn't have noticed if Monkey hadn't mentioned it.* He climbed in. Monkey breathed a sigh of relief and said with a smile, "Well, what do you think? Great, isn't it? Now you can look to your heart's content."

"There are some electric wires here. Wonder if they're hot?"

"Probably not, but don't touch them."

"Think they'll come looking for us?" Ah-li looked down at the steel mesh floor of the basket. He fantasized that he might shrink so small he'd slip right through a hole in the mesh, or else he'd turn into water and drip through.

"Don't be such a damned fool. We're on our own time now, they can't tell us what to do."

Ah-li was still looking down at the street below, his hands gripping the edge of the basket. "Monkey, do you think anyone can see us?" Ah-li spoke in hushed tones, unconsciously fearing that the steel basket was overloaded. Monkey didn't hear him. He tugged on Monkey's clothes, and as Monkey turned around, the steel basket swayed with the shift in weight. "Aiyo! Don't move!" Ah-li seemed afraid to breathe.

The look on Ah-li's face made Monkey laugh. The basket swayed more violently, but now Ah-li wasn't as frightened as he'd been a moment before.

"Monkey," he said calmly, "don't laugh at me like that." Although the basket was still swaying slightly, he kept telling himself not to be afraid. But this forced him to be even more attentive to the movement of the basket. Noticing how serious Ah-li was, Monkey stopped laughing and even felt a little embarrassed.

"Okay, I won't laugh. What did you want to tell me when you tugged on my shirt?"

"I was just wondering if anyone can see us up here."

"What are you afraid of?" Monkey knew at once that this was the wrong thing to say. Ah-li got to his feet, having huddled there in the basket ever since crawling over from the balcony.

"You think I'm a coward. Well, let's just see how brave you are, all right?" He had a wounded look on his face.

Seeing him like this, Monkey knew he'd have to stop making fun of him.

"Not me, not me," he said again. "I wasn't making fun of you."

"You weren't? That's exactly what you *were* doing."

"No no, I swear!" Monkey raised his hand as a sign of his oath, but he presented a ridiculous sight.

Ah-li could barely keep from laughing. "You've got the nerve to swear?"

"I swear. May the pipe holding this basket snap in two if I meant to make fun of you."

That did it—Ah-li burst out laughing.

"Yow! That shows what kind of friend you are! You'd swear another man's life away!"

"I'm in the basket too, you know!"

"You sure are."

"What difference does it make, since we're pals?"

They were both laughing happily by now. Ah-li sensed that the basket was swaying more violently than ever; forcing himself to keep his fear in check, he couldn't stop laughing. He cast a quick glance below when Monkey wasn't looking.

"Look down there," Monkey said.

This threw a fright into Ah-li, who thought that Monkey had noticed him. But Monkey continued, "We're directly above the roadway, so the people and cars down there are closer to us than anyone else. They don't even know we're here. What chance is there that we could be spotted by anyone off in the distance?" Their eyes were riveted to the ground below.

"Look, the people down there are just specks, and the cars are like matchboxes. How could they possibly see us?"

"What do you think, doesn't everything down there on the ground look like the works of a machine? That's it! It looks like the works of a wrist-watch. Some of the parts are big, some are small, some fast, some slow; back and forth they go, each moving in its own sphere. Hey, have you noticed how neat and tidy everything down there looks from up here?"

"Of course it does," Monkey said with a laugh. "Even if a man and a woman were up here stark naked, I'll bet no one would notice."

"Give it a try."

"You try it. You first."

"I didn't say it."

They laughed again.

"You're afraid someone might see, aren't you?" Monkey asked.

"You mean afraid they'd come up and stop us?"

"Never happen."

Ah-li paused a moment to think, then said, "I wonder what my mother would do if she saw me up here."

"I think she'd probably faint."

"Let's drop the subject—it bores me."

"Got any cigarettes?" asked Monkey as he searched his own pockets.

Ah-li took out a pack and handed him a cigarette. They lit up and lapsed into silence. Finally Monkey pointed over to the train station and said, "The train from our hometown is about due at the station."

Ah-li looked off into the distance to see the train slowly pulling in.

"How long have we been here?" Monkey asked in a muffled voice. "I've always hated figuring out time."

"What?" Ah-li couldn't make out what Monkey was saying. He too was speaking in muffled tones.

"What I said was, how long has it been since we left home and came to Qishan? It's been a long time, hasn't it?" Monkey took a long puff on his cigarette. "It's gone by so fast. We arrived at just about this time of day. I remember it turned dark soon after we stepped off the train."

"It's been two years and seven months."

"That long?"

"You figure it out. When do the anemones bloom at home? You remember you told me to meet you early in the morning in the clump of anemones behind the temple? I waited so long for you to show up that I'd picked almost all the flowers on the riverbank. When you finally did show up you told me your uncle had lost back all the money he'd won two days before and had even lost your aunt's bracelet in the game, so there hadn't been any money for you to steal." Ah-li paused before continuing. "I asked you 'What are we going to do?' and you answered me by asking the same question." They laughed.

"Damned if you don't have a good memory."

"At the time, we made plans to sign on as deckhands on the boat my uncle worked on. But then I asked how we were going to get to Qishan on the little money we had between us. What would be left after we bought the train tickets?"

"No problem! Didn't you say we could look up your uncle?" Monkey spoke excitedly, his voice filled with confidence and hope.

"That's it! That's just what you said then, and exactly the way you said it. You've got it down perfect!"

Monkey gave Ah-li a heavy slap on the shoulder and laughed heartily. "And then what?"

"And then . . . and then we became sign painters," Ah-li said uneasily.

"Let me tell you what happened." Monkey was watching Ah-li puff incessantly on his cigarette. "We looked for your uncle for three days without finding him, until our money ran out. You said you wanted to go home, and we started to argue. Since we didn't have the money to return home, I said we should keep looking for your uncle. But then you told me you'd never actually seen him, that you'd only heard your mother talk about him. So then we became sign painters and now we've paid our dues. The boss has us working on the biggest painting in the world and has given the two of us the most important part of the whole thing." When Monkey was at his happiest, his laughter sounded like someone pounding a table.

"You said you didn't hold it against me."

"I don't—I'm only trying to be funny."

"It dawned on me recently that there must be lots of young people like us who are treated badly at home and run away to follow some pipe dream."

"Look there! I'll bet there are some on that train. They step down, bundles in hand, mouths agape as they stare blankly all around. That's what they all look like." Monkey was struck by the humor of the scene he'd painted.

"Off the train and onto a ship of thieves."

"What ship of thieves?"

"Once you get on one, you can't get off! You go where it takes you."

"All you know are expressions you've picked up from the old-timers. The other day you used one that I was going to ask you about, but I forgot."

"The old-timers' expressions may be corny, but they say it best."

"What do you mean, say it best?"

"I mean they're right on target!" Ah-li said. "Just leave it at that!"

"How come I'm not aware of that?" Monkey teased him. He flipped his cigarette butt away toward the riverbank. "Give me another one."

"I'm not sure myself, but that doesn't matter." Ah-li fished out another cigarette and continued, "If you told me to go back east and live in the mountains again, I couldn't do it. I don't think I could stand it for a single day." He took out his matches, and since the wind was up, he lit his cigarette first, then took a deep puff. "A cigarette up here sure tastes good." He handed his cigarette to Monkey to light his own off of. "Could you do it?"

"Didn't I already say that I, Monkey, would never again set foot on land where my uncle had shit?" He passed Ah-li's cigarette back.

"That's not what I mean." But he didn't know how to express what he meant. "The first time I went home, they treated me like a man from outer space, crowding around and asking me a thousand questions. The village chief even said to me, 'I'd be grateful if you'd try to find a job for my Ah-mu when you go back.' You wouldn't believe it, but they seemed to respect me. It didn't seem right. I never figured that the second time I went home, over New Year's, the village chief would ask me if I'd found Ah-mu a job yet. I felt terrible. They think we've really got it made here."

"Why can't you go back now?"

"I don't know." Ah-li was troubled. It wasn't that he was afraid to say why but that he didn't know how to express what was in his heart. "To give you an idea, I've got this feeling that I can't go back till I've made some money. But the way things are, there's no chance of that. So I'd lose face if I went back." Noticing the disapproving look on Monkey's face, he quickly added, "That's not the only reason, of course, but I can't find the words for the others right now."

"Forget it! Why talk about boring things like this?"

The sky was growing darker, the winds had picked up, and the empty paint buckets were rattling and sliding around with each gust of wind. Monkey unmindfully began humming the folk song about the centipede, the toad, and the snake.

"Ah-li, let's quit this job, okay?" Monkey said, coming out of his deep thoughts.

"Why?"

"I knew you wouldn't go along with it," he said despondently. "Forget it, just forget I said anything."

"How do you know I wouldn't go along?"

"The boss is really counting on you for this job."

"Didn't I just say that if we keep going like this, I'll be surprised if we don't go crazy? Have you forgotten that?"

"That only goes for this job. Once it's finished, won't you be in good shape? There won't be any more jobs like this afterward. This lousy painter's job just doesn't suit me."

"To tell you the truth, I'm not sure I'll even be able to finish this job."

"Have you got something in mind?" Monkey asked, happiness written all over his face. "You thinking of quitting?"

"Nope."

"Well then, say what you mean!"

"All we can do now is let things take their course. I don't know what's going to happen."

"Then what did you mean when you said you wouldn't be able to finish this job?" Monkey was obviously edgy.

"Who knows what can happen when you run into a dumb job like this that can drive you nuts?"

"Maybe we really will go crazy. Maybe we'll be so fed up we'll up and leap to our deaths."

"It's not *that* bad," Ah-li said with a laugh. "Who knows, maybe someday we'll just say to hell with it all and quit. Either that or we'll keep putting in our time and see how things turn out."

Monkey reflected for a moment, then said, "Ah-li, let's not worry about doing everything together, okay? I think I might quit tomorrow!"

"Don't jump off the deep end." Ah-li couldn't think of anything better to say. "All of a sudden you're jumping off the deep end. Of course, if you had a better job lined up, I'd shut up, but I know you haven't."

"If I don't show up anymore, you and I are still best friends. And besides, we're roommates."

"That's not the problem. Do you think you can just do anything you want?"

"Now?" Monkey cried out resentfully. "As I see it, nothing we do for the rest of our lives will be our own choice!"

"Didn't we leave our hometown together and come to Qishan?"

"That's the only time. And look where that got us!" Monkey was getting angry. "I don't give a damn—I'm quitting tomorrow."

"What then?"

"Who cares?"

"How could anything be that easy?" Ah-li said with a laugh.

"I said who cares, and that's that!"

"Everything's fine. Why get so touchy all of a sudden?"

Neither man said anything for a moment.

Ah-li took out his cigarettes. "One left. Here, you take it." Monkey shook his head. "Then let's split it," Ah-li said, breaking the cigarette in half. Instead of giving half of it to Monkey, he put the two halves in his mouth and lit them both. Then he handed one to Monkey. "Boy, was I dumb a minute ago; that's how I should have lit them." Monkey accepted his half of the cigarette but didn't take a puff right away. Ah-li smoked his cigarette as he studied Monkey.

"Let's climb down after we finish this cigarette."

Just then a strong gust of wind blew one of the paint buckets over the ledge. Ah-li yelled, but Monkey froze. They stared blankly at the bucket as it was tossed by the wind past them and down to the ground. For what seemed to be an eternity they were in a state of fearful shock, staring down at the bucket and at the pedestrians on the street below. The bucket shrank to the size of a small speck; then, when it had nearly disappeared from sight, a crisp clank resounded from the street. They looked at each other.

"It didn't hit anyone, did it?" Ah-li asked.

"I don't think so," Monkey said, staring downward with wide eyes.

"No, it didn't. If it had, someone would be lying on the ground," Ah-li said. "A few people have walked over to take a look."

"It didn't hit anyone." Monkey seemed to be reassuring himself. "Did you hear the sound it made when it hit the ground?"

"Yeah. *Clank*. It wouldn't make that sound if it had hit someone."

"It couldn't have hit anyone. Those damned people down there, why are they sticking around? Here come some more. Look at them!"

"I see them. Goddamn them!"

"Look at them! They're not leaving. What are they looking at us for?"

"I think we'd better climb down."

"What're you afraid of? It didn't hit anyone."

"More and more people are gathering down there."

"Who cares?" This was spat out with the same anger as his reply a moment earlier. Monkey thrust his head out over the edge of the basket and shouted at the top of his lungs, "Get away from there! If you don't watch it, I'll jump and squash you all!"

These shouts startled Ah-li. "What the hell are you doing, yelling like that?" He was getting angry.

"Look, they're moving away, aren't they?" Monkey said triumphantly.

"Moving away? There are more people than ever now. How can you say they're moving away?"

"Damn them!"

"The ones in the center are moving back, but more and more people are gathering around the edges. Look over there! Cars are stopping too. We're in trouble now."

"We didn't hit anyone."

"Look, there's a clearing opening up right beneath us."

"Damn them, they think we're going to throw something else down."

"No, they think you're going to jump."

"Me?!"

"Isn't that what you just yelled down?"

"Let 'em wait!" Monkey said.

3

Before long, traffic on the road beside the river was snarled at the intersection of Shengsen Street. More people continued to crowd around until there were even groups forming along Shengsen Bridge and on the opposite bank of the river. A police car drove up to the area, siren screaming, lights flashing.

"Here come the busybodies," Monkey said.

"Let's get out of here."

"Let's go!"

When they looked back up to the roof, they saw four men come running up to the ledge from the stairwell. They froze, and before they knew it, the four men had reached the edge of the roof. One was a uniformed policeman, two were stocky men in civilian clothes who looked like wrestlers; the fourth was also in civilian clothes but was much slighter than the other two.

"Now you two stay put," the policeman blurted out. The other three men, who seemed to be surveying the situation, were speaking in hushed voices, but even if they'd been speaking normally, Monkey and Ah-li couldn't have heard them. With the howling wind, shouts were all that worked.

Ah-li and Monkey were terrified, though they forced themselves to present a calm outward appearance.

The apparent lack of concern on Monkey's face made the policeman especially fidgety, for experience told him that such a calm expression was the kind worn by a person who wasn't afraid to die. In his flustered state, the first thing he said to them was, "Why do you want to commit suicide?" He was a couple of meters away from them but had to shout to be heard over the gusting winds.

"We're not suicides!" Monkey answered him.

"What? Speak louder!"

"We're *not* suicides!" Monkey shouted.

"Not suicides? That's fine! Stay put!" The policeman turned and said, "Mr. Ji, come over here and talk to our friends."

The slight man walked over and said politely, "What's the problem, my friends? Maybe I can help."

"We are *not* suicides!" Monkey shouted again. He was beginning to lose his temper.

"Don't listen to them," interjected the policeman, who was on his haunches nearby hooking up a radiophone. "Whether they're suicides or not, it's always safer to treat them as if they were."

"I know you're not suicides," the slight man said.

"Then you guys stand back and let us climb over there," Monkey said.

"Uh, hold on now, just hold on." The policeman quickly put down the radiophone and turned around. "We're going to help you in just a moment," he said. "Now please don't move."

"Hey, why don't you say something?" the man asked, pointing to Ah-li.

"I've got nothing to say," Ah-li answered lazily. They couldn't possibly have heard him.

As the policeman rigged the radiophone antenna, he kept watching Ah-li, saying in a low voice to the man named Ji, "Keep a close eye on the silent one there."

"What are your names?"

"What?" Monkey asked.

"I asked you your names."

They were taken by how courteous the man was.

"We're both named Jin," Monkey replied. "Now if you'll let us climb over there, we'll be happy to answer all your questions." He turned back to Ah-li and said in a normal speaking voice, "What'll we do? They don't seem to believe us."

"What *can* we do? We'll just have to sit tight and let them do whatever they want with us."

"What can they do? Come and carry us on their backs?" Monkey turned back and shouted to the men, "Since you won't let us climb up there, do you plan to come and carry us over on your backs?"

This gave the men on the roof a scare.

"That's the same tone of voice the guy who jumped off the Insurance Building used."

"That's right. Be very careful. If another one jumps, it won't look good for us—and this time there are two of them!" the policeman commented.

"The way things look, the strongmen we brought along won't be of any use," Mr. Ji said. "The fire trucks and ambulance haven't arrived yet. See if you can hurry them along."

By this time more people had begun to congregate on the rooftop, some of them reporters with cameras hanging around their necks. They pressed up to the edge of the roof as close as they could to the two men and started taking pictures.

"What's your full name, Mr. Jin?" the slight man asked Ah-li.

Monkey nudged Ah-li with his knee. "Ah-li, he's talking to you." Ah-li rested his chin on his arms and looked at the man but said nothing.

"His name is Jin Ah-li. Mine's Jin Wanggen, but most people usually call me Monkey."

The people on the roof laughed.

"So that's why you're not afraid to climb so high," a reporter chimed in. But they couldn't hear him.

"Gentlemen, would you cooperate by letting us ask the questions, please? I'd rather you didn't ask anything just now, since people's lives are at stake here. This is no laughing matter, so please cooperate," Mr. Ji said to the reporters.

"Are you brothers?"

"No."

"Then it's just a coincidence that you're both named Jin."

"In Jin Village on the east coast, everyone's named Jin," Monkey said.

They could hear the bells and sirens of the fire trucks below. Ah-li and Monkey looked down to see several men descend from three fire trucks and begin rigging a safety net directly beneath them. An ambulance was parked to the side. Everywhere they looked they could see throngs of people.

"Mr. Jin," the policeman shouted.

They raised their heads and looked back up at the roof.

"Don't worry about all that, it's just there to protect you."

"We're not worried!"

"That's fine."

Monkey began to wonder what was going on. He noticed that the roof was nearly packed with people. The man who'd been talking to them so pleasantly was now surrounded by a group of reporters, and though he could see him gesturing, he couldn't make out what he was saying.

"Do you have any relatives in Qishan?"

"No."

"How about him?" he asked, pointing at Ah-li.

"He doesn't have any either."

"Where do you work?"

"At the Giant Sign Painting Company. We painted those huge breasts on VV on the sign down there."

The policeman asked Monkey all the routine questions he needed for his report. Monkey was getting annoyed. Ah-li asked softly, "Do we have to answer all their questions?"

"I guess so."

"We're going to be famous. We're sure to make tomorrow's headlines."

"To hell with the headlines! We haven't done anything wrong."

"How much longer is this going to take?"

"Who knows? I never dreamed there'd be this many people with so much time on their hands."

"What'll we do?"

"What'll we do? We sure can't climb up there now, so we'll just have to see what they have in mind for us."

"Yeah, that's what we'll have to do!" Ah-li agreed.

The sky had now completely darkened and two lights were shining down on them from the roof. The ladders from the three fire trucks below extended only as far as the fourteenth floor. Spotlights were aimed at the two men from three separate angles. All Ah-li and Monkey could see clearly was each other. Just as they were beginning to grow uneasy and impatient from the effect of the lights, another bright light appeared right in front of their eyes. Two objects suspended from the end of a bamboo drying pole, along with an electric cord, inched toward them.

"What's going on?" Monkey shouted.

"Don't be afraid! They're only microphones for the Qishan and Shengsen TV stations." The voice came to them through a loudspeaker. "Don't worry, we're not going to hurt you."

"Damn it, don't let them trick us," Ah-li said softly to Monkey.

"I promise we won't hurt you. We're here to protect you. We're not going to trick you." The voice over the loudspeaker was crisp but soft.

Ah-li and Monkey were startled.

"Can they hear us?" Ah-li asked.

"That's right, you're coming through loud and clear. Didn't you hear me when I said that those things hanging from the bamboo pole are microphones? We can hear every word you say." The voice through the loudspeaker continued, "Now do you believe we're not going to trick you? I told you we were using microphones. This way we won't have to strain to talk to each other."

Flashbulbs were popping, and there was a great deal of activity on the roof. Some of the background noise was picked up by the loudspeaker.

"Chief Du, would you give us an interview? We're from Shengsen TV."

"All right."

Another bank of lights suddenly flashed on the roof, and Ah-li and Monkey could see some of the people up there. Chief Du, the policeman who had spoken with them, was surrounded by a group of reporters and was answering their questions. Mr. Ji had resumed talking to Ah-li and Monkey through the loudspeaker, but they were still able to overhear some of the interview going on behind him, things not meant for their ears.

"Chief Du, do you think this will remain at an impasse?" a reporter asked.

"I'm sure it won't," Chief Du answered with assurance.

"What do you feel is the safest means at your disposal?"

"We'll do everything we can."

"Chief Du, we need more concrete answers. You understand that both Qishan and Shengsen TV cameras are on you right now, and that people all over the country are waiting in front of their sets for your answer."

The reporter's comment brought Chief Du up short; after a momentary pause, he stammered, "Er . . . um . . . it's like this. Um . . . ever since they started putting up high-rises, uh, suicides have, uh, steadily increased. Over the past several years, uh . . . a dozen or more people have leaped to their deaths. We've, uh, managed to save two of them . . ."

"Chief Du, could you be a bit more specific, please?"

"Very well. Uh, one of them we rescued by using a ladder, the other was saved by a net. But, uh, there's always some danger with a net. We missed several who fell to their deaths and one who hit the net but was killed when he bounced off. Um . . ."

"What's being done to protect these two men?" a reporter asked.

"Uh, as I see it, the ladders are out, since they only reach up to the fourteenth floor. We're twenty-four stories up right now. . . ."

"Camera! Take a shot of the ladders!"* the reporter shouted. Then he turned and asked Chief Du, "Since the ladders are out, will you use a net?"

"Not if we can help it. Uh, we're going to try to find out why they want to jump, then we, uh, we'll try to help them solve their problems so they won't have to."

---

* The first two words are in English in the original.

"Chief Du, a moment ago they said they had no intention of jumping," a newspaper reporter said.

"Hell, you can't believe anything a potential suicide says. We've been there before. They say they're not going to jump, then the minute you lower your guard, they're over the side. Heh, heh, this, uh, is a heavy responsibility we have."

"What if they're really not going to jump?"

"How can we be sure?" Then Chief Du added, "Even if they're not planning to jump, we have to operate on the premise that they are. Don't you agree? Uh, that's the humanitarian way. Don't you agree with that?" He gave a smug look at the camera.

They continued talking, Ah-li and Monkey overhearing every word and growing terrified when they heard Chief Du say that a tranquilizer gun was one of the means at their disposal.

"Would you tell us your names, please?" Mr. Ji asked.

"Didn't you just ask us that?" Ah-li responded impatiently.

"Yes, of course. And you answered everything just fine. But, well, it's like this. Everyone here is very concerned about you two, so I'm asking you some of the same questions for our TV audience. Please don't be angry."

"Are we on TV?" Monkey asked in amazement.

"We're going to be famous," Ah-li said. "Monkey, who said we'd never make a name for ourselves?" Ah-li was feeling emotions he could not express. At least now he had a desire to talk.

"How long have you been in Qishan?"

"Monkey, you did all the talking last time, so now it's my turn to answer."

"Go ahead!" Monkey too felt a change in himself. "Ah-li, being on TV makes me feel like talking."

"Me too."

"You go ahead."

"What should I say?"

"Hey, Mr. Jin and Mr. Jin, you haven't answered my question yet," the loudspeaker demanded.

"What question? Go ahead and ask!" Ah-li answered.

"How many years have you been in Qishan?"

"Two years and seven months."

"You have a good memory." Then the loudspeaker asked, "What have you done in those two years and seven months?"

Just as Ah-li was about to answer, through the loudspeaker he heard the voice of someone in the background.

"It still doesn't look to me like those two are set on committing suicide." It was one of the reporters.

"I don't think so either," another agreed.

"Don't you be fooled by their cheerful manner. That's just an indication that a man who's been thinking of suicide has made up his mind," Chief Du said to them.

Since the loudspeaker was pointed straight at them, if Ah-li and Monkey strained, they could hear the soft voices in the background. The people on the edge of the roof also heard part of what was being said, but since it was coming to them unamplified, they never dreamed that Ah-li and Monkey could overhear the interview.

"Hm? What have you been doing these two years and seven months?"

"We've been working together as painters the whole time," Ah-li answered. He was trying to hear the interview taking place in the background.

"Not bad. You must have painted a lot of houses in that time."

"Now you know better than that, so what are you up to?" Ah-li said testily. He sensed that the interview in the background was more important to him, and he strained to pick up some things not meant for his ears. "I told you we're sign painters. For instance, we did those big billboards in front of the train station." He was growing impatient.

"That's some fine work, like the ads for White Oil, Rose Soap, and for those refrigerators," the voice over the loudspeaker praised. "Then you two are artists!"

"Call us whatever you like."

"Really, that's good work. A lot of artists' work goes unnoticed, but just think how many people see your handiwork every day!"

More snatches of the ongoing interview filtered through.

". . . of course there are things we can do, like offering them food, for instance." Chief Du was answering a reporter's question. "Then we could lace the food with knockout drops or something . . ." The remainder of his comments were drowned out by the loudspeaker.

"I'll bet there are a lot of people around town who know that you two painted those beautiful billboards in front of the train station," the loudspeaker said.

". . . let us reporters interview them?" one of the reporters was asking Chief Du.

"You'll have to understand that there's a purpose in our chatting with them. We must avoid spooking them. We're trying to keep them calm."

When Ah-li heard this part of the interview in the background, he shouted, "We want to talk to the reporters."

A commotion broke out on the rooftop.

"All right. Answer a few more questions, then you can talk to the reporters," Mr. Ji said through the loudspeaker.

"No! We want to talk to them now," Monkey said.

Chief Du led the reporters away from the microphone and spoke to them for a while, after which one of them came over and took the microphone from Mr. Ji.

"I'm a reporter from Shengsen TV," he said. "My name is Pan Ming."

"Mr. Pan, how many years have you been a reporter?" Monkey asked. His question took Ah-li by surprise. He stared hard at Monkey. The question also took the people on the rooftop by surprise.

"Not long, just a couple of years."

"During those two years have you covered any hot news items?"

"Um . . ." While reporter Pan was puzzling over his answer, some of the people beside him urged him to say yes while others told him to say no.

All this greatly displeased Monkey. "Well, yes or no?"

"No!"

"So today's your big chance, isn't it?"

When Chief Du saw that the tables had been turned and that the reporter was stuck for an answer, he grabbed the microphone, nearly ripping it out of the man's hand, and said, "Let's not get into this. Let's change the subject, all right?"

"No! I want to talk to reporter Pan!"

Pan reluctantly took the microphone back; he was coached by Chief Du. "Tell him that this isn't a hot news item."

So Pan said, without giving it any thought, "No! This isn't much of a story."

"Oh, I understand. It's only a big story if I jump." He turned to Ah-li and said, "Ah-li, they're disappointed, can you see that?"

Confused by Monkey's remarks, Ah-li was growing uneasy. Just then an argument broke out on the rooftop. ". . . just who's interviewing whom around here?" Chief Du was noticeably distressed. "Will you take the responsibility? I certainly won't!"

"Monkey, what's on your mind?" Ah-li asked.

"I'm not sure. I'm all confused. One minute I think this, and the next minute it's something else."

"Me too."

"I wonder if my uncle ever bought a TV set," Monkey said pensively. "I really doubt that he could afford one with his gambling problem."

"But someone else might have one."

"As I recall, your folks don't have one either, so they'd have to go over to the neighbors' to watch TV."

"Oh God, I hope my mother isn't watching!" Ah-li said.

"I'm sure she is."

Someone on the roof was talking to them again. "Now what's your problem?" It was Chief Du.

"Problem? I've got nothing *but* problems!" Monkey said. "How about you, Ah-li, any problems?" Ah-li had been stunned by the issue of his mother and was too distraught to speak.

"Just tell us your problems and we'll help any way we can." Seeing the look of despondence on Ah-li's face and the complete dissipation of his spiritedness, Monkey responded lethargically, "What good would it do to tell you?"

"Try us and see."

"We've boarded a ship of thieves." When he said the words, even Monkey himself didn't know what he meant. They somehow just slipped out.

"What does that mean? Make yourself clear. I'm sure we'll be able to work things out for you."

"Ask Ah-li, those were his words." Monkey was getting fed up with the whole business.

"Ah-li, tell us, please, what were you referring to when you said you'd boarded a ship of thieves?"

Ah-li ignored Chief Du's question. He imagined that his mother was seeing everything on TV, and he was not going to answer any more of Chief Du's questions.

Tension was growing on the edge of the roof.

"Wanggen, you tell us your problems, okay?"

"Didn't I just say we'd boarded a ship of thieves?"

"All right, all right, can you tell me how much you earn a month?"

"Monkey! Don't tell them!" Ah-li blurted out. When Monkey saw how tense Ah-li had become, he swallowed the words he was about to utter.

Someone standing behind Chief Du said, "Get to the point. The best idea is to get them to talk about their problems."

"Do you make three thousand?"

They didn't answer.

"Two thousand? Well, how much?"

"Don't ask us that!" Ah-li shouted. He was visibly agitated. "All right! Let's talk about something else."

"We'll talk about nothing!" Ah-li spat out.

Ah-li's outburst brought the whole situation to an impasse. Monkey didn't know what to do. Several times he wanted to ask Ah-li what was going on, but he stopped short each time. The reporters' flashbulbs kept popping. The winds howled around the rooftop.

"First, zoom in, zoom in."* The speaker must have been one of the live-coverage reporters. There was a sudden heaviness in the atmosphere; the pressure was starting to build. Everyone in the area was finding it a little hard to breathe. Ah-li began to sob, a heartrending, uncontrollable sob. The photographers clambered up to the edge of the roof. Monkey was muttering to himself, but no one could understand him.

"Ah-li . . ."

"Leave me alone!" Chief Du was just about to say something to save the situation when Ah-li unexpectedly started to scream hysterically. He got to his feet, stared up at the roof, then began wailing pitifully and uncontrollably. By this time, Monkey's mutterings had become intelligible: he was saying over and over, "I don't care, I'm going down, I'm going down, I'm going down . . ." Without a break in his muttering, he rose to his feet and grasped the edge of the steel basket, preparing to go back down the same way he'd climbed up. Ah-li knew he was going down. Monkey raised his leg to hook it on the edge. The loudspeaker blared out: "Wanggen—Wanggen—" The area was lit up by the frantic popping of flashbulbs. Monkey shielded his face from the glare with his arm. Chief Du was shouting for all he was worth. Monkey suddenly released his grip and stood up straight in the basket.

An ear-splitting "AHHH" of disbelief rose from the invisible crowd below and reverberated against the mammoth wall—Monkey had fallen. In that instant, Ah-li shouted hysterically for them to douse the spotlights, and the ensuing darkness engulfed him like a child in the womb, moaning softly. The wind that had been howling around them could hardly be heard now above the frantic screams of the people on the roof. But through it all, the shrill cry of a television reporter shouting "Camera! Camera! Camera!" was heard as it pierced the heavens.

* English in the original.

*Sayonara / Zaijian*<sup>*</sup>

o

## THE HUMAN CONDITION

I can't help but feel pleased with myself when I reflect on how I handled two onerous affairs over the past couple of days. The first was taking seven Japanese men out whoring with some of my countrywomen; the other was erecting a false bridge between those seven Japanese and a Chinese youth—in other words, the perpetration of a gigantic hoax.

This is how it all came about. Late yesterday morning our general manager placed a long-distance call to Taipei from our branch office in Kaohsiung, telling me to be at the airport by 12:10 to meet a Mr. Baba and six other Japanese. He told me repeatedly and in no uncertain terms to treat them well, as they had close business ties with our company. They had decided to go directly from the airport to the hot springs in Chiao-hsi. Since Chiao-hsi was so far out of the way, I recommended the hot springs of Peitou as a better choice.

---

* The title is the Japanese and Chinese for "good-bye." The four sections of the story are titled after popular Japanese films.

"Everyone knows Chiao-hsi is way out in the country, that the girls there aren't as pretty as those in Peitou, and that the tourist accommodations leave a lot to be desired. But you see, they're looking for something out of the ordinary. Baba and his bunch are a '*Sennin gin kurabu*,' a so-called 'Thousand Beheadings Club.' They've been to Taiwan five times already—this makes the sixth—and Baba said he wanted the hot springs of Chiao-hsi added to their itinerary."

"Why not ask Assistant Manager Ye to accompany them, sir? I've got work piling up."

"No, no! Chiao-hsi is your hometown, so I want you to take them."

"But . . ."

"This is company business, and important business at that," the general manager said somberly. Then he began to laugh. It probably struck him as funny that he was turning pimping into "important company business." At least that's what I figured.

At first I assumed there was no way I could refuse, but when I heard him laugh I mustered up the courage to try to get out of the assignment, just as the time signal blared in my ear and the operator asked, "Do you want to continue your conversation?" The general manager and I answered almost simultaneously: I said yes, he said no. Unfortunately for me, it was his call, and he hung up. I distinctly heard the click but instinctively shouted "Hello! Hello!" several times before dejectedly replacing the receiver. Unless I decided to quit and go home, it looked hopeless.

In my wildest dreams I never imagined I'd be a pimp someday. But in fact, this turn of events was neither as lightly achieved nor as simple as it sounds, for at the time I was in the throes of a painful psychological struggle.

As I slammed the receiver down, Assistant Manager Ye and my office-mates all turned to look at me. Assistant Manager Ye already had an inkling of what had transpired, especially since I'd mentioned his name during the conversation, and as soon as I hung up he said in a loud voice, "So the general manager wants you to take a group of Japanese to the hot springs at Chiao-hsi, huh?"

"He wants me to be a pimp!" I said angrily.

Except for two female co-workers who lowered their heads, all the others burst out laughing. I sensed from their looks that they'd thrown down a challenge. Most of the time they considered me to be the most principled and straitlaced person among them, and in my speech and actions that's what I wanted to convey. So it seemed to me that they were eagerly waiting to see how I'd handle this pimping business. I hadn't expected to be put into such an awkward position by people who revel in the misfortunes of others. Actually, it wasn't simply a matter of doing a little pimping; if that had been all there was to it, I could easily have laughed at myself then and there and let it go. I could surely have managed that without any damage to my principles. The problem was, not long ago, a newspaper article had spurred me into attacking the Japanese in front of these people in a fit of nationalistic zeal. Now I was expected meekly to take a group of seven Japanese men out whoring with some of my countrywomen. I was acutely aware that my colleagues would prefer to see me throw up my hands and quit. They'd reward me with looks of respect and envy and even be so magnanimous as to honor me with a round of hearty praise. Naturally, some would only be going through the motions, pretending they were really intent on my staying.

I knew that if I went ahead stolidly and met those Japanese, my image would suffer in my co-workers' eyes, and my work at the office would be affected. But all this was nothing compared to my deep-seated inner struggle.

My position as someone who has a pretty good grasp of recent Chinese history has led me to abhor the Japanese. I was told that my grandfather, whose stories I'd loved listening to, had had his leg smashed by the Japanese as a young man. Then there was my middle-school history teacher, an unforgettable man we all respected, who had tearfully related to us episodes from the 1937–1945 War of Resistance against Japan. He told us how the invaders had come to China with battle songs heralding their heavenly mission of rooting out the unrighteous, euphemistically giving this vicious and evil war of aggression the title of "holy war." Meanwhile they had swept across China butchering and brutalizing untold numbers of innocent civilians. This history teacher, who was himself from Nanking, showed us a foreign magazine with photographs of the "rape of Nanking." We saw decapitated Chinese, pregnant women whose bellies had been slit open, and, most unforgettably, lines of Chinese, including mothers clutching their children, walking hand in hand into huge pits to be buried alive. I recall that my body grew rigid and hard as stone when I saw those pictures. Tears flowed as we listened to him, and we hated ourselves for being too young to have participated in the war, searching out the "Jap devils" and avenging our countrymen.

Who could have predicted, with all the changes in the world situation and the transformation of society in the twenty years that followed, that the seeds our history teacher had planted in our hearts as part of his educational mission would reach the present stage of development? Though I felt an occasional embryonic stirring, no opportunity for the seeds to sprout ever presented itself; or perhaps this awareness of mine had long since been washed away by the tides of time. Still, there is no way that something so deeply rooted in my conscience could ever be completely eradicated.

Now, however, not only could I not be hostile to Japanese but also, on the general manager's orders, I was being forced to accompany them to the hot springs at Chiao-hsi and keep them well entertained. Granted, any Chinese would have felt the same sort of contradictions if given such an assignment, but my position as someone from the town of Chiao-hsi added another layer of ineffable difficulty. What was I going to say to hometown friends when they asked me why I'd come home? The general manager had emphasized that he wanted me to take them *because* I was from Chiao-hsi.

*Damn it, I'm going to quit!*

*Quit?*

Since coming to Taipei ten years ago, I've changed jobs at least twenty times, doing whatever I pleased. Several times during that period I didn't even have money to pay the rent, and there were occasions when I had to pawn things to get money to take my sick baby to the doctor. The clouded expression that settled upon my wife's face during those fearful days hasn't completely left her. If I refused to take this assignment, where would I find another job? Then there are the chest pains that have been bothering me in recent nights. I can no longer cope with these things as easily as I could in the past. In all honesty, this job has given my small family its first chance for stability. And the clouded look on my wife's face, the picture of fear and foreboding, is gradually giving way to wrinkles of laughter with our child's nascent attempts to speak and some other new tricks. Even his chronic bronchitis seems to have disappeared.

*Damn it! I've got to stay on!*

*Stay?*

Principles I've held on to tenaciously for many years and that have formed my unique personality and temperament—are they to be cast aside now? Then why have them in the first place? It wouldn't seem like the real me without them. I know that my close friends would be surprised if I did this thing, and after having grown accustomed to hearing their praises, what would I do once their vision of me lost its luster? I figure that the hardest compromise to strike would be with myself, for if I put aside my principles, what would I have left?

But on the other hand, if I take that stance, wouldn't I be placing my ego above everything else? Wouldn't that be the shortsighted way to look at things? Am I so great that I need sacrifice nothing, even for my family? Especially since my wife and child don't necessarily share my principles. For even though she's an adult who can understand her husband's beliefs and their worth, and can even support them regardless of the strain they impose upon her, what about our son—a child who understands nothing at all? When he's hungry he has the right to cry for milk. When he's sick he has the right to be given medical attention. He has the right to demand of the world that he be allowed to grow up and become independent. I know I could not bear to shortchange my own child, for who knows, he may someday accomplish something great, and if not him, maybe his children. And it might turn out that the key to his future rested solely on whether or not I did this thing.

When my thoughts reached this point, I suddenly discovered what a bastard I'd been in the past. The greater part of those so-called principles of mine could in fact be summed up as a game of esteeming myself by looking down on everything else and prizing only those things that elevated and satisfied my own ego.

"I guess I've got to do this pimping job after all," I said in answer to the stares of my officemates, who were eagerly anticipating a quick resolution. Although I said it jokingly, I'd actually come to the decision with grim seriousness. I knew what they were thinking and had to construct a ladder to let my self-respect descend carefully if it were to remain intact. "Don't laugh. I'm going to try my hand at being a pimp. Why not?" I didn't really care if they were listening or not, I had to finish this simple but important speech. "If I don't take those seven Japanese today, someone else will. One way or another, seven of our countrywomen are slated for the chopping block." At first they were speechless; then they exploded into laughter.

"Hey! Huang, what's wrong? What kind of talk is that? You're not dealing with some antiprostitution commission." This statement by Assistant Manager Ye was followed by more raucous laughter.

"Now wait a minute. Listen, will you?" I didn't have anything else to say, but I couldn't just drop the subject. "As far as I know, not one of those girls chose this line of work. They're victims of their environment—sacrificing themselves for their families. Since I'm going to be a pimp, I'll show them how to bleed those Japanese. You know that the price of women is a gauge of national development—the cheaper the women, the more backward the place. There are countries in South America, for example, where a girl earns only eight pesos for a day's work picking coffee beans, whereas a fourteen-year-old can earn sixteen pesos by sleeping with a man, the exact price of a cup of coffee in one of the big hotels. Don't laugh, that's the truth. In the eyes of the Japanese we're a backward nation. Even though we've made great strides, they hold us in contempt. Damn it, when I see them coming to Taiwan with all their airs of superiority, it makes my blood boil!"

"So you're going to help them get their kicks at Chiao-hsi?" This bold comment by the shy Miss Chen, who was obviously moved by what I said, came as a complete surprise. And it sparked another outburst of laughter; I laughed with them, though in fact I was troubled by the comment. After my efforts to build a ladder in order to gently lower my self-respect, the bottom had been kicked out from under me.

I couldn't let her comment pass, but what was I to say? My reaction of "Uh huh, uh huh" must have seemed pretty comical, since they all laughed.

Just as I was finding myself falling into a state of total embarrassment, I had an inspiration. I asked her, "If the general manager had given you this assignment, would you have taken it?" My heart let out a secret cry of alarm. If she said no, then what?

But before I had time to give it any more thought, she replied, "I'm a girl, so the general manager wouldn't ask me to."

During the laughter that ensued I shifted the object of my attack. "Assistant Manager Ye, would you have done it if the general manager had asked you to?" He stammered something as he laughed, and I continued, "During our phone conversation just a moment ago he said this was company business, important business!"

With an embarrassed laugh, Assistant Manager Ye said, "No question about it. Who'd dare refuse?" As I stood looking at them, smiles frozen on their faces, I was aware of how crafty a person I'd become.

### THE SEVEN SAMURAI

By mid-day I was standing at the airport exit holding up a large piece of white paper on which I'd written WELCOME MR. BABA in big letters. I waved it feebly and with considerable embarrassment in front of arriving passengers. Before long a Japanese came up, looked at the sign in my hand, gave me a smile, then turned around and shouted in Japanese, "He's come, he's here. He's over here!" Out came four more, all of whom gathered around the first man, then turned to look back inside. They were jabbering back and forth:

"What about Baba *kun* and Takeuchi *kun?*"* asked the first man out.

"They're still in customs."

"I wonder why they're giving us so much trouble this time."

"It looks like they're only nit-picking with us Japanese."

"They're real bastards!"

"They even checked inside my pants."

"Me too!"

"Really? Ha ha . . . they didn't check mine."

"Come on now, they checked all four of ours!"

"Did they really examine your crotches?"

"Mm-hm. They made us take down our pants too. What's so embarrassing about that? Why not admit it?"

"Heh, heh . . . now, if it had been young Taiwanese girls doing the examining, I'm sure we'd have been happy to oblige."

They laughed delightedly, laughter that appeared to wash away the anger caused by the inspection.

They were standing across from me, separated by a railing and five or six steps. I figured we'd made contact, so I might as well fold up the paper and put it in my back pocket—I could still see myself standing there a moment ago waving it in the air. "I made a goddamned fool of myself!"

The one who'd come out first thought I was talking to him. "Baba *kun* hasn't come out yet," he said. "Wait a moment, please." Once again they seemed anxious. "Do you think Baba ran into trouble?"

"How could he? He wasn't bringing any contraband in."

"Maybe on account of those nylon stockings and pantyhose?"

"No, of course not! We've brought them with us before without any trouble."

"Maybe so, but we brought in eighty pairs this time!"

"Those things are dirt cheap. If they want them, they can have the whole lot as a gift."

---

* The Japanese word *kun,* like the word *san,* means "Mister," though the former is much less formal and is used by friends.

"This is such a letdown."

"Those sons of bitches!"

". . ."

". . ."

". . ."

Since we were separated by some distance, I couldn't make out all their grumbling and wasn't sure what they were talking about.

The other passengers from their flight had all debarked and were on their way, and these men were still waiting for Baba and Takeuchi. One of them started toward me to say something, but a couple of the others called out at the same time, "They're coming out!"

Two short, stocky Japanese, their faces set tightly, emerged.

"Any problems?" asked their friends.

"What kind of problems could there be? They were just trying to make things tough for us. Damn, that makes me mad!"

"Oh, Baba *kun*, he's here," the man said, pointing to me.

A smile quickly appeared on Baba's face, and he led the others over to where I was standing. We exchanged business cards across the railing.

"Mr. Xu is in Kaohsiung . . ." I stammered.

"Never mind, we're aware that your general manager is henpecked."

"No, honestly, he couldn't make it back from Kaohsiung this time."

"What difference would it make if he could, since he's so henpecked?" Baba asked with a chuckle. "But the trip won't be wasted as long as we have Huang *kun* to accompany us."

"No . . ." I didn't know how to respond to him. Although not intended to, Baba's words had reminded me of my role as a pimp. Troubled as I was, I managed to say, "Well, I'll do my best, and I hope I don't disappoint you."

"Just looking at you, so young and handsome, we know you won't."

*Damn, that sounded terrible!* I wondered what they were thinking.

"Baba *kun*, what are we waiting for?" they pressed him.

"Nothing at all!"

"Well, let's go then."

"Okay, let's go!" Then Baba said to me, "Huang *kun*, the success of this trip depends on you."

Their luggage was very simple: each had a bag slung over his shoulder, a parcel containing two bottles of imported liquor in one hand, and another small bag in the other hand. Since there were eight of us in all, we hired two taxis and headed directly from Taipei Airport for Chiao-hsi.

Although we'd exchanged business cards at the airport, I still wasn't sure who was Ochiai, who was Tanaka, and who was Ueno. The only ones I knew were the last two to come out—Baba and Takeuchi—and Sasaki, whose name I learned later. I remembered him because he had a particularly long face, and because he'd been the first one out of the airport, the one who'd nodded to me. I was in the first taxi with Baba and two others whose names I didn't yet know, while Takeuchi, Sasaki, and the rest followed in the second car.

"Huang *kun*, how far is it to Chiao-hsi?" Baba asked.

"Well, if we don't run into any rain or fog on the mountain roads, two and a half hours should do it," I said.

"That's pretty far!" said one of the others—the bald-headed one.

"How's that?" the man sitting between Baba and the other blurted out with a laugh. "It looks like Ochiai *kun* is getting impatient!"

"Bullshit! You're the one who's getting impatient!" But he was laughing.

"If you want to know the truth, Tanaka *kun* is getting impatient too." Baba joined the others laughing.

I turned in my seat in front and said, "No, I'm afraid Baba *kun* isn't telling the *whole* truth. He ought to have said *everyone* is getting impatient."

They laughed and shouted their approval.

"I was right, wasn't I? This trip won't be wasted as long as we have Huang *kun* with us," Baba said. "He knows what's on our minds."

*Damn him! God damn him . . .* I cursed to myself, though my face was all smiles. I was conscious of the fact that in ten years of working in the business world I had acquired the habit of masking my true feelings, which I'd always despised in others. Nonetheless, this sort of societal influence on an individual's habits was no different than the instincts of camouflage, protectiveness, alertness, and imitation that animals have developed in order to survive.

From our light banter of a moment before I learned that the bald-headed man was Ochiai and that the other one was Tanaka. As the taxi passed around the statue on Tunhua North Road and onto Nanking East Road, Tanaka looked behind him and said, "Tell him to slow down. The other taxi can't keep up." The others turned around to look.

"He's caught up—he's right behind us now."

"Don't worry," I said. "Both drivers know the way." They turned back around and quieted down for a moment. Baba blew out a puff of smoke.

"What's going on with the Taipei customs people lately?" he asked, looking exasperated. "They're coming down pretty hard on us Japanese."

"Yeah, I wonder why!" said Ochiai.

"It's a case of Tel Aviv guerrilla-phobia," I said reproachfully.

"Tel-a-what? What phobia is that?" asked Ochiai as he leaned over.

I could see that neither Baba nor Tanaka had understood either, so I said, "Last month at Israel's Tel Aviv Airport, wasn't it four of your countrymen who . . . ?"

"Oh, that! We know," Tanaka said in a subdued voice, while the others leaned back in their seats and nodded.

"That damned bunch of animals murdered all those innocent people in mere minutes." Then I added, controlling my anger, "So who can blame the customs people here?"

"Oh, of course," Baba said, "of course. But still it seems they're more sensitive here in Taipei. . . ." Baba, Ochiai, and Tanaka tried to conceal their distress, but I could see it in their faces.

"If they're so sensitive in Taipei, why didn't they just refuse to let you off the plane?" I paused. "Tel Aviv guerrilla-phobia is a worldwide phenomenon these days."

"Um, you've got a point there," Baba said softly.

"The Japanese youth of today are absolutely lawless." The look on Ochiai's face showed that he was trying his utmost to absolve himself of any blame. "Day in and day out they're shouting their opposition to one thing or another. All Japan is in a state of anarchy. As I see it, if things continue this way, the end result is going to be chaos."

As Ochiai finished, I felt an urge to settle some old accounts by reminding him that the previous generation of Japanese wasn't much loftier than the youth of today. The blood and stench of their aggression in China had left an indelible stain on the annals of history. But after seeing the unhappiness on their faces and a complete absence of the looks of superiority that Japanese people usually bring to Taiwan, my thoughts went unspoken and I let the matter drop. Instead I smiled and asked, "Why so glum?" I paused. "Did they confiscate anything of yours?"

"As a matter of fact, they didn't."

"We certainly didn't bring any contraband in with us."

"Then everything's fine. I was afraid they'd confiscated your swords," I said in jest.

"What swords?" Baba cried out nervously. The others stared tensely at me without making a sound.

"Huang *kun*, don't make jokes," said Ochiai. "What swords are you talking about?"

Seeing how edgy they'd become, I laughed even harder. "What swords do you think?" I asked. "The swords you use in your 'Thousand Beheadings Club,' of course."

They exploded into laughter as they caught the joke.

"Ha ha . . . that's right, our 'thousand beheadings' swords! Ha ha . . ."

"We couldn't hijack an airplane with those, could we? Naturally they wouldn't confiscate them! Ha ha . . ."

Baba felt himself ostentatiously down below. "I'd better make sure," he said. "Maybe mine was confiscated without my knowledge."

To be honest, no matter how mischievous I was feeling or how much I wanted to get under their skin, this struck me as pretty funny.

Then Baba assumed the pose of a stage comedian and shouted in the loud and peculiar voice of a Japanese samurai:

> The Way of the sword is the Way of man;
> With the sword there is man;
> As the sword perishes, so perishes man.

Ochiai and Tanaka were sitting beside him laughing. Ochiai informed me that Baba was incanting the final lines of their "Thousand Beheadings Club" manifesto. They were a happy bunch now.

"How many years have you had this 'Thousand Beheadings Club'?"

"Eight years. We seven are the only members," Baba answered.

"Why only seven?"

"Well, we were schoolmates in elementary and middle school, then we were together in the army, now we're business associates. How about that? Not something you see very often, is it? A lot of people want to join, but we won't let them."

"We may not have a large membership, but in Japan we're famous," added Ochiai with great pride.

"What's the special significance of the so-called thousand beheadings?" I asked.

Baba squinted conspiratorially and said, "In former days all samurai had but one wish, and that was to kill a thousand men during their lifetime."

"I don't imagine any of them ever made it, did they?"

"No, but it was the samurai's ideal, and anyone who didn't subscribe to it was not a good warrior. So in order to kill his thousand men, he had to constantly practice his art."

"What about your 'thousand beheadings'?" I pretty much knew already but asked just in case there was more to it.

"Heh, heh." Baba laughed cunningly. "The days of the Samurai Code are gone forever, and we can never again wander the earth wearing swords, killing and being killed. Besides, we wouldn't be samurai even if we could. What we mean by our 'thousand beheadings' is that we hope during our lifetime to sleep with a thousand different women. Heh, heh, do you follow me?" Baba looked smugly at the other members.

I was struck by how loathsome they were, but a smile must still have shown on my face, or they wouldn't have been so openly licentious. The terrible thing about it was, I didn't have to feign the expression.

"Have any of you reached your goal?"

"Not yet!" Ochiai blurted out. "A thousand may not sound like many, but in fact it's hard as hell. . . ."

"A thousand is our ideal, so every time we get the chance, we travel: South America, Southeast Asia, Korea, Taiwan . . . these are places we visit often."

"You must spend a lot of money!"

"We weren't born with any, and we can't take it with us. As long as you look at it that way, it's not so bad. Life is short, and you have to take your pleasures when and where you can. Isn't that right? That's something else all seven of us agree on." I never imagined that such a concept could be supported by a tragic-heroic philosophical foundation. Baba had given this explanation in complete seriousness.

"And that's not all. We have a principle that except for our wives, we can never sleep with the same woman twice," added Ochiai.

"Does it count as a breach of the club's rules?"

"No, but you see, there's a limit to every man's vitality. Doing it a thousand times is no mean task, so in order to achieve our club's objective, self-restraint comes naturally."

Even Tanaka, who had been sitting quietly in the corner of the seat, leaning back with his arms folded and a smile on his face as he listened to the others, added a comment. "Huang *kun*, there used to be a basement coffee shop in the downtown area by the name of . . ." He thought for a moment. "I can't remember the name. Let's see, did it have a barbershop upstairs . . . yes, it was a barbershop. Do you know if that coffee shop is still there?"

"Hm, a basement coffee shop . . ." I pondered for a moment. *The Barbarian doesn't have a barbershop upstairs, nor does the Literary Salon; then there's . . .*

They sat there talking as I pondered. Baba looked over at Tanaka and asked excitedly, "You mean the place where Akiko worked?"

"Right! Akiko's place." Tanaka too was growing interested.

"Huang *kun*, listen to me and you'll know right away what place he means," said Baba as he tapped me on the shoulder. "There's a very narrow door next to the barbershop," he said, using his hands to help describe it, "that's easy to miss if you aren't looking for it. That door is the entrance to the coffee shop. Now do you know where I mean?"

I shook my head. "No, I can't place it."

"That's strange!" Baba replied. "It's a famous place, very well known in Japan! How could you not know it?"

"I'm sorry, I just don't. What makes the place so famous?"

"Heh, heh, heh. There are girls there from all over, and they can do absolutely everything. Now are you sure you don't know?"

"No." I really didn't. Baba and Tanaka eyed me with knowing looks.

In his role as the upholder of fairness, Ochiai said, "I believe Huang *kun* when he says he doesn't know. In matters like this, tourists are better informed than local residents. Those places cater to tourists, not locals, so it's not so strange after all."

By rights I should have been grateful to him for getting me off the hook and saving me from embarrassment, but it seemed to me he'd attached entirely too much importance to the whole affair. What was the great loss of honor in not knowing about such a place? In fact, in Chinese society, this knowledge was in itself a loss of honor. I wondered how Japanese looked at such things and experienced a mild, passing anger.

"Ochiai *kun*," I said, "there's no need to make explanations for me. If you were to ask me something like where the Palace Museum is, or the History Museum, and I couldn't tell you, then I might be embarrassed. But in matters like this, well . . . ha ha ha . . ." I laughed then because I sensed that I was being too grim and that my words were making them tense. They nodded repeatedly, expressing agreement with what I was saying.

"Huang *kun*, you're right, of course. We didn't mean any harm."

"That's right, we didn't mean any harm."

I was quite adept at pretending. I laughed loudly, as if it were all a joke, and gradually they were affected by it. I was even able to squeeze out a few tears of laughter, and as I wiped my eyes I said, "So? Now who's being serious, you or me? I'll tell you the truth," I said with a smile, "I do know that basement coffee shop you're talking about. It's not there anymore. The police closed it down a while ago."

There was nothing the three of them could do but look at me and smile. Ochiai seemed about to say something, but just as he started to speak, something told him to let it pass. He sat up straight, then fell back against the seat.

"Huang *kun*," Baba said, "you're really something!" Afraid that this would lead to another misunderstanding, he added, "What I mean is, I really admire you."

"No, no . . ."

They began talking among themselves.

"I was right, wasn't I?"

"That's for sure."

"Oh, come now," I said.

Tanaka still sat there in his corner, smiling and nodding his head.

I was generally pleased with things so far, having gotten in at least a couple of licks.

"There are three of you ganging up on me," I said jokingly. "That's not fair." I looked at my watch. "We still have more than an hour before we get there, so if you can sleep, you ought to try—you need to conserve your energy."

"No, I'd rather chat with you. But maybe you feel like sleeping," Baba said.

"No, I'd just as soon chat too."

"Huang *kun*, if we say anything out of line, don't let it get under your skin," said Ochiai with a grin.

"I won't, and the same holds true for you."

As the taxi passed through the mountain area known as Sea of Clouds, the driver put a cassette in the tape deck, a Chinese rendition of a popular Japanese tune.

Maybe due to the effects of the music, Tanaka looked out at the mountain scenery and exclaimed, "Would you look at that! This place looks just exactly like Aomori Prefecture!"

"I was thinking the same thing myself," said Ochiai a little incredulously. He lowered his head to look out the window. "Except there aren't any roadside apple orchards."

"Those grass huts look the same too. See, right over there." Baba pointed to some huts we'd just passed.

"Even the song the driver's put on is authentic," I said.

"That, and your fluent Japanese," added Baba with a smile.

*Damn it, that does it!* I cursed to myself out of anger and a sense of injustice. If Baba's comment had been a calculated one, then I'd lost this round. I secretly observed his expression to see if he'd had any intention of wounding me. If he had, then I'd have responded with some verbal jabs of my own. But my observation told me he had no such intentions, even though I still felt uncomfortable. I couldn't help thinking that in their subconscious they still considered Taiwan one of their colonies.* No, not only in their subconscious; in reality, Japanese who come to do business in Taiwan, with their haughty, disdainful attitude, strut around as if Taiwan were their economic colony. I turned back around and looked at the mountain road ahead. Throughout the trip I'd been troubled by feelings of loathing. Baba and the others behind me talked and laughed as before, and although it seemed they were talking about me, I didn't pay any attention to them. I sat there with anger boiling inside me and a meek expression on my face; even if they were telling wondrous stories, it sounded very unpleasant to me.

*Damn it! A pimp! I'll quit!*

*Quit?*

I should have put my foot down the moment I finished my conversation with the general manager in the morning. But how could I just up and quit?

The psychological struggles that had raged in me after the morning phone call were upon me once more. Unable to bear the pressure of these contradictions, I rolled the window down, stuck my head out, and let the wind beat against my face. After taking a few deep breaths, I felt a little more comfortable. The taxi was just then passing above a mountain valley. I began taking in the scenery: I could see the floor of the valley below and a long, narrow mountain stream flowing through it. The strange thing was, the sight of this watery thread far down on the valley floor brought vague thoughts of history to my mind. Historical something? Something historical? I didn't know. I felt as if the stream were flowing through my heart, bringing with it feelings of depression and sadness.

* Taiwan was occupied by Japan from 1895 till 1945.

Baba patted me on the shoulder and said, after I pulled my head back in the window, "Huang *kun*, would you please ask the driver to stop. We have to relieve ourselves." As our taxi pulled to a stop, the car behind us with Sasaki and the others also drove up. Giggling and laughing, they all got out of the cars, formed a line at the side of the road, and began relieving themselves. I stayed in the car, watching them, and as I noticed two tour buses approaching I began to be a little anxious for them. But just as the tour buses, which were full of passengers of both sexes, passed by, the men not only continued to leisurely joke and talk, some of them even turned around as they were taking a leak and smiled at the passengers. Years before, whenever people of the older generation spoke of the Japanese, they talked about how the men loved to piss by the side of a road. At the time I hadn't thought it was such a big deal, but seeing the men standing there in a row, oblivious to everything but taking a leak, I finally understood why the older generation had been so preoccupied with this idiosyncrasy, and why the Chinese called the Japanese "dogs" or "the four-legged ones."

After the tour buses had passed, the men were laughing loudly, and I could even hear Baba shouting out in that strange voice:

> *The Way of the sword is the Way of man;*
> *With the sword there is man;*
> *As the sword perishes, so perishes man.*

## YOJIMBO

It was three-thirty in the afternoon when we arrived at the Evergreen Hot Springs Lodge in Chiao-hsi. After they'd picked out their rooms, the seven of them debated for a while whether to eat first or to take a bath. Ultimately they agreed to have food and wine delivered to Baba's room.

Two middle-aged women in uniforms and wooden clogs quickly and efficiently brought a large round table into the room, after which they moved in the right number of stools. When they came in again carrying the dishes and chopsticks, they brought along three seventeen- or eighteen-year-old girls.

"These three are on duty," the waitress, whose name was Ah-xiu, said to me. The girls stood timidly off to the side. Ah-xiu pointed to the nearest one. "Her name is Xiaowen, the one next to her is Ah-yu, and the

last one there is called Yingying." As their names were called out, the
girls nodded for lack of anything better to do, then crowded together and
began to giggle.

I gave a cursory introduction all around. The seven men looked the
girls over from head to toe, causing them no little embarrassment.
Xiaowen lowered her head and seemed to be looking at her own unat-
tractive feet, with their short, stubby toes and painted nails, trying her
hardest to draw them back in. My experience told me that these girls
were fresh from the countryside; deep suntans acquired from years of
working out in the sun hadn't faded much. I also had an occasional
glimpse of dark scars left by insect bites and sores all over their calves.
Though they were professional girls now, their timid expressions produced an effect of freshness in the eyes of those seven Japanese battlefield
heroes. I could hear their muted discussion:

"Not too bad."

"Sort of earthy," said Baba, "but that might be just what we're
looking for."

"They're all pretty young."

"They look to be about sixteen or seventeen."

Sasaki said something—what, I'm not sure—that made the others
laugh, and laugh hard. The three girls stayed huddled together and even
looked a little frightened, though for some reason they couldn't keep
from laughing along with the men. The one called Xiaowen even turned
and pinched Ah-yu and Yingying on the legs, causing them to scream
out. Puzzled and startled, the Japanese asked me what was going on.

"You three dimwits," Ah-xiu yelled to the girls as she set the table,
"why aren't you over here helping me? I'll give you hell if you don't
watch out!"

"Xiaowen here pinched us for no reason at all!" complained Yingying
as she reached over between Xiaowen's legs. "I'll get even with you!"

"Help! Don't!" Xiaowen screamed and ran toward us.

"Madam! Look! Look here at your Xiaowen!" Ah-xiu yelled at the top
of her lungs.

The waitress who'd come in with Ah-xiu joined the conversation,
saying earnestly, "If you're not going to help, then at least sit down and
behave yourselves. What do you think you're doing? These men here are
Japanese guests, you know!"

The girls calmed down.

"They're still children," Baba said with a smile.

"Look here," Ochiai said as he embraced Xiaowen, who had gone over to him. "She's got quite a body. I want her." He lowered his head and looked at her cradled in his arms. "I like you. Do you understand?"

Xiaowen nestled softly in Ochiai's arms and asked me what he was saying. I told her. Suddenly she raised her head and pointed up at him. "Sex fiend!"

"Xiaowen! Watch your mouth!" Ah-xiu warned.

Ochiai's curiosity was piqued. "What?" he asked.

"I was just teasing him," Xiaowen said.

Ochiai asked again.

"She said you're a sex fiend," I told him.

He and the others laughed when they heard this. "That's right, I am." Then he gleefully pointed to the others. "And so is he, and so is he, and so is he . . . all seven of us are sex fiends."

Sasaki, who was standing next to Ochiai, nonchalantly reached over to feel Xiaowen up, but she pushed his hand away.

"What makes you think you can do that?" she said. Then she struck the pose of a comic character in a Taiwanese opera and said with a smile, "'A man takes no advantage of a good friend's wife.' Don't you know that?"

"Oh, you're a mean one, you are!" Sasaki said with a laugh in response to her actions.

"Huang *kun*, what's this child been saying?" Ochiai asked.

When I told him what she'd said, he was, of course, delighted, and proceeded to hug her even more tightly. "She really is a good girl!"

Sasaki, amused by all of this, reached out again and touched Xiaowen on the thigh. She promptly hit his hand, and they went back and forth like that while the others looked on with amusement.

"Sex fiend!" Xiaowen shouted. She wanted Ochiai to come to her defense, but he was trying to get her to hit Sasaki.

Naturally, Xiaowen hadn't meant anything in particular when she said "A man takes no advantage of a good friend's wife," but she wouldn't let any of the others except Ochiai touch her. I thought, *Xiaowen is, after all, Chinese, and though she may be a prostitute, in a contest to see who was more civilized—her or the Japanese—they'd lose. Maybe that's why we Chinese deride the Japanese by calling them "dogs."*

Before too long, Yingying and Ah-yu were also in someone's arms. It was then that the situation arose that caused me more discomfort and embarrassment than any other in my whole life. I was expected to translate all their meaningless small talk, and not just for one but for all of them. As I was not personally involved in a sexual liaison, most of what they were saying grated on my ears. Nonetheless, I had to translate all their comments for them. We have a saying in my hometown that goes: "The pig-stud farmer earns his pleasure." It means that someone who raises a boar to service others' pigs doesn't earn much, but at least he can get some vicarious thrills. In a rural society this kind of occupation is not looked upon as respectable and is usually reserved for old men who live alone. Although they don't have wives or children to keep them company, while the pigs are mating they remain alongside them, assisting in the process, using their hands to keep everything running smoothly, which is the source of some vicarious pleasure. Well, that's where this local saying comes from. Now that doesn't mean I'm using rural standards to look down on pig-stud farmers, for they at least get pleasure from their work. What was I going to get from mine?

*Damn it!* The more I thought, the angrier I got. But then, how could I lay all the blame at their feet? They weren't forcing me to do this. On the contrary, they'd treated me with politeness and courtesy. Their constant "Huang *kun* this, Huang *kun* that" was more or less designed to get on my good side. Then just what was it that made me feel I had to do it? Normally my understanding of society's influence on the individual is more theoretical than practical, but this time my comprehension came from personal involvement. Just as I was squaring off with the Gargantuan society, unhappily it sneezed, blowing me away to the very heavens as if I were caught up in a violent windstorm. Naturally, before me was not society in its entirety, only that portion under the control of Japanese economics. I think that must be why the Japanese come here with such feelings of superiority.

"Huang *kun*, have them send in a few more girls," Takeuchi said.

"Have them all come in. Tell them we have presents," said Baba as he turned and picked up a bag. "Look, we have all these presents."

I told Ah-xiu to send them in, and she said they'd be coming right away, just as soon as the meal was served.

As promised, as soon as the first course arrived, twenty or so girls came to the room—some stood inside and some remained just beyond the door. Ah-xiu played the director, calling out, "You girls inside the room, step in closer. You girls outside, come on in." Then she said to me, "The three duty girls are already agreed upon. In addition to them, why don't you all choose one more apiece. You might as well have a few more." As she finished, she noticed there were still some girls who hadn't come into the room, so she yelled, "I told you to come in, but you just stand there! Well, don't accuse me of playing favorites when it's too late!"

Although several moved inside the room, at least seven or eight remained outside. The girls' faces were generally expressionless, but I could still tell who among them had been successful in their occupation and who had not. The ones inside the room manifested more confidence and pride than those outside. As I went out to ask the others to come into the room, I spotted one leaning up against the wall, her head lowered as she toyed disinterestedly with her fingernails. When she saw me coming out of the room, she looked up, then dropped her head even lower than before and turned her face to avoid looking at me. In that brief moment I had a good look at her face—one side of it was covered with an aboriginal tattoo. I vacillated for a moment. If I asked her to come in, her inferiority feelings would be even stronger than they were now, but if I didn't ask her, she'd be thinking, "The customer doesn't like my face," and would feel even worse. What to do?

In the midst of my indecision, not knowing how best to handle the situation, I took her hand gently and said, "I want you. Now won't you come in?" I saw the expression on her face—she was both startled and pleased—and in that instant her mind seemed to be cleared of many of its contradictions. Taking courage from this, I spread open my arms and affectionately herded all seven or eight of the girls into the room. My attitude toward them seemed to erase the feelings of inferiority they usually carried with them.

Baba was standing on a chair and weaving back and forth, causing everyone to laugh lightheartedly. He unzipped the bag draped around his neck and pulled out several pairs of nylon stockings, which he held up over his head as he shouted, "Is everybody in? Come on over! There's a pair here for everyone."

I urged the girls to go up and take them, but I never figured that as they surged forward, the six Japanese sitting on the floor would join the fray. Twelve hands reached out to begin feeling the girls up, resulting in a great deal of laughter and shouting. The men could not have been busier or happier, saying to themselves proudly as they probed:

"Aha! I felt it."

"Hey! Don't run away, those are nice titties."

" . . . "

I went up and grabbed several pairs to pass out to the few girls who wanted some but didn't have the nerve to go up and get them. They were all so delighted to get their hands on these things that even the ones who were molested during the handout felt it was worth it. Actually, stockings like those weren't that different from the ones sold in little stalls near the supermarkets in Taipei for about twelve dollars a pair—the packaging was a little nicer, and that's about all. Whatever this exchange between the Japanese and the girls constituted—whether it was to be a part of the whole deal or just a welcome gift—I couldn't help being reminded of their countrymen's posture in so-called Sino-Japanese economic and technical cooperation. *Damn it*—as these thoughts crossed my mind, I began feeling uneasy about myself again.

It was during all this grabbing and feeling that each of them selected the girl of his choice and began embracing her. Baba had his eye on one for himself, so he jumped down and threw his arms around her. The girls who remained, knowing they hadn't appealed to anyone, started to drift away.

"Hey, wait a moment!" Ah-xiu called them to a stop, then said to me, "Ask the Japanese to select a few more to join the fun. They're all so cute." Then she turned to the girls and shouted, "Just look at you— about as lively as bumps on a log. You don't laugh, you don't cry . . . you know, I'm not going to starve if you don't make anything, and I won't get fat if you do. I've got a bigger heart than any of you. . . ."

Baba responded to the suggestion by saying there were already ten girls, including the three who had been assigned, and they didn't want any more. At this the girls started walking out of the room again. One of them grumbled as she passed through the door, "I could have told you they wouldn't want any more, so why did we have to stay behind and lose face. . . ?" I didn't hear the last part of the sentence, since she was walking out of the room as she said it, but Ah-xiu, who'd been helping inside, dropped what she was doing and ran after them.

"You bunch of tramps!" she screamed from the doorway. "You're a bunch of sluts!"

They asked me what Ah-xiu was yelling, but I couldn't translate that for them. All I said was, "She told them to have the kitchen hurry up with the food."

"Oh, I thought it was an argument. Japanese is still the best-sounding language, especially when spoken by women. It's just beautiful," said Ochiai proudly.

"That's for sure," agreed Sasaki. "Plenty of foreigners feel that way. How about you, Huang *kun*?" The others were nodding in agreement.

I'm afraid that even if an enlightened Japanese were to come to visit Taiwan, one of his ex-colonies, it would still be difficult to keep from exposing his feelings of superiority. How much more so then for Baba and the others of his generation, who come here, do what they please, attain their goals with money, whore around with our countrywomen, and even make fun of our language! With a forced gentleness to my voice, I said, "That's right, the Japanese language is just like your packaging designs—very attractive. Japanese has a nice sound to it, but its application is a whole different matter."

I stopped and looked at them for a moment. I could tell they didn't understand what I was trying to say. I was about to explain myself when another idea came to me; I said jokingly, "There's another facet to the Japanese language: take, for instance, sexual intercourse. Here in the countryside the people use the word 'screw,' while our soldiers say 'shoot your wad,' both of which you feel lack elegance and sound simply awful. But if you say 'have sex' in Japanese, or just use the foreign term that has been imported and swallowed whole, '*meiku rabu*' (make love), you think it's elegant and romantic-sounding."

I could see this struck them as funny, so I continued, "But in fact, with 'screw,' 'shoot your wad,' 'have sex,' or '*meiku rabu*,' aren't we dealing with the same thing? Can it be that if you say '*meiku rabu*' you're talking about doing it differently somehow? Or maybe it lends the act respectability? Or perhaps it means that you can join bodies and souls as one and rise to the heights of supreme bliss?"

At first I had secretly reminded myself to sound as friendly as possible, but as I went along I grew more excited until I couldn't hold back. Fortunately the only parts of my discourse they paid any attention to were the vulgarities and the humor, so they laughed even harder. I didn't think it was all that funny, and it suddenly occurred to me that this analogy should not be used to criticize the Japanese language. It should be used as a criticism of the ego-pleasing and phony conduct of the intellectuals. When I saw that they'd mistaken my intent, treating my comments as a laughing matter, I felt uneasy. But something inside told me to just drop the matter.

When the food arrived, the topics of conversation began to expand. The girls sat down beside the men and started pouring wine and serving food to their customers. The girl with the tattoo, who had been standing the farthest from the room, was now sitting beside me and seeing to my needs enthusiastically. It occurred to me that I had a moral responsibility here, since her friendly attitude toward me had sprouted at a moment when her self-esteem was at its lowest and I'd said, "I want you. Now won't you come in?" She had been moved by that. For someone like me who feels keen hostility toward Japanese, having to play the pimp in order to keep my job, making arrangements for them to whore around with my own countrywomen, had created immense inner conflicts. If I hadn't had the capacity to mask my feelings with a happy exterior—like a clown—I'm sure I couldn't have withstood the bitter struggle. Under conditions like these, how could I have any desire for a woman?

My heart cried out with the injustice of it all. If I didn't have her come to me that night, she would feel slighted; even though she was a prostitute, if I disappointed her after my actions had stirred up her emotions—even if it were only a one-night stand—I'd be guilty of trifling with her. I turned and looked at her. She returned my look shyly, then turned her face away again in what seemed to be a manifestation of her inferiority complex. Seeing how simple and unworldly she was, I didn't have the heart to disappoint her. *Okay, we'll see what happens tonight.*

A while earlier, before the other girls had come in, I'd interpreted the exchange between the first three girls—Xiaowen, Yingying, and Ah-yu—and the men, and I was fed up with the role. Suddenly I had an inspiration: I'd open a provisional language course to teach the Japanese some Chinese and the girls some Japanese. But I'd only teach them the words for "good," "no good," "yes," and "no," and they could all learn them together. As soon as I mentioned my plan, they promptly agreed, and within three or four minutes had mastered their lessons. They were having a great time: a constant, uninterrupted flow of "yes," "no," "good," "no good" emerged from their mouths until they got so noisy I found it hard to continue my own conversation. I stood up, clapped my hands loudly, and shouted everyone down.

"Okay, now," I said, "you can say the words. From now on, communicate verbally and with hand and body language. Please, I beg you, don't bother me anymore." Things really began to heat up then. Even the most taciturn among them decided to try their hand, and as a result, whether they were getting through to each other or not, this became entertainment to go with their food and drink. The sounds of laughter alternately rose and fell, and even I was laughing so hard my sides were splitting. The girl on the other side of me said to Ochiai, "You're a son of a bitch."

"Good, good." Ochiai nodded vigorously to show how happy this made him. The girl, whose name was Meimei, was so overcome by laughter she collapsed over onto me. Ochiai asked me what she'd said. "Didn't you just say 'good'?" I asked. He said he guessed that what Meimei said must certainly have been interesting.

"It most assuredly was," I said. "She said you were a little chubby, but cute."

Ochiai was so happy he grabbed Meimei's hand and said, "Really? Hee hee hee, you're pretty cute yourself." There were many more of these comical exchanges, until soon they all began to suspect that they were being had and I was once again interpreting every word.

"Hey, friends," I said to the Japanese with a smile, "treat me like a human being too, all right? I can't just sit here and watch you have a good time, can I?" I reached over and put my arms around Ah-zhen, the girl with the tattoo, to give her a hug. Then I held out my wine cup and said, "I'll drain this cupful to express my apologies to you gentlemen." So saying, I drained the cup.

"Won't that make things difficult for us?" Baba asked good-naturedly.

"How could it? Doesn't your 'Thousand Beheadings Club' roam the world relying only on your swords?"

"Huang *kun*, you're the wittiest person we've met among the locals. We're no match for you."

"You flatter me." I picked up my wine cup again. "Here, let this represent my gratitude for your flattering remarks." Again I drained the cup.

I could sense that from our first meeting at the airport till now their attitude toward me, or at least insofar as their speech and their conduct reflected it, had undergone quite a transformation. By this time they no longer exhibited any sense of superiority in front of me, and even Baba seemed a little intimidated by my presence.

As I observed them at the meal, I could see they were no longer inhibited by the language barrier, had turned it into a form of entertainment. And the knowledge that they were in a foreign country made them feel as if they were floating on air. Then they began to get the itch. Squinting his eyes and holding Qiuxiang in his arms, Baba said, "Huang *kun*, I'm afraid we can't avoid imposing upon you now. Do you know their price?"

I asked Ah-zhen, but she only stammered and was unable to say anything. Eventually, the girl sitting next to Tanaka, Baimei, was pushed forward by the others to speak for them.

"Are you interested in a 'rest' or a 'mooring'?" she asked. Actually, she had no idea of the real significance of the Japanese words *kyukei* and *tei-haku*, which were remnants from the Japanese occupation. In this context, a "rest" meant a short time, and a "mooring" meant an overnighter.

"How much for a 'mooring'?"

"It's like this: if it's one of our own people, it's two hundred." Then she looked at the Japanese and asked softly, "They really don't understand what we're saying?"

"Not a word. Say anything you want as loudly as you like."

Nonetheless she continued in a low voice, "For Japanese it's four hundred."

"All right." Then in a loud voice I said, "We'll make it a thousand for a 'mooring.'"

"Hey, not so loud!" one of the girls blurted out. The others laughed.

"How much of it do we have to give you?" Baimei asked.

"None."

"How could we allow that?" several of them asked in unison.

"Don't worry about it." Then I said in Japanese, "One thousand for the night, and that's not a bad price. You can use your revalued yen and enjoy both convenience and economy."

"All right, let's decide." Baba nodded to the others with his head cocked to one side, indicating that he was asking for their opinions, although the inference was that he'd already made the decision for them.

"Baba *kun*, you still haven't asked Huang *kun* to take care of the arrangements for our trip to Hualien, have you?"

"Oh, I almost forgot," Baba said, striking himself on the forehead. "Huang *kun*," he said to me, "I'm going to have to ask another favor of you. We've heard that in Hualien you can find real aboriginal girls. . . ."

"I'm not sure," I answered calculatedly.

"You really don't know? Heh, heh, heh . . ." Ochiai asked teasingly.

"It doesn't make any difference. Huang *kun*, we plan to stay in Taiwan for a week, and Hualien is one of the places we want to visit. Call your company and have someone buy eight tickets for tomorrow's noon flight."

"Don't you mean seven tickets?" I asked.

"The eighth one is for you."

"I'm afraid I'll be busy tomorrow."

"Don't you want to come along with us?"

"It's not that. I really have things to do. But don't worry, if I can't make it, the company will send someone else to accompany you. Okay, I'll make the phone call," I said as I walked off.

"Sorry to trouble you."

When I returned to the room after making the call, nearly all the girls had left. Only Yingying and Xiaowen had stayed behind to clear the table.

"What's up? Where is everyone?" I asked.

"We asked them to leave for a while so we could make our preparations," Ochiai said with a mysterious grin. "Huang *kun*, how about you?"

"What preparations would I have to make?" I had an inkling of what he meant. I smiled, and Ochiai and the others smiled back.

"What about the phone call?"

"The plane takes off at 12:30. We'll leave here in the morning on the 9:31 train."

"Fine, no problem." Baba looked at the others. "That's it then."

Ochiai reached into his pocket and pulled out a little gold object that looked like a lipstick, only slightly larger. "Ever see one of these?"

I took it from him and opened it up. They were all standing around snickering as I examined it.

"A cologne atomizer?" I asked, putting my thumb on the button.

"Hey! Don't press it!" Ochiai yelled. "Don't press it!" They laughed.

"What is it anyway?" I hadn't a clue.

"Haven't you ever heard of the magic oil of India?"

"No."

Yingying and Xiaowen, thinking it was a cosmetic of some sort, dropped what they were doing to come over and take a look. "What's that?" Xiaowen asked.

"Hey! Don't tell them." Ochiai grabbed it away from me, but then he must have remembered that they couldn't understand what he was saying. When he continued, he appeared to relish talking about it with them present so as to add some spice to the drama. He said, "An hour before we get to work, we spray a little of this stuff on the turtle's head— just a little. There's nothing like this stuff—the pleasure it brings is almost endless!" He smiled lecherously at the girls. "You know what I mean?"

Xiaowen reached over to take it, but I snatched it away. "This is an ointment for aches and pains," I said to her. "Hurry up and clear away the dishes." The girls walked away disappointed.

"Huang *kun*, you can try a little if you'd like," Baba said.

"I don't think so," I said, handing it back to Ochiai. I experienced a strange sort of anger.

"Huang *kun* isn't like us, he's still young. He probably doesn't need it."

By then they'd finished the food and wine, so they headed back to their rooms, to make their so-called preparations, I suspect. I went back to my room and lay down on the bed to sort out my feelings. My thoughts went around and around without ever coming together. Then they turned to Ah-zhen, the girl with the tattoo. I was sure that if I summoned her that evening, she'd be happy to come and would be nicely submissive. Beginning to get aroused, I abruptly recalled that I'd be doing it along with the Japanese, and my anger was rekindled. *Should I not call her then? As self-debasing and simple as she is, she must certainly think that I want her tonight. If I don't call her she'll be hurt, and this hurt will go beyond just the missed chance to earn some money.* I thought and thought about it. *Damn it, I'll wait till tonight and see what happens!* Just as I was lying there feeling miserable, Baba knocked on the door and came in.

"Excuse me, Huang *kun*, sorry to disturb you."

Whatever the situation, they were always polite and courteous. But I was still disgusted with him. Once politeness and courtesy become habits and lose their spontaneity, what you're left with is blatant superficiality. He grinned as he said, "Can we call the girls now?"

"Now?" I sat up.

Baba nodded. I glanced at my watch.

"But it's only a little after six o'clock!" I said.

My startled reaction seemed to cause him some embarrassment. "You're right," he said with a smile, "it is a little early, but we've finished our preparations."

"You mean you've already sprayed on your magic oil of India?" Though there was a smile on my face, I wasn't feeling very happy.

He nodded. "And some other stuff as well. You see, since the potions are effective only for a period of time . . ." The smile on his face suddenly retreated and was replaced with a pathetic look.

"They don't have any side effects, do they?" My expression of concern was a complete fabrication.

"Of course they do, if you use them too often. But think about it— we're all in our fifties, and a thousand 'beheadings' is no simple task." As he said this, the last trace of a smile disappeared completely.

I stood up and patted him on the shoulder. "All right," I said, "I'll go."

"I'll be in my room." The smile he'd entered with started to make its return. But I knew that their smiles were dependent on the support they received from the magic oil of India and other stuff.

I walked out of my room against my own inclinations. Had there been someone behind me forcing me on, no matter how strong his arms, I'd have surely turned back to resist even if I were to die in the attempt. But when I turned back, there wasn't a thing in sight, and in that blur of time the cold, still corridor—almost deathlike—gave me a fright. In that fleeting moment I seemed to have moved from a strange and distant place back to reality. Unwilling though I was, I had no choice but to walk downstairs. At the desk at the foot of the stairs I ran into Ah-xiu, who had been serving us just a while before.

"Huang *san*," she addressed me in Japanese style, "what can I do for you?"

I was momentarily speechless, for I suddenly realized that I could not avoid asking her to have the girls go straight away to sleep with those Japanese. A while earlier, when I was negotiating the price, I hadn't felt so keenly what I was involved in, since I was able to more than double the going rate. In fact, I even experienced the stirrings of national consciousness—the illusion of serving my fellow Chinese. Whether or not such behavior and feelings were justified, I still experienced the thrill of dealing a defeat to my enemy. But not at this moment. As I stood there before Ah-xiu, I knew with absolute clarity that the moment I opened my mouth to speak, I'd be a bona fide pimp. "Damn it! Those Japanese want the girls to come to their rooms now," I said to her, showing my anger.

"Huh! Now? They can't go now. Why, it's only . . . what time is it?" She looked up at the clock on the wall, then at the girl behind the counter. "It's only six o'clock. How can they go now? Our girls aren't here to serve them alone."

"I know that, damn it! But . . ." I couldn't finish.

"We're not trying to take advantage of anyone," Ah-xiu said, "but the general rule is that a 'mooring' is from midnight on."

"We can't do that. No one expects a girl to spend the night starting this early," added the girl behind the counter.

"That's right! I know that," I said.

"Tell you what. I'll have the girls go up half an hour early, at eleven-thirty. How will that be?"

"That'd be fine, of course, except . . ." I paused for a moment. "Would you go upstairs with me and tell them personally? Just tell them what the general rule is."

"You'll have to be my interpreter."

As we walked upstairs, Ah-xiu said to me, "The girls here say you're a good guy." After a pause, she added, "Aren't you originally from Chiao-hsi?"

"Who said so?" I answered with a start.

"Your home is next to the temple, and you're Uncle Yanlong's eldest son. Am I right?" She smiled.

"How did you know?"

"All the older people in our place recognized you."

"Uh-oh!"

"It doesn't matter." Then she asked me in a very lighthearted tone, "Did you go to Taipei right after you quit teaching? What sort of business are you in now? You must be doing well."

"Not really. I just work for a company."

"It's been years already, but Yumei still talks about you. She says you were the best teacher she ever had."

I stopped in my tracks and asked in a trembling voice, "Who's Yumei?"

"My eldest daughter. You were her fifth- and sixth-grade teacher."

I remembered her and suddenly felt somewhat relieved.

"Oh! So Chen Yumei is your daughter! Where is she now?"

"She's in her first year at a girls' high school. She's changed quite a bit since you knew her. She's tall, taller even than me."

"Mrs. Chen, I have a favor to ask. Please don't tell Yumei I came here," I said awkwardly.

Mrs. Chen thought this was pretty funny. "I won't, but what difference would it make?"

"No, please. Just say you ran into me somewhere—anywhere."

"I won't tell, I won't breathe a word," she said with a giggle.

We talked for a while longer at the head of the stairs. I still felt a slight heaviness in my heart, though I was more at ease than when Chen Yumei's mother first told me she knew who I was.

I took Mrs. Chen to find Baba and informed him of what she had told me.

"So that's how it is!" he said. "What a damned nuisance."

"I'm terribly sorry, but those are the rules around here." Mrs. Chen nodded apologetically.

"How about this, then: suppose we throw in a little more money, could we have them come now?"

"I'm sure that would be all right, but it might not be worth it."

I asked how much more each one would have to give for the girls to come now.

"At least two hundred."

"Let's tell them five hundred. After all, the Japanese are so rich they won't miss a few hundred."

After I informed Baba, he said, "Well, if that's how it is, we have no choice. I'll ask the others."

He knocked on each of the doors and called the others out into the corridor; once they were all together he opened the discussion. When they arrived at their decision, Baba represented them. "I guess that's how it has to be. Huang *kun*, tell them to come right away." When it came to business and money, the Baba who had up to that moment given me the impression of someone who treated others politely had been transformed into a person just like everyone else.

Before long, all the girls they had requested, excepting Xiuxiu, whom Takeuchi had wanted, arrived in the rooms. Mrs. Chen and I took the thoroughly displeased Takeuchi downstairs to the resting quarters to. select another girl who appealed to him. After the longest time he grudgingly settled on a girl named Meijun. It seemed to me that my conduct had been abruptly and severely restricted ever since Mrs. Chen had told me that most of the people in the hotel knew me. I experienced an unremitting anxiety: had I said or done anything out of line in the presence of my fellow villagers? *Damn it, I'm here with Takeuchi, picking out a girl as if she were a piece of goods.* He continued the process a while longer. By rights I should have been doing something for the girl, but seeing the exasperated look on Takeuchi's face, I stood frozen off to the side, embarrassed to death.

After Takeuchi walked off with Meijun, Mrs. Chen came up behind me. "How about you, Huang *san?*" she asked with a smile. She had the best of intentions; if I'd wanted the company of a girl, she wouldn't have thought anything of it, working as she did in such a place. But her smile brought me unbearable discomfort. I knew what she had in mind.

"No, not for me, thanks."

"You don't have to be so straitlaced. Ninety percent of those who take it on the chin are straitlaced people."

*Hai!* I had to laugh inwardly. *God knows if I'm an honest man!* But all I said was, "That's all right. This has nothing to do with being straitlaced or not."

She laughed and let the matter drop as she followed me upstairs. Naturally, that took me by surprise, since I'd hoped she'd press the issue, giving me the opportunity to ask her advice on how to handle the matter of Ah-zhen, the girl with the tattoo.

"Mrs. Chen," I said, pausing at the bend in the staircase, "I'm sure Ah-zhen is under the impression that I want her this evening. But actually . . ."

"Don't you worry about it. I'll find a nice girl for you."

She'd misunderstood me. Of course, I'm no saint, but in my complex and totally self-contradictory state of mind I couldn't come up with a single decent idea.

"No. I'd like to give her five hundred and not have her come to my room tonight."

"That's not necessary. I'll tell her and it'll be all right."

"But I . . . I made arrangements with her earlier." This was the best way to handle it. If I were to say I was fearful of injuring Ah-zhen's self-respect and adding to her low opinion of herself, Mrs. Chen might laugh at me, I thought. At the same time, I was terribly afraid of running into Ah-zhen. I took five hundred dollars out of my pocket and gave it to her.

"If that's how you want it, you don't have to give so much. One hundred is plenty." She kept one of the bills and gave me four back.

I took three and handed back one. "How's this? Give her two hundred."

"Ha ha! She makes a hundred percent profit, just like that," she said with a laugh as she took the money.

I went back to my room, lay down, and stared blankly at the ceiling. I had nothing to look forward to but a long evening alone in my room, and I didn't know what to do with myself. How could I go to sleep so early in the day?

Since I'd been away for a long time, I thought about going home to have a look around. But Father would ask me when I'd arrived and what I'd come home for. If I told him the truth, that I was accompanying some Japanese on a pleasure excursion to Chiao-hsi . . . ai! I wouldn't even try. I'd only be looking for trouble. Years earlier, when I'd chosen not to take over his brokerage and even quit my job as a teacher, a scene had erupted that had left a lingering bad taste. If I were to tell him now that the job I'd gone to Taipei for was bringing Japanese here to the hot springs to whore around, nothing I could say would make any difference; even plunging into the Yellow River could not wash the stains away.

I didn't want to dwell on it any longer. There was no going home!

Instead, I thought of other places I could go. But wouldn't it be the same? If I ran into any friends, wouldn't they ask my reasons for coming home? They might even let my father know, and things would be even worse. To travel to Chiao-hsi and not even come home! It would be like two years ago, when he'd screamed, "When the ancient sage emperor Yu was taming the Yellow River, he passed by his home three times without entering. But you! Who the hell do you think you are?" If he were to fly into another rage because of me, this time he might die of apoplexy. No, that was no good either. I decided to just lie there.

I rolled over and noticed a photograph of a foreign pinup girl hanging on the wall. She was straddling a chair backwards and cradling her chin in a waiting pose. As I was looking at it my train of thought quickly turned in a new direction. I figured that those Japanese—*Damn them*— were just then reaching their climaxes. I wondered what effects the magic oil of India had. Who knows, if I hadn't been recognized by Yumei's mother, maybe Ah-zhen would already be lying beside me. There's a saying men have: "Ugly women are great in bed."

With her low opinion of herself and my expression of interest in her, I'm sure she'd have shown me a terrific time. *Damn it! I wonder what she's doing right now.* But no matter how overcome by my own desires I was, something inside me maintained awareness. It was this that kept me from daring to face myself, and the less I dared to do that, the fewer my chances of escape. As a result, I felt ill at ease and so pained that I jumped violently to my feet. I lit a cigarette and paced the floor. Suddenly I noticed the telephone. I reached out and took it off the hook; the girl at the desk answered.

"Front desk, may I help you?"

"Oh, I'm sorry, it was nothing." I hung up. But I was immediately aware that what I'd just done was very unusual, and if the girl at the desk were to mention it later to anyone—especially Yumei's mother—it would be the object of a lot of speculation, and even my private thoughts would become common knowledge. Ai! More cause for embarrassment! I figured the best thing to do would be to leave my tiny room.

I went downstairs, apologized to the girl at the counter, then went into the restaurant, found a table, and ordered some food and a bottle of beer. I sat there trying to figure out what sort of lie I could tell my wife to avoid having her suspect me of being unfaithful. Thoughts that had sprung from my own imagination and those that had their origins elsewhere came to me one after another for some time. Eventually I was like a lonely long-distance runner undergoing slow and agonizing physical and mental torture: I finally reached the finish line, dead drunk and empty.

## JAPAN'S LONGEST DAY

When I opened my eyes the following morning I saw Ah-xiu, Baba, and the others standing around my bed. In a dazed state of mind, I was shocked awake by the anxious looks on their faces and by their apprehensive comments. "Huang *kun*, there's nothing wrong, is there?" I sat up with a start.

"What's happened?" I asked.

"You scared us. We thought you were sick."

"No, I'm fine. Look!" I sat up and threw a couple of punches in the air. "There's nothing wrong."

They laughed. Then Mrs. Chen told me they'd knocked repeatedly without being able to awaken me. They couldn't even get me up by ringing my telephone. Finally, they'd asked her to bring the passkey.

"It's getting late," Baba said. "Didn't you say we'd be taking a train a little after nine o'clock?"

"Mrs. Chen, did you get the tickets for us?" I asked.

"Yes, the 9:31 train. I'll get them for you in a minute."

"Hm, 9:31." I looked at my watch. "There's no problem, we still have about an hour. The train station is close by." Then I said to Mrs. Chen in Taiwanese, "Will you get our bill ready, please? Have they paid the girls?"

"Yes."

I took out another two hundred and gave it to her as a tip. "My goodness, how embarrassing to be tipped by Teacher Huang. Thanks a lot," she said as she left.

"Huang *kun*, you must have had a great time last night, eh."

"Um, I had a good time." In matters of this kind, no one believes you if you say you didn't do anything. And even if you manage to convince them, you'll be laughed at and suffer a considerable loss of face. So it's better just to say yes.

"No wonder you couldn't get up," Baba said with a look of envy in his eyes. "You must have had quite a time—a night of pure enjoyment!"

I grinned at them, secretly pleased that these dimwits were so easy to fool.

"How about the rest of you?" I asked.

"Not bad!"

"Well, I didn't enjoy myself!"

A voice full of displeasure came from somewhere near the window behind me. The others were convulsed with laughter, but it took me aback. It was Takeuchi. He stood there looking out the window, keeping his back to us.

"What's the matter, Takeuchi *kun*?" I asked him.

"Go ahead, tell him. It won't hurt," Baba said.

Takeuchi turned around with a forced smile as Baba said with a laugh, "In the years since we founded our 'Thousand Beheadings Club,' we've made one discovery. Most people, maybe even you, would probably call it superstition, but what happens is that whenever one of us encounters bare skin . . . uh . . . a bare surface . . ." He grinned as he paused. "What I mean is, if he makes a girl without pubic hair, then unfortunate things begin to happen to him."

"Are you kidding?"

"Last year, after I had one in Hong Kong, I lost a thousand U.S. dollars. Ochiai had one, after which his factory burned down. Sasaki had an auto accident and spent two months in the hospital. And then there was . . ."

"That's enough!" Takeuchi interrupted.

"Yes, that's enough," I agreed. "Those are coincidences. You don't really believe in such superstitions, do you?"

As I was talking, I observed Ochiai looking for something in his bag. Happy as could be, he pulled out a little memo book with a red sateen cover, walked over, and flipped through the pages.

"Take a look at this," he said.

I took it from him and was startled when I realized what it was. I began to silently curse them. The little book, it turned out, was a record they kept for the "Thousand Beheadings Club." Each page recorded the time and place, the name of the girl, a description of her figure, how the lovemaking went, and what happened, followed by a critique. The bottom half of the page was left blank so they could use a piece of transparent tape to affix one of the girl's pubic hairs.

"Get it now?" Ochiai said with a grin. "Takeuchi's page for today won't . . ."

"All right, all right, I guess you're happy now!" Takeuchi shouted.

Why was he so angry? There was a lot I didn't know about their "Thousand Beheadings Club."

Later I learned that each of them had one of these little books, which they used to exchange experiences. If they made some sort of discovery this way, then everyone could perform experiments based upon it.

Once they were on the train they began discussing their experiences of the night before, holding nothing back.

"Hey!" I interrupted. "There are people all over Taiwan who speak better Japanese than I do, maybe right here beside us."

"We're not discussing politics or anything," Baba responded.

"I know you're not, but we Chinese aren't accustomed to talking about sex so openly and are embarrassed to hear such things in public places." I knew my words were a little inflammatory, but what the hell, those are the breaks! It wouldn't do any good to suppress my feelings any longer. But I still had a smile on my face.

They were speechless for a moment; then Baba said with a nervous laugh, "Huang *kun*, you're not angry, are you?"

I laughed and said, "How's that? If I were angry, I'd keep my mouth shut. It's just possible, however, that someone might be offended and come over with mayhem on his mind."

They were frightened by this prospect, at least a little, and after taking a look around they turned back to me.

"Could that really happen?" Sasaki asked softly.

"We don't have to worry about such things in Japan," said Ochiai.

"But that's Japan—this is not Japan!" I said.

"Naturally," said Baba, "but I don't necessarily agree with Ochiai *kun*. In Japan we too . . ." Obviously trying to salvage some dignity for his country, he quickly realized that he was on shaky ground, so he paused momentarily.

Ochiai picked up the conversation, saying with some displeasure, "Baba *kun*, is that really necessary?"

I returned to the attack, responding to what Baba had been about to say, remembering to keep a smile on my face.

"Baba *kun*, no matter what the situation, if there's something that embarrasses you in Japan or something you don't dare do for fear of injuring others, then you shouldn't do it when you go abroad, at least in regards to what we're talking about. Isn't that right?"

"No, hold on a moment, Huang *kun*, I didn't make myself clear. What I meant was . . ."

"That's enough, Baba *kun*, that's just about enough. Let's everybody speak for himself. Who asked you to be Japan's spokesman?" Then Tanaka said to me, "Huang *kun*, please don't be so sensitive. Heh, heh . . ."

I laughed along with him. "Tanaka *kun*, who's being sensitive? But you make it sound improper to be sensitive about things. Besides, since you're Japanese, under certain circumstances or in certain situations you can't avoid representing Japan. But I agree—everyone should speak for himself."

"You see! I said all along that Huang *kun* is the sharpest Taiwanese we've ever met, didn't I?" Baba said.

"Let's just forget it," I said. "And let's all take it easy."

"How can we take it easy now? Huang *kun*, you're really something. You created the tense situation, and now you want *us* to take it easy!"

"You've got it all wrong. But okay, do what you want." Then I added, "Don't worry about me. In case anything happens, I'll still be here beside you."

"Then we can put our minds at ease," Baba said.

But after my warning, they seemed to run out of things to say. They sat there like blocks of wood. I had no idea what they were thinking. When the train pulled into Ting-shuang-hsi, Ochiai asked, "How long before we get to Taipei?"

"Another hour."

"We still have that far to go?"

"Mm-hm."

A young man who'd evidently boarded at T'ou-ch'eng was standing near us. I noticed right off that he was tuned in to our conversation. I'd cautioned them not to talk about their sexual experiences on the train partly because I felt they were being too flagrant about it and partly because I'd noticed this young man who was engrossed in their comments. As our eyes met, he smiled and nodded. I nodded back.

"Excuse me, sir, you're Chinese, aren't you?"

"Yes, I am."

"It's hard to believe that someone as young as you can speak such fluent Japanese."*

---

*As a rule, only Taiwanese educated before 1945 speak Japanese fluently.

"You're too kind. I barely manage."

"My name is Chen, and I'm a senior in the Chinese Department at Taiwan University. After I graduate, my father is going to find a way to send me to Japan for advanced study. So could I trouble you to ask these Japanese a few questions for me?"

Just as I was thinking to myself that he might be a little too brash, he asked abruptly, "What do those men do in Japan?"

*Damn this young fellow! If I ask some of the questions he has in mind, they might laugh at the presumptuousness of our young people. Besides, isn't it all topsy-turvy for a student of Chinese literature to leave Taiwan and go abroad to do advanced study?* Then I had an inspiration. Why not take this opportunity to hurl a few barbs at the Japanese and teach my young friend a lesson at the same time? The prospect of a little sport nearly made me laugh out loud. Serious though the matter at hand may have been, I figured this would be a good chance to have some fun.

I told the young man they were a fact-finding group of Japanese college professors.

"Oh, that's perfect!" He was delighted. "Would you mind helping me out?"

Though the others couldn't understand what we were saying, they were watching our expressions closely and with great concentration, especially when the young man was speaking.

When I turned back to the Japanese, the young man nodded to them, and they timidly returned his gesture. "He's a college senior," I said. "His field is history, and since he's writing a thesis on the War of Resistance, he'd like to discuss a few things with some Japanese."

They were momentarily speechless. Then one of them said confidentially, "As businessmen, we don't know anything about that."

"That doesn't matter. Besides, I don't know what he's going to ask." I turned to him. "They'll be pleased to answer your questions, though they're afraid you might not find their answers satisfactory. Also, before you begin, they'd like to ask you something first. They want to know why someone studying Chinese literature would want to go to Japan to do research."

"I've heard there are lots of original editions there," he said. Uncomfortable with this answer, I felt like responding right then and there. But I kept my feelings in check and pretended to give his answer to the Japanese.

"He'd like to know if you were born around 1916," I said.

They looked at one another with shocked expressions, wondering how the young man could have guessed so accurately and why he seemed to be investigating them. Actually, I'd already learned this from registering them at the hotel.

"What does he want to know that for?" Baba asked with an expression of displeasure. "Huang *kun*, this can't have anything to do with the thesis he's writing. Besides, that's personal."

Seeing that the young man had observed the look of displeasure on Baba's face, I quickly told him, "Professor Baba is disappointed with your response, even a little upset. He said that research in any field of knowledge doesn't depend upon the edition one uses. For example, if you're doing work on the *Book of History*, using both an original and a later edition, will you gain a deeper understanding from the former?"

"But your mood and feelings while you're doing the research won't be the same. Also . . ."

"Hold on there," I interrupted him. "If you say too much at one time, I won't be able to interpret for you, so let me tell them what you just said first." I turned to the Japanese. "He offers his apologies for asking this sort of question, but he wants to gain an understanding of the background of those days, that's all. He'll understand if you don't feel like answering him." Then, speaking for myself, I said, "Were you, as a matter of fact? What difference could telling him make?"

"Well, if that's all it is, actually, all seven of us were born in 1917. We're from the same town and we were classmates in elementary and high school." When Baba finished, the others stared intently while I spoke to the young man.

"Many people who do research in Chinese are under the impression that they're doing research on Chinese words. But what's really worth researching is Chinese society and the great Chinese thinkers. He said that your wanting to go to Japan to do research in Chinese literature is actually just a pretext, isn't it?"

An embarrassed smile appeared on the young man's face. "No, it isn't. I really want to go to Japan to study. But what the professor says is certainly worth thinking about. Could I ask if he's a sinologist?"

"No, he's a professor of Japanese literature, but anyone in Japanese literature has a solid foundation in sinology." I was beginning to get a little flustered. I hoped I wouldn't forget what I was supposed to be asking the Japanese and wind up giving apple answers to questions about oranges.

"My papa's always telling me that Japan is a pretty good place, so I'd like to see it for myself."

Baba and the others were looking at me, waiting to hear what was being said. I turned to them. "He said you must have been just the right age to be drafted into the army and take part in the war of aggression against China, right?" I looked first at the pale face of Ochiai, then at the composed Baba. I said with a laugh, "This fellow doesn't care much for others' feelings. But there's no harm done. Ochiai *kun*, you seem a little touchier about this than the others. What's wrong?"

"Nothing's wrong." He paused for a moment, as if troubled. "In those days everybody but the disabled was drafted into the army. Naturally, we were no exception."

"A great war isn't caused by common folk. I don't care if you call it a war of aggression, because it was initiated by the Imperial Government in power. Me, I just followed orders." Baba looked at the others. "Isn't that right?"

"To listen to you now, you'd think that you opposed that war down to your marrow. But what about those days? Weren't you right in there singing about how you represented the Way of Heaven in its destruction of the unrighteous, marching onto the continent of China as you sang, and calling it a 'holy war?'" Then I forced a smile and said, "If I'd been in your shoes, I guess I'd have done the same."

Suddenly feeling as if a great weight had been lifted from their shoulders, they all laughed nervously.

"So you've been to the China mainland? When you were in the army, that is?"

"All except Takeuchi *kun*."

"I seem to have gotten interested in the subject myself, but actually these are his questions." I smiled, then turned to the student and said, "The professors hope you'll forgive them if they sometimes seem impolite by being critical of your thoughts in this matter."

"Oh, don't worry about that. I should be thanking them," he answered.

"They say it's understandable that your father has good feelings about Japan, because people of his age grew up under a Japanese educational system that kept them ignorant. But someone of your generation shouldn't have such thoughts."

"It was my papa who told me . . ."

"Let me finish. Professor Baba also said that supposing Japan is a fine place, or America is a fine place, or somewhere else is a fine place, what you seem to have in mind is to go to a fine place somewhere to enjoy yourself, or perhaps just to escape from reality. What he wants to ask you is this: granted that Japan is a fine place, just what have you done for Japan? If the answer is nothing, then you'd best not make plans to reap the benefits of her accomplishments." I smiled. "But the professor says this is just a personal reaction to your comments, and if you really want to go to Japan, he says you'd be welcome."

"I wouldn't go there just to have a good time! I'd go to study!"

"Going to study is fine, and that's your business. What the professor says is not intended as a criticism of you but is aimed at today's youth and their dissatisfaction with reality, which makes them all want to run off to a better country that exists only in their imagination. These are the people he's talking about. Only you know whether or not you're one of them."

"What he says is right, and I respect him for it. How many days will they be here looking things over? It would be wonderful if they could speak at our school."

*I'll be damned! So this is what our young students have come to.* It's the sort of common-sense talk you can hear anywhere, but in the mouth of a foreigner it somehow gains credibility. *Hmm. "Only monks from afar really know the Scriptures!"* Although it struck me as funny, it unnerved me a little as well. I'd started out wanting to poke a little fun; how could I have guessed that I'd soon be attacking both parties? I knew I didn't have enough understanding of these matters to keep it up forever, and sooner or later I'd slip up. I figured it was time to put on the brakes. But how? Since I didn't know, I decided to keep it up until the young man got off the train.

The strange part was, I hadn't expected that in using my limited knowledge of history to settle some accounts with the Japanese I'd actually induced these men with their superior airs to simply acknowledge a debt by slowly nodding their heads.

"This student has made his position clear, and I think we can accept it."

"I hope that in his thesis he won't use our viewpoint as a critique of Japan."

I was elated to hear Sasaki say this, for I could see how little remained of the pleasures they'd bought the night before. But I wasn't quite ready to let them off the hook yet. I wanted to turn their pleasure into anguish, no matter how ephemeral it might be. "I don't think he will," I said. "To draw general conclusions from an isolated situation is taboo in scholarly work. I'm sure a college student understands that."

"I hope so," Sasaki said. Then he continued, "Not long after the war, when TV came to Japan, we were finally able to witness the past in documentaries about the war we'd been involved in. . . ."

"Did you see any of the fighting in China?"

"Sure! Quite a bit, as a matter of fact." He looked at his friends. "Isn't that right? It was then that we were able to really see what kinds of things we'd done."

I feigned a confused expression. "How could you have a clear picture of what you'd done after seeing documentaries?"

"Oh!" Ochiai, his face looking drawn, showed signs of real discomfort. As for the others, although they exchanged glances, their attention never strayed from our conversation. Sasaki blurted out almost painfully, "We saw the rape of Nanking, we saw bodies floating on the Whampoo River, we saw the bombing, we saw . . ."

"Sasaki *kun*, that's enough," Baba said, shaking his head, "that's enough, that's enough."

I agreed, he'd said enough. They'd been parties to it, and if they'd truly seen documentaries giving irrefutable proof of their ruthless persecution of the Chinese, there was no need for me to pursue the matter any further. This reminder that I'd given them was all any humane, conscionable human being could stand. Seeing the mental anguish written on their faces, I could tell I'd achieved the desired effect. But what could I say at this juncture to the young fellow beside me, who seemed so terribly eager to know what was going on?

I continued having my sport with both parties for a while longer.

"Young fellow, please don't be angry."

"I won't."

"Just now they wanted to ask you something else. You told them you'd never been to the Palace Museum; that came as quite a shock. And a real disappointment. You say you're a college student and that your major subject is Chinese, that you even live in Taipei. Then why haven't you taken the time to go have a look?" I could see he was still swallowing the bait; he lowered his head slightly with an expression of shame. "They said that even though they're in Taiwan for a visit of only a few days, they've already been to the museum twice. They said their minds have been troubled as they wonder how a magnificent race of people that was able to produce the cultural treasures in the museum could in recent years have dried up so completely."

"Mr. Huang, I'm so ashamed."

"But then, you're too honest. When you meet foreigners who are so concerned about China, you should lie and say you've been to the museum. And if that sort of thing embarrasses you, then why not just go there someday and take a look for yourself? But no matter, what's happened today is no real loss of face—at least you're sincere. But isn't there something you'd like to ask them about Japan? Before you could even start, their questions kept you from asking them anything."

"I did have some questions, but after listening to what they've said, my questions don't seem so important any longer. I feel this has been a lucky day for me—I've learned at lot."

"As a matter of fact, you can hear people right here saying the things they were telling you today. It's strange: if your own people say something it's a fart in the wind, but if a foreigner says the same thing it's a message from the gods. Isn't that right?"

"But honestly, I've never heard any of this before."

"Sure, I know. I'm saying that it happens a lot."

I glanced over at the Japanese; they were sitting there as if they were about to hear a judge pronounce a sentence. When I turned to talk to them, they changed their posture slightly to concentrate on what I was saying.

"I hope you'll forgive this brash young man . . ." I didn't have a chance to finish.

"What do you mean? We couldn't respect him more!"

"Youngsters his age are on the romantic side and generally more patriotic. I already told him not to ask any more questions, since it's all history anyway. You've come here to enjoy yourselves, and talking about the past like this can only cause you unhappiness." I paused for a moment. "But he did say that after the Japanese put down their weapons, they switched to economic aggression, where they don't have to see their victims' suffering. I told him he shouldn't say that, but he said it *is* economic aggression, and from certain angles . . ."

"Huang *kun*, that's enough," Baba said, shaking his head, "that's enough!"

Sasaki said agonizingly, "Huang *kun*, I'm so sorry."

"Why should you be?" I said with a smile.

"We all feel very guilty. Please tell this young man how much we respect him. If the postwar Japanese youths were at all like him, I think there'd be hope for our country." From the very beginning I could sense that Sasaki was more deeply affected than the others. The situation this time, in which their reveries had caused such pain, had started with him and spread to the others.

The train pulled to a stop at Pa-tu. The young man broke in on our conversation.

"Mr. Huang, this is my station. Thank you, thank you all." He bowed to me and to the others. This so unnerved the Japanese that they jumped to their feet and returned his courtesies, almost as if they had received a great favor.

"This is where he gets off," I said.

"*Sayonara!*" It never occurred to me that the young fellow knew a word or two of Japanese. This was the first time I hadn't mediated their conversation. They were actually communicating with each other.

"*Zaijian!*" Nor had I suspected that these Japanese had learned to say a word or two of Chinese.

Each of them shook hands very gravely with the young man as they parted.

"*Sayonara.*"

"*Zaijian.*"

The young man left, and they all sat down. Sasaki, deeply moved, sighed. "There's a Chinese youth you can be proud of."

"And how about me?" I asked playfully.

There was a hint of returning smiles as they said, "You too, naturally."

*God only knows!* This struck me as pretty funny.

"I was right, wasn't I? You have to mind what you say in public. If that young man had understood Japanese, things wouldn't have turned out as they did."

"Huang *kun*," said Baba, "let's not talk about it anymore."

They leaned back languidly against their seats. Ochiai asked, "Huang *kun*, how much longer?"

"About thirty minutes."

"Still thirty minutes to go?" he blurted out, as if the remaining half hour of our trip would take forever.

*Bibliographic Note*

o

Huang Chun-ming's earliest short stories were published primarily in the literary supplement to the *United Daily News* (*Lianhe bao*) and in the literary magazine *You shi wenyi*. Several of the stories translated in the present volume first appeared in the literary quarterly *Wenxue jikan*. Huang's first volume of stories, entitled *His Son's Big Doll* (*Erzi de da wanou*), was published by the Dalin Publishing Company in 1974 and includes four of the stories translated here: "The Fish" ("Yu"), "The Drowning of an Old Cat" ("Nisi yi zhi lao mao"), "Ringworms" ("Xian"), and "His Son's Big Doll." In March 1974, two volumes of Huang's stories were published simultaneously by the Yuanjing Publishing Company: *The Gong* (*Luo*), which includes the title story, "Xiaoqi's Cap" ("Xiaoqi de nei ding maozi"), and "The Two Sign Painters" ("Liang ge youqi jiang"); and *Sayonara / Zaijian*, which was the source for that story and "The Taste of Apples" ("Pingguo de ziwei").

.Other titles in the
*Modern Chinese Literature from Taiwan*
series

**Chu T'ien-wen—*Notes of a Desolate Man***

A Taiwanese gay man reflects on his life, loves, and intellectual influences

A *New York Times* Notable Book of the Year

A *Los Angeles Times* Best Book of the Year

"Superb. . . . A strong and perceptive voice now arises from Taiwan."
   —*New York Times Book Review*

"By turns richly erotic, humorous, and devastatingly forlorn."
   —*The Seattle Times*

"[A] stylish meditation on marginalization, radicalization, and decay."
   —*Los Angeles Times*

**Cheng Ch'ing-wen—*Three-Legged Horse***

Twelve deceptively simple stories about Taiwan and its people by one of the island's most popular "nativist" writers

Winner of the Kiriyama Pacific Rim Book Prize

"A rare jewel." —*Pacific Rim Voices Book Review*

"Written in simple language yet rich with vivid details."
   —*New York Times Book Review*

"The finest examples of modern Chinese fiction I have come across in
   English." —*South China Morning Post*

### Wang Chen-ho—*Rose, Rose, I Love You*

A ribald satire of a Taiwanese village that loses all perspective—and common sense—at the prospect of fleecing a shipload of lusty and lonely American soldiers

"Delightfully irreverent."—*World Literature Today*

### Li Qiao—*Wintry Night*

An epic historical novel tracing the fortunes of a Hakka Taiwanese family across three generations from the 1890s through World War II

"A work of epic proportions." —Howard Goldblatt, award-winning translator of Chu T'ien-wen's *Notes of a Desolate Man*

"One of the most influential classics in Taiwan's contemporary fictional world."—Liu Jianmei, University of Maryland

### Michelle Yeh and N.G.D. Malmqvist, editors—*Frontier Taiwan: An Anthology of Modern Chinese Poetry*

Nearly 400 poems from 50 poets spanning the entire twentieth century of Taiwanese poetry

### Chang Ta-chun—*Wild Kids*

Two funny—and tragic—stories of youth from Taiwan's most famous and best-selling literary cult figure

"An addictive little literary treasure." —Mo Yan, author of *Red Sorghum* and *The Republic of Wine*

"Ghoulish, playful, totally subversive." —Emily Gordon, *Newsday*

"In two jaunty, disturbing novellas from Taiwan . . . Chang Ta-chun presents us with disaffected adolescents who roam city streets, complain about school, fantasize about gangster life, and wear Chicago Bulls T-shirts." —Maureen McLane, *New York Times Book Review*

### Hsiao Li-hung—*A Thousand Moons on a Thousand Rivers*

A prize-winning Taiwanese best-seller about love, betrayal, family life, and the power of tradition in small-town Taiwan